THE SOUL WARS

COLLECTED EDITION

J.D. BLACKROSE

To my husband and children,
who have allowed me to dare to dream.
To my brother,
who is a one man cheerleading squad, complete with pom-poms.
To my mother,
who shows me what unconditional love looks like every day.
To my father,
who told me "Jack the Horse," was good,
and
To my cousins Deborah and John,
for showing me art is worth doing.

PART I

SOULS COLLIDE

1

"Holy Mother of God," muttered Adelaide Beauchamp (née Rochon), using the strongest language she ever allowed herself. "That...that...vampire thinks he can buy my land, my *family's* land? He's too big for his britches." She sliced a piece of pecan pie and nicked her left thumb, her hands unsteady with age and anger. She sucked her bleeding thumb and abandoned the pie.

She continued to talk to the ghosts in the house. "I may be the last of our line," she said, walking through the mansion, caressing the priceless antique furniture, "but no perversion of nature is getting his hands on Rochon or Beauchamp property." The house ghosts rattled the chandeliers in agreement. "Stop that!" Adelaide admonished, hurrying to the dining room to check on a crystal light fixture from the 1800s. "They may not stay up."

At eighty, she stooped over with a widow's hump and a belly pooch that looked as if all the fat in her body had either traveled up or fallen down to her midsection. She lived with a Creole woman a short ten years younger than her employer, who now stood at the entrance to the kitchen. "Ma'am, a few more wall tiles fell, and the paint is peeling badly. Should I call the repairman?"

"Too expensive, Mathilde. Let's make do for now."

"When Mr. Beauchamp was alive, we kept the house in pristine condition."

"That was twenty-five years ago, Mathilde. Louis has been gone for over two decades."

"But with the house falling into disrepair like this, we cannot have any parties or teas. It just wouldn't do. You have a *reputation* to protect."

"My days as a society lady are long gone. Do what we always do—hide it with a painting."

"Yes'm." Mathilde sniffed, turned her back, and exited in precise, crisp steps.

Adelaide studied the woman's back as Mathilde exited, and then she extracted a parchment envelope from her pocket, running her uninjured thumb over the wax seal, and read the contents for the umpteenth time. The message was delivered by a human, of that she was sure, since it was dropped off in the middle of the day. The deliveryman had exquisite manners and spoke in a lyrical Old-World French. She fumed at the memory. Employing formal etiquette made it impossible for her to refuse the envelope. That Gaspard Bessette had out-maneuvered her.

Adelaide sat at an old escritoire, an antique writing desk that she still used, and compared Bessette's note to another from the Historical Society. The Historical Society had agreed to consider the home and its trappings as a Louisiana Heritage Site.

The photos of her ancestors rattled in their frames. "Hush," she said to pictures on the desk. "That creature is not getting this land or this house for a long time, hopefully never." She pounded her walking stick on the hardwood, picked up the receiver of her antique phone, and called for her driver. She was going to meet the lion in his own den. She patted her hair, straightened her pearls, and took measured strides to the car, concentrating on keeping her breath steady. Rochons and Beauchamps don't show fear.

The main entryway of Gaspard Bessette's mansion was heavily guarded, and cameras recorded activity from every angle. *The tall, blond Nordic woman who drove that monster truck was most likely responsible for the extra security*, Adelaide thought.

The guard at the gate stopped the car, and her driver, Noel, the eighteen-year-old son of her first driver, handed the guard her greeting card. The guard motioned for her to roll her window down as well.

"Sorry, ma'am, but I need you to exit the vehicle so we can inspect it and check you for weapons."

"You must be kidding, young man. I'm not getting out of my own car so you can pat me down like a common criminal!" The whip crack of her voice made the guard step back and mutter "sorry, ma'am," a reflex programmed into children of the South from birth. He hurried into the guard box and placed a call. Meanwhile, the other guards swept the underside of the black Town Car for bombs. She seethed. Who did he think he was, this vampire?

The guard on the phone gave a thumbs-up.

The other guards did a visual inspection of the interior of the vehicle and completed the scan of the external body. Then, the head guard said, "You can go in, Mrs. Beauchamp. Monsieur Bessette is expecting you."

As she and Noel waited for the gate to slide open, she heard the head guard say, "Kara is not going to like this breach in protocol."

A second guard replied, "Well, I'm not going to be the one to tell her. She'd kick my ass."

"Can you believe she carries an actual sword?"

"She has a shield, too."

"I don't think she's human."

The drive up to the house took another ten minutes.

"Noel," Adelaide said, "did you know that this house originally belonged to the Leroux family? They died out years ago."

"No, ma'am, but I'm sure my pa remembers."

"They had the most extravagant balls held in this house. I can still recall kissing the Leroux boy in the rose garden."

The teenager swallowed and willed that mental image away. "Sounds fun, ma'am."

She knew the house's electricity and plumbing had been completely replaced, and she assumed the kitchen was re-done. The exterior and the gardens were returned to their former glory, but the statues had been replaced with more security-friendly low stone walkways and benches. Adelaide felt like she was moving into a beautiful bunker.

Noel opened the car door for her, and she exited the vehicle holding his hand. He walked her to the entrance, where a butler and more security greeted them. A suited man with a crew-cut held Noel back. "I'm sorry, son, but you can't come in with Mrs. Beauchamp."

Noel raised his eyebrows and glanced at Adelaide. She patted his hand. "It will be all right, Noel. I won't be long, so please stay with the car." Noel nodded.

Reminding herself that she was a Rochon and a Beauchamp, Adelaide entered the vampire's lair. The entryway was illuminated by lights that somehow mimicked both the warmth of the sun and the elegance of the stars. The ceiling soared, revealing an arched staircase leading on both sides to the second floor balcony. The floor tile was a white and black pattern, and the walls were painted a light blush. Ornate mirrors graced both sides of the entrance to further refract the light, creating an experience of floating through the mid-day sky.

A voice said, "Welcome to my home, Madame Beauchamp."

Adelaide turned her head toward the voice, which emanated from the entrance of the sitting room.

His baritone was silky smooth with a slight edge, like whisky on ice. The man who addressed her wore a custom blue pinstriped suit with a lighter blue tie and matching pocket square. His long dark hair, marred only by a white streak from his left temple, was pulled back into a queue held by a blue ribbon. The last time she had seen him, his hair had been cut short. She wondered how a dead person grew hair.

His eyes matched his tie, a sparkly blue that had undoubtedly charmed many ladies in the past. His mouth was quirked into an amused smile as he walked toward her with his arm out as a signal that he would escort her into the sitting room.

She ignored the arm, walked right past him, and settled herself on a long chaise.

Startled by her poor manners, Gaspard Bessette lowered his arm and followed her, his eyes now glinting with both amusement and some annoyance. He sat across from her, taking a moment to unbutton his jacket and inhale a small breath.

"Madame, how may I help you?"

Adelaide did her best to straighten her shoulders. "You can start by ceasing to offer me money for my house and land. I am not selling." She tossed his latest missive on a side table.

Gaspard pursed his lips and stared at her as if he could see through her soul. The seriousness of his scrutiny combined with the luxuriousness of his lips reminded her of those secret embraces with the Leroux boy. Parts of her that were way too old to be tingling sat up and noticed. She found that irritating.

He settled back on the chaise and asked, "Isn't your maiden name Rochon?"

"Yes, my family has been here for generations. Unfortunately, I am the only remaining member of my family." She grasped her hands together at the last.

"I knew a Baron de Rochon in the 1700s, who lived in Franche-Comté. Are you from the same family?"

"You *knew* him? Personally, knew him?"

"Yes, Madame, I am somewhat older than you may think."

Adelaide knew vampires lived a long time, but it was difficult to imagine the man in front of her, who looked to be a virile forty, as centuries old.

"Yes, our lineage goes back that far," said Adelaide. "We have few records, but he was indeed my distant, very distant, ancestor." Leaning forward, she said, "I would love to know any details you could share about him and the family."

Gaspard closed his eyes a moment and then torqued his head in a brief nod.

"Le Baron was a portly man as he aged, but he started slim and was quite a good horseman. He was known for being fair and honest to the villagers, but ruthless when it came to criminals. As a result, his barony had little crime. A story followed him for his whole life about how he came upon a horse thief stealing from his barn. He, it is said, singlehandedly captured the criminal and then personally drew and quartered him. It is reported that he buried the head and left the other pieces on the main traveling road as a warning for others."

Adelaide was rapt. "Is the story true?"

"After a fashion. His son, not him, did come upon a horse thief and capture him, but in a moment of mercy for the poor soul, the son declined to kill the thief and placed pig parts on the main road instead."

"How do you know this?"

"Because I was the horse thief."

Adelaide's jaw dropped.

"I was human then, not yet turned, aged forty and knew better, but my son and wife had died from disease, and in my mourning, I took to drink and lost my position as a cook. Forty was old in those days, and between illness and famine, I was weak and desperate for food. I couldn't ride well, but I thought to steal the horse and sell it. Your ancestor had other plans. He warned me not to try to steal from the family again, gave me an apple from his pocket, and sent me on my way with a few coins. He felt sorry for me, and that one moment of kindness saved my life."

Adelaide sat back and lifted her chin. "It's a nice story, and it may even be true, but I am still not selling to you. In fact, I have deeded my house, land, and belongings to the Historical Society with a promise that they will maintain the property as a museum for one hundred years."

Gaspard raised one eyebrow. "Then I shall wait another one hundred years."

"If you live another one hundred years. You are quite hard to kill I understand, but not impossible."

"Are you threatening me, Madame?"

Adelaide laughed, gesturing at her frail frame. "No, Monsieur, I am no threat to you, but I do not want a vampire owning my property. I am doing all I can to prolong that occurrence."

Gaspard stood, buttoning his jacket. A man dressed in a butler's uniform appeared at the entrance, apparently summoned by some invisible signal.

"Please escort Madame to her car. She has made her case quite plain."

"Yes, I have. Good evening, sir."

Adelaide followed the butler out, once again refusing the proffered arm, and tottered to her car where Noel was waiting. She entered the car with as much grace as she could muster because she knew that Gaspard watched her. Once inside the vehicle, she let out a wheezy breath and allowed the fear to seep in.

The vampire's entire being screamed power. She could feel it in his look, his voice, even the posture of his body revealed him to be the dominant force in the room. How was she, an old human woman, supposed to oppose that? She wondered how many vampires lived in the mansion. She'd seen several in the past but surmised that since she didn't frequent the grounds at night, she would not have an accurate estimate. It could be dozens, hundreds even. Was the only thing keeping them in control Gaspard's sheer will? She hoped not, even though his will was formidable, because that seemed too thin a thread to hang on. Which brought her to her other question. The human muscle and weaponry was equally as intimidating as his presence, but she couldn't help but wonder why he needed all that security. Who could a man like Gaspard Bessette possibly be afraid of?

2

Gaspard stood at the living room window and watched as Adelaide drove off. As a master vampire, the small amount of fading light didn't bother him, and he took a moment to enjoy the view from his window before full dark.

Adelaide was a proud lady, something he could appreciate. It took a certain kind of toughness to approach him in his own home. He didn't understand the reason for her refusal. His financial offers had been generous, but he could afford to wait longer if need be.

He thought back to those days long ago in the Burgundy region of France and the junior Baron de Rochon, not yet of title, who caught him thieving. Despite all the generations between them, Adelaide had his nose and his spirit. Of course, he hadn't told her the whole story, and he doubted he ever would.

She did not need to know that the person who turned him was the then residing Baron de Rochon. When the hale and strong son found the desperate and frail Gaspard, he beat him to a pulp and dragged him in front of his father. There were already rumors about the reclusive Baron and his penchant for only appearing in the evening. The stories claimed that the father was a blood drinking monster of the night and that is why the son ruled the day. They weren't too far off.

Gaspard tumbled on the floor of the Baron's study, bleeding everywhere from the son's assault. He remembered it like it happened yesterday.

"Henri," said the father to his son. "Good work. Leave us." Gaspard recalled the look on Henri's face as he realized he had miscalculated. Nevertheless, disobeying his father was impossible, and he retreated. As he did, he cast a look at Gaspard and mouthed, "I'm sorry."

When Gaspard glanced up at the Baron, his bowels loosened and he pissed his pants. The Baron's face was stretched and pale white. His eyes were bloodshot, and most frightening, his fangs were two inches long.

Despite his injuries, Gaspard scuttled backward toward the door attempting an escape. He left a trail of blood along the floor and shivered when the Baron bent down on one knee, ran his finger through the blood and sucked, reveling in the taste.

Gaspard grasped the door handle, but it was locked. He was gasping for breath now, physical injuries forgotten. His mind was ripe with fear, and panic told him to run, run, run. His back hit the door, and he stood, whirled around, and pounded on the wood, yelling for help.

He swirled back around to face the monster but saw nothing because the monster was already at his throat. He collapsed to the floor, held in the Baron's arms like a child, losing his senses, and crying inside for the mother he could barely remember.

He woke with a pounding headache, a mighty thirst, and the feeling that the room was too bright. He blinked several times and covered his eyes with his hands against the light.

"You will get used to that in time," a voice said. "Your senses are heightened."

The Baron stood off to the side holding a glass of wine. He handed it Gaspard. "Drink this. You will feel better."

Gaspard gulped the wine down, his thirst driving him past delicacy. "Merci, Baron. What is this vintage?"

"Scullery maid number three, I believe."

"I don't understand."

"It's human blood."

Gaspard dropped the goblet to the ground and put his hand to his mouth. He felt his own fangs, and the events of the past hour returned to him.

"Oh, my God."

"No. Don't believe He had anything to do with it. Maybe more of the Devil, if you ask me."

"You've turned me into a monster."

"That is a matter of opinion. I need a student, an heir. You seemed to fit the bill."

"You have an heir. Your son."

"He takes care of daytime duties. I need someone to learn my night-time responsibilities. Together, you will run the barony when I am required to leave."

"What am I?"

"A vampire. A fledgling so your powers are minimal, but I will teach you to be strong."

"I can't eat food." It was a statement, not a question.

"You can. It is not an enjoyable experience, but you can get by at a dinner party. You will require blood on a daily basis for a while."

"I don't want to do this!"

"I'm afraid you have no choice."

"Where will I get blood?"

"Why, scullery maid number three, of course. She will be yours, since you seem to like her taste. And because this will be a nightly thing for you, I'll add her sister, whose name I also don't recall. We'll just call her scullery maid number two."

"Who's number one?"

"Their mother. She's mine."

"What about their father?"

"That's me."

"You don't know the names of your own daughters?"

"Should I?"

"I would think so."

"Well, I don't. When you learn them, you can share that information with me. And since I am to be your teacher and your father, you can call me Luc."

"You are in your thirties, far younger than I am. How are you to be my father?"

The Baron guffawed. "I am over two hundred years old, certainly old enough to be your father. I am your father in this new life, and you will treat me with the respect due your sire, who also happens to hold your life in his hands. Besides, you have changed, too, my son." He gestured to a looking glass on the wall.

"It's a lie that vampires cannot see their reflection. I'm not sure where that tall tale came from, but it has stuck and is quite useful. Those who believe that nonsense will dismiss you as completely human simply because you can be seen in a mirror! Isn't that delightful?"

Gaspard swallowed and collected his courage to look in the glass. His once stringy black hair was now thick and luxurious, and he had a white stripe that ran from his temple down the hair's full length. His face, once angular from starvation, was now aristocratic, and his wide blue eyes were more intense, with a shock of dark eyelashes framing each eye. His skin was paler than before but smooth, showing little signs of age or the scars from the burning embers so familiar to cooks. The thought brought him to look at his hands, once mangled from knife cuts and scalds, now unblemished. He wondered what else might have changed and looked down at his trousers.

The Baron chuckled. "Afraid the changes are cosmetic, boy. Nothing has, uh, grown or thickened, 'fraid to say."

"But, does it…ah…work?" Gaspard asked, unable to blush but very embarrassed.

"Yes, my son. It does work and quite well. You will find your libido to be as when you were young."

"You said that the maids are your daughters. We can have children?"

"Vampires, with a bit of proper and uncomfortable ceremony, can sire children the natural way. I fought quite hard to have those girls, and several boys you will find working about. I needed stock that could never be taken away, married off, traded, or sold."

"You had children to ensure a blood supply?"

"Why yes, it gets difficult to govern if villagers keep disappearing. I have bought children, too, letting them grow to mid-teens and then using them for sustenance."

"You have a herd."

The Baron tilted his head as if thinking hard. "I guess I have. Humans have sheep and chickens. We all need a food supply."

"But those are animals, not thinking, feeling people!"

"I fail to see the difference, and after a while, you will fail to see the difference, too. Humans get addicted to the bite. It is a wondrous feeling on their end, sometimes quite sexual, other times a feeling of total completeness, a type of overwhelming fulfillment. Our bite fills the empty places in their hearts. It is a blessing for them, really."

"You said the ceremony is uncomfortable?"

"An understatement my boy, and it involves consorting with witches, something you should avoid at any cost. Black-hearted things."

"But I should like to have another child."

"Once you are at full strength, you can sire a vampire if you so desire. Having children of your body has a high cost, one which I have paid. I did it, but I don't recommend it."

Baron Rochon refused to discuss this again, and Gaspard lost interest in the subject. Mortal life seemed fleeting after a while, a speck of time in his long existence.

Luc Rochon taught him the nighttime duties of running a barony with a sizeable vampire population, a world hidden from those who walked the day. Gaspard learned about vampire politics and how to tell a burgeoning master vampire from ones that would always be subservient. He himself continued to grow in power and was soon able to influence vampires older than he.

Henri became his brother, and they shared as many moments during the evening as possible, until Henri had to retire and Gaspard had to work. The elder Baron simply left one day, with no forwarding address, and Gaspard never saw him again. They buried an empty casket and mourned his passing with the villagers, and eventually thoughts of Luc fled from the town's mind and memory.

Now, as he came out of his reverie, Gaspard struggled to remember the names of the scullery maids who were once so important to him. Did he have the equivalent of scullery maids now? What were their names? He made a mental note to find out.

He nodded to the butler. "Fetch Marc, please."

"Very well."

Gaspard paced as he waited for his assistant. His sense of the house was always accurate, and he could feel that it was unsettled. Something was wrong, and he couldn't tell what it was. There was an uneasiness in the air that he couldn't place.

A well-muscled man with long brown hair and the pale skin of a vampire knocked on the door.

"Good evening, Gaspard," said Marc. "Are you ready to go over your appointments?"

Gaspard's back was turned, so the vampire assistant kept on speaking. "You have a meeting with the visiting coalition from the Northeast Region. There are also several younger vampires that we've taken in to care for, and three are finding it hard to control their thirsts. Two sanguineers aren't enough, so I'm assigning three to each, and..."

"Three should be enough. If they need more, they will have to be staked. They will never gain control. The Northeast Region is your thing. You represent me. I have no interest in meeting with that little potato of a vampire. He simpers like a sycophant in the old courts. But this is not what I want to discuss."

"What then?"

"What I want to talk about is the disquiet I sense in the house."

Marc cleared his throat. "We've had some accidents with the reconstruction of the guest house and gazebo during the day. The architect and workmen are spooked."

Gaspard turned to stare at his assistant. "What do you mean, accidents? What did Marie say happened?"

"When Marie and I did our nightly handoff, the main topic of our discussion was that no matter what the workmen did, the gazebo wouldn't stand. They called in the architect, but he found no problems in the plan or the construction. They would build it, turn around to get more supplies, and the pieces would fall."

"Let me see the report."

Marc handed Gaspard a folder that contained the update from the day staff to the night staff. Marie and Marc worked together much as he had with Henri.

The note was written in Marie's precise handwriting.

At eleven o'clock in the morning, and then again at three and four, the supportive struts on the new gazebo collapsed. Contractors and architect are baffled by the continuing failure of the wood to hold. Despite careful review, they cannot determine why the construction continues to fall. They are bringing in wood with a steel core to see if that will solve the problem.

Gaspard read the note three times.

"Why do you think this building problem is what I am sensing?"

"I'm not sure, but it is the only thing I can pinpoint."

Gaspard shifted topics. “Did you know that Madame Beauchamp came to see me this evening?”

“I heard. What’s she like?”

“Honorable, proud, stubborn.”

“I take it she didn’t accept your latest offer?” Marc asked.

“No, she did not. She tossed it aside, literally.”

“What are you going to do?”

“For now, wait. I need Lisette.”

As if she heard, Lisette slipped into the room. She wore long, silver negligee, and her auburn hair was styled in an up-do so he would have clear access to her neck. She was his special sanguineer, a volunteer blood donor who was taken care of financially for her service. He had also paid for her law degree.

Without being asked, Marc bowed out of the room. Lisette smiled at Gaspard from the corner where she reclined against the wall. The slit of her negligee went all the way to mid-thigh revealing gorgeous tanned legs. Her toes were painted a deep red, and her green eyes teased him from afar.

“Well, my love, what is your need?” she said.

“Come here, Lisette.”

“Hummmm,” she purred. “What if I don’t want to?”

Gaspard smiled. “You want to.”

Lisette slid along the wall another few feet. “Make me.”

Before she knew it, before any mortal could see, he was in front of her. He stroked her face and then pulled her close. Just the smell of him was enough to arouse her. She licked his neck showing him what she wanted. He licked hers, and she trembled in response. He stroked his hands down her back, grabbing her hips and pushing them toward his arousal, which he released with one tug. He slowly, oh, so slowly, lifted her silk nightgown, pleased to learn she was naked beneath it. He lifted her by the hips and held her against his body. Her head dropped back and her eyelids fluttered. She dampened with an intense, animal need and thrust forward to make him move faster. He slipped into her in one stroke, biting at the same time. The flow of blood pulsated with the flow of their lovemaking, and for a moment, she saw the world from his eyes, and he from hers.

She saw the room in Technicolor, her skin so detailed she could see each of her own eyelashes and thought *I am beautiful.* He saw with dulled human eyes, but experienced her orgasm, an unexpected, delicious joy. Until that moment, he hadn't understood how breathtaking the experience was for his partner, the release of the body, the high of the bite, a soaring of spirit. In that moment, that exact moment, he finally glimpsed the full power of the addiction.

3

Kara stood outside the door, hand raised mid-knock. She'd been with Gaspard's household for a few months, assigned to Gaspard to provide protection, security upgrades, and training for security personnel.

She'd intended to update Gaspard on some of the protective measures she'd put in place, from the additional outside cameras to the hiring of extra guards, and the krav maga lessons she'd instituted. She'd procured new equipment, focusing on knives, swords, and for the larger men, the Viking axe, a particular favorite of hers. While guns were great for some things, the fool-proof way to kill a vampire was to behead it. Sharp, honed edges did that best, and she rubbed her hands together with glee at the thought. Oh, and she'd better tell him about the flame throwers. Fire was effective, too, and so much fun to use.

The thought of all those weapons and the hard training to follow made her giddy. Battle is what she lived for. She'd been almost happy as she approached Gaspard's office. Now she was disgusted.

The sounds from within the office were unmistakable, and while she was no prude, she was repulsed by the sheer exhibitionism, the renunciation of privacy, and the flaunting of their sexuality. The man was sex on two feet with fangs, but he'd never hear her say it. She specialized in icy stares, and that was all he was going to get.

She strode away, heading for the training room she'd established next to the new security headquarters. Four people were inside practicing with bo staffs, another weapon she insisted they learn how to use. She stepped inside the training room and watched the two men and two women spar.

The women stood opposite one another, as did the men. The male-female pair with their back to her attacked first. The woman adopted a horse stance, raised the bo over her head, brought it down and across the inside of her body, aiming for her opponent's ribs.

The man, taller than she, took a different route. He lifted the staff in both hands, one palm up, the other palm down. He lifted his right leg to his knee, held the bo stick above his shoulder and lunged forward intending to deliver a powerful front strike. The other man jumped back into a cat stance, widened his hands on the bo, and raised it to block the attack.

Kara watched the next few minutes, observing the intricate swirls and twists the opponents used.

"Stop!" Kara ordered.

Kara pointed to the man who had lunged into a deep front stance. "You're getting your overhead front strike mixed up with your front thrust. You only lunge that deeply for a thrust. For a strike, you can't step as far, which is why you lost power. Also, your bo starts parallel to the ground over your shoulder not angled backward," she said, gesturing for him to demonstrate that he understood. The man corrected his starting stance, and Kara gave a nod of approval.

"Now you," she said, turning to the woman. "Your overhead rib strike was executed well. Good job."

The woman grinned and shoved an elbow into her colleague's side.

"But after that, you guys all got twirly. These are bo sticks, not lightsabers, and they are for *battle*, not choreography. The twirls and circles are pretty, but they waste time. Focus your efforts on learning the basics and being able to block hard and fast."

The man said, "Are you saying we can't have fun?" He gave her a wink.

Kara closed her eyes, said a prayer to Odin to protect her from fools, and stepped deep into his personal space. "I am teaching you to be lethal. You want to be in a movie, go elsewhere." She stepped even closer.

The man blinked, leaning his torso backwards, his workout sweat switching to fear sweat.

Kara hissed the last part. "Do. You. Under. Stand?"

All four nodded.

Kara stepped away, relaxed her shoulders, pointed to the staff, and asked, "How do they feel?"

The woman who had been in the defensive position clapped her hands together. "They are so light! Flexible but strong. What are they made of?"

Kara replied, feeling a little smug. "Oak hard wood over teak. The oak makes them sturdy; the teak makes them light."

"I like the two tapered ends," added the woman with a wicked grin. "Much better for shoving through a vampire's chest."

"That's why they are made of wood, no foam or metal."

The fourth person, a man about six feet tall, ventured a question. "But there is metal. What are these for?" he asked, pointing to two small metal divots, one on each end of the staff.

Kara really smiled now. "My special surprise. Let me show you."

Kara was also six feet tall, so she borrowed the man's staff. She nodded to the smaller woman, who held up her staff in a protective stance.

Kara whirled her bo stick in a lightning fast foot sweep and followed with a thrust to the woman's chest. The woman backpedaled, off balance and stumbling, trying to bring her stick up in a high parry, but it was clear that in real battle, she would be dead.

That fact was punctuated when they all looked at the tip of the staff a few inches from the woman's heart and saw the hidden blade Kara had loosed as she attacked. The tip of the blade was only *millimeters* away from piercing the woman's body. Kara repressed the button, and the dagger slid back inside its sheath, within the tip of the bo staff.

"Oooohhh," breathed the woman. "I likeee. Handy-dandy for vamps."

"Exactly. Practice with them as much as possible. We don't want anyone slicing their own necks."

She exited considering the word handy-dandy. She liked it. She'd have to remember that one. Modern English was such an interesting language.

4

Adelaide tossed and turned, battling the primordial soup of age and worry. Visitors from the Historical Society were coming to see the house today, and she worried that they might back out of the deal. She hadn't been forthcoming about the state of disrepair.

She felt the ghosts on her skin and hoped there weren't any sensitives in the visiting party. She spoke aloud. "I'm trying to do what is best for all of us. Please behave!"

Precisely at eleven o'clock, two representatives from the Historical Society appeared on her doorstep.

"Hello, and welcome to the Beauchamp mansion. I am pleased to have you," Adelaide said as she accompanied them into the sitting room.

The man of the pair, a portly fellow named Beaumont Landry sported an anachronistic handlebar mustache. He gestured in what he must have thought to be a magnanimous manner and announced, in his most important voice, "I've always wanted to see the inside of this home. So many deals brokered in these rooms. This was once a place of power." He belched as he lowered himself onto the antique red velvet love chair.

Adelaide held her tongue, but thought, *this is still a place of power, you fat bastard.* Apparently, the resident ghosts agreed. She could feel their animosity deep in her bones, their cold fury sinking into her soul as they gathered in the sitting room, lowering the temperature by several degrees.

Beaumont's companion, a tall thin woman, shivered and drew her wrap tighter. She introduced herself as Harriet Alva and inclined her head toward Adelaide as she said, "Mrs. Beauchamp, we thank you for having us. This historic house must be preserved."

That made Adelaide smile. "I agree, Miss Alva. It is what my husband would have wanted. May I ask, with your last name, are you related to the celebrated Alvas from Spain who settled here in 1769?"

"Why, yes," Miss Alva said, fluttering her hand as if this was a trifle. "My family goes back generations."

"It certainly does. Wasn't much of your family's property burned down in the Great Fire of 1788?"

"It was, but it turned out to be a blessing as my family was able to rebuild and support the construction of our dear St. Louis Cathedral. There is a plaque to the Alva family's generosity in the rectory to this day. The Bishop has us in once a year to commemorate."

Adelaide gave her a thin smile. "How lovely for you. It is best that history be remembered."

"Yes, on that we can agree."

"Which is why I am so thrilled to have your promise to restore and preserve this wonderful home after my death," Adelaide said, drawing the conversation toward the most important topic. She offered a tray of canapés.

"Well," harrumphed Mr. Landry, "we will agree to preserve, but to restore," he said, waving his chubby index finger in the air, "that is what we have to see. There is a limit to our funds, you know."

"Why don't we take a tour of the house, Mrs. Beauchamp? Then we can discuss our next steps," said Miss Alva. "Drafty, isn't it?"

Adelaide's heart sank because she knew that they wouldn't like what they saw, and the ghosts were making things more difficult. It wasn't her fault that she and her husband had never had children. Or, maybe it was, but Louis never had children with any of his other companions either, and she was sure that if one of them could have conceived a child, they would have done so, if only to snare Louis for themselves and flaunt it in her face. Of course, she knew about his dalliances, but as any wife of the time, she turned a blind eye. Men would be men, and the women in their lives simply had to live with it.

She shepherded her visitors through the upstairs bedrooms where the paint was peeling, revealing water stains on the walls, and ushered them past a hall bath whose faucets had rusted right off. She waved away the comments about the broken wall tiles and the listing chandelier in the dining room and prayed they didn't trip on the uneven flooring. She kept up a steady flow of chatter as she escorted them room to room.

"And here," she said, gesturing to the scarred oak desk in the study, "is the very desk where Nathan Beauchamp signed freedom papers for all of his slaves. Many of them stayed on as help."

"That was generous of him to keep them on," remarked Miss Alva.

"Not really. They moved from slavery to indentured servants. It was a shameful time in our history. Tell me," said Adelaide, struggling to hold back her unladylike snark, "when did your family finally free their slaves?"

"After the Battle of Forts Jackson and St. Philip, of course. Like you said, it was a shameful time in our history."

By this time even Mr. Landry was blowing on his fingertips to keep them warm. He motioned to hurry things along.

Adelaide led them back to the sitting room, adding, "Luckily, the city itself was spared a battle, so we have many historic buildings to protect, isn't that true?"

"It is! And that is why we are here, though I am afraid, Mrs. Beauchamp, that though we would like to hold this building, it will require that you invest in some restoration. We had no idea the extent of the damage. The walls are cracking, and the floors seem warped. There is a shocking current of cold air even with the windows closed. The furniture is gorgeous, but what has happened to the house structure? It must be fixed, and I am afraid the Society cannot manage this all by ourselves."

Adelaide grimaced. She had a backup plan, but it would require selling her jewelry, a process she didn't want to do. But there was no choice, and anyway, she thought to herself, who would she give it all to?

Mr. Landry gazed at Adelaide and said, somewhat more kindly that he had spoken before, "Mrs. Beauchamp, I am a sincere admirer of your husband's family and their influence on the sugar industry in New

Orleans, but it is true. We cannot shoulder this burden. Please think about what you can do, and we will revisit the subject."

After the Society people left, Adelaide wept, a ghostly hand holding her own. The Rochons and Beauchamps didn't give in; they survived. They had made it through the Civil War, yellow fever, massive floods, early frosts, sugar mill fires, and intense negotiations with the DeBore family over land rights for sugar cane crops. She'd been childless at a time when fertility was a measurement of a woman's worth. More recently, she and her home had survived Katrina. She straightened her shoulders. She would do what she had to do and be glad it was an option.

The contractors blamed the unprecedented foundation damage on the shifting, swampy grounds native to Louisiana. Adelaide and staff needed to leave the property for a month while the experts lifted the house and rebuilt the foundation. Moving specialists arrived to package breakables and secure furniture.

While the contractors fussed over the soil on her plot, checking its acidity and debating whether it was more or less loamy than the neighboring land, Noel took Adelaide eighty miles away to Baton Rouge.

They arrived at an elegant storefront with discreet lettering announcing the location as Southern Estate Jewelry. The owner of the establishment was a man older than Adelaide herself and was someone she known since childhood.

"Paul, it is so nice for you to receive me," said Adelaide as the wizened man kissed her on both cheeks.

"Adelaide, you are still a beauty."

"Hush. We all know that isn't true," Adelaide said with a small smile.

"It is true, my dear. Allow me to introduce you to my son and grandson," Paul said, gesturing in a genteel manner toward the younger versions of himself that hovered nearby. The son clasped Adelaide's hand and brought it to his lips. The grandson nodded to her, wiggling back and forth in what appeared to be too tight shoes.

Paul locked the door and took Adelaide's arm. "Let's move to a private room in the back where we will be more comfortable."

As she walked across the floor, Adelaide was taken back to an earlier time and for a moment imagined she was once again the debutante of old. She gazed at the diamonds, gold, and other precious gems that lined the cases on either side of her, admiring their beauty, although some of the modern settings were not to her taste. Once, she would have been in here to buy, happily flitting from one case to another as Paul and Louis chatted, Louis prepared to indulge her every whim. *Those were good times*, she thought, *but times change.*

Paul gestured to a chair at a small table and sat in an opposite one, the son and grandson lingering in the background. He pulled out an artfully hidden drawer and withdrew a black velvet square, which he placed in front of Adelaide.

"Show me what you've brought, my dear," he said, sympathy in his eyes.

Adelaide wouldn't have tolerated sympathy from anyone else, but Paul had been a part of her life forever, a best friend to Louis and her close companion when Louis died, visiting on weekends, until both decided that the trip was too long for either of them.

Adelaide extracted a silk bag from her purse and handed it to Paul, who unwrapped it with care and placed the items on the black velvet. When he saw what was inside, he caught his breath.

"The star sapphire broach, Adelaide! And your wedding ring? Are you sure?"

"I have no one to give them to, Paul."

"I was there when Louis chose each of these pieces for you."

Adelaide reached up and touched Paul's face. "We both know you picked this ring out for me, Paul. Louis had terrible taste in jewelry."

Paul cracked a wide smile. "That is true. He thought bigger was better."

"Remember that ruby?" Adelaide said, letting forth a girlish giggle that would have shocked Gaspard.

"I never thought I'd say a ruby was ugly, but the cut was all wrong," Paul responded. "But Louis wanted you to have it."

"I'm glad you talked him out of it."

"He bought the gold bangle bracelets instead."

"I love them. I'm not ready to part with those yet."

"And yet, we have your diamond engagement and wedding ring here, the star sapphire from Burma, and your father's Elgin pocket watch."

"The chain is the original."

"I can tell," Paul said softly. "The gemstones have increased in value, especially since the rings are set in platinum. The pocket watch will sell for a few hundred."

"Whatever you can do, Paul, and thank you."

The son and grandson stared at the sapphire broach, eyes wide.

"How big is that?" asked the grandson.

His father estimated, "Fifty carats?"

Paul replied, "Forty carats, about eighteen carats smaller than the Rockefeller sapphire."

"What's the Rockefeller sapphire?" asked the grandson, leaning over his grandfather's shoulder, hand outstretched but floating mid-air as if he were struggling to restrain himself from feeling the jewel's glistening surface.

"John D. Rockefeller bought it from an Indian maharajah in 1934. That sapphire sold for over three million dollars at its most recent Christie's auction. I think this one, though smaller and missing the glamour of the Rockefeller provenance, will still sell a bit below that price. But I will need to send it New York, Adelaide."

"How will you sell it?"

"It will go on private auction with Christie's. They have a special list for people who want and can afford these things. They will take their cut and then you will get the rest. I don't know how long it will take. I'll sell the rings and watch from here."

"What about your cut, Paul?"

Paul narrowed his eyes. "Adelaide, I do this for you as a friend. After all these years, you think I'm going to charge you money?" The son, standing behind him, recoiled at this statement.

"Thank you, Paul."

"It is my pleasure, beautiful lady."

The two walked to the door holding hands. Adelaide spared a glance behind her to see Paul's son and grandson gaping at their retreating backs. Paul walked Adelaide to her car and opened her door. He leaned in and gave Adelaide a soft kiss on the forehead. "I still love you," he whispered.

Adelaide clung to him for a moment, then took her seat in the car. As Noel drove off, Adelaide wiped away a tear. Noel did a good job pretending he didn't see.

5

Adelaide paid Mathilde her wages for the month and waved as the maid set off on a trip to Disney World with her grandchildren.

"Okay, everybody," Adelaide said to her family ghosts. "We are out of money at present, and all living residents have to be out in a week. My only choice is the guest house."

The ghosts surrounded her, their anxiety bleeding into her body. Her blood ran cold, and she shivered in the warm air. She hadn't visited the old place in a long time and was afraid of what she would find, or what she would hear.

Placing one foot in front of the other and balancing with her cane, Adelaide made her way down the stone path to the cottage. She despaired just looking at it. Left to its own devices for years, the cottage tipped to the right. The roof had a sizeable hole, and as she entered, she could smell mildew in the main room. Surprisingly, the bedroom was in better shape, and there were linens in the closet still wrapped in plastic. The running water worked, despite the rust stains on the sink and tub. Once she plugged in the washer and dryer, they turned on, and she ran a load of towels she'd located under the bathroom sink just fine.

She placed a large bucket under the hole, shook out the bedding in the closet, and cleaned with some old rags she found in the kitchen. It was slow, painful work. Her back and hips screamed in agony. Her knee swelled, and she sneezed because of the thick dust. Using her cane meant one hand was occupied at all times, so she had to clean with the other. Nevertheless, after several painstaking hours, the house was dust free, the bed made, and the old icebox was cooling.

She stopped at nightfall and walked back to the main house, wanting to avoid staying in the guest house for as long as possible. Besides, she was physically and mentally exhausted and yearned for her own bed.

Adelaide was in the kitchen the next morning choosing what necessities she would carry to the guest house. She ached all over and was thinking that she might have a rolling cart somewhere when a loud knock on the door caused her to bolt out of her chair.

She caught her breath, smoothed her hair, and walked to the front door, which she feared would give way with the force of her visitor's pounding. Adelaide composed her face, as her mother trained her, and opened the door.

Nothing could have surprised her more.

A Nordic goddess stood on the step. She was six feet tall with blond hair, almost white, cut close to her head on the sides and back, but long over her eyes. Her eyes were ice blue, and the muscles showing from beneath her racerback T-shirt proved she was in formidable shape. She had a belt slung low around her waist with a knife sheathed on the left side and seven Japanese throwing stars on the right.

Kara turned her eyes on Adelaide. "You know who I am?"

Adelaide drew her shoulders up and lifted her chin. "You are Gaspard Bessette's assistant, Kara something-or-other."

"Svarstal. Kara Svarstal. And yes, I am his assistant, his First."

"What does that mean?"

"I am his top assistant, second in authority only to him."

"Why the weapons?"

Kara stilled. "I am also his bodyguard."

"You don't seem like the kind of woman who likes being ordered around by a man, or a vampire."

A frisson of distaste crossed Kara's face before she schooled herself. "I'm on loan."

Adelaide decided not to pursue that statement. She wasn't sure she wanted to know who was powerful enough to own this woman and lend her to someone else. Instead she asked, "Are you Swedish? You have a slight accent."

"Something like that."

Adelaide gestured the woman in, noticing that there was a bronze disc, about the size of a silver dollar, attached to the back of Kara's belt at the bottom of her spine.

Kara turned in a circle, taking in the packing boxes and plastic furniture coverings.

"Mr. Bessette noticed that you had contractors here."

"Mr. Bessette should mind his own business."

"He is concerned about your well-being. Lifting the foundation of an old house is no simple matter. Where will you stay?"

"None of your business! It is time for you to leave."

"There is a guest cottage on this property, yes? Is that your plan?"

Adelaide was fuming, but she nodded yes.

"I shall look at it."

"No. You do not need to look at it. Please go and tell Monsieur Bessette that I appreciate his concern, but I am fine."

Kara ignored her, walked on past, and exited through the kitchen door and to the back garden, following the stone path to the cottage. Adelaide tried to hurry after her but couldn't possibly keep up with the younger woman.

"What are you doing?" she yelled at Kara's back. "I did not give you permission! You need to leave!"

Kara whirled on her from several feet away, mouth set. "My employer directed me to ensure your health and safety. I *will* see this cottage if you mean to stay there." She strode off like a Spartan to war, without a look back. Adelaide decided to wait in the kitchen. She considered calling the police but shuddered at the thought of making a fuss. No, she could handle this. She fixed a cup of chicory coffee to keep her hands moving and her mind calm.

Several moments later, Kara burst in through the back door and said, "That house is simply unserviceable. It has a hole in the roof, rickety furniture, and I am certain there are mice in the walls. There was this constant scurrying just at the edge of my hearing. Gaspard will not allow this."

"Gaspard has no right or ability to do anything about it. It is my house, not his. And as far as the sound you heard, those aren't mice or any other living creature. Those are the daytime sounds of the ghosts who live there."

"I would have sensed ghosts," said Kara, matter-of-factly.

Adelaide raised one manicured eyebrow. "Is that so?" She flicked a finger to the corner of the room in a beckoning manner, and the ghost that hovered there floated forward and shifted *through* Kara's body. The lithe woman straightened to her full height and, in one fluid motion, unsheathed the knife with her right hand, whirling to look behind her and then spun in a full circle to locate the source of her discomfort. Adelaide wasn't surprised that Kara felt the ghost, nor that she felt it so acutely that she unsheathed a weapon.

She was surprised to see the knife stretch into a golden sword.

And she was *stunned* to watch Kara tug on the disc at her back, snap it open, and twirl it around in one smooth motion. Even the athleticism that it took to do that wasn't surprising. No, the shocking part was that the small disc expanded into a full bronze and silver shield.

The woman standing in front of Adelaide was something out of Norse mythology. Her entire body radiated with an ethereal glow. The sword and shield were decorated with runes and polished to a fine shine. Her body moved with the grace of a leopard, and her breathing stayed even and calm as a trained warrior's would. In the distance, Adelaide heard a horse whinny.

The two women stood frozen in place, staring at each other with curious eyes. Kara sheathed her sword and replaced the shield, once again a small disc that connected to her belt at the small of her back. She bowed to Adelaide.

"Well played, Madame."

"What are you?"

"A Valkyrie."

Adelaide poured two mugs of coffee, reached under the cabinet, grabbed a bottle of Kahlua, poured a healthy amount into each mug, and handed one to Kara. Both women sank into chairs and leaned their arms on the scarred wooden table.

"I knew you were something, but with all the fairytale creatures coming to light these days, it is hard to know what is real and what isn't. I was originally thinking Amazon."

"No, too Wonder Woman. Valkyries are real."

"Why is a Valkyrie working for a vampire?"

Kara sipped her coffee, scrunching up her nose at the question. "Let's just say I lost a bet." She shrugged. "But Gaspard isn't bad once you get to know him. He's got an old-world charm and code of honor that I respect."

"Why couldn't you feel the ghosts here?"

"That is an excellent question. I should have been able to, but maybe since they weren't fallen soldiers…? I have no answer now. Who was that, by the way?"

"Nathan Beauchamp, my husband's ancestor who owned this house during the Civil War. He is the one who got the Beauchamps into the sugar industry, making the family quite wealthy—which was easy since he used slave labor. He freed his slaves toward the end of the war, and the family had money troubles for awhile, but they were able to make it."

"Why is he hanging around?"

"Several individuals are still here. I get the sense there is unfinished business of some kind, but I don't know what it is. They've been present since I moved in. They keep me company."

"You can see and feel them?"

"Mostly feel them. They don't adopt a substantial shape, but I can perceive them. I've never personally seen a ghost manifest in the physical plane. That is a peculiarity of only the strongest hauntings."

"Why?" asked Kara.

"The ghost has to hold strong human emotion to tie itself to the physical world. Something has to feed that emotion, be it love, anger, shame…whatever. It is rare to see more than a gauzy haze or a translucent outline."

"Interesting. I've never met a sensitive like you."

"It's a family quirk," Adelaide replied. "Now something interesting about you. You said you can sense ghosts but couldn't sense this one…" She gestured with her hand for more information.

"I'm learning that there may be a number of things I can't perceive," said Kara, frowning behind her coffee mug. "But we digress. You can't stay in that cottage. It's in shambles."

"I am staying in that cottage, and it isn't your choice. And by the way, how did that exasperating man know that the foundation needed to be replaced?" Adelaide's temper rose, and it was only years of strict, knuckle-cracking instruction that allowed her to place her mug onto the table rather than throw it.

Kara drained the dregs of her coffee, unimpressed with Adelaide's anger. "He knows something about old houses and guessed. Let me suggest a compromise. Please allow my employer to fix the hole in the roof, clean up the place, and provide food and cooking utensils for you."

"I don't want charity."

"Oh, for goodness sake, Mrs. Beauchamp, he has more money than he could ever spend. Let him help you. It will make him feel better and make you safer."

"Why will it make him feel better?"

"I told you. He has an old-world honor. He wouldn't rest knowing that an elder lived next door in squalor. It would bug him to no end."

Adelaide's eyes sparkled. "If it will drive him crazy, maybe I should do it."

Kara placed her hand on Adelaide's. "It would make *me* feel better to know you are in a safe, secure place."

Adelaide considered her options. She had no way of knowing when Paul would call, so though money was coming, she had no idea when. Something had changed during her visit with Kara. It was as if she'd made a new friend. That hadn't happened in so long she'd forgotten what it felt like.

She inclined her head. "I accept, with thanks, and Kara?"

"Yes?"

"Call me Adelaide."

6

At least the woman would allow him to help her. Gaspard owed her that much. It was her ancestor after all that shepherded him into this life. He would have died a starving pauper if not for the Baron de Rochon.

Lisette ran her hand down his back, scooting up behind him so she could massage his shoulders and the strong muscles in his upper arms. She'd adapted to his nighttime hours, sleeping later into the morning so she could take afternoon classes during law school. Now that she was an associate at a local firm, she needed to be in early, and their schedule was becoming troublesome. He liked Lisette very much, but his insight the other night into her addiction coupled with the necessities of her career made him think it was time to let her go.

But not now. He twisted and brought his right hand up to cup her head, pulling her mouth to his. While maintaining the kiss, she moved around him so she was sitting in his lap, his groin next to hers, both of them aroused, but he didn't want a hard, fast encounter. He wanted to make it last, since he realized this would be the last time. He wanted to seduce her.

He broke the kiss and nipped her bottom lip, massaging her shoulders before he slipped her robe off. He massaged her arms and then, in one movement, lifted her off him and lay her down on the bed so he could gaze his fill. He skimmed his hands down her body, teasing, tempting, but never letting his touch fulfill her desires. She arched her back, thrusting her breasts up for his touch, and brought her hands up above her head to grasp the bedstead, a sign of her surrender.

Their lovemaking was a languid dance that took them both to the brink, brought them down, and started up again. It was long, beautiful, and for Gaspard, bittersweet. He held back his bite, an act of self-denial unsurpassed in its difficulty. He plunged into her, mouth at her neck, scenting, breathing, but didn't even nibble, no matter how she pushed her neck into his mouth, twisted to give him better access, and begged.

"Why?" she demanded, after it was over, but the tears in her eyes told him she already knew.

She left that evening, and Gaspard called for a sanguineer he did not know.

The woman who entered was middle-aged with a strong frame and, he couldn't help but notice, a beautiful bosom. She was shaking like a leaf but managed a wan smile.

"Come here and sit beside me," Gaspard said, patting the sofa next to him.

"Thank you, sir."

"What is your name?"

"Sarah."

"What made you volunteer for this job?"

She looked away for a moment. Gaspard reached out, placed one finger under her chin, and turned her to face him.

"It is okay; you can tell me."

"My son."

"You have a child?"

She had tears in her eyes. "Yes, he's four, but his father is abusive, and I don't want him near me or my boy."

"And you came to me thinking that we could protect you if you became a sanguineer?"

"Yes, your staff told me this was possible." She was wringing her hands by this time. Her knee bobbed up and down with anxiety.

"Marc!" Gaspard called.

"Yes, sir?" Marc said from the door.

"Have we looked into Sarah's situation?"

"Not yet, sir."

"Please do so, and have Kara do it."

"Oh," grinned Marc, "that's evil. He won't stand a chance. Sarah, where does your husband like to hang out? A bar? A pool hall?"

"Skeeter's Tavern. He drinks and plays darts. He's quite good." Her knee stopped bouncing, but she was rubbing her hands together as if to keep warm.

"Marc, please ask Kara to make sure he knows that Sarah and their boy are under our protection. Let's make it very clear. Not deadly, but she should leave no room for doubt."

Marc chuckled. "She's going to love this."

Gaspard turned to Sarah. "You may stay here until we are sure you are safe. In the meantime, I want you to be certain about taking on this position. We will provide protection for you whether you are a sanguineer or not. It is your choice. You should know that there is a chance you might become addicted to the bite. I'm going to make sure all sanguineers are rotated to lessen the chance, but in all honesty, I can't guarantee it won't happen."

"I knew what I was doing when I applied," she responded. "I'm just nervous because I've never done this before. I have no idea what to do."

Gaspard looked deep into her eyes and said, "Ah, *mon ange*. Relax." She took a deep breath, closed her eyes, and he could hear her heart rate slow. He brushed her neck with the tips of his fingers, and her head lolled to one side. Moving closer, he breathed on her neck, bringing his left arm up to steady her head. His right hand rubbed gentle circles on her upper back between the shoulder blades, providing a gentle, reassuring pressure. Her breathing slowed and her body relaxed into his embrace. He bit into her but with as much care as possible, and she didn't flinch. She didn't seem to even notice.

Her blood was sweet with the depth of fine wine. This wasn't the blood of a young girl fresh out of school and ready to take on the world. This was the blood of a woman who had loved, laughed, and grieved. He savored it before swallowing, breathed in her scent, and with an effort of pure willpower, moved away from her when he'd had enough. *I could drink her down,* he thought, dragging himself away with one last inhale and a shake of his head. His thoughts flew to a woman he'd known in Paris. *I shall have to be careful.*

Sarah recovered from her stupor, like a woman coming out of a pleasant dream. She nodded to Gaspard and slipped out the door.

After dinner, Gaspard called for Marc.

"Are you ready to discuss the evening's schedule, Monsieur?"

"I am."

"I understand that Lisette has left us? Should I arrange a severance salary for the period of one year?" the executive asked, looking down at his feet so as not to cause Gaspard any embarrassment.

"Yes. And we need to discuss the sanguineer policy."

"In what way?"

"The addiction is worse than I understood. I am afraid for our sanguineers' mental health. I think we should try rotating them so they don't give more than once a week, and not to the same vampire. How have our longest sanguineers managed?"

"They are addicted, but they volunteered for this position and have been well compensated. They show no desire to leave."

"Drug addicts don't want to leave their heroin, either. I want a doctor to visit Lisette tomorrow to see how she is doing. We may need to wean Lisette off the bite in stages. Now, what appointments do I have this evening?"

"The contractors working on Mrs. Beauchamp's property want to give you a short update. They are waiting in the front room."

"I shall go to them now."

Gaspard walked the few steps from his office to the front room, finding two of the contractors waiting for him, looking uncomfortable sitting on an antique chintz sofa in their sawdust-covered work boots and carpenter's pants.

The two men stood and shook hands with the vampire. The head of the team spoke.

"Mr. Bessette, we wanted to let you know that the foundation on the Beauchamp mansion is even worse than we thought. There are the normal fractures that one would expect on a house that old, but it is almost as if someone dug tunnels from the main house to the grounds, or perhaps the other way. It is very odd. We will have to fill in quite a bit of dirt."

Gaspard nodded. "I am sure that Madame is not prepared for that extra cost."

"She is not, which is why we came to you as you requested."

"You did right. I will pay for the extra work, but do not tell Madame. She wouldn't accept my assistance in this way. You must do it without letting her know."

"Yes, sir. That is generous of you."

Kara walked in on the tail end of the discussion and stood by as the contractors left. Her hands were crossed in front of her, hip jutted out to the right, a small scowl on her face. She wore jeans and an old T-shirt that read, "New Orleans: Lestat sucked here."

"You summoned?" she said, dragging out the word with an acerbic flair to show how she felt about being called like a dog on a leash.

"I need you."

"What for? And by the way, Adelaide is not going to like it if she finds what you are doing."

"So, let's ensure she does not find out."

"Why do you think there is all of this extra damage?" she asked. "You must have a theory."

"I do not have a theory, but I'm going to ask you to help find the answer."

Kara made a face. "What do you want me to do?"

"Do what you do best. Explore, study, research. Listen. See if there is anything that we don't know about that property that we need to know. Fault lines? Sand pits? What is causing that level of destruction to the property?"

Kara gritted her teeth and said, "You know damn well that is *not* what I do best. What I do best is search for and gather the slain on the battlefield. What I do best is serve Odin. What I do best is fight in hand-to-hand combat, or on horseback with a sword. I do *not* babysit older society ladies and investigate mundane soil shifts in this swamp of a state."

The air around her roiled with an unnatural energy. She was furious, bored, and more than a little annoyed that she'd landed in this spot, despite it being her fault. It amused him. He liked to watch when she got like this. The energy she released reached out and touched his aura, tickling it at the edges. It was arousing and provocative, like nothing he had ever experienced before. She intrigued him, and if he wasn't so afraid of, nay...not afraid, *cautious* of upsetting her true boss, she'd already be his.

Maybe. He wasn't sure he could make her be anything if he was honest with himself.

Gaspard reclined with a languorous, leonine air on the chintz sofa while the Valkyrie in front of him protested. He watched her with half-closed eyes, enjoying the show. The air was crackling around her, sparks flying from her heels. He wondered what it would be like to be inside all that energy. Would it be like being in the calm of a tornado, or plunging into the full force of a hurricane? He hoped to one day find out.

His feigned air of indifference infuriated her even more. The house shook, and the chandelier in the nearby living room tinkled in protest.

"Kara! Control yourself before someone gets hurt. Or, before I have to spend more money fixing things."

Kara took a deep breath and shook the tension out of her arms, rolling her neck to release those muscles. She paced three steps one way and three steps back, forcing the energy into physical release. The antique rug she was pacing on smoked as the energy grounded itself like electricity. He sighed. Yet another thing to replace.

"Why is it that I have to do this task? Aren't there others who would be better at this job?"

"Stop pacing! The rug you're burning a hole in is worth at least ten thousand dollars. I have money, but I don't like to waste it because an employee has a temper tantrum."

Kara looked down at the scorched, ruined rug. "Sorry, but it's your fault."

Maybe he had baited her. He'd burn a hundred rugs if he got to see her in her full glory, even once. If he got to share that energy with her. Got to hold her in his arms and have her look at him with a burning desire.

Moving on, he said, "Madame likes you, and you have to admit she is clever. She got the best of you, didn't she? Tricking you into revealing yourself like that."

The old woman had gotten the best of her. She had to admire Adelaide's spunk. Kara hadn't felt the house ghosts, and the eighty-year-old used that to her advantage.

"You haven't sensed any ghosts here, have you?" Gaspard asked. "Ghosts don't usually like to hang around vampires. We're both dead, yet vampires are still living. I think it frustrates them."

"Ghosts are remnants of the past, with not fully capable minds and bodies like vampires. It is not true to state that a vampire is dead, technically speaking, at least not to people like me," responded Kara, arms crossed. Her posture said this was a subject she didn't care to discuss.

Now Gaspard was curious. "How do you sense us?"

"Vampires take up space in the physical realm. You aren't dead, you are undead, or perhaps altered-living," Kara explained. "Ghosts exist solely in a metaphysical realm."

"Altered-living," mused Gaspard. "Perhaps I should petition the city council to accept us as a special interest group, like the physically disabled, albeit with an expanded life-span and a severe allergy to sunlight."

"I'm sure if you wanted that, you could get it passed through the legislature," Kara responded with a grimace. "You own the city council."

Gaspard stood up and stepped toward Kara, lowering his voice. "It is true," he whispered. "But there are many things I want and don't yet own."

He took another step toward her and waited for her response. When she didn't move, he took another, and then still another so that he was inches from her body. He could see the pulse in her neck, sense her heartbeat, and feel her breath. Her scent was intoxicating, and he breathed it in, savoring the taste of it on his tongue. He reached out one hand and caressed her cheek, locking gazes with her for that one moment, his eyes searching for something, anything, in hers.

She never budged, never flinched, but her glare told him not to move one millimeter closer. He wondered how quickly she could move. Was she faster than he was? Did he dare?

"We can't get everything we want," she snapped, ducking under his arm, sliding past his body and out the door.

Gaspard crossed his arms over his chest and let out a deep breath. How ironic. The ladies' man couldn't get the one lady he wanted.

7

Once Adelaide agreed to accept Gaspard's help to restore and move her things into the guest house, she took to it like the society lady she was.

"You there, young man, handle those dishes with care, please! They are real china, not paper plates!"

"Your hands are rather dirty, sir. Would you please wash them before touching my clothing? And for goodness sake, wipe your feet off before you enter the house. You are tracking mud everywhere."

Once the four beleaguered movers left the cottage, Adelaide settled about making the cottage as homey as possible. She puttered with plants on the windowsill, fluffed pillows, made some tea, which she then let get cold, and delayed the inevitable.

Finally, she walked the perimeter of the cottage. When she reached the back, she stopped and saw in the waves and valleys of the grounds what others might not, but she knew was there.

The remnants of the slave pen.

Nathan Beauchamp and his father and grandfather before him were masters of the slave trade. The pen had been thirty feet long and twenty feet wide, with two floors, made of logs bound with iron bars. The floors had been covered in straw, but the straw was never changed or cleaned so it was soaked in urine, feces, and blood. In the middle, on both floors, was a long iron post running the length of the room, to which slaves were shackled. Some were shackled so tight they couldn't sit or lie down and were locked in a permanent upright position. Thousands of slaves made their way through this crowded, fetid, odorous pen. Men and women were separated, and if they cried out or protested, they were whipped. They stayed in this cruel structure until it was time for them to walk, still shackled, to the old St. Louis Hotel for auction.

The Beauchamp's wealth was made on the backs of these poor people, and the Rochons knew and approved. She carried this guilt with her every single day.

It was their cries she heard at night down on this part of the grounds. It was their ghosts who haunted her dreams, and Adelaide would have done anything to avoid having to face them. Did Gaspard Bessette know a slave pen also existed on his land? It was the sale of human cattle that made the Leroux family wealthy. They traded human flesh as well as horse flesh, and they valued the horses more. The Leroux racetrack and their history of winners was a byproduct of the slave trade. The stud fees alone made them rich. It was why she couldn't stand horse racing to this day.

"Well, nothing for it. Must face this if I am to have any peace down here," she said out loud. "If you choose to visit me this evening, please know that I feel your pain and am sorry that my family had anything to do with your suffering."

The ground shifted beneath her feet, making her unstable. She caught her breath as the darkness closed in and the temperature dropped. She hurried into the cottage and locked the door, all the time knowing that such flimsy barricades had no effect on the injured souls that still dwelled here. She headed to bed, shivering while sweating, shaking while resting, trying to hold back the onslaught she knew was to come.

It came in the form of a ghost so fully realized that she thought she could touch him. He told her his story, forced her to witness the cruelty of that time. And as he recounted his tale, the scenes played for Adelaide like a movie where she was the star, so that each feeling, each emotion, each pain dug into her bones and mind, ensuring that she didn't just see the movie, but felt it raw, unfiltered, and true.

My name is Amos. I was married, not legal o'course, but in my heart, to

Betsy. We were born into slavery in Virginia, but our master sole us, leaving our son and daughter, eight and five at the time, alone on the cotton plantation.

My Betsy begged to keep the chirrin with her, but she was beatin' for beggin'. She didna care. She lay on the floor, hands in supplication, promisin' to be the best slave evah, if the chirren could come with us. Our master kicked her in the head, and I whispered to her to stop. The chirren were nearby and didn't need to see their mama kilt. Two of the women slaves remainin' behind hugged the kits and moved them away. We hoped they got taken care of.

Adelaide's chest heaved with the heaviness of their grief, almost crushing the breath out of her. It was her children left behind. She was abandoning them.

We were shipped down hereah and kept in this pen 'afore bein' sole at auction. The first night the roof leaked bad and the rains almost drowned us. We couldna move, shackled to the bars like we were, and the only thing that kept me goin' was knowing that Betsy was up floors helpin' with the cookin'. I dinna wanna leave her, so I forced myself to stand, head above the water until my legs gave out.

Adelaide's legs quivered with the effort of trying to stand. Her lips moved with the Lord's Prayer.

After the rains came the skeeters, bit'en us every wheah and leavin' us scratchin' and itchin'. It was tons painful and most of us got sick from it and several died. We were fed bits o'bread, cornmeal mostly, but not enough. We were sick, wet and starvin' and just waitin' for the day when it was time to be sole again.

The itching was unbearable, and she scratched herself all over, welts rising like flames. Her belly growled with hunger.

By the time that day came, I learned that Betsy wouldna be comin' too. She was to stay heeah and work the shuga' fields. I begged to stay and work the processin' and that Sylvester Beauchamp, Nathan's daddy, 'lowed it since I was strong. The processin' was damn terrible work, with insects everywheah and more rats than people. The frost came early one season and we stayed up four nights in a row tryin' to save the crop.

The rats crawled across her feet, and she slapped at the gnats in her eyes.

While I was processin' Betsy was workin' the fields. I hardly saw her, but I done know where she was, so I'd look to the fields hopin' to catch a glance of her. We could see each other as we passed in the evenin', she to the women's quartas' and me to men's. Someatimes we could almost touch hand, skatin' fingertips over one anothas 'afore someone saw.

Betsy's fingers brushed Adelaide's, and she was consumed by an unbearable want.

One night I caught sighta Betsy and couldna believe what I saw! My wife, my wife, *had a iron colla on with three horns sticken' outta it and a bell in each horn so you could heah her comin' wherever she are. No hidin'. Her face was black 'n blue, and I knew wannah must o'happened.*

The rage was barely banked. It rose up in her in a wave and pushed out all reason.

I was fightin' a mighty anger inside and was askin' which one was it. Doncha ya know it was lil old' Nathan Beauchamp hisself. Yeah, you got that right. Nathan decided to take advantage of my wife, and when she fought, she got beaten and punished with the colla. The colla was heavy and she couldna sleep with it so she grew weaker and weaker. I was tole to make peace wit it and be glad she didn't get the mask with the muzzle, but I was watchin' her die, and couldna stand by no longa.

Grief. Sadness. Exquisite pain.

When we passed in the evenin' I broke the line and grabbed her, tryin' to unhook the colla. I was pulled off and taken' to the side o' the house where I was whipped. I yelled bad things at them and they just kep' goin' at it. They marked my back so bad I couldna stand. I collapsed on the ground and otha slaves drug me to the slave house.

The rage broke free and flowed like a dam released, accompanied by the crack of the whip in her ears and the bite of the whip on her back. She writhed with it, screaming aloud for them to stop.

My wife was killed that night as punishment to me. She was suffocated. Her air cut off. She suffaed! She cried for me, I know, but I didna come. Afta that my heart was broken and I gave up. I died of infection from the whip marks on my back and they threw me in an unmarked grave and heah I've stayed, my anga growin' for years now. And isn't jus' me. Theah are hundreds of us and we getting' more powerful wit time. Soon, you'll see.

She was consumed by an unbearable anguish until she was spent, limp and focused on one thing. Justice.

Adelaide's head whipped to the right as a ghostly, yet impossibly physical, hand slapped her across the face. She could still feel the whip marks on her back. Somehow, she knew that she always would carry those scars.

Amos disappeared.

Adelaide, at age eighty, wet the bed.

8

Being a ghost, Nathan floated along unaware of time. When he died, he rose out of his body, drifted to a corner of the room and watched while the doctor pronounced him dead. He observed his own funeral preparations, tried to comfort his wife until he realized she couldn't sense him, and after the hubbub was done, he...lingered. There was nowhere to go and nothing to do, and he got tired of watching generations pass, and he set about fading to almost nothing.

Then Adelaide came, a member of the Rochon family, who were known for being sensitives. She brought the ghosts out of their slumber. He hadn't realized others were lingering, too, including his father Sylvester, and Slinky, the field boss during his time. The biggest surprise was that his most trusted house servant, Martin, a free colored man from up north, lingered, too.

He pondered why the four of them hadn't moved on. He'd witnessed his wife's crossing and his children's, and countless others as they entered the Door, and yet, he'd never been drawn to the Door and didn't believe Sylvester, Slinky, or Martin had either.

What he did feel was something he now recognized as anxiety, a puzzling development. He had been confused by the feeling at first and was slow to realize what it was. The unsettled feeling took hold the day Adelaide talked to the Historical Society and hadn't left, exhuming him from his sleep inch by inch until he was aware, mindful of his surroundings and the comings and goings of everyday life. Adelaide had moved out to allow the refurbishment to begin, and he was unhappy that he couldn't keep an eye on her, but he was trapped within the house. His apprehension grew each passing moment, and it was creeping into fear. Sylvester, Martin, and Slinky felt the growing dread as well, and the four ghosts gathered in the kitchen, staring out the back window, watching for something they could not see.

9

Skeeter's Tavern was full, men drinking draft beers with one another, clapping each other on the back, and laughing like everything was funny.

She could smell the desperation that lay under the jovial facade, the frustration, the failures, and the violence. It was right there for the taking, shimmering under the surface of banal civility. The niceties of society spread a fragile layer over the seething mass of anger that roiled beneath.

These men were angry at everyone. Their bosses, their former bosses, the fathers and mothers who raised them with high expectations. They hated with ferocity, and no one was spared, not even their children and wives.

She drew on her power to keep her camouflage in place, throwing dark brown hair over her shoulder, loathing that she was six inches shorter than normal. But she was there to do some damage, and she wanted to take him by surprise. Walking in as a six-foot armed warrior wasn't ambush material. It would have been satisfying but a tactical mistake. Kara didn't make tactical mistakes.

"Hey lovely lady," slurred one of the men, a barrel-chested guy with a copper mustache. "You lookin' for company? You must be in all that leather and your titties hanging out like that. What do they call that? A boob picker-up?" He shimmied his upper torso back and forth in the mistaken belief that he needed to illustrate what he meant.

"A bustier."

"Whatever," said the man, waving his hands in the air and swaying back and forth on his barstool. "I like it!"

Another man, more gut than chest, spilled his beer on her feet. "You're not her type, Bud. This lady is cla-ssssy. You can tell by them boots. No low-life woman can afford boots like that. Maybe she's got a shuga daddy somewhere. But mebbe not. I don't see anyone lookin' after you, baby girl."

The man grabbed her by the waist and tried to pull her in for a kiss. Kara turned her back to avoid him, but he shoved her up against the bar and rubbed his crotch along her backside, flaunting nothing as he was so drunk an erection was impossible. Kara looked around and realized the other guys had moved on to new distractions, so she decided to take some action. She jabbed her head back into his nose, and he jumped back like a bear stung by honeybees, shaking his head as if to make sense of the situation. His nose bled down his shirt, and Kara was certain he'd have two black eyes.

She used his confusion as an opportunity to drum the message home. She grabbed his crotch with her right hand and exerted pressure on his Adam's apple with her left.

She looked him in the eye and said, "Go. Away."

By this time, the bartender had rushed around the bar to push the man off her, but when he saw her handiwork, he looked her up and down and realized this was a woman who didn't need help. The bartender had been around a long while. He knew Gaspard, not personally, but by reputation, and was perceptive enough to know this lady belonged to the Master.

"Wh...what are you doing here, Miss...?"

"Layla," she said, using the name she'd chosen for that night.

"Miss Layla. I believe you here for a specific reason. Wouldn't see you in here normal-like. Does Mr. Bessette need something I can provide?" He swallowed hard and looked down at his feet, trying to keep his gaze from Kara's chest.

"Who's the jerk-off cockroach that married a woman named Sarah and likes to beat on her and their four-year old son?"

The bartender shrunk away from her but whispered, "That'd be Bobby, over there talking to the blonde. Look lady, I don't want no trouble, so whatever your business with him, do it elsewhere, okay? Just make sure Mr. Bessette knows I helped you."

Kara gave him a cold stare. "Mr. Bessette *expected* you to help me. You've done no more than the minimum, which allows you to keep all of your body parts connected together."

The bartender stammered, shifting his eyes left and right to avoid her glare. "Fair enough. Understood. Uh...yeah, well, he's over there." He gestured his head toward a muscular gentleman in jeans and an old concert T-shirt, a pack of cigarettes rolled up in his left sleeve, then he scurried away.

Kara rolled her neck, put a little sway in her hips, and approached the cockroach, letting a little desire seep out of her core and float its way toward him. He turned to her as quick as a boy smelling a fresh-baked apple pie cooling on the window sill. When he turned, Kara saw his left arm tattoo and had to fight not smack him right there and then. Who the hell puts a pig hugging a dancing beer bottle on their arm?

The other arm was imprinted with a heart and the name Sarah. Maybe he wasn't a complete douche. Kara felt a smidgeon of anger leave her body, but that smidgeon returned, with friends, when the cockroach held both hands out in a grabby-grabby motion and said, "Can I feel those?"

"Maybe later, baby," Kara purred, pulling at his arm and placing it around his waist. Kara looked at the blonde, who hadn't taken the hint and loitered nearby. "Take a hike." The blonde flounced off and found a new target.

Kara could read the cockroach's face like a dime-store novel. The cockroach couldn't believe his luck. He was staring down at the most perfect set of boobies he'd ever seen, and a hot chick was begging for his attention. If he'd been sober, he may have recognized the warning signs of a situation going downhill fast, but as it was, his beer-addled brain couldn't see past those luscious mounds of flesh. He was visualizing burying his head in between them when Kara leaned in and nipped his lower lip. He almost came right then.

"Come with me, lover," Kara said, guiding him off the stool and toward the back door. The other men in the bar hooted and hollered, some in admiration and a few in jealousy. The beer gut guy from earlier held ice to his face and clutched his draft, knuckles reddening with the force of his grip. His eyes never left them, and he stared hard until they walked out the door.

"Hey gorgeous. I can't take it no longer. Come here and let's pull that thingee off of you and set those bambas free."

Kara winked and pulled him farther away toward the back of the parking lot. She doubted anyone would hear them, but she didn't need to take chances.

Cockroach stopped walking, bent over, and heaved. What sloshed down smelled foul, and what stayed on his clothes smelled worse. Kara rolled her eyes and decided to finish it.

She grabbed him by the T-shirt and pulled him up in front of her, slamming him against a car. She wondered if a car alarm would go off and then looked at the piece of shit vehicle and realized it would be a blessing to whomever drove it if it got totaled.

"Whatcha doin?" Cockroach asked. Kara slapped him.

"I have a message for you. Are you listening?"

"Uh huh." Kara slapped him again.

"Sarah and your boy are off limits to you. You go near them again and you will regret it, I assure you."

"She's my wife!"

"Consider this your divorce notice."

"She can't keep me from my son!"

"She might not be able to, but I sure as fuck can, and I will make mincemeat out of you if you so much as look at either of them, much less raise a hand to them."

"It was the one time," Cockroach whined.

"One time too many."

Cockroach was sobering up and decided he'd be tough. He pushed Kara and held up his fists in a way that he thought was threatening. Kara yawned.

"How's a little thing like you going to stop me from getting to my family, bitch? You think 'cause you're hot you can tell me what to do? You can't! I've got rights under the law and under God 'cause it is the righteous way of things." He swung his right fist, spitting vestiges of throw up in her face. Kara sidestepped.

He followed with a ham-fisted punch with his other hand. She side-stepped again.

Kara was delighted. She'd been hoping for this. When he punched a third time, she grabbed his fist and flipped his arm behind his back, pulling the arm up so there was maximum pressure on his shoulder. "I'm stronger than I look," she hissed. "And I'll dislocate your shoulder without a second thought if you don't promise to stay away."

"Hey!" a big voice bellowed at her from halfway across the parking lot. Beer Gut and his cronies were there, six men in all, lumbering toward her like bulls.

Kara grinned and yanked Cockroach's arm up and out, dislocating the shoulder and breaking the wrist. He screamed, went down, and stayed there.

Beer Gut barreled toward her but stopped dead when she let go of her camouflage and flashed into her full glory. She drew her sword and held the point at Beer Gut's throat, the other men falling to their knees.

"It's an angel!" one of them said. "A real angel from Heaven."

"Not quite, but you're in the right ballpark," Kara said. "I came to warn this man," she pointed to Cockroach slumped on the ground, gibbering to himself, "to stay away from his wife and son. They are under my protection. And that goes for any of you who think beating your wife and kids makes you a man. You want to get on my good side, stop drinking, stay home, and take care of your families. You have been warned!"

Thunder crashed as she finished, lighting up the night behind her, haloing her in a nimbus of light that made the men prostrate themselves on the ground. Cockroach passed out.

Figuring her work was done, Kara stalked away, not looking behind her.

She got to her truck, smiling to herself, looked at the sky, and said, "Thanks, Thor. Appreciate the assist." A rumbling roll of thunder laughed its way by.

10

While Kara was taking care of business, Gaspard was finishing paperwork like any normal businessman when the guard house radioed in that a big man was at the gate with Lisette in the car. "Something is wrong with her, Mr. Bessette. She looks sick."

"Send them in."

The butler opened the door a crack. "May I..."

"No, you may not, but your master can," thundered a big, burly man, pushing right past the butler and into the foyer. The man was six-two-ish, wearing workman's boots and painter's pants in size huge. He had a bushy beard and could have passed for a lumberjack. Or a tree.

Gaspard came out to see what the disturbance was and stopped cold. It wasn't the size of the man. It was what he held—a limp, lifeless Lisette, dressed in a T-shirt and panties.

"You did this to her!" the man accused. "You have to fix her!"

Gaspard blinked once and then said, "In here, hurry."

He led the man to his study and motioned for the man to place Lisette on a couch. The man lowered her flaccid body, and Gaspard checked for a pulse.

"She's breathing and her heart is beating, but it is very fast and she won't wake up. This started after you sent her away," the man said, staring at Gaspard's back. Gaspard was on one knee next to Lisette.

"What's your name?" Gaspard asked, unbuttoning his shirt at the wrist.

"Ned. I'm Lisette's brother. People call me Tiny." The man was pacing, and the tension danced around his body in flashing sparks. You didn't need to be a vampire to sense it.

"You may want to leave, Ned. I think she is suffering withdrawal, and I'm going to have to feed her blood. My blood."

"I'm not leaving, so do what you can, but if she dies, so help me, you will answer for it. I might not have mentioned this, but I'm the smallest of her four brothers."

"I shall endeavor to save her, so I do not have to face that particular threat," replied Gaspard, who rose to fetch a letter opener.

This could be done with teeth, but it was so uncouth, and why do that when a sharp letter opener was available?

Gaspard knelt next to Lisette's head and sliced his wrist with the letter opener. He held the dripping appendage over her mouth and encouraged her to drink it.

"Come on, sweetheart, you can do this," he murmured. Lisette didn't move to drink, and her breathing became more labored.

"It's not working!" raged her brother, already making a fist. Marc, who had been watching from the doorway, slipped in and covered the man's raised fist with his own. He pushed downward, and Ned's arm collapsed to the side. Ned's eyes were wide and his mouth open.

"Gaspard is doing what he can," Marc hissed showing some fang. "You will not threaten him again."

Gaspard ignored it all. With a vicious move, he picked up the letter opener and slashed the tip of his own tongue. The blood spurted on his shirt, the couch, and Lisette's face as he crushed his lips to hers, forcing the blood deep into her mouth, making her swallow. It was a savage taking that was nothing like the joyous love-making of before. This was hungry, feral, and fierce. This was life and death on the edge of a knife, and the next two minutes would show which prevailed.

Lisette moved her own head and answered his kiss with equal ferocity. The blood pumped between them, his death blood giving her life while she grabbed at his hips pushing up in a desperate move to deepen the joining.

Marc tugged on Ned's sleeve and said, "She will live, but now, it is time to go."

Ned nodded and lumbered out of the room, following Marc.

Gaspard grabbed at his pants, using one hand to push them down. He yanked his underwear down, and his erection sprung free, thickening and lengthening with every second. Lisette's tiny panties mattered not. He tore them off her and still kissing, plunged into her, forgetting to be gentle, wild with want. She met him with equal desperation. Animal, rough, and running along a tidal wave of desire, they both orgasmed in an explosion of heat. He once again saw from her eyes and looked at his own face, a mask of blood and violence, and was surprised how much she liked it. He felt her anxiety and pain began to fade, and as he left her mind, the last of it ebbed away.

"How are you feeling?" he asked her. She lay there covered in blood, a smile on her lips, eyes half-closed.

"Much better," she murmured. Then...

Her eyes flew open, and she shot up on the couch, pushing him to the floor.

"You did this to me! You sent me away knowing I wanted to stay, knowing I was hooked on your blood like some street corner junkie, and you let me suffer!"

"I didn't understand the extent of the addiction. I've never thought about it before. In the old days, food didn't leave. They just stayed until they died. Addiction wasn't a part of the problem."

"Food? Food! You arrogant French asshole! Is that what I am to you, *food*?" Her voice increased in both volume and pitch.

Gaspard winced at his choice of words. He hadn't called sanguineers food in a long time. It was an old-fashioned, provincial, and insulting term, and he'd used it without thinking.

"I'm so sorry, my darling. It was a stupid phrase." He reached out to hold her, and she pushed him away, getting to her feet, back ramrod straight as she whirled on him.

"Tell me how to break this addiction. I do not want to be connected to you for the rest of my life. In fact, I am going to leave New Orleans and get as far away from you as possible!" Her cheeks were flushed red from blood and anger. Her eyes flashed in fury, but also pain. The guilt just about overwhelmed him.

"Lisette! I am very sorry. I didn't understand. That is why I had the doctor check on you. You are very special to me. I pushed you away in order to avoid this very thing, but it was too late."

"I told the doctor to go away. I said I was fine. In reality, I was throwing up on the bathroom floor, shaking like a leaf. I thought I could quit cold turkey, leave, and never see you again. You *hurt* me!"

"I know! I'm sorry! I didn't know this would happen. Please, Lisette, calm down and let's go shower. We're a mess," he said, gesturing to the blood and torn clothing.

"I will shower. Alone. Have someone bring me some clothes. How did I get here anyway?"

"Your brother Ned brought you."

"Ah, Tiny. Always looking out for me. Please tell him I'll be down in a few minutes so he can take me home. And, Gaspard..."

"Yes?"

"I never want to see you again. This is your fault." She turned toward the bathroom, and he heard her whisper, "But I'm trapped. I'm a lifetime junkie. God help me."

Gaspard showered in the hall bath, dressed in jeans and a Tulane sweatshirt. He descended the stairs and raised his eyebrows at Marc, who gestured toward the sitting room.

Ned sat on an overstuffed chair, head in hands. His enormous feet splayed out to the sides. His beard was quivering, and Gaspard realized the big galoot was *crying*.

"Your sister is going to be fine," he said.

Ned lifted his head, eyes red-rimmed and cheeks stained with tears.

"Thank you."

"You're welcome," replied Gaspard. He crossed his arms and sat across from Lisette's brother, a brother who loved her so much he risked entering a vampire's lair without invitation to save her. A man who threatened and begged for her and would sit here for as long as it took to ensure she was well. Gaspard thought of Henri, killed in a landslide while on a hunting expedition with friends. His body had been buried under a mountain of rock, and they had left him to rest where he fell. Gaspard deserted the estate the following week breaking generations of tradition by establishing one of the Baron's granddaughters as its mistress.

"You might not thank me when I tell you what must happen next."

"What do you mean?"

"Lisette is addicted to my bite and my blood. She no longer wants to see me, which is understandable. But she will get sick again without regular infusions."

"So how do we do that?" Ned's voice now dripped with sarcasm.

"I will fill seven vials with my blood every week and have it delivered to her house every Sunday. She will need to take one every day of the week, at least for a while. Perhaps she will be able to wean herself off. I hope so."

"So, you made her into a vampire crackhead."

"No, she'll be in control of her mind, and her life will continue at her firm, with no negative side effects. Think of it as taking a pill a day to control cholesterol."

Lisette walked in at that moment wearing some borrowed clothes.

"I heard what you said, Gaspard. Fine. As long as I don't have to be near you, I'll take your blood. Ned, let's go."

They walked out, Lisette slamming the door behind them before anyone could catch it, so angry that neither she nor Ned noticed the shadow of a figure leaning against an old cypress tree situated opposite the house, beyond the fences, hidden from the cameras.

Inside, Marc stared at his boss in disbelief.

"How are you going to send her vials of blood every week?" he asked.

"I am going to cut my wrist, fill seven test tubes, and have someone take them to her every Sunday."

"Do you think that will work?"

"It won't be as good as having the actual bite, but the blood itself should keep the worst of the symptoms at bay."

"You will need to feed after losing that much blood," worried Marc.

"That is why we have sanguineers, my friend. Now, let's switch topics." Gaspard strolled to the window to stare out into the night. Then he turned, leaning against the sill, a picture of elegance. His jeans draped low on his hips; his hair was loose and hung to his shoulders. The only sign that he was concerned about the evening's events was a slight tapping of his index finger on the wall behind him.

"What is happening with the construction?" Gaspard asked. "Are we still having trouble nailing boards together?"

Marc squirmed a little, and said, "Ah...actually, yes. The gazebo will not stand."

Gaspard's gaze sharpened. "Is there magic afoot? What would explain this? Have you consulted with the local fae?"

"The fae swear they have nothing to do with it, the contractors cannot explain it, and Marie is tearing her hair out trying to make the deadline."

Gaspard rubbed his chin. "Perhaps we should see how Madame Beauchamp's construction is doing. I wonder if she has the same problem."

11

Kara's clothes were soaked in sweat and clung to her body in the hot, late afternoon. The stickiness was irritating but no more so than the damned vampire she served, through no fault of her own. Okay, maybe a little fault of her own. In fact, one could say she was at least fifty-percent responsible, but that wasn't the point. She couldn't return to Valhalla until her service was done. At least she'd been allowed to bring her horse. They couldn't deny her that. Rikassa was a part of her.

She reached down and smoothed the white horse's mane. Rikassa was a Wild One, a breed created for Valkyries and for Valkyries alone. She was loyal to Kara and no one else. Right now, she was breathing hard from their run through the estate so they could both burn off some energy. Now at the farthest corner of Gaspard's land, Kara dismounted and fed her beloved Rikassa some apples. Anyone watching would have been surprised because there were no apple trees around and Kara carried no pack. Kara opened her palm, and the apples were there. Rikassa didn't care about magic. She *was* magic and was used to getting treats from Kara's hands. She nuzzled Kara and then concentrated on eating her sweets.

Kara sat on a stump and thought about Gaspard. The man was exasperating. He had caressed her face, a liberty she allowed *no one*, except the greatest of heroes rescued from fields of battle. And even then, she chose them. They did not choose her, particularly after the battle that landed her here. This latest affront was infuriating.

She wasn't even sorry about the rug.

She slapped at a mosquito and noticed the sun. She had let her mind wander a long time. It was almost dusk. Time to go back.

She meandered back, giving Rikassa time to rest and ensuring she herself had enough time to calm her mind. When she arrived at the house, she dismounted, gave Rikassa a caress, and whispered, "Run, Wild One, run," into the mare's ear. The horse took off, freedom on four hooves, tail flying. No barn for a Wild One. None could hold her and Kara wouldn't have wanted to pen her in anyway. Kara watched the horse glide away and envied her.

Straightening her strong shoulders, she strode into the house, blowing by the guards who greeted her and the day keeper, Marie. Marie was most anxious about something, but Kara waved her off with a curt, "Not until after I shower."

She stripped naked, waiting for the water to run hot. She looked in the mirror. She carried several scars, most of which could be healed by the water baths at her home, but she liked them. Her body was muscled and sinewy. She heard one of the guards call her "ripped." She wasn't sure what it meant, but he said it in a complimentary manner, so she knew it wasn't an insult.

She stared at the one long scar on her stomach. It was a slash across her mid-section, higher on the left and angling down to her right hip. That was a scar she would always keep. She'd lost her freedom for it.

An efficient fifteen minutes later, dressed and armed, she went downstairs and met Marie. The minute woman was fluttering with anxiety.

"Miss Kara! Monsieur Gaspard told me to give you this message, but I have been unable to find you all day. You weren't in your quarters."

"I sleep as much as possible during the day as my employment requires me to be up all night."

"But you weren't in your room!"

"I slept outside. I prefer the open sky."

Marie flapped her hand at Kara. "Never mind, it doesn't matter. You are here now. The message is a simple one. He wants you to go check on Madame Beauchamp and find out how the construction is going. As you know, we are experiencing some difficulty getting the backyard building done, and Gaspard believes there may be foul magic about. He wonders if it is affecting her, too."

Kara sighed, whipped out her cell phone, and dialed Adelaide's home. She didn't know if Adelaide owned a cell phone, but she doubted it. An unfamiliar man's voice answered.

"Beauchamp residence."

"Where is Adelaide?"

"Excuse me, but who is asking?"

Tapping her foot, Kara snapped, "This is Kara Svarstal, Adelaide's friend and Gaspard Bessette's employee."

"If you are her friend, then I am sorry to tell you that Mrs. Beauchamp has been injured. I am her personal physician and made a house call on her behalf."

Kara was already rushing to her truck. "What happened?" she demanded.

"I am unable to tell, and Mrs. Beauchamp won't tell me. She appears to have been whipped."

Kara stopped with one foot in the truck.

"Whipped?"

"Yes. Someone beat her, and she won't tell me who." The physician's voice was grim. "Someone hurt this frail woman, and I'd like to make a report so the police can arrest whomever is responsible, but she is stubborn and says that I wouldn't understand. Wouldn't understand! What is there not to understand about being lashed? Maybe you can talk some sense into her."

"I'm on my way. Oh, and one thing. I wouldn't say the word frail in front of her face."

Despite his frustration, the doctor chuckled. "True, true. I shall be more discreet."

Kara jumped the rest of the way into the truck and drove as fast as she dared to the Beauchamp estate. As she reeled into the drive, she noticed that the house was ready to be lifted. She ran into the main house, passing plastic-covered furniture, her long legs moving at not quite human speed.

A man with a white beard and wire-rimmed glasses greeted her.

"Miss Kara, I presume."

"Yes. You are her doctor?"

He held out his hand to shake. "Yes, at your service." He grabbed a bag that was lying on the floor and said, "I will be back tomorrow to check on her. She's in the sitting room on the couch. Let me know if you find out what happened. I am anxious to have the perpetrator behind bars."

"I will."

He headed out the door, stopping for a moment to turn and say, "And make sure she takes her medication. I don't want those welts to get infected."

He left, and Kara walked into the sitting room ready to give Adelaide hell for not having called her when she was hurt. She halted when she saw the once indomitable woman, whose spirit and energy were enough to stare down a master vampire in his own lair, lying on the couch swaddled in blankets despite the warm temperatures. There were red swellings on the woman's face and she looked...diminished.

"Adelaide."

"Hello, Kara. I'm glad you are here. You're the only one who'll believe me."

Kara strode over, bending on one knee beside Adelaide, feeling somewhat relieved that the woman's voice was still strong.

"What happened?" asked Kara, brushing some hair from Adelaide's forehead, making sure to avoid the red marks.

"It's the ghosts, Kara. The ghosts."

"Which ghosts?"

"The ghosts of the slaves who died in the slave pens that existed on this estate and Gaspard's."

"Restless ghosts did this to you?"

Adelaide laughed, then winced at the pain. "Look at my back, Kara."

The older woman struggled to sit up. Kara guided her the rest of the way, sat on the couch, and lifted the woman's light blouse to see a swath of white bandages.

"Take one of the bandages off, Kara."

"That will hurt you."

"You need to know."

Kara chose a bandage toward the top of Adelaide's back, near her right shoulder. She pried the bandage off, gasping at what she saw. Adelaide let out a hiss of pain.

"This is a real whip mark!"

"Yes. It is the whip of the slave owners on a slave's back. A ghost came to me last night and told me his story. It is a terrible story that brings shame to my family. These ghosts aren't just restless. They have been gathering energy for over a hundred years, seething with their need for revenge. They have manifested, Kara. Manifested. And they mean to cause a massacre."

Kara helped the woman back down on the couch, chewing on her lip, not believing what she was hearing. She dragged a chair close to the couch and asked, "They are the reason our construction won't stand?"

"I suspect, yes."

"They are the reason for the excessive deterioration of this house?"

"Yes, again."

"And they are now strong enough to do this to you?"

"They are, and they mean to avenge their treatment and murders by killing as many people as they can."

Kara considered this for a moment. "I think it is time for you to come to Gaspard's house. You need care and we have a lot to talk about," Kara said, expecting an argument.

To her surprise, Adelaide nodded. "Yes, I think that is a good idea."

Kara arranged to have Adelaide moved to Gaspard's mansion and indicated that Adelaide would need 'round the clock nursing care. She then called Gaspard and told him what happened.

"Ghosts did this?" he exclaimed.

"I think by now we can call them specters. They have gained access to the physical world and can manipulate objects."

"Adelaide says there were slave pens on these grounds, too?"

"Yes, and she thinks that is what is causing the buildings to fall. You have placed them right on top of the slave pen remnants."

"What if I move them?"

"My bet is that by now it will not be enough."

"You are bringing her here, yes?"

"Yes. We'll see you soon, and Gaspard?"

"Yes?"

"None of our security measures are prepared for this type of assault."

12

Lisette held onto the kitchen counter, hands shaking, knees trembling. She was trying to fight the addiction, but like any addict, her body craved its poison. She held on, gasping for breath. Her chest was tight and her body was hot, burning from the inside. *I'm dying, I'm dying*, she thought. She bit her lip and held on a few more seconds.

She could stand it no more. She'd made it five minutes. One more minute than last night.

Reaching for the mug of tea near her right hand, she uncorked a vial with her left, dumped it in, and drank it all down in one long swallow. She threw the mug across the room and felt a sense of satisfaction when the ceramic exploded into shards.

She wiped her mouth with the back of her hand and turned at the sound of a knock. Anxiety clawed her throat as she walked to the door. What if Gaspard had changed his mind and wouldn't supply the blood? What if he wanted her back? Both thoughts made her stomach churn.

She put her eye to the peephole and saw a man, well-dressed, trimmed beard, wearing a cravat instead of a normal tie, backlit by the outside light.

"Yes?" she said through the door.

"Mademoiselle, I wish to speak to you," the man said.

"Who are you? What do you want?"

"I will explain when I come in. I promise that I will not hurt you."

"You swear?"

"I do."

The way he made that promise was different. Something about his manner of speaking gave the word weight.

"What is it that you want to talk about?" she asked.

"I believe you have had some association with Gaspard Bessette, have you not?"

Her eyes narrowed. "Yes..."

"I, too, have known him, and I believe you and I share the same experience. Mistreatment, negligence, carelessness. I believe we have mutual interests when it comes to Monsieur Bessette."

Lisette opened the door.

The man was taller than she'd thought. His cravat was silver and paired with a crisp white shirt and gray suit. His shoes were immaculate, gleaming with the polish only money could provide. Whoever he was, he was loaded.

"I will stand here on the step and speak to you. At this moment, you cannot come in."

"Ah, you see me for what I am."

"A vampire, yes. I've known quite a few. You forget to blink."

"My tell, I'm afraid."

"What is your business with Gaspard?"

"I owe him some recompense. I saw his servant deliver blood to you. You require his blood now?"

"That's none of your business."

"True, but it makes us allies, I believe. You are addicted to his blood, through no fault of your own, I am sure, and I owe him for some...challenging moments of life."

"What did he do to you?"

"Left me for dead."

"Gaspard wouldn't do that."

"Ah, but he did. This would be easier if we were inside."

"Tough. When was this? What happened?"

"It was some years ago, but to me it seems like yesterday. I was buried, alive. Gaspard walked away. I was near death when a vampire found me. He heard my heartbeat, faint as it was, and turned me. My body suffered severe injuries, and it took two excruciating years to recover."

"Vampires heal fast."

"Not when their spine is crushed. That takes some time."

Lisette eyed the vampire. "What is it you want?"

"Revenge, of course. I want him to feel what I felt. I imagine you might, too. If we work together, perhaps we even the scales."

Lisette considered this for a moment. She recalled the nausea, the shakes, and the self-loathing of a few moments before. The thought of Gaspard feeling that same way was like a sugar rush, electric and elating.

"You may come in."

"Thank you," the man said, entering her home. "Allow me to introduce myself. My name is Henri."

13

Confusion. That is what Gaspard felt. It was such unusual feeling that he took a moment to recognize it. Certainty was his normal state, the settled feeling in the gut that said you were correct and that everyone would do as you commanded. This quivering gelatinous mass that was his stomach now was unfamiliar and unpleasant. It made him resentful.

The pencil holder on his desk fell over and hit the floor. The room cooled by several degrees, and he could feel the presence of the specters. The ghosts on Gaspard's land became even more active after Adelaide moved in. The gazebo and guest house still would not stand. Things within the house developed minds of their own and shuffled around. The kitchen, where slaves had labored to provide food for their owners, was unusable.

A scream from the kitchen caused him to pop up and run. As he entered the hallway, he smelled smoke and realized the kitchen was on fire. The smoke alarms blared, and a security officer grabbed him by the elbow.

"Sir, we have to leave now."

He shook him off. "Is anyone in there?" he yelled.

"Not sure, sir, but we have to go *now*."

A sword whizzed through the air missing his face by less than a quarter inch and buried itself in the kitchen door. It impaled a diaphanous figure who now hung by the chest screaming a blood-curdling shriek. Kara ripped the sword out, swung upper right to lower left, and the figure disintegrated, flowing away like ash.

"Run!" she screamed, shoving Gaspard forward. The security officer pulled Gaspard along, pushed him out the front door, and collapsed. Firefighters, summoned by the alarms and an urgent call from the guard house, gave the officer oxygen and pulled everyone back to a safe distance.

A cloud of spectral bodies whirled about the front door, unable to go any farther. They whispered promises of death. A shining sword tip slashed through them, slicing them to ribbons.

The Valkyrie emerged from the ash, fire raging behind her. Gaspard couldn't believe what he saw. She was wearing full body armor, held her sword in her right hand and her shield in the left. A nimbus of light encased her, and Gaspard could have sworn she'd grown taller.

There was a shout from upstairs that caught his attention, and Kara's. Sarah, the sanguineer who lived at the mansion with her son, was leaning out the window.

"I'm afraid to come down the stairs! There is so much smoke!"

"Stay there!" yelled Kara, and then she whistled.

Rikassa came running, one minute not there, the next, in full shining white glory. Kara mounted the horse in one fluid leap, turned, sheathed her sword and shield, turned the horse, and backed up several yards. Then she sent the horse running at full speed, yelling to Gaspard, "Be ready to catch!"

The horse raced toward the house. Kara stood up on the horse's back, and as they approached the mansion, Kara vaulted off of the horse and flew through the air to land on the balcony below the one that held Sarah. She then leapt up, a vertical leap of several feet, and seemed to hang in the air without falling. She used those moments to grab the boy and drop him to Gaspard, who waited below.

To Gaspard, time stopped. His reflexes were preternaturally quick and the secret, he had learned, was slowing down time in his mind. He saw Kara grab the boy, watched her hang in the air for an impossibly long time, and saw the boy fall in slow motion. *His feet are down*, he thought. *I'll have to catch in a vertical position*. Moving fast but what felt slow to him, he positioned himself underneath the boy, held out his arms, and readied himself as the boy fell, fell, fell, like a feather in a rainstorm, and caught him just as he would have hit the ground. The boy was wailing, and Gaspard handed him off to the EMTs.

Kara returned to the balcony and leapt a second time, pulling Sarah off the balcony and again, dropping her to the vampire beneath. Sara made the same long fall, but Gaspard caught her with both arms and placed her on the ground. She gave him a peck on the cheek and ran to her son.

Kara jumped, alighting on the ground with the grace of a cat. Gaspard couldn't help but think, *ten from the Russian judge*, but he didn't dare joke out loud. Not at this moment. Rikassa came over and nuzzled Kara to make sure she was okay. Kara sat on the ground, watching as the firefighters got the fire under control.

One foot in front of the other, legs heavy and heart full, Gaspard approached her, and then with her look of permission, sat next to her on the grass.

"That was amazing, what you just did," he whispered.

"I couldn't have done it if you hadn't been there to catch them," she murmured back. "No one else could have caught them from that height."

He wiped soot from her face and said, "I guess we make a good team."

His heart leapt when he was rewarded with a smile.

Gaspard had no way of knowing that a shadow lingered in the distance, observing, studying, and planning.

14

Henri walked Adelaide's property, feeling the unrest of the entombed spirits. The ghosts didn't appear to him, but he could feel their anger, churning, hot, and most of all, self-righteous. He drank their fury in, enjoying the rush.

The darkness welcomed his wicked thoughts, and he released the fly on his pants, reaching in to rub himself. It wasn't enough, so he shimmied his trousers lower and let the night breeze caress him as well, using both hands to fondle himself up and down in long strokes.

The physical friction still wouldn't bring relief, but the memory of his last conquest got him to the right place. She'd been studying at the library and had the misfortune of staying until close. She was waiting outside the building for her boyfriend, or maybe her father. She was about twenty-five but so slim, so petite, she could have been younger. He'd loved the way her straight, black hair tickled her neck. It was enthralling.

He relived the night as he rubbed, getting faster and faster, pulling at the tip, coming so close, so close. He encased his balls with one hand, still pulling with the other and sank into the memory.

She'd been scared and begged him in rapid Japanese, not English. She was slight with tiny breasts, like little rosebuds on white snow. Her shirt lay on the ground, ripped and discarded, and she was holding her arms over her chest, trying to protect her modesty. He let her turn and run a bit, while he climbed a fire escape so he could watch her from above. Once he was sure he had given her the impression of freedom, he leapt down, landing in front of her. She shrieked, and he relished how her tiny breasts bobbed up and down with her screams.

He couldn't take it anymore and grabbed her, cradling her to him, pulling her tiny body to his own. Dipping his head, he sucked at one of those glorious nipples and bit her right above her left breast. He let his fangs go full length, slipping them through the ribs, and sucked her heart's blood as it pumped faster to stave off her death. It had been glorious, and just as he remembered the sensation of drinking from a beating heart, he orgasmed so hard he sank to the ground.

Encased in his own afterglow, he lay on the cool lawn and rolled onto his back. With his pants still at his knees, he lay in the darkness and reveled in the memory of his conquest.

The spirits around him quieted as if they disapproved of what he'd done to the girl. "What's it to you?" he yelled at the specters. "You wish to cause death! Why can't I?"

Amos materialized out of the shadows and stared at the half-naked vampire. *We wish death for our tormentors. You wish death on anyone.*

Henri scrambled to his feet and fixed his trousers.

"You might warn a body before you do that!" he said, facing the translucent ghost.

Why are you heah?

"Revenge takes time to plan."

Amos cocked his head in an inquisitive look.

Revenge? What for?

Henri kicked at the earth like a five-year-old boy being punished for stealing a cookie.

"For my death! My suffering! And my rebirth! You know the vampire who lives on the adjoining estate, Gaspard?"

Only by name. We ain't got no quarrel with him, but methinks other ghosts up that hill do.

"He left me for dead, left me to suffer."

Well, you are dead.

"Not that kind of dead, you fool! I was mortal then. I wanted my father to turn me, not Gaspard, but he wouldn't, claiming that I wasn't suited to being a vampire. I never learned what he meant by that because he'd wave me off any time I asked. Then he turned Gaspard and made me call him brother."

How didya become vampire?

"I was buried under a heap of rock, crippled but not dead. My so-called brother walked away. I lingered like that for days, starving, parched, and praying for death or for my brother to return."

Amos paced back and forth, and Henri noticed that he left a physical imprint on the grass, creating a line of trampled greenery where he stepped.

"How do you do that?" Henri asked, pointing to the worn path.

We are old ghosts, fueled by the need for justice. It gives us strength.

"Ah, then you will understand my story. We are the same. Aren't revenge and justice two sides of the same coin?"

No. And we's not the same as you. But let's all heah more.

"Can you give me your hand?"

Mebbee.

"Try." Henri held out his left hand, and although he was non-corporeal, Amos was reluctant to take it, given where it had been a moment before. But a white man was giving him an order, and despite himself, he obeyed.

Amos' translucent hand floated into Henri's solid one, and the part of them that shared a living death connected them like a live wire. The two hands melded into a space that lay in between realities, merging their minds, erasing them as individuals and creating something new.

Henri tried to shake loose but could not. He felt the rock on top of him all over again, the weight of it on his back and shoulders. Blood streamed into his eyes from the gashes on his forehead. His legs were numb, and he couldn't wiggle his toes. He wondered if his toes were even there. Maybe they were crushed into little bits, pulverized and smashed into a delicate pattern of blood, skin, and bone on the ground. He couldn't tell.

Pain crept forth an inch at a time and blossomed into a tornado of agony, screaming along the nerves in his upper shoulders and neck. His arms were useless, and all he could do was turn his head from the left to the right, his nose scraping the ground each time he shifted. Part of him blessed the pain because it let him know he was alive, but as the first hours passed, the pain mocked him. It became a physical thing dancing in front of his vision, and he spoke to it.

"Why are you tormenting me? Stop hurting me."

The pain intensified.

"Stop! Stop...stop..."

A stinging sensation raced down his arm to his elbow, where it discontinued into a numbness scarier than the pain.

"Just let me die."

A passing breeze stole through a crack in the rocks and blew dirt in his eyes and nose. He spat some out on the dust in front of him and then had to lay his head in his own saliva. Parched, he reached out his tongue to lick his own wetness from the dirt, only to swallow more dirt that scraped his throat and increased his misery.

His voice cracked as he began. "Hail Mary, full of grace...*Je vous salue, Marie*...Our Father, who art in heaven...*Notre Pere, qui es aux cieux*..."

He finished the Rosary and blacked out, waking when it was cold and dark. Moonlight slipped through chinks in the rock. His stomach gurgled, the sound loud to his ears in the small space, a space he now believed would be his crypt. The gurgling was replaced by convulsions as his empty stomach cramped. He resigned himself to death, beseeching the Lord to stop his suffering.

His prayer was answered, but not in the way he expected.

"*Mon ami*? Is there someone in here? I can hear a heartbeat."

"I'm here," Henri whispered, hoping that someone who could hear a heartbeat could hear his voice. "Gaspard? Brother?"

"Non. But soon you will call me Father..."

That was when Henri knew he'd been discovered by a vampire.

He squeezed his eyes shut as the vampire shifted boulders and scraped away at the sediment. Henri then watched as a thin, white hand with long, filthy nails scooped dirt, removing enough so that the vampire could lay on his side and look Henri in the eye with his own.

The vampire's eye was an unusual hazel framed by silky, thick lashes. He spoke in a raspy voice that hurt Henri's ears.

"I will get you out, but you must promise me one thing."

"What?" mouthed Henri, too dry to speak.

"You must stay with me forever."

Henri closed his eyes in an unspoken consent, not knowing if he had five more minutes much less forever.

At every slip of the rock, Henri believed it was his end. As the vampire moved them, the boulders bounced farther down, booming in the night, and twice a slab fell down near his head, blocking off even the moonlight, leaving him encased in his stygian tomb, turning each moment of vague hope back into despair.

It went on like this for an endless amount of time until Henri's entire head was clear of the debris, then his torso. The vampire leaned in, shoved his hands under Henri's armpits letting Henri's head drag to the ground, and hauled the rest of Henri free. The vampire rolled Henri onto his back and did a survey of the damage.

Henri lifted his head and looked at the vampire, shocked at what he saw. The vampire's hair was long and oily and hung over his right eye. When the vampire brushed his hair back, Henri gasped in horror at the gaping hole where the vampire's eye should have been and the ropy scars that ran from the vampire's forehead to neck.

Henri lifted his head and gazed at his own body, numbly noting the mutilation. His torso was twisted almost ninety-degrees to the left, his hips dislocated and separated from his lower spine. His legs were crushed, knees pushed to hyperextension, and as he had imagined, his feet were compressed into crude triangles, giving him the appearance of having bloody flippers.

The vampire spooned Henri's broken body, cuddled next to him like a lover, and then bit into Henri's neck and drained him dry.

Henri had woken with blood in his mouth, a stunning vision of the night sky, and a prickling in his feet.

The memory ended. Then...

Henri felt the rock on top of him all over again, the weight of it on his back and shoulders. Blood streamed into his eyes from the gashes on his forehead.

"No!" Henri yelled, flinging himself backward, cutting the link between his and Amos' hands. Amos staggered back, his hand burning in a blue glow, a remnant of the merging that had allowed Amos to live Henri's nightmare.

Lawd almighty that was a bad'un. That happen'd to you?

Henri nodded, unable to speak, perspiring a crimson sweat,

wondering if that was his eventual fate, to live that experience over and over again. His knees knocked at the thought. He stilled his shaking extremities and regained his feet.

What happen'd to your vampire daddy? You ain't still with him so guessin' that forevah thing didna work out.

"We parted company." Henri wiped his brow and shook his hand, flinging the blood-laden sweat onto the ground.

Amos' eyes went wide, and his body stretched like an image in a fun house mirror, then he collapsed to the ground, writhing like a catfish on the line. He flashed in and out of the physical plane, a ghostly candle caught in a breeze. Other ghosts, ones Henri hadn't even known were there, surprised him by filtering forward, arms outstretched, dripping ectoplasm in glistening waves onto the lawn. It clung like morning dew to the blades of grass only to evaporate in an eye blink. These specters flared into reality for a second and then disappeared back to the metaphysical plane, like stars winking out of existence.

Henri watched the specter's mouth open and back-stepped several feet. His bloody sweat ran in rivulets now, and as each drop hit the ground, the ghosts flickered back into the physical sphere, staying a bit longer each time.

Yer blood feeds us! It makes us stronger! Give us more.

Henri hesitated for a moment, thinking of what this might mean. He licked his lips and said, "What's in it for me?"

We gettin' justice soon. Gotta think anythin' makes trouble for the lady Beauchamp gotta rile up your brotha.

Henri crossed one arm over his chest and used the other hand to cradle his chin, then gave a jerky nod.

"Blood for you now equals chaos for Gaspard later?"

Dozens of ghosts shimmered in the night, nodding their heads. They hovered near him, and though he didn't have to breathe, he had the sensation of being suffocated. He lifted his wrist to his teeth, readying to tear the skin when the ghosts swarmed him, biting and sucking, stealing the life force that he himself had stolen. They raked his arms and gnawed on his face, slurping his blood as if they were vampires themselves.

The ghosts depleted Henri until he was unconscious, crumpled on the ground, arms and legs askew. They departed without a backward look at their benefactor, baying their defiance to the night.

Their howl carried up the hill to the Beauchamp mansion, and the house ghosts shivered in fear. Sylvester, Martin, and Slinky stood next to Nathan, minding their post in the kitchen, floating along, transparent wisps framed by the window. The echo of the ghosts' shrieks sank into their center, and their anxiety became something more. It became full-on fear, that burning fear that catches your breath and makes you want to stand still like a rabbit, begging God that the monster won't see you, bargaining everything you have to escape whatever demon was in your path.

The strength of that fear consumed them, encased them, and wormed its way into their hearts. They absorbed it, soaking it up like a dry plant in the rain. The fear escalated to panic, panic for Adelaide, for themselves, and for anyone who would meet the creatures who made that deranged howl.

Disturbed beyond anything in their memories, the ghosts did the equivalent of pacing. They wandered back and forth through the hallways, up the stairs, through the bedrooms, and back down to the living room, dining room, and kitchen. When they completed a circuit, they started again, having no other way to fight terror. The walls shook, and the chandeliers loosened in their casings, knocking crystals together in a discordant tune.

Nathan glided through the kitchen on yet another sweep of the house and kept going on his rounds. He slipped past the big kitchen table, the shelves of collectable mason jars, the pantry and...bumped into the swinging doors that led to the dining room. The other three ghosts flew around the corner, saw Nathan, and careened to a stop, bumping into *each other*. They stared at each other in stunned surprise. Nathan reached out one hand toward the door and pushed the right panel, shocked when he could feel the wood under his fingertips, and the door responded to his touch, swinging open.

The four were dumbfounded and terrified. *What magic is this*, they wondered. What was happening to them, and why? The alarm at this new development added to their fear, and when Nathan looked down, he realized he could feel the floor under his feet.

This can't be good, he thought.

15

Henri came to when his fingers started to burn. He logrolled under a tree, steaming at the touch of the rising sun, and dug into the earth, pulling clumps of dirt and grass over his body. He snapped out an arm and caught a squirrel, bringing it to his lips in distaste. Its mate came searching, and he repeated the act. With enough sustenance that he wouldn't die a true death, he let the sun draw him down.

"Hey, buddy, you okay there? You don't look so good." A man prodded Henri with a stick.

Henri opened one eye and saw the man pointing at him with a cane, a spry older gentleman with a tiny poodle on his post-supper walk. Henri had always hated poodles. The French were obsessed with them, always naming them something stupid, like Fifi.

"Fifi..." he said out loud.

"Yeah! Howdya know? This here's Fifi. She's a toy poodle and cute as a button, aren't you, Fifi?" Fifi lifted up her front legs and balanced on her back ones.

"Good girl! Let me give you a treat," said her owner, pulling a nibblet of something out of his pocket and hand-feeding it to the dog.

"Anyways, how you doin'? I walk my dog here 'cause Adelaide don't mind. She likes Fifi and says it's better for me to walk her here than on the side of the road with all them cars goin' by. Anyways, came 'pon you here and thought you could use some help. No place to be sleepin' outside at night without a tent. The skeeters will eat you up! Hey...!"

The man said no more as Henri reached up, grabbed the man's leg, and yanked him down, pouncing on the man's neck. Fifi yapped and ran away, her leash trailing behind. Henri buried the body in the wallow he'd made for himself, and, feeling much refreshed, decided it was time to pay Lisette a visit.

He walked toward Lisette's house, thinking about how scared she'd been when she'd opened the gate for him the other night.

"Promise you won't hurt anyone."

"My dear, I will hurt Gaspard, but none other."

"I wish I could see him suffer. He's like a drug pusher with the very best crack and sculpted abs..." She trailed off.

Henri had controlled his impatience. "I don't think it is a good idea if you are there. You might change your mind. We must be firm in our actions. Gaspard hooked you to his bite and then threw you to the wolves. He left me when I needed him most, just as he left you. For this, he must suffer."

"But...he didn't throw me to the wolves." Lisette's voice trailed off.

"Lisette, would you need to drink blood every day if it weren't for him?"

"No."

"He manipulated you. Now, get me in the gate."

Lisette drove up to the back gate and used her card key to open it. Henri jumped out and headed toward the mansion.

"Don't kill him!" Lisette had yelled after him. "He's not so bad..."

Henri had ignored her and crept toward the house, carrying through with his original plan. Truth was, he didn't care if he killed every living and undead being that resided there. If it all went to plan, he'd... what was that odd phrase... have a weenie roast over the smoking remains of the house and its occupants.

16

"The cameras show a woman with a man driving in the back gate," Kara said.

"That gate is a private entrance and secret to almost everyone. Who was it?"

"Did you take Lisette's card key away from her?"

Gaspard closed his eyes with the realization.

"Lisette is in on this? Who was with her?"

Kara placed a photo in front of him.

Gaspard froze staring in disbelief at the image. He attempted to speak but choked on his own words.

"Gaspard? What is wrong?"

"This cannot be! That is Henri, my brother. He died decades ago."

"And yet, he started the fire. Lisette just let him in."

Gaspard stood, and Kara could feel him draw his power to him. She heard the lesser vampires in the house grunt at the sudden shift in energy. His eyes glittered with restrained fury, and his fangs dropped to their full length. The air around him crackled, and the force of his power pressed on her and made her stumble a foot back. For the first time, Kara saw him as the master vampire that he was.

Without making a sound, Gaspard strode out of the room. Kara watched his back, not sure what he wanted her to do. She decided it didn't matter what he wanted; she was his bodyguard, and it was her duty to follow. She hurried after him, cursing the whole time. There was no way this would end well.

Outside, Kara could see that the vampire was so furious he couldn't be bothered with human niceties. His face was drawn taught, chalky white, and his cheekbones stood out in harsh relief from the rest of his face. His lips were a virulent red.

Kara caught his arm, and Gaspard whirled around, eyes glittering, capturing her in his gaze. She stared at him, caught, trapped, and yet, she felt that this was the only place she wanted to be. An owl hooted in the breeze, moonlight bathed them in a warm glow, and Kara's world tunneled down until all she could see or feel was Gaspard.

Rikassa whinnied in the distance and galloped to her Lady. She shoved her nose into Kara's face, releasing her from Gaspard's spell. The horse turned her attention to Gaspard, spun, and in a most deliberate motion, kicked Gaspard with her right back hoof.

Gaspard jumped and lunged at the horse, who rose in the air ready to trample the vampire. Coming to her senses, Kara stepped between them, heart beating fast, and caught Rikassa by the mane with one hand, shoving Gaspard back with the other.

"Stop!" she yelled. She turned to Gaspard, tight with fury and embarrassment. "What did you do to me?" she demanded.

The vampire was as still as a statue. "I did nothing."

"We *will* talk about this again," Kara promised, a sharp edge to her voice. "Now, however, we will drive to Lisette's house and deal with the real danger."

Kara listened to the wheels crunch on the road gravel as she drove, breathing in even lungfuls of air to force herself to calm. *What the hell was that*, she thought. Had she been mesmerized, hypnotized? Was that an enthralling? She gripped the steering wheel to hide her trembling hands from Gaspard. *Valkyries don't tremble*, she thought.

She counted her breaths as she drove. In, one-two-three. Out, one-two-three. By the time they arrived at Lisette's home, she was back in control and praying none of her sisters found out about this little incident.

Gaspard was not in control. He leapt from the truck, moving quicker than the human eye could see, and walked in Lisette's home without knocking. The door had been locked, so walking in was an understatement. He splintered the door and pulled it off its hinges.

"Shit!" Kara said and hurled herself after him. The scene in front of her was so surreal it looked like a high school production of *Macbeth*, with Lisette in the Lady Macbeth role. Lisette was staring at the blood on her hands, not paying any attention to the blood gushing from her neck. Henri crouched beside her, fangs out, hands up in what looked like claws. His eyes were narrowed, and his mouth was in a bloody sneer, his clothes covered in grass stains and dirt.

Gaspard's face didn't change at all. He was still in that way only vampires could be—until he wasn't. In a flash, he pounced on Henri, grabbed him by the lapels, and threw him across the room into the brick fireplace. The mantle fell on Henri's head with a sharp crack. Henri shook off the attack, jumped back up, and tackled Gaspard, slashing at his face with his talon-like nails. To Kara, this took place in a blur of action accompanied by blood spatter worthy of a TV show.

Knowing she could do nothing about the vampire pissing match, Kara turned to Lisette. "We need to stop that bleeding. Come into the kitchen with me." Lisette followed, docile and spellbound. Lisette sat in a chair and allowed Kara to place pressure on her neck wound, which had already started to coagulate.

"What happened, Lisette?"

Lisette seemed to come to a bit and turned her head to look at Kara. "He said Gaspard hurt him, like Gaspard hurt me, and that if I helped him, I could hurt Gaspard, the way Gaspard made me hurt. I didn't know he was going to set a fire that could have killed a lot of innocent people."

She continued. "He came back to my house, and I confronted him. He got angry, really angry."

A huge crash came from the living room followed by the sound of broken glass. *That was the sliding glass doors to the back porch*, Kara thought. *I hope she has insurance.*

"Henri grabbed me by the arms. He was so strong that I couldn't fight. He used one hand to twist my neck so that it hurt and then, then..."

"Yes," said Kara.

"He raped me. I don't mean physically like the regular kind, you know? I mean he bit me, making sure it hurt, using his powers to make me stay still. I was screaming inside but couldn't move. He ripped away when Gaspard broke the door."

Lisette blinked, and Kara could see her mind was returning. She knew it was back when Lisette started to scream. Kara reached down to hold her, but Lisette pushed her away. Not knowing what else to do, Kara fetched Lisette a glass of water and stood next to her, waiting out the panic and feeling useless.

Lisette rocked back and forth in jerky movements, gasping for air and tearing at her hair. Alarmed, Kara tried again and this time held her still, using her size and strength to keep Lisette from hurting herself until Lisette's screams deflated to moans. Lisette closed her eyes, wrapped her arms around her knees, and keened, "No, no, no," repeatedly. Kara reached out to hold her hand, but Lisette shot to her feet and ran up the stairs. Kara heard a door slam.

Knowing that there was nothing more she could do for Lisette, Kara walked into the living room and followed the trail of destruction to the back yard. Once, the yard had been manicured with a small fountain in the middle. That fountain was rubble, and anything that had been a flower bed was vaporized. The two vampires stood across from one another, both bleeding from multiple scratches, but Henri fell to his knees and laughed.

"You know that you left me for dead?"

"I thought you *were* dead. You were buried under a mountain of rock!"

"Buried alive!" Henri snapped, wiping blood from his lip with the back of his hand.

"I didn't know! For this, you use my friend and attack me and mine in my home?"

"Yes!" screamed Henri. "Yes! You owe me. You owe me time. My spine was crushed, *imbécile*, and you left me there to perish. But I didn't die. Instead I became like you, but without the power, money, or good looks. I was the insect of the vampire world, thanks to you. When my arms worked, I scraped my body across the floor to move from room to room, pulling myself along on my belly. You. Left. Me."

"This was a long time ago, and I didn't know you were alive. Besides, now you can live forever. What's two years?"

Henri sat on the ground, snickering with glee. "Well, ask your old lady friend if she would like two more years and see what she says. She's not going to get two more years though," he sniggered. "You know you have some very angry ghosts on that property? Thanks to me, they are wide-awake now."

Kara's blood turned to ice.

"What have you done?" demanded Gaspard, leaning down to hold Henri by the chin.

"Nothing that wouldn't have happened anyway, with a little more time. They had manifested by themselves. I just gave them a little blood to egg them on a bit. Rile them up. They were angry. Now they're bloodthirsty." He sneered and then fell to his back holding his sides with laughter.

"Adelaide!" Kara exclaimed. "Gaspard, Lisette is hiding upstairs. Go to her, she needs you. I've got to see to Adelaide."

She ran to her truck, heart in her throat, praying to Odin that the old woman was all right.

17

Adelaide had observed the kitchen fire from a separate wing of the house. *Could the ghosts have set that blaze*, she wondered. It seemed unlikely, but if they did, she had to try to stop them from hurting anyone else. She dressed, every movement sluggish with remorse, believing that she was responsible for the fire.

Noel drove to Gaspard's to pick her up and was stopped by a guard wearing a ripped uniform with slashes of soot on his face.

"You can't go in, son."

"I'm here to pick up Miss Adelaide. She called for me."

The guard leaned down on the open window, and Noel saw the fatigue in the man's eyes.

"Look, you can call her at the house."

"I do recognize you. Go around the back; you'll never get through here. I'll open the gate remotely."

Noel held out his hand in a fist, and the guard bumped him back. "Thanks, bro."

"Don't bro me, son. Get yourself around the back and pick up that nice old lady. Then skedaddle. We've got enough going on."

Twenty minutes later, Adelaide stood in front of her own home, a place she'd lived in for years, one she had considered a refuge, and now it was a place of dread.

She was quivering with fear, back still hurting from her last encounter, terrified of what might happen next. But she was the only one who could communicate with the specters, so it was up to her to stop them. She stiffened her resolve and stepped out into the middle of the estate.

The ghosts swarmed, their presence so suffocating that she felt as if her mouth and nose were stuffed with cotton. She tried to speak, but it was impossible. The ghosts were stronger than before, and there was a blood lust that hadn't been there prior. It was like revenge wasn't enough. Now, blood needed to run in rivers.

The ghosts grabbed her arms and pulled her down to the ground. She hadn't even been able to get a word out. Mustering a resilience she didn't know she had, she called to Amos.

"Why did you start the fire? You could have killed many innocent people!"

The ghosts hesitated.

Amos came forward, so real now that she could see the color of his skin and the whip marks on his torso. An ugly scar made her think of a knife wound.

What do you mean, old woman?

Adelaide struggled to sit up, but the ghosts held her down. Amos tilted his head to the side, listening to something or someone. He nodded and then leaned in and straightened her skirt. He motioned for the ghosts to let her sit up.

Betsy says this is no way to treat an elder, slave trader or not. Now tell me 'bout the fire.

"The fire at the vampire's house. It caused a lot of damage."

We didna start it.

"We saw ghosts in the kitchen doorway."

Ghosts that haunt that house mebbee, partly solid like us tryin' to 'scape the flames. But I donna care. You can all burn, talkin' for myself. You tryin' to blame us for somthin' else? You who did all the hurtin'? You who did all the whippin, punishin' and your men doin' the rapin? You know how many mullato chiles we have in our number? Lots, 'cause your white men like to get randy wit our women and then you mistreat the offspring.

The blood lust rose in Amos and his entire retinue. Sounding less like a wounded, wronged man looking for justice and more like a bloodthirsty killer, Amos lowered his voice and hissed, *I think we'll start with you.*

If he intended to scare her, it didn't work. Adelaide didn't hear him because she was so engrossed in pondering the situation. *If it wasn't the ghosts, who could it be*, Adelaide wondered. There must be another party involved, an X factor she hadn't accounted for. Her mind buzzed with possibilities. Maybe it was...

Adelaide careened out of her reverie by the ghosts pulling her down again, their hands plucking at her clothes. They shoved her onto her back, and a strong pair of hands grabbed her hair and dragged her out onto the lawn, into the slave pen, which was now visible to the naked eye, a red stain on the face of her property and heritage.

The smell was unbearable, and she felt the brush of spiders on her legs and the burrowing tics in her ears. The wooden floor scraped her back, and she jerked with pain when they manacled her to the middle bar. She wondered if they would whip her again and could only utter, "No, no, no."

She closed her eyes, believing this was the end, hoping for a quick death when she heard the clang of a sword hitting the metal of a spectral chain.

Adelaide opened her eyes and saw Kara struggling with a phantom, a ghost so far gone in his rage that his entire being sucked in light like a black hole, a veritable absence of spirit. Adelaide hadn't known this could happen to a restless ghost, and despite her pain, Adelaide was so horrified she said a quick prayer that the phantom slave found his way.

Kara fenced this black spirit with her sword as he flashed in and out of the physical world, each time getting closer until he hit Kara's shoulders with the chain, knocked her to her knees, and then slashed her arm with a knife—a real knife—pulled out of the mist.

Adelaide tried to call out, but diaphanous hands held her down. Adelaide noted that the ghosts smelled pungent like fruit left out in the sun too long. Ghostly leg irons chained her feet, and a multitude of hands pinioned her arms to the ground.

Kara now battled the entire army of ghosts, and even she could not win that on her own. She whistled for Rikassa, and the horse came running so fast that Adelaide wasn't sure her hooves hit the ground. Kara leapt onto the horse and used her height to her advantage, swinging in wide downward strokes, not quite destroying the ghosts but pushing them back. Kara nudged Rikassa closer to Adelaide and stabbed at the ghosts who restrained her friend. The ghosts melted back, muttering curses, calling Kara a she-devil. As long as Kara guarded her, the ghosts stayed back, but Adelaide knew this was a stalemate that couldn't last.

Their attention turned with the arrival of the vampires.

Gaspard zipped toward Adelaide and Kara, another vampire hot on his heels. This new vampire's fangs were down full length, and before Gaspard could get to the women, the other vampire tackled him from behind forcing Gaspard to turn and engage. The two vampires moved at a blinding speed, so much so that to Adelaide's eyes, they were flickers of color with vaguely human shapes. The other vampire's colors were brown, gray, and purple while Gaspard's were red, orange, and yellow.

An onslaught of ghosts welled up from the slave pen behind them, bearing talons like birds of prey, distorted features twisted with hate. They charged Adelaide, and she hunkered down, whimpering in fear as they drove toward her. Kara readied her sword and shield, blocking Adelaide with her body. Rikassa lowered her head and stamped a challenge.

They were surprised when the ghosts passed right on by and entered the house instead. It was if a bomb had gone off with a pounding drum-beat to follow. The house ghosts—Nathan, Sylvester, Slinky, and Martin—charged the slave ghosts in a fantastic clash of spectral power. Lights flickered, and Adelaide could hear the shouts of Amos and his clan as they fought their former masters and the black man that had turned his back to their plight. Their anger pulsated through Adelaide's body, and she closed her eyes to push out their rage and pain. Sylvester and Nathan received the bulk of the blame, but it was Slinky who'd performed the beatings and Martin who'd turned a blind eye.

Adelaide heard her dishes hit the floor and the tinkling of the dining room chandelier as it gave in to the inevitable. Something that looked like pillow fluff floated out the back door followed by a dozen tea cups.

The slave ghosts ripped the house ghosts from their anchor inside the mansion, and a clash of phantasms exploded on the lawn. It was impossible to keep track of who was who, but Adelaide could hear the shrieks, the thuds, and the weeping. A cadre of slave ghosts veered off and encased the two vampires, who were both bloody from multiple bites and gashes, and held them fast. Kara dismounted and charged, throwing all her effort into rescuing Gaspard. Several of the ghosts snickered and blinked out of existence only to reappear next to Adelaide. Kara stood dead center looking right to left, determining how to get to them both.

Adelaide could take it no more. With an effort of extreme will, she shoved the ghosts of off her and yelled, "Amos, STOP!"

The world stopped. Amos emerged from the miasma and approached her, so solid she could see the faint tinge of his blue cotton pants and the outline of his bare feet pressing into the grass.

What is it you hope to achieve, old woman?

"These people are innocent. Leave them be. Kara wasn't anywhere near the sugar plantation during your time. Both she and the vampires were in the old-world."

But not Nathan and the other house ghosts. They owe us. Adelaide could feel Amos' power pressing on her temples, and she staggered beneath the weight.

Nathan stepped forward, separating from the haze of ghosts, blood, vampires, and Valkyrie.

I offer myself.

Amos turned to him. *What do you mean, slave master?*

I offer myself. I will let you destroy me so that I am spent and cannot go through the Door. But you must let the others go and then move through the Door yourself. We did you wrong, it is true, and I will pay for that, but the rest of you should leave this plane. It is time.

Amos floated back to his compatriots, and the ensuing conversation happened at a level almost beyond hearing. What they could hear was so disturbing that Adelaide, Kara, and Gaspard winced in pain. The other vampire covered his ears but still struggled against his ghostly captors, fangs snapping like an injured lion on the savanna, useless but defiant.

Amos returned. *Nathan and Sylvester. Both of you. Nothing less.*

Sylvester floated to stand beside Nathan. *I accept, but you must promise to leave and let our descendants and neighbors live in peace.*

We agree.

Kara pulled away from the ghosts, snarling in fury. Gaspard and the second vampire backed away, free but wary of both the ghosts and each other. Adelaide bowed her head and said, "So let it be."

Nathan and Sylvester moved to the center of the ghostly crowd, which separated to let them in and then enclosed them in a circle. No one breathed or made even the tiniest sound. There was silence and a quiet acceptance that this was the end.

Violence exploded in nightmare of sound and motion. The crowd converged on the two slave masters and tore them to pieces in a frenzy of destruction. White filaments of spectral substance flew in every direction. Ghostly fluid ran in rivers on the ground and pooled at Adelaide's feet. Most disconcerting, she lost contact with Nathan's consciousness, his soul destroyed forever. Sylvester followed, passing out of existence and out of Adelaide's reach. It took a few seconds.

Adelaide's stomach turned, and she fell to the ground, heaving. Kara ran to her side. The ghosts stepped back, still angry, but their fury was banked. Amos inclined his head at Adelaide.

We depart now. Vengeance is ours. Justice is done.

A female ghost slipped forward and placed her hand in his. Betsy, Adelaide guessed. Together at last.

There was a glow in the distance as if a window had opened so the light could shine in and illuminate places it had never touched before. The ghosts floated toward it in a spectral line, disappearing into the light's radiance. As the last one entered, the glow dimmed and then winked out.

No one noticed Slinky and Martin float back to the house.

Adelaide and Kara each let out a sigh of relief, but then Kara yelled out, "Gaspard, watch out! Henri...!"

Adelaide watched, mouth open in shock as Gaspard roared in pain. The vampire, Henri she now knew, jumped on Gaspard and latched onto his throat. Kara picked up her sword and rushed toward Gaspard, only to be pushed aside by a figure in black, who grabbed Henri by the scruff of the neck and threw him to the ground.

18

Gaspard thought he was done for. Henri's fangs were buried deep in his neck, and he couldn't shake him off. He was flooded by sadness, and a deep heaviness overtook his body. *He will get my blood*, he thought, *and it will make him stronger. At least I can stop that. Oh, how I wish I had held Kara, at least once.*

Feeling powerless for the first time his long life, Gaspard reached up to tear out his own throat and deny Henri the satisfaction of absorbing his strength, but Henri was not there, pulled from him by a force unknown.

Gaspard staggered to regain balance and looked at the scene before him, not believing what he saw.

"Luc?" he gasped, strengthening as his wound began to close.

"Hello, son," said the black figure who held Henri in the air by the back of his shirt like a kitten in its mama's mouth.

"What is happening? Where did you come from?"

"I followed Henri here. When he lay in the ground under that mountain slide, covered in rocks, dirt, and debris, he called out for as long as his strength lasted. He was turned by a lone vampire who believed he could mend Henri and keep him as a companion. For two years, this vampire nursed Henri back to health, providing his own blood as well as that of human donors. Once he was strong enough, Henri drank his master down and hunted for me."

Luc placed Henri on the ground and shoved his boot on Henri's neck, using his heel to strain Henri's head up in an awkward position.

"He blamed me for turning you and not him. We...quarreled. He stormed out, injured by my hand and determined to scent you out. I arrived a day ago, but thankfully, just in time."

"Why is he so strong?"

Luc closed his eyes. "He drinks the blood of children."

A rock settled in Gaspard's stomach.

"That is forbidden!"

"By every rule and law, yes."

"The Assembly will kill him!"

"Yes, I am to take him back to answer to them, and I will, even though he is my son." Luc's face was a portrait of pain.

Adelaide burst forward.

"You're Luc Rochon, my ancestor!"

Luc bowed his head and said, "Yes, my lady, and glad to see the bloodline remained so... so... what is the word?"

Kara stepped forward and offered, "Spunky?"

Luc pressed his finger to his lips. "No."

"Spirited, plucky, brave, determined?" Kara said.

"I was going to say courageous."

Adelaide rolled her eyes.

"No, I mean it. I know our bloodline ends with you, my dearest, but what a way to end!"

"I'm not dead yet," quipped Adelaide.

Luc laughed. "Just so, and I love that movie. Son," he said turning to Gaspard, "I must leave and take your brother with me."

Adelaide and Gaspard both said, "No, you just got here!" The two looked at each other in surprise.

"And yet, now I must go."

He picked up Henri and placed a pair of odd, thorned manacles around his wrists. "Come, Henri, there are vampires expecting you."

Henri spit at his father.

"Classy," Luc said, and whipped out a muzzle and tightened it across Henri's mouth.

Luc turned to Kara. "A Valkyrie? My, my, Gaspard. What did you do to deserve this?"

Kara snapped, "He didn't do anything."

Luc raised an eyebrow. "Odin doesn't lend out Valkyries for no reason. One day, I will hear this story."

Gaspard schooled his features and swallowed the sense of abandonment he felt at Luc's stunning arrival and immediate exit. He stepped forward and held out his hand.

Luc ignored the hand and leaned in to give Gaspard a kiss on both cheeks. Then, he seized Henri and vanished.

Kara asked, "How did he do that?"

Gaspard turned to look at her, smiling at her astonishment. He was glad he was still here to see it. "He's a very old vampire. God knows what his abilities are."

Adelaide butted in. "This was a nice reunion, but can we go inside now? I'm exhausted, and my kitchen is a mess again. I think I'll need to burden you with my presence a little longer."

"My kitchen is no better, but lead on, my ladies."

The two women, one holding the other by the elbow, made their way to his car. Gaspard watched Kara as she assisted Adelaide and thought, *maybe I need to be bold—time is short.*

19

Gaspard asked Adelaide to visit Lisette, hoping the older woman's nonthreatening manner would allow Lisette to release some of her anger, and her heartache.

Lisette talked to Adelaide, telling her the whole story, and Adelaide held her as she cried. She rocked the younger woman and promised her, "Henri is done for, don't worry, he won't be back. You're safe. You're safe."

Inside, Adelaide wasn't so sure. What proof would they have that Henri was dead? She had to trust an unseen, unknown, mysterious Assembly of old-world vampires? She wasn't stupid enough to trust in that. She swore to herself, if that snake of a vampire slithered his way out of his punishment, if Luc wasn't strong enough to kill his own son, she would see to it that Henri was destroyed.

Kara was thinking similar things while on her ride. The rhythm of Rikassa's trot soothed her. The events of the last few days were tiring. She hoped she could soon return home.

She heard the caw of a crow and looked up at the nearest tree. There were two ravens sitting there.

"So," she said, "am I able to come back?"

She inclined her head and listened for a moment.

"You've got to be kidding me! He still needs me? What about *my* needs?"

The ravens blinked their yellow eyes and flew off.

Kara threw up her arms in frustration and turned Rikassa toward Gaspard's mansion. She rode the horse hard and jumped down from the saddle as soon as she got close. She charged by the guards and stalked into Gaspard's office, where he was holding a meeting with men in suits. She didn't care.

"It seems my tenure here has been lengthened!"

Gaspard stood up with a smile, walked around his desk, and took her hand. "And it is my pleasure to have you." He kissed her palm.

Kara glared at him, turned on her heel, and stormed out. Gaspard's grin widened.

Adelaide overheard this exchange with satisfaction. They were good for each other, even if Kara didn't know that. Gaspard didn't either, believing his interest was lust and nothing more. Adelaide followed Kara down to the sparring room. The Valkyrie was already beating a punching bag, and the floor sizzled with sparks from her feet.

Adelaide took a seat on a bench and watched.

Right jab, left hook. Left jab, right hook. Low right kick, high right kick, footwork in a circle around the heavy bag. Knee strike, knee strike, followed by a spinning back kick that separated the punching bag from the stand, sending it soaring across the room where it landed with a heavy thud.

Adelaide couldn't believe it. The heavy bag was shredded at the seam, and sand spilled out onto the floor.

"Awwww... crap!" Kara threw her gloves across the floor, tearing at her hand wrappings. "Now I have to clean this up."

Adelaide cleared her throat to get Kara's attention. "I am not an expert by any means, Kara, but is that supposed to be possible?"

"Hard to do, but, as you can see, not impossible."

"Kara, what brought you here?"

Kara didn't reply, just grabbed a bo staff and started working through basic combinations. The staff moved so fast it made an audible swishing sound that echoed in the stillness of the room. Adelaide had no idea what Kara was doing, but she did know she was glad she wasn't Kara's enemy.

Marc sauntered in the workout room and blanched when he saw the heavy bag. Without missing a beat, Kara chucked a bo staff at him and said, "Fight!"

She launched a vicious combination, starting with a rib strike, spinning for extra momentum, moving into a series of figure eights to push Marc back and ended with a forward thrust.

Marc recovered and gave back as good as he got. Other people, vampires and humans, gathered in the room to watch the spectacle. Adelaide heard several of the vampires betting on Marc, cheering him on, hoping that the blond intruder would get her comeuppance. The guards who reported to her bet on Kara and clapped every time she landed a strike.

Marc took the advantage when Kara slipped in a pile of heavy bag sand that had migrated across the floor. He executed a perfect four-point strike hitting her three times, missing on the last target. She scrambled out of the way and came up with a handful of sand, which she threw at Marc's eyes. The crowd gasped.

Marc dropped his staff and rubbed at his eyes, blinking to clear his vision. He staggered, unable to see, and in pain. Someone ran to him with a wet cloth, and he used it to wipe the sand from his face. He held the cloth against his eyes and shuffled to the bathroom to wash the sand from his face.

An emaciated vampire who looked very young to Adelaide, and not all there, pointed a finger at Kara and shouted, "You cheated!" The rest of the vampires contributed with their own taunts. They didn't notice when Marc returned from the bathroom, face and eyes red, accompanied by a serious Gaspard.

Unaware or uncaring that his Master was present, one of the more rash and egotistical vamps made a move toward Kara, attempting to get behind her and hold her by the torso and shoulder. Kara flicked her eye at Gaspard, who gave a minute nod. Without another beat, Kara shoved the staff behind and released the dagger.

"Kara did not cheat," Gaspard announced. The room quieted, the shocked vampires looking anywhere but at him. The guards stood at attention.

"Marc, please tell them why Kara didn't cheat."

Marc faced the crowd and said, "Because the aim isn't to play fair. The aim is to win. When in battle, use everything you have and end the fight. No games. No show-boating. It is life and death, people. Kara was brilliant. I wish I had thought to use the sand myself. I lost fair and square, and in a real fight, I'd be true dead."

The emaciated vamp said, "Yeah, so what? She killed one of ours," gesturing to the pile of ash that had settled in a neat pyramid topped off by yellow rubber charity bracelet.

"I was attacked, and I defended myself. Anyone who doubts my skills is welcome to try at any time, using any weapon. But I assure you," Kara said, stalking the line of vamps, "if you attack, I will end you. Make no mistake."

She continued. "Anyone interested in learning fighting techniques should sign up in the security office for our night classes. Smart vampires don't rely on their vampiric powers alone."

"They've always been enough before," the emaciated vamp replied.

"Well, Toothpick, I have three words for you."

Insulted, Toothpick crossed her arms. "What?"

"One lit match."

A shiver traveled through the vamps, and Adelaide watched as several vamped out, dropping their fangs and unhinging their jaws. Adelaide scrunched on her bench, making herself as small as possible. A guard noticed and slid in front of her. Two more guards offered her their hands and together, they moved her within their ranks, out of harm's way in case a full riot broke out.

Gaspard pulled on his power, using his position as Master to augment his power with theirs. The vampires weakened, several falling to their knees, one mewling in discomfort.

Gaspard's voice boomed like he had a microphone. "Kara is our security expert. She is my trusted guard, and if I hear that any vampire in my seethe tried to kill her, I will send you into the sun myself. Is that clear?"

The vamps assented through nods and quiet affirmations.

"Good. Then go."

The vamps filed out, some holding their heads as if they had a migraine. The guards led Adelaide upstairs.

Kara whirled on Gaspard. "You didn't need to do that. I can take care of myself."

"But you are precious, my dear Kara, and I dare not return you to your home in anything but pristine condition. While you are here, Kara, you are mine, and they needed to know that." Gaspard exited, Marc on his heels. Kara glared at his retreating back and said, "I'm not yours, Gaspard. Not now. Not ever."

Gaspard paused and, without looking back, said, "We'll see."

Kara marched out of the room and up a back staircase to the kitchen back door, and threw the screen door open.

"Thor, brother, can you help? Sisters, please!"

A quiet rumble was all she heard, followed by silence and the distant caw of two ravens.

PART II

SOULS FALL

1

"Vampires don't have souls! They cannot be collected to serve."

"They can, and this comes directly..."

"No! It is a perversion!"

Pain raced across her stomach as she was almost rent in two by her own elder sister.

Kara jerked awake, gasping for breath, holding her stomach over the scar.

Well, that was fun, she thought, still feeling the phantom pain. *Let's do that again. Why not every night since it is so much fun?*

The phone rang.

"Miss Kara, this is your four p.m. wake up call," said Emmie, a middle-aged human staff member who had afternoon phone duty. "May I ask why you want to get up so early? You could sleep in. Gaspard won't be downstairs for a while yet."

"I know, but working on a vampire's schedule makes it hard to get any vitamin D," Kara quipped.

"You could take vitamins."

Kara shook her head; grateful Emmie couldn't see. "I was kidding. I want to ride my horse for a while. It helps me clear my mind."

"Oh! Well, in that case, have a lovely ride."

Kara descended the stairs, glancing at the damage from the kitchen fire started by Henri, Gaspard's vampire brother, who had, for all intents and purposes, returned from the dead. Gaspard had no idea that Henri was alive, and turned, until he showed up and tried to kill Gaspard and everyone in Gaspard's home. Plus, there were some pissed off ghosts. Trying to keep track of it all gave Kara a headache.

That wasn't the only thing that gave her a headache. Odin had ordered her to continue serving Gaspard instead of returning home where she belonged, so there was no chance of life returning to normal any time soon.

Rikassa waited for her by the back gate, pawing the earth in anticipation. Kara leapt onto the back of the horse, and the two galloped, Rikassa's tail high, Kara laughing to the wind.

Kara directed Rikassa toward a swampy part of the grounds she had never visited before, where the mosquitoes were the size of dragonflies. Today, though, it wasn't as muggy as usual, and she had been curious about the place. It was a traditional bog with gators and snakes, but she could see a shimmer of hard top behind it. Rikassa would be highly offended if Kara suggested that the horse couldn't handle a few reptiles, so they proceeded through, Kara eventually dismounting when the trees got too low and close. They both sloshed through the swamp, getting wet to the knees, tripping on the undergrowth, and swatting insects left and right. Kara saw a crawling, flying mass of black writhing on a rock and went closer to look, regretting it the instant she realized it was a throng of flesh flies feasting on some dead creature. As a collector of the slain, she had seen more than her fair share of maggots, flies, and other scavengers, but it still grossed her out.

She saw the road.

Correction, she thought to herself. It wasn't really a road. It was a roughly paved path about a car's width covered in a mixture of pebbles and shells. The shells glinted in the sun, and the reflection created a dizzying rainbow that hovered over the surface. The horse liked the sensation of the crunchy layer under her hooves and danced back and forth, like a dog would roll in the grass, simply to enjoy the feel. Kara petted her flank and whispered soft words into her dearest companion's ear.

They were both dripping wet, and Kara's boots squelched as she and

Rikassa followed the path, the noise obvious as the sound reverberated in the silent air. Kara stopped for a moment and listened. She heard no birds, or insects, even the trees seemed to stand still. The stagnant, stale air carried nothing outside of the sound of their feet, not even the flop of an alligator moving off a log.

What manner of magic is this? Kara was excited that maybe she'd found a secret, and her natural curiosity carried her onward. She wasn't so reckless that she didn't unsheathe her sword and hold tighter to Rikassa's mane, but brazen all the same. She kept her eyes peeled for danger while she continued, step-by-step, along the path.

A wet, sloppy *thunk* broke the silence causing Kara to juke to the left and bring her sword arm up on the right. Nothing exited the dense trees, so she crouched a little lower, in a fighting stance, and continued walking.

A similar *thunk* came from the left, and Rikassa whinnied and pulled to the right. Kara soothed her with long strokes on her back, and the horse calmed. It bothered Kara to see Rikassa uneasy. The horse wasn't afraid of anything.

They both heard it. *Thunk, slither, thunk, slither*...an eerie combination of heavy footsteps and a serpentine glide of scales against the shells and rocks, followed by the whisper of displaced maidencane grass and cattails that got louder every second. Kara's breath came a little faster, and she focused on slowing it down, realizing that whatever this creature was, it was coming closer. Her training told her to leave and return with reinforcements. Curiosity, that minx, kept her fast.

A fetid, rotting smell reached their noses at the same time, and Kara saw a bit of a brownish-green snout before Rikassa made the decision for them both and bolted backward. Kara ran after her, grabbed Rikassa's mane, and threw herself up on the back of the fleeing horse, shocked at the war horse's behavior. She'd never seen Rikassa flee from anything.

An enormous sound emanated from the creature behind them, something between a growl and a yawn, topped with a hiss so high pitched it hurt her ears. The growl that followed rang across the swamp, and Kara saw birds rise from the trees miles in the distance. It was if the sound traveled faster than sound should, farther than physics allowed.

Rikassa, normally surefooted, skidded on the loose ground and almost pitched Kara headfirst. Rikassa righted herself, raced forward, and plunged headlong back into the marsh, unerringly heading toward the mansion grounds. Kara slipped off Rikassa, so as not to hit her head on branches, and splashed behind her mount. The horse whinnied, and the horses in Gaspard's barn whinnied in response, sensing her anxiety. Kara stopped a moment to catch her breath and get her bearings, knee deep in swamp muck. It was only then that she saw the white sign, hanging askew from one nail on a large bald cypress tree, practically swallowed by Spanish moss but still readable. "No Entrance! This means you! Fear your death!"

Someone must have put that up there to keep trespassers out of Gaspard's land, Kara thought. The sign was ridiculously dramatic. Gaspard wouldn't hurt anyone for wandering on his land by mistake, and he most certainly wouldn't kill them. She reconsidered for a moment, revised her opinion, and spoke out loud to her horse. "Okay, he might kill someone, but it would be for a very good reason, and after a lot of thought. I wonder who put up that sign?"

The horse shivered, her withers shaking and her tail swishing in unease, letting Kara know that she didn't care about the sign and it was time to go. Kara led Rikassa away from the bank, comforting her with her hands and voice until they reached the barn. Usually, Rikassa didn't sleep in the barn, but they both smelled bad and the horse needed a bath and brushing. *Horse first, myself later*. It was one of the first things her sister Valkyries taught her when she was brought into Odin's service.

As she tended to her horse, a niggling thought squirmed its way to the forefront of her brain. That overly dramatic No Entrance sign hadn't been facing the swamp to keep people *out* of Gaspard's land. It had been facing *inward*, warning Gaspard's guests and residents not to enter the wetlands at that spot. Whatever that creature was, it must be a killer.

2

Kara took a shower to clean off the detritus of the swamp. While the hot water fell on her head and back, loosening tight muscles, she ruminated about the creature. It seemed like an alligator or a lizard, but the sound it emanated was the cry of a far larger creature. She couldn't make sense of it and wished she'd seen more. She was kicking herself for losing control of Rikassa and not standing firm in front of the whatever-it-was. She'd make sure Hildr never heard about it.

She dressed by rote as she almost always wore the same exact thing: custom-made heavy blue jeans with skinny legs, wide belt loops, and a modified belt to accommodate her weapons. She attached a bronze and silver disc to the belt at the base of her spine, several Japanese throwing stars on her right side, and her sword, camouflaged as a small knife on her left so she could draw it quickly.

On her top, she wore a black racer-backed tank, which showed off her toned arms and muscled shoulders. When needed, her battle armor simply appeared, a part of her magic that she gratefully accepted and appreciated.

If it had been cool, she would have added a fitted black leather jacket, but it was warm, even in the early evening, so she left herself as she was and made her way to the door of Gaspard's office, where she gave a small knock. Gaspard barked, "Come in," and she entered, stopping dead as soon as she set foot inside.

Gaspard stood, shoulders back, fangs slightly down, with a dreadful glower. His two assistants, Marie, who handled daytime duties, and Marc, a vampire who handled nighttime duties, were standing in front of him with the body postures of people who had delivered bad news. They weren't scared, exactly, but they were... wary.

As usual, Gaspard was well dressed, this time wearing a charcoal gray suit and a pink and gray paisley tie. He'd braided his hair in an old-fashioned queue and tied it with a silver ribbon. The ribbon intensified the silver swash of hair that ran down from his temple to the tip, the only mark of color in what was otherwise jet-black locks. His blue eyes snapped in irritation, and the aristocratic lines of his face looked more drawn than usual, a sign that he was letting his vampiric nature shine through.

"Gaspard... Master," started Marc, "you know that they..."

"Impose on my hospitality and then make unreasonable demands!"

"I was going to say, believe in an old-fashioned etiquette."

"I am certain we can make things right and smooth any hard feelings, Gaspard." Marie wrote a note on her clipboard, pressing hard with the pen.

"What is it about angry, destructive ghosts, the appearance of my formerly dead brother, and a fire that do they not understand?" Gaspard demanded.

Marc coughed into his hand. "They feel that your problems should not have interfered with their formal welcome. It is a feint, perhaps, to get you in trouble with the American Assembly, but it is a small thing. No worries, Gaspard. We will invite the Northeast contingent here for a small, intimate party, and I'm sure we can make amends."

Kara stepped forward. "Would someone tell me what is going on?"

Gaspard's face relaxed, and he gave a very French shrug, just a move of the shoulders, expressing exasperation with a touch of *c'est la vie*.

"The Northeast contingent of vampires arrived before our, ahem, activities of last week and have lodged a formal complaint with the American Assembly about my lack of manners."

Kara tried hard to hide her smile. "They are angry because you attended to an emergency and didn't make nicey-nicey?"

"That about sums it up."

"We will invite them for a soirée of some kind and make this go away, Gaspard. Let me and Marie take care of it," said Marc.

"Fine, but you know how I feel about Simon Whitleigh. He's sycophantic little troll of a vampire..."

"Who may be more than three hundred years old and holds one of the largest seethes in the Americas," reminded Marc.

Gaspard plopped with an unusual lack of grace in his chair. "*Oui, oui, oui. D'accord.* Let's entertain them and as Kara says, make nicey-nicey."

Marie, who was at the end of her daytime shift and looked exhausted, her face wan and strained, let out a large exhale, scribbled another note on her clipboard and said, "It shall be done, Gaspard."

As Marie and Marc left the room, Kara approached Gaspard's desk. "How can I help with this get-together?"

Gaspard waved his hand at her. "Do the usual. Check on the security and make sure the backyard is safe for visitors. With the fire damage, the party will have to be outside."

"Yes, sir," Kara replied, biting her lip to keep from laughing out loud at his discomfiture. "We'll make it festive and safe. Those Northeastern vampires will be singing your praises."

Now Gaspard did laugh. "You know, vampires are supposed to love etiquette and old world, European parties. I hate them. All of them. I have my seethe here in New Orleans and don't want anything else. Why do these...*politicians*...have to make my life more difficult?"

"I guess it doesn't matter what circle you run in, there are always politicians." Kara crossed her arms. "Do you have any idea why they came here? What they want?"

"To strengthen ties, create an alliance, yada yada. Bullshit, bullshit, bullshit, *merde, merde.*"

Kara's smile was huge by now. "I've never heard you like this before, Gaspard. I like this more relaxed side of you. I recognize that TV reference. Did you actually watch *Seinfeld*?"

"No soup for you."

Now Kara was belly-laughing and sat down in a chair to keep herself from falling. Gaspard joined her, and Marc popped his head in to make sure everything was all right, mouth tight, eyes wide, the very picture of alarm.

Gaspard caught his breath and reassured his employee, “All is fine, Marc. Don’t worry.”

“Yes, sir. If you ever decide to have a fit of giggles again, warn me first, okay?” Marc said, eyes twinkling. “It’s a shock to the system.”

“I do not giggle. I chuckle in a mature manner.”

Now Marc giggled. “Yes, sir, of course. I will leave you to your chuckling.”

With Marc’s departure, Kara decided to turn the conversation to her adventures of that afternoon, conveniently leaving out the part where she and Rikassa ran away like squealing children. That was between her and the horse. She’d have to make sure Rikassa didn’t tell Hildr or any of her sisters either.

3

Gaspard was intrigued. "Did you actually see the creature?"

"Not really. I smelled it, and I think it had a snout and scales of some kind. It had a distinctive walk that makes me think it was injured or maimed in some way. Do you know what it is?"

"No, I don't. The locals here insisted we keep that sign up when we bought the land and warned us not to go into that section of the fen, but I never gave it much thought. We have no need to go there, and whatever lives there is free to do what it wants as long as it stays there. But I didn't think there was a mystery to it. I thought maybe a particularly large alligator lived there, or a nest of poisonous snakes. It really didn't concern me." He steepled his fingers and closed his eyes, silent for a moment.

"I bet Adelaide would know," he said. "She has already retired for the evening, but you could ask her tomorrow."

"I think I will." Kara pushed herself up from the chair. "I've got to make sure our backyard is ready for visitors." She started toward the door.

"Kara."

She turned. "Yes?"

"You said *our* backyard."

Her face hardened, losing the light and humor it had moments before. "*Your* backyard, Gaspard. Yours." She stalked out, sparks flying from her heels, a sure sign that she was annoyed.

Gaspard couldn't help it. This time he did chuckle, a low sexy sound that followed her as she left.

Pushing that growl out of her mind, Kara walked the perimeter of the lawn making notes about shrubbery and a grassy hillock that practically screamed sniper. She would make sure she had a team placed there, both to ensure no one else decided to use the knoll for the same purpose and to keep the advantage for her team. She wondered how many vampires were in the visiting party and headed for the security headquarters located next to the safe room in the lower level of the house.

Twenty minutes later, she pounded up the stairs and stalked into the Marc's office, situated off Gaspard's.

"Tonight? The Northeast vamps are coming *tonight*?"

Marc looked up at her from his paperwork, taking off his reading glasses with his left hand as he did so. She scoffed at the affectation. Vampires didn't need reading glasses.

Marc answered, "Given their current mood, it seemed expedient to get it over with. Simon and twenty of his seethe will arrive in a few hours, at midnight."

"You realize that gives me no time to plan."

Marc placed his reading glasses on his nose. "You go do the voodoo you do so well, Kara. It is because we have you that I felt comfortable even suggesting this."

"How many of Gaspard's people are attending?" Kara asked, pacing and letting little embers fly as she did.

"One more than however many they bring. They have told us twenty, but we will be prepared for more."

"So, at minimum, forty vampires..."

"Forty-one."

"Forty-one, but how many humans?"

"We will provide one sanguineer for each vampire."

"We have that many?" Kara stopped pacing and stared at Marc.

Marc grimaced. "Just."

"Any humans that aren't food?" she asked, resuming her pacing. The embers flew in abundance now, trailing her heels, and Marc pressed a small button under his desk.

"Servants, of course. Once our guests dine, they may want a small sherry or cognac. We will have servants to help with this."

A small red-haired woman with a smattering of freckles across the nose appeared at Marc's door carrying a damp mop and wood polish.

"Kara," she chided. "You're sparking again."

Kara looked down at the floor. "Sorry, Emmie, don't think anything is scorched, and on the plus side, I didn't set the throw rug on fire this time."

"Thank God for small favors. What's this vampire done now?" she asked, gesturing her chin toward Marc.

"Now, Aunt Emmie..." said Marc.

"Don't Aunt Emmie me. I helped raise you, child. I know how you think."

Kara cocked her head at Marc. "Emmie is your aunt?"

Marc nodded. "Raised me with my father once my mother died."

"Ummm hum, gives me a few sips of blood now and then to keep me young. Offered to set me up in a house of my own, but what on earth would I do there? I'd be alone. Rather work for my supper and housework is all I know. Still," she said, holding her chin in her hand, "I like being able to pick and choose my chores." Emmie poured some wood polish directly on the floor and started scrubbing with the wet mop. The small spark marks buffed away.

"Well, your nephew and Gaspard set up a party with forty vampires..."

"Forty-one," Marc corrected.

"Forty-one and even more humans for *tonight* so that I have no time to prepare. I'll have to call in extra staff from paid leave, and you'll be paying them golden overtime, princess," Kara said, poking Marc in the chest.

Marc's eyes grew wide and his fangs descended a quarter-inch. "Don't touch me."

"I'll touch you, Marky-mark, if I want. You should have consulted with me about this. Sorry, Emmie, about the sparking."

As she stormed out, she could hear Emmie say, "You asked for it. You know you should have consulted with her."

"Yeah," replied Marc, "but she would have said no."

4

Kara summoned every guard available. Some grumbled about lost vacation time promised after the ghost fiasco; others were more sanguine, compelled by a sense of duty. All were seduced by the double overtime. She requested they meet in the training room where she had recently staked an impudent vamp who had challenged her authority. Marc and Gaspard had backed her up, intending to strengthen her status, but Kara knew all their words did was submerge the animosity where it would simmer and grow beneath the surface.

Several vampires were vexed enough to want to kill her, taking umbrage with the idea that she could be more powerful than they. Kara wasn't sure if this was because she was female or because they simply disliked everyone and believed vampires to be the top of food chain. She didn't know, and she didn't care, but she was counting on someone making a move.

Twenty guards assembled, fewer than Kara wanted but all she could get on such short notice. They were in full uniform, weaponed up, and ready for assignments.

"Sarge!" Kara commanded.

A stout, dark-skinned former police officer who'd gotten sick of the bureaucratic bullshit inherent to the New Orleans Police Department stepped up. He'd been up for Master Sergeant but was passed over for a younger, skinny, white kid with a college degree. Sarge had thirty years in, took his pension, and signed up with Kara the next day, explaining to her, "I'm too young to retire for real but too old to take orders from a pissant Charleston college boy. Besides, my wife would kill me if I stayed home, and there is a lot of paperwork in a murder investigation. I'd hate for her to go through that."

"Sarge, if a vampire attacks from the front, what is your first reaction?" Kara asked.

"Shoot the sumbitch."

"Okay, but shooting a vampire may not cause much damage. It could stop some young ones, but might be completely ineffective against an older one or a Master."

"But you might be able to slow it down."

"True, but they are fast. Slowing one down doesn't mean much if you don't have a follow-up plan."

"Then, I'm not sure. I don't carry a sword," said Sarge, standing at attention, annoyed that he didn't know the answer.

"I'm giving you all a present," said Kara. "Feel free to shoot an attacking vamp, but once you do, follow-up with one of these to the throat."

She bent to the box at her feet and handed each guard a straight matte black tanto knife in a nylon sheath. The sheath didn't have a fold-over snap so the knife was a quick pull. Sleek and elegant, the knives had strong tips for stabbing but sliced well enough to cut anyone's jugular down to the spine. The guards examined their new toys, eyes wide with excitement, reminding Kara of kids on Christmas morning.

"We'll have training sessions with them later, but for now, attach them to your belt and keep them with you."

A skinny, scrappy, pock-faced little dude spoke up. "One thing, ma'am. If we are using the knives, that means the vampire is too close in for my liking."

"Good point, which is why you will always be in teams. Find your partner, stay with your partner, never leave your partner, and if you haven't gotten it by now, attach yourself to your partner so that you are never more than a few feet away from each other. One can shoot and the other can stab."

"That won't end them," said the skinny guy.

"Nope, but this will," said Kara, reaching down to the second box. She handed them each a specialized cigarette lighter that created a very tall flame.

In a fierce, clear voice, Kara said, "If a vamp is attacking, your orders are to shoot, stab, and flame 'em. What is that emergency number? 911? Protocol 911. Got that?"

The guards nodded.

"Let's try not to have any drama here tonight, but you know what to do if one comes at you or your partner."

The guards said in unison, "Shoot, stab, flame 'em."

The skinny guard smiled wide. "We should get that printed on T-shirts."

A few of the Marines demonstrated different knife holds to their counterparts, keeping things focused on the stab part of Kara's new security motto. One gloated to the team, "We'll get to the slicing part later. These knives are like buttah, I tell you. Buttah. Uncle Sam gave us some primo knives, but these are beauties."

Kara went from one to the other helping to position partners in the best positions for the shoot, stab, and flame doctrine. Were both partners right handed? Do it this way. Was the vamp between you? Reposition for gunplay so you don't shoot your partner. One had more experience with knives from military work? That person gets the stabbing part. Ready to flame but not sure where to place the lighter? Try the neck collar on a male wearing a dress shirt or anything cotton.

One guard queried, "What if they aren't wearing cotton? What if they are wearing that shiny disco crap the young ones seem to love so much?"

Kara replied, "Start with the hair."

The guard grinned and high-fived his neighbor. "Yeeeaah, that *could* ruin a day."

His neighbor replied, "You know the saying. Teach a man to start a fire, and he's warm for a day. *Set* a man on fire, and he's warm for the rest of his life."

Another guard broke in, "Set a vamp on fire, and he is warm for the rest of his death. I tell you, vamps light up like Molotov cocktails thrown into a nail salon. They burn, baby. Burn."

The first guard said, "I don't get the nail salon."

"Never walked into one?"

"Nope."

The second guard explained. "They make your eyes water. The acetone fumes could kill you."

"Acetone is highly flammable."

"Yeah, Sparky, that was kinda my point."

The group's laughter echoed through the room as they practiced for another few minutes, intent on each other and their training, a sense of camaraderie taking hold. Kara watched them, pleased. They were becoming a unit. Now they needed to fight together, and the cohesion would set in.

So, she stood alone at the back of the room, near the changing rooms, waiting.

Kara heard a whisper of movement behind her and thought, *ah, they do not disappoint.* It took all her self-control not to turn around. A foot slammed into her back, and she flew across the room, landing with a scream and a thud. She was proud of the scream. It almost sounded real.

Four vampires stepped out, fangs descended and mouths stretched in gruesome caricatures of smiles. One stalked forward, dressed in black from head to toe, a white shirt with a wide collar under his leather jacket. Kara thought he'd taken the whole creature of the night thing too much to heart. He held a hand out to the guards in a flat-palmed stop motion.

"Don't come near her. She challenged us, and we are here to take our due. Don't interfere." He flicked his hair over his shoulder, head angled just so, pausing for all to admire.

"Hey, Lestat, get your butt out of here. Kara may get angry," replied one of the guards.

"Shut up, human. She doesn't frighten me."

"Well, there are an awful lot of us guards as well."

The eighties hair band wannabee snorted. "*You* don't scare me at all."

The guards ran out of patience and shifted forward, causing the three other vamp poseurs to lean in, straining in their excitement to get to the guards and Kara, wanting a blood bath.

The guards didn't usually engage in chit-chat, but the banter had achieved its objective. Sarge and his skinny partner had slipped out the main door and circled to the restrooms unnoticed. The two guards re-entered through the changing room doors, approaching the vamps from behind. They moved soft and silent until they were in position.

"Kara, move!" shouted Sarge, and Kara rolled behind a pile of mats where she could peek out to see what happened next.

Sarge fired and the bullets ripped through the vamp's chest and slammed into the back wall. The other guards spread out in low positions, out of the line of fire, taking cover where they could, getting positioned to shoot.

The holey vamp stared at his chest in shock and was still standing when the skinny guard pumped another round in his chest. A third guard advanced from the side and jammed his knife into the vamp's spine. The vamp toppled, blood gushing from its neck. Sarge motioned to skinny guy who ran forward and stuck the lighter into the vamp's flowing locks. *Whoosh*! The wood floor wasn't ever going to be the same.

The other vamps turned to attack, but by then, the guards had gotten the message and worked in pairs. One shot, one stabbed, and the other followed up with flame. It was all over in five minutes, start to finish.

Kara emerged from her observation post, clapping. "Nice job, everyone. We'll need to get faster, and you can't count on a third person being available, but not bad. Not bad at all."

Sarge was covered in ash and waved his hand in front of his face to clear the flecks away. He coughed. "This was a live training exercise. How did you know they would show?"

"I didn't," said Kara. "But they were itching to kill me, and I was certain they would learn of our training and note the absence of other vampires. I gambled that they would see this as an opportunity. I appreciate that they made themselves available." She winked and exited, gesturing for the guards to follow. They proceeded to their positions, high on adrenaline but also warier than a half hour before.

Kara whistled her way into Marc's office, informing him of the damage to the training room and the loss of four of Gaspard's seethe, and then sauntered out leaving him open-mouthed. She waited a beat after she closed the door and was rewarded by the creative swearing that followed.

Serves him right.

5

Kara's staff placed themselves in strategic locations around the property. A double team manned the front so that they could expedite the search of each vehicle and individual. Every guard was armed with both regular and silver bullets. She didn't expect weres of any kind, but it was prudent to be careful.

Kara dressed in black fire-retardant tactical pants with a thin layer of Teflon fabric protection, which muffled sound and was good for silent operations. She packed gear in every pocket, including a custom flashlight made from aerospace grade metal with special LED sunlight synthesizing bulbs and extra nine millimeter rounds for her Glock 19. She donned her camouflaged sword, throwing stars, and shield and shoved the gun into a sleeveless holster top. A black fitted cotton jacket concealed her weapons. She preferred her sword to guns, but it was better to be prepared. If things got extra rough, none of this would matter and she'd generate her armor, but she hoped the shit wasn't going to come close to hitting that fan. In fact, she wasn't certain anything bad was going to happen, but her Valkyrie spidey-sense was tingling, and she had learned long ago to listen to it.

The vamps arrived precisely at midnight in black Town Cars driven by creatures passing for human. There were twenty-one vampires, a fact she noted and communicated to Marc by radio. The first two cars held flunkies dressed to the nines, whose purpose was to look pretty. They looked young for vampires, meaning that their skin held some of its original softness and they hadn't yet given up the habit of breathing. They were a distraction.

The real power arrived in the third car, a black sedan like the others, but the driver was armed and the three men in the back were vampires of considerable age. She could smell the guns, and old vampires had complex, whirling auras that spoke of centuries on Earth, not decades. She whispered a warning to the guards and slipped into the shadows to observe the newcomers.

"Mr. Whitleigh, welcome. Your bodyguard cannot come into the mansion armed, I'm afraid, but we'd be happy to store his weapons here, and he can retrieve them when you leave," said Sarge, who had taken the lead.

The bodyguard cast a glance toward the back and received a nod from the man in the middle. He handed over his handgun to the guard.

"Please exit the vehicle so we can search you." The bodyguard, a giant of a man, once again got a nod and cooperated while being searched. Kara couldn't see him clearly from her observation post, but she was surprised to realize he wasn't a vampire.

"I will take this thin wire I feel hidden in the lining of your jacket, sir. I believe this is a garrote, is it not?" The bodyguard stood stony-faced.

Simon Whitleigh said through the car window, "One can never be too careful."

Sarge nodded. "We agree, which is why you will understand that we also need you to exit the vehicle."

Kara heard Simon's intake of breath and listened as he let it out to the count of ten.

"Of course." Simon and his two companions exited the vehicle, and Kara peered through the gate to get a good look at them, focusing her attention on Simon.

Gaspard had once called Simon Whitleigh a little potato of a man, and Kara could see why. His build was round in the middle, narrower up top and below, giving him the unfortunate shape of a bowling pin, although not a very tall one as he was, at most, five-foot seven. In the lights, his skin was florid and his lips were full and fishy. Kara had never seen an unattractive vampire before and wondered at it as she walked back to the house, knowing Sarge and team had things well in-hand.

Precisely twenty-two vampires from Gaspard's seethe settled in the backyard in a loose circle surrounding a fire pit that had been turned into a bonsai planting, creating a stunning tableau. They were situated near entry and exit points and had already fed on bagged blood earlier in the evening so as not to stress the sanguineers.

The sanguineers sat on chairs, backs stiff, licking their lips in anticipation and apprehension of the service required. Feeding could be pleasurable for the sanguineer, but the pleasure was not guaranteed. The members of Gaspard's seethe were always gentle, but no one could promise that Simon's seethe would be as generous. Marc placed a hand on one sanguineer's shoulder and whispered in her ear, "Sarah, I will keep an eye out for any mistreatment, I promise. You will be safe." Sarah schooled her face into a polite mask but gave Marc's hand a quick squeeze.

Marc met the Northeast vampires with a bow. His grand gesture was overshadowed, however, by the state of the vampires' feet.

Kara had been certain the Northeastern vampires' intent was to sweep onto the back lawn in all their grace and glory, which was why she'd ordered that the lawn be cut and watered. They might have intended to swoop in like old Hollywood film stars, but it was hard to do that when your feet were covered in wet grass and you were forced to stop to wipe your shoes on the stone walkway and pick wet clover from your ankles. Marc waited while the vampires dealt with this insult, a small smile on his lips.

As the Northeast vamps scraped and shuffled, awkward and annoyed, Gaspard exited the expansive, gold filigreed back doors, hands out in an old-world gesture of welcome. He noted the grass and caught Kara's eye with a grin. Point one, Kara.

"Simon! So good to see you," said Gaspard. "I am sorry we couldn't meet last week. We had some issues that needed to be addressed."

Simon stepped forward and grasped Gaspard's hand in a shake. "It was unprecedented to allow us to enter without official welcome, but of course, we understand. When you have a tiny seethe and not enough staff, you have to take care of everything yourself."

Kara knew Simon meant this to be an insult, but Gaspard didn't rise to the bait.

"I have wonderful staff, Simon, as you know because you were welcomed by my right-hand man, Marc."

"That is not the same as the master himself, but again, why argue about trifles?" Simon fluttered his hands at his own magnanimity. "It is difficult to live up to high standards of protocol when you are just getting on your feet. I remember being your age, although I was always careful to behave with decorum."

Kara bit the inside of her cheek and stifled the desire to punch Simon in the mouth.

Gaspard, unfazed and unruffled, smiled wide, showing a lot of teeth. "Let me introduce you to Kara, my head of security." Gaspard gestured for Kara to come forward.

At Kara's entrance, Simon stilled. Kara felt his look on her and was alarmed by the intensity of his contemplation. It scorched her skin, and despite the heat of the examination, she got goosebumps on the back of her neck. In the distance, Rikassa responded to her discomfort by moving closer to the lawn, still out of sight, but within quick reach.

Gaspard noticed Simon's scrutiny and frowned in response, placing an arm around Kara's shoulders for a moment to lay his claim. Kara was irritated by the gesture but stifled her objection, understanding Gaspard's logic. Simon was not an average vampire. Moving this close to him, she could feel his power lying under the surface, raging hot, contained by his strength of will only. He was like a lava pool that had been temporarily iced over.

Kara didn't offer her hand, but Simon reached forward and claimed it anyway, bending down to as if to give it a kiss. Immediately, Kara's left hand clapped down on his right shoulder, and she pressed a thumb into his supraclavicular nerves. The pain stopped his descent to her hand, and he inclined his head ever so slightly. She let him go with a similar nod.

"I meant no offense, Kara," Simon said. "I was honoring a beautiful woman and a warrior."

"Who chooses not to be touched," Kara replied. "In my line of work, I require both of my hands to be free at all times."

"Of course, of course," said Simon, waving her words away. He absently patted his right pocket. "Damn it, seems I've misplaced my pocket watch. What time is it?"

Gaspard answered, "About 12:30 a.m."

"Ah, time is fleeting, is it not?" He continued, "Gaspard, this is quite a beautiful setting you have here. Please let me introduce my lieutenant, Jarius." He turned from Kara, showing her his back in a display of confidence, and gestured to his bodyguard, a bull of a man with the nose of a heavyweight boxer. Now that she could study him unimpeded, she realized he may not be a vampire, but he was powerful. Everything about him was huge. His shoulders practically tore his suit jacket at the seams. His hands were the size of dinner plates, and his legs were so muscled he couldn't put them fully together and stood in a slight straddle. Jarius shook Gaspard's hand, glanced at Kara with hard, vicious eyes, and took his position at the right-hand side of his boss.

Kara stepped to Gaspard's left side and walked with them to the center of the lawn where the Gaspard's vampires waited. She felt the gaze of the trailing Northeast vampires on her neck.

Gaspard gestured to the sanguineers. "Please, take advantage of our hospitality. The sanguineers are available, one for each of you. I have promised them that you will abide by hospitality rules as well and take one sip."

"Thank you for the generous welcome, Gaspard. Of course, we will abide by the rules. A vampire who doesn't is in peril from the Assembly, and we wouldn't want that, would we?"

Kara swallowed hard at Simon's tone, wishing she had psychic powers so she could force a cobblestone to shift in the walkway and trip the potato. Or, maybe she could tie his shoelaces together? Or...

Her reverie was interrupted by Gaspard, who responded with a controlled, "No, we wouldn't. I didn't realize you were so involved with politics, Simon. Have you always been in the Assembly's pocket?"

Simon gave Gaspard a hard stare. "I stay *aware*, Gaspard, something you should do as well if you don't want to mold here in this backwater."

"I'm happy in this backwater."

Kara moved closer to Gaspard, angling her body so that her right arm was free and within one sword length of Simon. Her disdain for disingenuous chit-chat was legend among her family, as was her habit of saying what she thought without thinking first. Her temper was also well-known. She was afraid her arm might fly without her permission and wondered if Odin would accept that as an excuse for killing a vampire without provocation. Probably not.

At Kara's move, Jarius shifted his position to be closer to Simon and placed his bulk in between Kara and his boss. Kara slid closer still until the two were almost nose to… chest if she was being honest. Jarius' mangled nose was a good two heads farther north.

Marc jumped between them both and said, "Why don't our guests enjoy the hospitality we have provided for them? Simon, please direct your seethe to fulfill their thirsts." He tugged on Kara's sleeve. Kara fake lunged at Jarius and laughed when he jerked back.

"I don't think Jarius liked that much, Kara," Marc whispered in her ear. "Why provoke the man?"

"That's not a man, Marc."

"What is he?"

"Hybrid, human and something else."

"Troll?"

"Maybe. His eyes *are* close together."

"Well, you think about that. In the meantime, try not to start a war, Kara," Marc said, leading the way to the sanguineers. Kara shot a look at Gaspard. His face was blank, which Kara knew meant he was furious.

6

Tensions abated, the Northeastern vampires each chose a sanguineer. A tall female vampire with the most gorgeous sepia colored skin, approached Sarah and glided toward her, undulating like a cobra trying to mesmerize its prey. Kara wanted nothing more than to shove the cobra back in her basket, but she wasn't in charge of this part of the party. But, her job was to ensure that no one got hurt, so she kept a close eye on cobra-vamp and made sure the vamp knew it. From the look of contempt on the vamp's face, it appeared that the cobra-lady didn't care what Kara thought and maybe even liked the audience.

Another vamp from Simon's seethe closed his eyes and turned in a circle as if judging each of the sanguineers by smell. The sanguineers shifted in their seats, made nervous by the eeney-meeny-miney-mo technique employed by this sharp-nosed showoff dressed in an actual tuxedo with a cape like a phantom of the opera gone wrong.

Gaspard's sanguineers weren't used to this. Except for some of the younger vamps that joined Gaspard's seethe recently, now four down in population, Gaspard's seethe was polite and made an attempt to ensure any feeding was a pleasure for the sanguineer. The deliberate attempt to unnerve the donors was off-putting and unfamiliar.

What is it with this seethe, thought Kara, *that makes them all so bizarre*?

She whispered her question to Gaspard, who smiled his answer at her, though his eyes were hard. "It is a symptom of their leadership. They take on the characteristics of their Master."

That's lovely, thought Kara. It told her all she wanted to know about Simon. She had a dog once, one who liked everybody except this one woman. The woman always seemed friendly enough, but Kara felt unnerved every time she came around. Turned out the woman was a witch who enjoyed kidnapping children and making them into stew. Since then, Kara had learned to trust her instincts and watch for the signs. If the apples were rotten, it was because of the tree that bore them. Kara turned her attention back to the feeding.

Cobra vampire had taken Goth to a new level, and on anybody else, it would have been too much, but on her, it was successfully creepy. She stalked Sarah, who shrunk from her, pulling back with the instinct of prey knowing it was in a predator's grasp. The vampire smiled, showing her fangs, and grabbed the woman by the neck, squeezing so that Sarah whimpered, and whispered, "You are right to be afraid. Give me more of that luscious fear."

Kara and Marc moved to intercept but halted when Simon seized his vampire by the upper arm and yanked her away, pulling her into his grasp. He placed his other hand on her shoulder and pushed her down to her knees, his long nails digging into her neck.

"We abide by the rules, Vanessa! You have embarrassed me in front of our hosts. You are not allowed to drink tonight. Go over there near that copse of trees and wait until it is time to leave."

Vanessa tried to stand, but Simon instructed, "Crawl," and every vampire and human watched her crawl across the stone walkway and onto the wet grass, dragging her long black dress behind her, pink tears flowing down her face.

Well, if she's crying, she can't be too dehydrated, thought Kara. She should be able to retain control, but she flicked a finger at two of the guards to stand between the banished vampire and the rest of the party.

Meanwhile, Phantom-vamp had chosen an overweight man who usually had a laid-back attitude and a great sense of humor. Now the sanguineer's face was rigid with terror, and he had scooted off his chair and backed up several feet. Kara was done. She stepped between Phantom-vamp and the sanguineer.

"Hey there, oh lover of musical theater, I see that you get off frightening your sanguineers. We don't allow that here, so if you don't dial it back, I'm going to take your actions as a threat and act appropriately."

The vamp stopped in his tracks. "I do love musical theater. How did you know?"

"The cape sort of gave it away."

"Really? I even left the mask at home."

"You might want to consider toning it down a bit. I don't think it's working for you," said Kara.

The vamp's face dropped. "That is disappointing. I have a Pirate of Penzance look, too. Do you think that would be better?"

Kara appeared to give it some thought. "Not sure, maybe though. You know these things can be very tricky."

"It's the nose, isn't it? I can't escape this damn nose. Even in life it kept me from playing the leading man."

"I feel sorry for you, really, but right now you're going to have to decide what you want to do. Feed nicely with this gentle sanguineer here," Kara said, gesturing at the man behind her, "or, back off. It's up to you."

The vamp placed his hand to his lips, considering his options.

There was a moment of silence.

The vamp leapt at Kara, fangs out, crying, "What I want is to feed on you!"

Kara reached back and pulled the sanguineer out of the way with her left hand while slipping beneath the vampire's arms, getting out of reach. She took a quick glance at Simon. The master vamp had his face in his hands, even he not believing how stupid this vamp was.

The vamp strutted toward Kara, eyes wide, sending out waves of temptation, seduction, and promises of rewards beyond imagining. Kara had experienced true mesmerization once, from Gaspard, and this vamp didn't have a fraction of Gaspard's juice. She batted the compulsion away like one might dismiss a fly.

The vampire stopped in front of her, face crestfallen.

"You weren't affected."

"Nope."

"What if I do this?" the vamp asked, narrowing his eyes like an eight-year-old trying to use the Force.

"Still nothing," Kara said.

"But being with me would be sweet. We could make sweet, sweet love," the vampire wheedled. He tried his compulsion yet again, holding out an arm. "Join me."

"Okay, snickerdoodle, we're over. It isn't you. It's me. I just can't imagine us in a relationship. So be a good boy and walk over there to the back of the line, and we'll forget this ever happened."

"It was always like this when I was alive!" the vampire said. "Always an understudy, never the lead."

Kara patted him on the shoulder. "I get you, big guy, but rehearsal is done for today."

The vamp hung his head as he shuffled away, muttering, "It's not fair. I gave up sunlight for *this*?"

Simon turned to Gaspard. "My apologies for my charges' lack of manners."

"Totally understandable, and as you can see, no harm done. You, however, have not partaken of our offerings."

"I have no need at this moment, thank you, unless..." Simon glanced at Kara, who flashed him an icy glare.

"Kara?" said Gaspard to Simon, eyebrows to his hairline.

"It is too much, never mind," Simon replied.

"Yes, it is," said Gaspard.

Gaspard took a moment to reign in his exasperation. "Now that everyone else has fed, perhaps we can sit down and discuss the reason for your visit."

"So forward! Are you always in such a hurry?"

"Only when I am certain that there is a specific reason why I should be. You didn't come to New Orleans for the ambience."

"No, I didn't." Simon walked toward the back of the lawn, motioning for Gaspard to follow. Kara and Jarius moved with them.

"Does she have to be here?" Simon asked.

"Does he have to be here?" Gaspard retorted.

Simon sighed. "Well, I guess it is proper since my interests lie with her, and Jarius goes wherever I do. He is extremely loyal."

Kara studied Jarius for a moment, wondering why this enormous man would serve such a pathetic excuse for a vampire as Simon

Whitleigh. There had to be a story there. Her curiosity was piqued, but she pulled herself back to the conversation at hand.

"What do you mean, your interests lie with Kara, Simon?" Gaspard kept his voice even.

"I have need of a new security consultant, and the word is that she's the best," Simon said, *sotto voce*. "I'd like to retain her services for a short time to review the Northeast's current security plans and contingencies."

"No."

"That fast? Why? It would be a consultant position for, say, a month."

"She is not mine to give," said Gaspard, mouth tight.

"She is your employee?"

"She is a consultant, and she is needed here and cannot leave."

Simon pouted. "Maybe we should ask her directly?" He turned to Kara. "The money would be very good."

"No."

Before Simon could respond, an odd sound came from the far end of the lawn. It was a scraping sound followed by a *thunk*, then a *scrape* and a *thunk*, and a fetid smell blew upon the breeze. The next sound was a scream, followed by two shots and the sound of something heavy hitting the ground.

"Vanessa!" said Simon. Kara was already moving.

7

"Stay here!" ordered Kara. "You two," she said, pointing at the two closest guards, "get Gaspard in the house. The rest of you, move the humans to safety." She raced toward the sound, hoping it wasn't what she imagined. Another scream lit the air as the guards who had been standing watch over Vanessa met their ends. Kara got there just in time to see what had attacked them.

It was about seven feet long, or tall, depending on whether it stood upright or on four feet. It was a yellow-green color, the color of bruised, dying flesh, with scales covering its body. Three of its feet had talons like a hawk's although several inches bigger, but the fourth, the front right, was a stump. The creature slavered like a rabid dog with sharp canines, glowing red eyes, and a two-foot serpentine tongue. The tail added another four feet to its length, and the spikes down the ridge and at the end reminded Kara of a dinosaur.

Vanessa's body lay on the ground in two pieces, the top part trying to crawl away, the head bubbling blood while entrails oozed out of the bottom. The first guard's body was also rent in two, and Kara watched as the creature took an enormous bite and gulped it down. The second guard was simply missing a head, which explained why Kara only heard one guard scream.

Kara pulled her Glock and aimed, firing off three shots. All three bullets bounced off the creature's hide. Two teams of guards arrived in tight formations of four and poured bullets into the creature, with little effect except to aggravate it. It turned toward them, pushed off its back legs, and charged.

"Back up!" commanded Kara.

A vampire from Simon's seethe flew over their heads and landed on the creature, riding it like a bull. The animal reared up, knocking the vampire to the ground, but the vampire managed to land lightly on his feet. What he could not do, however, was avoid the spiked tail that crashed through his head, turning his brains to soup.

Kara and her guards were in a disciplined retreat, firing as they went in an attempt to keep the creature at a distance, so she almost didn't notice when Gaspard flew by her in a blur of motion.

"What the hell, Gaspard! You are supposed to be safe in the house!" she yelled, motioning her men to stop, take cover, and hold the ground. Gaspard was whirling around the creature faster than the human eye could see, but not too fast for Kara. She could see that his intention was to buy the guards time to determine a more effective plan by confusing the thing, whatever it was, but even as lithe and quick as Gaspard was, the creature had multiple weapons to deploy at once, and he got scratched across the torso by a talon. Gaspard's blood ran hot down his shirt and he slipped, falling to the grass.

At the sight of Gaspard down and injured, Kara abandoned any thought of using traditional weapons. She leapt forward. There was a flash of light, and in that split second, she dropped her normal clothes and emerged from the glow fully armored, sword aloft, shield out, and wailing a blood-curdling cry. She slashed at the creature with her sword and drew blood as she sliced the scales down its back, peeling them off like she was husking an ear of corn, revealing the vulnerable flesh underneath. She knew her efforts caused shallow wounds, and she stabbed once, injuring the creature, but she was unable to follow through with a killing strike.

The beast whirled around and snapped its teeth, making a screeching sound that hurt Kara's ears. She parried and thrust, forcing the creature to back away. With a final roar, it turned and fled. She hurled a throwing star at it, and the creature sunk into the swamp with a final yip, an odd sound that made Kara wonder where she'd hit it.

Kara caught her breath, and her sword dripped blood on ground. She wiped at the scratch on her cheek with the back of her hand and rotated in confusion at the sound of clapping. Simon stood several yards behind her, applauding as if she were a mezzo-soprano soloist at the opera. His vampires positioned themselves behind him, studying her like a new form of bug. Jarius also watched, silent, ready, and with a look that said he was aching to take Kara on.

Gaspard rose behind Kara and paused to put a calming hand on her back where no one could see. It was all she needed to steel her face and douse her anger.

"Brava!" exclaimed Simon. "That was extraordinary, my dear Kara. I had heard rumblings that you were something more than you seemed, but I never expected that display. The transformation into... into... whatever it is you are was magnificent. I must have you for consultant."

"No," Kara said. "Just no."

"But why for heavens not, now that I know your true nature? Well, not your *true* nature because I haven't determined which woman warrior clan you come from, but I will. I am sure your price will go up, but I'm willing to pay."

"I. Am. Not. For. Sale."

"This conversation is over," said Gaspard at the same time.

"No, it isn't," Simon snapped, showing his first real flash of anger. "You may not want to discuss Kara's services, but you cannot deny that I deserve recompense for the loss of two of my seethe. We came peacefully and were attacked. One of my seethe sacrificed himself trying to protect us all; the other lost her life in an ambush attack by an ugly, violent mystery beast on your property. As the host, you are responsible for our safety. Payment is due."

"Payment has been paid, in blood—mine, my guard's, and Kara's. Your true-dead vampires are to be honored. Now, it is time for you to leave." Gaspard marched forward, not bothering to look if Simon followed. Kara noticed that the talon cut on Gaspard's torso had already healed. *That's a nifty talent*, she thought, as she stepped behind a tree to return to her civilian clothes.

The retinue tromped back to the house so the Northeast vampires could depart, leaving poor Vanessa's head still snapping at the air. Kara could read Simon's face and knew his demands weren't at an end, *but for now*, she thought as she bandaged her cuts, *one problem at a time.*

The mansion was fully lit, all members of the household, human and otherwise, awakened by hurly-burly. News traveled fast, and Gaspard and Kara were welcomed as returning Spartans. Various residents reached out to shake Gaspard's hand and to simply touch Kara, whispering about her sword, shield, and armor. She heard the murmuring.

"What exactly is she?"

"A Viking? An Amazon?"

"I knew she was tough, but not this tough."

"Why is she here with Gaspard?"

"I'm sure they are lovers."

Kara moved through the crowd, eyes forward until she saw the one human she wanted to see.

Adelaide stood in a dressing gown, her body curved like a question mark, defiant as they come, and at that moment, she wore a stern look and was shaking a finger at Gaspard and Kara.

"You woke the Grunch!"

Kara said, "That thing is a Grunch?"

"Come into Gaspard's office," Adelaide demanded, turning on her heel. Gaspard followed, a wisp of a smile on his lips at the old woman's spirit. Kara's face held the same expression.

In the office, Adelaide waved for the door to be closed and spoke.

"The Grunch is a chupacabra from these parts. It's a serpent, maybe some amphibian, a little dash of mammal? No one knows, but it has haunted these parts for decades, maybe even centuries. For the last fifty years, it has been silent, hibernating in the swamp, and suddenly it is awake! You want me to believe neither of you had anything to do with this?"

Adelaide waited for an answer, hands on her hips.

Kara squirmed like a bad girl getting caught cutting class. Gaspard turned to Kara, barely restraining a laugh, and motioned for her to step up and answer Adelaide's question.

"I might have... you know, accidentally wandered into the far part of the swamp and disturbed the Grunch," Kara said, pulling at her left ear while avoiding Adelaide's eyes. "I saw this path, or road, and was curious so I followed it..."

"Curious! Little girl, your curiosity is going to kill you." Adelaide looked up at Kara, who was standing her full six-foot height but felt like she was shrinking with every one of Adelaide's words.

Gaspard decided to rescue Kara from Adelaide's wrath.

"We seem to be unaware of this creature's story, Adelaide, but we know you are the person to fill us in. Please sit. I'll order tea and you can educate us."

The topic was cut short when Marc knocked at the door demanding to be let in. Gaspard bade him enter and ordered tea from a servant.

"Simon and company have left, Gaspard, but it wasn't smooth," Marc reported, pointing to several scratches on his face and a virulent red ring around his neck that was starting to bruise.

"Marc, why are you injured? What happened?" Kara jumped to her feet to inspect Marc's injuries.

Marc suffered through her examination. "Some of Simon's seethe were angry. Simon departed first, and once he was gone, they decided to rough up our team."

"Rough up, how?"

"They attempted to feed on several guards and tried to take Marc's head, ma'am," said a new voice. Sarge stood in the doorway, covered in grime and blood.

Kara pivoted to Sarge. "Report."

"As Marc already said, Simon left first, and it was obvious that he was quite perturbed. He paid no attention to his charges and zoomed off in his car with Jarius. The older vamps that accompanied him in left in the second car. They never said a word."

"Which left the flunkies behind," said Gaspard.

"Exactly, sir."

Gaspard gestured for him to sit. Sarge shook his head. "I'm covered in filth, sir. It wouldn't be right." He shook his right foot, and pale flecks floated to the floor. Kara looked down at her feet, hoping Gaspard didn't recognize them for what they were.

He continued. "They attacked Marc first, two of them grabbing his ankles and another grabbing his head. I think they meant to literally pull his head off." Sarge scratched behind his ear and dust shook out.

Gaspard looked at Marc. "Are you okay?"

Marc rolled his eyes. "A little taller."

"Our boys jumped in and activated Protocol 911, ma'am," Sarge added.

Gaspard narrowed his eyes at Kara. "Do I dare ask what 911 stands for?"

Kara wasn't cowed in the slightest. "Tell 'em, Sarge."

Sarge shifted so he was facing Gaspard, creating a cloud of soot. He opened his mouth to speak, coughed instead, and was interrupted by Gaspard.

"Sarge, why do you smell like bacon?"

Sarge wrinkled his nose and said, "That is what I was going to explain, sir. Protocol 911, as in our emergency protocol, calls for us to shoot, stab, and flame attacking vamps. Didn't quite realize how much skin and ash would remain." He shook his head, releasing another waft of charbroiled meat into the air.

Gaspard pinched his nose. "How many did you kill?"

"Three, sir. The rest vamoosed."

"Our guards have to protect themselves, Gaspard," said Kara, standing up for her team.

"I'm not saying they did the wrong thing, Kara, but the greater the death toll, the greater the demands from Simon. No matter. We will deal with it when it comes." Gaspard turned back to Sarge, who was blowing fine dust off his uniform. "How exactly does one shoot, stab, and flame, Sarge?"

"It is Miss Kara's technique, sir, and a fine one at that. She gave us these beautiful knives! And the lighters! They're amazing. And you are right, Miss Kara. Going for the hair is foolproof, although more..." Sarge scratched his nose as he grasped for a word. "More... fragrant than expected."

Gaspard lowered himself into a chair.

"Thank you, Sarge. You and the team did well. Please go get cleaned off." Kara followed Sarge out to talk to the rest of the team and make sure someone stayed on guard duty for what was left of the night. As she stepped out, she saw Emmie standing in the entryway with a mop and bucket, ready to clean broiled vamp bits off the floor. Kara mouthed "sorry" to Emmie, who held out her hands in a "what can you do" gesture.

Some of the guards were leaning on tree trunks, and a few were laying on the ground when Kara got to the front gate. The former Marines and the one Navy Seal were patrolling in or around the guard house, as well as two army snipers settled on the mansion's roof. One of the snipers had been discharged from the army for an unsanctified kill. His spotter wasn't charged but left anyway. Kara still didn't know the story but wasn't surprised to see them still at their post, taking turns on the scope in a seamless rhythm.

One look from Kara and the lounging guards jumped to their feet. She stayed silent, waiting them out. They shuffled into a type of formation, straightened their uniforms, the scent of burnt vamp thick in the air. The Marines, Seal, and snipers stayed where they were and had the grace not to smirk.

"Gentlemen, the firefight is over, but that doesn't mean the danger has passed. Take a lesson from your military comrades and man your posts until relieved. Is that clear? Would you have relaxed this completely if Sarge were here?"

Their silence was enough of an answer.

"I understand you took out three of our guests."

The men nodded.

"Do you believe it was an emergency and that the sole way to deal with the vamps was Protocol 911?"

One of the guards spoke up. "Yes, ma'am. The vampires were trying to kill Marc and refused to let go. We had to shoot them."

Another one added, "Sarge gave us the nod, ma'am."

"Marine!" Kara barked at the Marine in the guard house itself.

The Marine stepped out. "Ma'am?"

"Do you agree?"

"Yes, ma'am. Those were righteous kills."

"Thank you. You are relieved. You," Kara said, pointing to one of the guards that had been laying on the ground, "you take over." The guard, a criminal justice major fresh out of security officer training, jumped to do as she asked, his face a mortified red.

"I'll call in the daytime staff who couldn't join us this evening and ask them to come in early. In the meantime, continue to man the perimeter. Do not go back by the swamp."

"Yes, ma'am," they replied in unison.

Kara turned to leave, but looked back and said, "Good job, though."

8

Kara rubbed her temples and sat in the sitting room, phone calls made, ready to hear about the Grunch. "Okay, Adelaide, let's do this. What's the Grunch's story?"

Adelaide fluffed her hair and sat up straight, unconsciously making sure her good side faced the audience. "When I was a teenager, everyone knew Grunch Road was a place to go for, let's say, privacy. It was a Lover's Lane, but there was always a mystery about the road, for it seemed to lead to nowhere and the farther in you drove, the creepier it got. Most teens stayed at the entrance of the road and didn't dare go any farther.

"But one day, a boy and a girl went in far and then backed out at full speed, skidding and throwing gravel. They made it to the girl's house, and her parents ran out to find out what was wrong. The girl kept muttering, 'Red eyes, red eyes,' repeatedly. The boy spoke of a dragon and later fell into a coma, not waking until weeks later.

"The next encounter was a fisherman. His wife reported her husband missing, and the police searched for him, eventually finding his car, his keys, and his pole and tackle box on the side of Grunch Road. He was never seen again.

"Then it was the goats. An entire flock escaped their pen and wandered down the road. The only thing the authorities found were a few bones. Everyone avoided Grunch Road after that and told the stories to their children to keep them away. It went on like this for several years, but every once in a while, some dumb kid would take a dare, head down Grunch Road, and disappear.

"The final disappearance was the straw that broke the camel's back. A hitchhiker came wandering through, and despite warnings generously offered at a local tavern, ventured down Grunch Road. As the others, he disappeared. No one really noticed since he was a stranger until they found his skeleton lying at the entrance with a few of his belongings."

"You mean his body," said Marc.

Adelaide shook her head. "No, I mean his skeleton. His bones were whitewash clean. There wasn't a speck of muscle, blood, or skin. There was some dried fluid on the bones and when analyzed, it was found to be a compound similar to our saliva, but a hundred times stronger. The police said that the monster literally ate him up and spit him out. The whole town felt like the placement of the skeleton was a warning from the Grunch not to enter his territory."

Kara, Marc, and Gaspard sat on the sofa, leaning forward, hanging on every word.

"So, what happened?" asked Gaspard.

"The community demanded a hunt, and eventually, the police agreed. Every able-bodied adult who could hold a rifle joined in, mostly the men, but a fair number of women as well. The Rochons and Beauchamps, my family, had several men in the party. They organized well, dividing the area into a grid and always going in teams, never alone, but volunteers dropped out left and right because the swamp and trees were so dark and disturbing. It was if the spirit of the thing infected the very air."

"A few intrepid souls kept at it, and eventually, they did flush the monster into the open. The reality of the Grunch was worse than the myths, and even these stout-hearted men lost their nerve. One, a long-time resident and a decorated veteran, got off one shot. It hit its mark, and the beast bellowed an unnerving howl and retreated. The men fled, wisely choosing not to follow it, and spread the word. Grunch Road was off-limits. The police put a chain and a No Admittance sign out there for a while. Nothing else has happened in the last fifty years, *until now.*" Adelaide shot Kara a look.

Kara squirmed in her seat but then remembered something.

"The Grunch has a stump for its front right leg. I bet that's where the shot landed."

Adelaide shrugged. "Seems likely. The bigger issue is what are you going to do about it? You woke it. You need to put it back."

"Or kill it," said Marc.

"Or kill it," said Adelaide. "Now, I'm going back to bed," she announced. "This one is past my pay grade. I'm an old, tired lady who needs her beauty rest."

Kara snorted. "Beauty, yes. Old and tired, definitely not."

Adelaide turned ever so slightly and gave Kara a wink. Marc walked Adelaide out saying he needed to go to the backyard to check on the clean-up.

Gaspard stayed on the sofa next to Kara. She hadn't pushed away from him yet, and he was enjoying the closeness. Even without touching, the heat of her skin warmed his own.

Kara pinched the bridge of her nose. "I'd rather not kill it, if it will return to the swamp and hibernate again."

"You may not have a choice, my love," Gaspard replied. "If the Grunch returns, you will have to destroy it."

"What if it doesn't return?"

"Then we leave it alone. Enough blood has been spilled."

"I'm going to bed myself. It is almost six a.m. I will think about this in the evening," Kara said, standing up and heading toward the door. "And Gaspard?"

"Yes?"

"I am not your love."

"You wound me," said Gaspard, looking at her with sleepy eyes, hands clasped to his heart.

Kara closed the door after her with a soft click.

And slammed back into the door face first. A red-haired vampire with the whitest skin Kara had ever seen leaned his entire body on hers, pulled back, and snared her neck in his right hand. Gaspard bolted out of the door, fangs descended, looking for the threat. He reached out to snatch Kara from the vampire's grasp, but Kara mouthed the word *no*.

She tossed her head back, into the vampire's embrace, which forced his grasp to loosen but most importantly, smashed his nose, which bled like a faucet. She used her right hand to cup his genitals, pausing a moment to wonder why young vampires always wore such tight pants, and squeezed. He let go of her neck, genitals and nose distracting him from his original mission. Kara whirled and, happy to give her toy a try, extracted her custom LED flashlight.

It lit the corridor like a lightning flash in the night sky. It was a burst of sunlight strong enough to grow plants, and it settled on the vampire's face. His hair and face smoked and then burned as he stayed hunched over trying to protect his nether region and his head at the same time. His nose stopped bleeding, not because it was healing but because it was on fire.

Kara switched the flashlight off, letting it hang at her side, and watched the defeated vampire smoke like a ham. Gaspard had withdrawn behind the sitting room door as soon as the light had flared to life, but now he poked his head out, took two quick steps, and pulled his wounded vampire up like a cat examining a tasty rodent.

"It was nice of Kara to leave you alive." That was all he said. He pushed the vampire away, who scuttled toward the basement door. Two of his companions who had been hiding behind the door grabbed him by the arms and pulled him down the stairs to the apartments below.

"Have there been other attempts on your life from within my seethe, Kara?" Gaspard inquired. His voice was mild, as if he asked what she'd like to eat for dinner.

Kara stored her flashlight and shrugged. "One other. Well, there were four vamps so maybe four others? Depends on how you count. They were very helpful in the end by serving as a live-action practice for my guards."

"Did you kill those?

"My guards did. We were practicing our new tactical approach."

"And exactly what is that?"

"As Sarge explained, Protocol 911. Shoot, stab, and flame."

Gaspard's head moved up and down in a slow, controlled manner, a thinking nod, while he sorted that out.

"Why didn't you kill this one?" he asked.

"Leave one injured to spread the tale," Kara grinned. "A faction of your seethe doesn't like me, and even with your orders, they are bound to try me out once in a while. Four are dead and this one is gravely injured with lifetime scars. The message will spread."

"I am… *unhappy* they disobeyed me," said Gaspard.

"They respond best to the direct approach, Gaspard," Kara replied. "And don't say anything to them. I find it curious that the five vampires who have attacked are all very young vamps. They are new to the seethe?"

Gaspard nodded. "This one was, and if the other four were a part of his group, then yes. They arrived a month ago, claiming to want to leave the seethe in South Texas. I am acquainted with the seethe, and if I were there, I'd want to leave, too. So, we accepted them."

"Their arrival is highly suspicious, Gaspard. Don't spook them. Let's watch them and see if we can't figure out what is happening in the larger picture."

"I will refrain from killing them but only because they may be useful. Once their use is gone, I will roast them over a spit, turning their bodies slowly, and I will make every other vampire watch as a warning. I will start at their feet and move inch by inch to their heads so they can watch their bodies charbroil."

Kara gulped. "That's harsh."

"I do not tolerate treachery."

9

Sleep brought clarity, and the next evening, Kara ordered the building of a fence along the back border of Gaspard's land. She patrolled the area with Rikassa in the meantime, looking for signs that the Grunch had returned. For the moment, she saw nothing. No tracks or broken branches. It seemed peaceful.

She rode in silence thinking through recent events. The arrival of the new vamps from the Texas seethe seemed too coincidental with Simon's arrival, and the Grunch was another complication but seemed unrelated to the vampires. Kara couldn't think of any connection between the ages-old Grunch and a bunch of newbie vampires from South Texas. Or, a seethe from the Northeast. She let her mind go blank allowing the events to filter through her subconscious assuming that some sort of pattern, if there was one, would reveal itself in time.

She rode along the whole back area, relaxing, when Rikassa came to a sudden halt, jerking Kara to attention.

There was an old, wizened man standing in front of the war horse. Whatever his original size, he was bent with age and now his height was no more than four feet. His skin hung from his frame giving him the appearance of a deflated balloon, and his clothes were ripped and stained. He wore no shoes. His skin was pale, almost white, and his eyes were pink. Kara realized he was an albino.

"Sir, do you need help?" she asked.

"No, not me, but you do," replied the old man in a surprisingly deep voice for his stature.

Kara dismounted and approached, kneeling so she could speak to him eye-to-eye. His eyes were rheumy but his voice was strong.

"What do you mean, sir?"

"The Grunch. The fence won't help."

"You know about the Grunch?"

"He and I are old companions in a way. We have achieved a certain mutual respect. He's been asleep a long time. I've sort of missed him."

"What is your name?"

The man looked up at the sky and then returned her gaze. "I forget."

"You don't know your name?"

"Haven't needed one in a long time."

"Where do you live?"

He gestured to the swamp.

"You live in there?"

He nodded. "There used to be a lot of us."

"A lot of whom?"

"Albinos. The locals pushed us into the swamp. They accused us of being devil-spawn."

"That seems cruel."

"It was," the albino said. He made the statement a fact, without rancor or resentment. "They also displaced a family of little people, dwarfs they were called then, and children with red birthmarks on their faces."

"Red birthmarks? Like port wine stains?"

The albino shrugged. "Whatever you call them now, it's all the same to me. Marks of the devil, they called them back when. We took care of the kids if we found them in time. Poor things."

"A lot of nonsensical superstition."

"New Orleans is like that," the man said with a sad smile. "But keep in mind we've lived through some weird stuff, including things like the Grunch."

"Are you the only albino left?"

The man nodded again. "I expect I am. I'll live the rest of my days out here. No need to come out. But that's not what I came to tell you, warrior lady."

"What did you want to tell me?"

"Now that the Grunch is awake, it has one thing on its mind."

"What's that?"

"To protect its eggs."

"Eggs! There's a female Grunch?"

"I've seen her once. She's a little bigger than her mate."

"Female reptiles often are," Kara said.

"The Grunch eggs lay dormant for years, but it must be time for them to hatch."

"So, if I kill it, I'm..."

"Possibly destroying the last Grunch family the world will ever know."

Kara covered her face with her hands. "Oh, Odin..."

"The little ones will be hungry," said the tiny man. "Just wanted to warn you." He scampered back into the trees without making a sound, leaving Kara to ponder his words.

10

"It has babies?" said Gaspard, leaning forward on his desk as if moving closer would change her words.

"That's what the man said."

"I can't believe there are any of the albinos left," commented Adelaide, taking a sip from her cold mint tea. "There was a whole colony forced back there at one time, but I would have thought they died out long ago."

"Long enough ago that he doesn't remember his name," said Kara. "He was easily over one hundred."

"Amazing what survives in the swamp," murmured Gaspard. "I'm sure these aren't the swamp's only surprises."

Marc knocked and entered without waiting for permission. "I have a letter for you, Gaspard."

"What is it?"

"You aren't going to be happy."

"Stop dilly-dallying and tell me."

Marc unfolded the parchment and read, "The United States Assembly commands Gaspard Bessette of New Orleans, formerly of France, to provide payment in full for the loss of two of Simon Whitleigh's seethe while they were on Monsieur Bessette's estate and supposedly under his protection."

"That was fast," said Kara.

Marc nodded. "Too fast. And we should note that it isn't signed by any individual member of the Assembly. It has all the personality of a form letter."

Gaspard walked to the window, turned, and leaned back on the sill. Kara couldn't help noticing how handsome he looked in his black suit and red shirt. His hair was free that evening, and he wasn't wearing a tie, showing his throat and a peep of chest hair.

"Kara?"

"Huh?"

"I asked what you thought."

"I think something about this stinks. How would the Assembly have time to learn about what happened and send this letter in one day? And if they feel they have a strong complaint against you, why not sign it?"

"Exactly right on both points. I think it is time to pay Mr. Whitleigh a visit. Where's he staying, Marc?"

"Hotel Mazarin, of course. They converted the Fleur de Lis suite and some neighboring rooms to be vampire friendly. Completely blocked from the sun, superb night staff, and room service."

Kara squinted at him. "Room service? Does that mean what I think..."

Marc gave a lazy grin. "Yes. Exactly what you think. For vampires, it's like ordering take-out, and all donors are cleared for disease before being added to the menu. Male, female, blood type, and of course, diabetics for dessert."

"That's disgusting."

"What? They're sweet, like a Moscato."

Adelaide interrupted their conversation. "Why would you want to go there, Gaspard? Wouldn't you want them to come here, on your territory?"

Gaspard shook his head. "No. We are going to pay a surprise visit. I want to see what that potato is up to. Let's go freshen up and look our best, shall we? Kara, dress up a little if you wouldn't mind. We are going to impress."

Kara stomped down the stairs wearing her one set of dressy clothes a spare fifteen minutes later. She wore a sleeveless black sheath dress with a thigh holster for her Glock and strapped her special flashlight to the other thigh. She paired the dress with a beaded jacket that had wide loose sleeves, good for hiding her camouflaged sword and a matte black tanto knife within the lining. She could easily slide her hand into the opposite sleeve, much like one would with a kimono, and rip the weapon out at a moment's notice. Her shoes were low black swede wedges with an ankle strap so she could run if necessary. She waited for Gaspard by pacing the length of the hallway, wishing she could put her regular clothes back on.

She heard the clearing of a throat and stopped pacing long enough to look up the stairs where Gaspard posed, ready to make his entrance. He still wore the black suit with the red shirt but had added a black, silver, and red striped tie and Italian leather loafers. He had braided his hair in its usual queue, pulled back tight, which emphasized his cheekbones. He must have fed because his skin had a faint blush, and as he glided down the stairs, he locked eyes with Kara, who thought he looked like the devil incarnate.

He kept her gaze, intense and piercing as he approached her, gliding along the floor until he was less than an arm's reach from her body. Keeping her eyes fastened with his, he reached out and slipped his arms up her sleeves and gently, ever so lightly, brushed his thumbs down her bare arms stopping to capture her wrists. He leaned forward, slowly, a millimeter at a time, a breath at a time, to brush her left ear with his mouth in a whisper of a kiss. Despite herself, Kara closed her eyes and swayed into his body so they were chest to chest. She was embarrassed that he could feel the increased beat of her pulse under his hands and the goosebumps he raised on her skin.

Gaspard, still holding her wrists, swept her arms behind her and used his body to shift her backward until he pinned her against the wall with the softest pressure, not dominating but holding, holding forever. He scented her neck, seeming to surrender himself to this point in time, this moment, right now.

Kara kept her head on his chest, enjoying the feel of his expensive suit and silk tie against her skin. It made her wonder if he would tie her up with that tie, or maybe he would use two? One for each hand? Behind her back or over her head? She smiled inwardly at these lascivious thoughts. What would her sisters say? But for once she relaxed into it, didn't question it, allowing herself to think, for a moment, that it could be real.

She cuddled up, ear to his heart and… she heard nothing. His chest was silent. His heartbeat was so slow that it was almost nonexistent. No stomach gurgles, even his breath was sporadic, air slipping in and out of his lungs only when he wanted it to.

Right, she chided herself. Back where she started. She pulled away with a frown, releasing the moment. Gaspard squinted at her, confused, but let it go. He held his arm out to her, which she refused to take with a shake of her head.

"Sorry, Gaspard. Free hands, remember?"

"All the better to reach the weapons in the lining of your sleeves, I suppose?" Gaspard said with an arched eyebrow.

"A girl can never be too prepared."

Adelaide popped out of the sitting room and gave them a once over. "You'll do," she sniffed but reached out to give them each a kiss on the cheek. "Be careful. I'm afraid the potato is rotten on the inside."

"We will be extremely cautious, Adelaide," said Gaspard. "It has become evident to me that we have enemies on all sides. It is time to use the, what did you call it, Kara? The direct approach."

Kara gave him an approving, and decidedly unromantic, fist bump to the shoulder and approached the front door first, Gaspard at her back, her head swiveling right to left in a scanning motion. She exited, standing on one side of Gaspard, back to him, using her whole body to provide him cover. The door was a mere few feet away within the compound, but it was smart to be diligent. No one was going to die because she was sloppy.

Kara sat next to Gaspard in the back. Marc took the driver's seat. Gaspard gave them a hard smile, fangs slightly descended. His blue eyes darkened until they were wholly black, and his body was in a state that Kara would call active relaxation. She knew it well. He was ready for battle.

He motioned to Marc to set off. "Let the games begin."

11

The Hotel Mazarin was a French Quarter luxe hotel a minute's walk from Bourbon Street. It was famous for its graceful open-air hallways, elegantly appointed rooms, and beautiful inner courtyard.

The management knew Gaspard well since he used the hotel when guests, welcome ones, came to town and because he had an agreement with the owners, so secret that not even Marc knew, to let him use the vampire rooms as a safe house in an emergency.

In fact, Simon would be aghast to know that Gaspard had paid to have those rooms renovated. It irked Gaspard that Simon was using the suite now.

When Gaspard, Kara, and Marc arrived, Joseph Willmott, the hotel manager, nodded to them and looked away, allowing them to progress to the second floor undisturbed. The two vampires stationed at the main entrance didn't intercept them either, and the bored vampire in the bar watching the lobby lifted a beer to his lips when they walked into his line of sight. They all simply turned their heads and looked the other way.

Kara mused over what this might mean but stopped short when Gaspard knocked politely on a door and announced, "Room Service." To Kara's surprise, Simon opened the door himself.

"It's about time, I'm starving..." Simon was saying, trailing off when he realized who stood in the doorway.

"Pardon my intrusion, Simon, but I desperately needed to see you this evening. May I come in, yes? Thank you."

Gaspard entered without waiting for Simon's consent and without a look back, headed into one of the two sitting rooms, making himself comfortable on the loveseat by the faux fireplace.

"Marc, would you please call down to room service and tell them that Mr. Whitleigh doesn't need them after all? I want us to have some privacy."

Marc hid a smile and used the phone on a side table to do as his master asked.

Simon gaped like a fish. Though it was well into the evening, he remained in his silk pajamas and matching robe. The balcony door was open, and the sounds of the revelers on Iberville Street floated through the air, but to Kara, it was the smell that told her where she was. The unmistakable smell was an unholy mixture of beer, vomit, urine, trash, and a soupçon of marijuana and cigarette smoke. She wrinkled her nose at the assault.

Simon drew himself up to his full five feet, seven inches, cinched his robe tighter, and regained his composure. Despite his bravado, Kara could tell he was nervous because he patted his robe as if looking for something, unsure what to do with his hands. He finally settled on crossing his arms.

"What is the meaning of this, Gaspard? You cannot come unannounced and cancel my dinner plans! This is outrageous. You have broken all rules of propriety, rules that the Assembly takes quite seriously."

"Simon, when were you turned?"

Simon jerked back. "When was I turned? What a personal question! What do you care?"

"I'd like to know. We don't know much about each other."

"I don't see why this matters."

Gaspard tilted his head. "Nonetheless..."

Simon sighed and threw up his hands. "If this matters so much, then fine. I was one of the English Puritans that settled at Plymouth Rock."

Kara startled. "Really, you came here in 1620?"

"Yes," Simon snapped.

Gaspard asked, "But when were you turned?"

"Shortly after arriving. There was a vampire on our ship, which explained the number of deaths far better than the scurvy you read about in textbooks, and when we landed, she wanted a scion. I fit the bill."

"Why did the vampire pick you?" Kara asked.

"I had demonstrated a certain ruthlessness during the voyage. She admired that quality."

"What did you do?"

Simon turned toward Kara, his eyes gleaming with the memory. "We had too many people and not enough food or water, so I threw several older people overboard in the middle of the night. It was a rational solution to the problem. Everyone assumed that these elders had gotten up to relieve themselves and hadn't been able to handle the rocky seas. *Voila*. Problem. Solution."

Kara couldn't keep the look of disgust off her face. "You are indeed a practical man."

"Exactly. I see the world as a series of problems that need to be managed in the most sensible way possible. And I do not let weakness get in my way."

"You mean emotion."

"I mean unrealistic attachments. You call them love, friendship, affection. I call them vulnerabilities."

"It is all black and white to you?" Gaspard queried.

Simon let out an exasperated breath. "Of course it is, Gaspard. Don't be such a ninny. There is power and helplessness. Dominance and submission. If you have one, you avoid the other. It's as simple as that."

"So, I can assume your arrival here is all about power?"

"Gaspard, I am tired of this. You are rude and obnoxious, and you cannot protect those under your care or those who come to you in the ancient rituals of host and guest. Frankly, I expected more. I will inform the Assembly of your failures."

"I know you will, and I don't give a damn. What I want to know is why are you truly here, Simon? What is your real game? The Assembly contacted me already about your so-called reparations, and I do not believe for a minute that this all happened by accident. They were waiting to send that letter."

Simon plopped down in a French Victorian armchair opposite Gaspard, taking care to keep his legs wide while staring at Kara.

"Really?" Kara asked. "Do you think what you have impresses me?"

Simon gave a wry smile. "Maybe. You don't know until you try."

"Seriously, Simon. You make me wish I could dry erase my head."

Gaspard cleared his throat. Marc slipped behind Kara to stand sentry at the door, giving her arm a squeeze as he passed. Kara moved sideways but within arms' distance of Simon, trying to get downwind of the stench from the street and away from Simon's little friend, which was peeking out of his robe.

Simon huffed. "Very well, if we are going to be plainspoken, which is so droll, I came here to check up on you, Gaspard."

"Check up on me?"

"The Assembly asked me to pay you a visit and see how you were amassing such power and learn what you are intending to do with it. After Paris, you can't blame them if they are cautious. I hate to tell them that they most likely overestimated you."

What the hell happened in Paris, Kara thought, but she didn't have time to dwell on it because Gaspard leaned forward, elbows on his knees, and stared at Simon like a viper ready to strike. Kara responded to his body language by centering her weight and crossing her arms so each hand was up a sleeve and close to a weapon. Her right hand grasped her sword handle, her left the knife.

"Paris is old history, Simon, so what do you mean, exactly? I have a small seethe, a relatively modest property, and am content with what I have. What power are you talking about?"

Simon turned his head to the right and raked Kara with his eyes. She was tempted to behead him right then, but Gaspard let out a breath that stayed her hand.

"Kara?" Gaspard asked Simon. "You are referring to Kara?"

Simon burst to his feet, his motion bringing him within a hair's breadth of being separated in two by a pissed off Valkyrie with a twitchy sword hand.

Without knowing how close he had come to true-death, Simon raged on. "Of course I am talking about Kara! Who is she, to appear out of nowhere and be in your service? And while you might be the most ill-behaved, toothless vampire I have ever met, having her here makes us wonder. Word travels fast, Gaspard. By bringing in an actual Amazon, you have shouted to the entire vampire world that you are preparing for battle."

"She isn't an Amazon," said Gaspard.

"Damn straight I'm not," muttered Kara. Marc, standing two feet behind her, snickered.

"Well, what is she then?"

"It is none of your business."

"The Assembly thinks differently!"

"The Assembly can go to Hell!"

The room went silent then. Even Kara knew that Gaspard's statement was dangerous. She could feel Mark straining to keep still behind her.

"If that is how you really feel, Gaspard, then perhaps you should announce yourself to be a *loup seul* and leave the rules, and security, that the Assembly provides."

Kara knitted her eyebrows. "A *loup seul*? A lone wolf?"

Simon turned toward her and sneered. "Exactly, my little mystery warrior. If Gaspard doesn't want to answer to the Assembly, he can announce that he is a *loup seul*. Of course, that little announcement would bring fire and brimstone in the form of challenges from other vampires who would want his little New Orleans hole in the wall territory, and you, Kara, of course, would be the biggest prize."

Kara pulled her knife, and in the quickest of seconds twisted Simon's left arm behind his back and placed her knife at his throat.

"I am not a prize to be traded," she hissed. She felt Marc at the ready behind her.

Gaspard held out a warning hand to Kara. "Kara, we cannot kill him. Please stand down."

"Name one reason why we can't," Kara demanded.

"Because he's right," Gaspard said with a whoosh of breath. Kara pulled the knife away from Simon's neck, proud of herself for only leaving a small nick, and stepped back. Simon touched the scratch with the tip of his finger, brought it to his mouth, and licked off the drop of blood it carried. Again, Kara wanted to punch him in the face.

"He's nothing, Gaspard!"

"He's an old vampire with a strong line of communication to the Assembly."

"He's a sociopath with a long lifespan."

"That too. My darling, we don't have the strength to win all the battles that would head our way. Not now anyway." He gestured for Kara to come stand next to him and whispered in her ear, "Not now, but not *never*."

Gaspard turned to Simon and said, "What exactly do you want?"

"Right now, I want my supper and for you to leave. I will send a note over tomorrow to tell you how we might reconcile this."

Gaspard gave a curt nod and gestured for Marc and Kara to lead the way out. Simon, hands on his hips, robe askew, stood in a portly salute of self-satisfaction and chuffed a snort of victory as Gaspard passed.

Before Gaspard exited completely, he turned back to look at Simon. "Simon."

Simon narrowed his eyes at Gaspard. "What?"

"Where are your guards?"

"I don't know what you mean."

Gaspard rotated his whole body, forcing Kara and Marc to turn with him. Gaspard focused on Simon's face and stalked forward. Simon took a step back and grasped the top rail of a nearby wrought iron barstool, then, realizing what he was doing, forced himself to halt the retreat. It was too late. Gaspard was inches from him, peering down at the little potato like a hawk watching a rabbit.

Kara shifted to stand beside the two of them; Marc stayed at Gaspard's back. Both he and Kara were breathing evenly, totally focused on the cock fight in front of them.

"I said, where are your guards? The guards at the main door saw me enter, as did the vampire who was pretending to drink in the bar. You would think that at least one of them would be suspicious about your dinner cancellation. Why aren't any of them here?"

Simon was silent.

"I'll tell you why," hissed Gaspard, leaning in even closer. "Because they thought I was here to bring a challenge, and they chose to step aside and see what played out. They abandoned you, Simon. Think on that."

Gaspard turned on his heel and exited, Marc and Kara following.

They switched positions as they exited the building with Kara leading, Gaspard in the middle, and Marc at the back, and the three worked their way toward their car, which was parked in a VIP space in the hotel's reserved back parking lot. Gaspard and Marc were talking together in low voices, intent on their discussion, so it was only Kara who sensed the danger.

She whirled, grasped Gaspard by both shoulders, and propelled him toward the car, instructing Marc to take point and cover their charge. Marc placed a hand on Gaspard's elbow and pushed him the rest of the way, throwing Gaspard in the back seat with an order to stay down. Kara watched this from the corner of her eye until a crushing hand came down on her sword arm, drawing her full attention to the big man who was making himself a nuisance. The last thing she heard was Marc shouting, "Let her do her damn job!"

Kara's right arm was numb from the blow to the nerves at her elbow, so it would do no good to draw her sword. She turned and ran, calling for Rikassa as Jarius emerged fully from the shadows and gave chase.

"I keep my master safe!" he bellowed. "And you are a danger to him. He's forbidden me from killing you, but he never said anything about hurting you. I'm going to rip your arms off at the sockets and..."

Kara never heard the rest of it. She leapt on top of a car and vaulted from car roof to car roof, using her agility to stay ahead of the human rhinoceros behind her. Jarius was human, or at least not a vampire, but he was unreasonably strong. It occurred to her mid-leap that he may be part jötnar, part giant. That made it all the more important that she stay out of his grasp. Jötnar, even half-breeds, were famous for compressing human heads between their huge hands, popping the brains out like pus from a zit.

Not a pretty picture.

Her hand tingled as the nerves returned to life. She hurdled over Jarius' outstretched arm and settled on Rikassa's back, who had flown at full speed to her Lady. Kara urged the horse to fly higher and used the ascent to transform into the Valkyrie she was, armor glinting with the light of the street lamps in the shadowed parking lot. The wild horse neighed a challenge to her Lady's attacker and veered to the right to give Kara time to draw her sword.

"I am no threat to you!" Kara yelled. "There is no need for this!"

Jarius looked up, face screwed tight in anger. He clambered on top of a Ford 150 with monster wheels, denting the hood with his weight, and jumped toward the horse, arms outstretched as if he thought he could catch Rikassa like a firefly. He landed with a thud on the concrete, a spider-web of tiny fissures spreading out from his feet. Rikassa flew directly at him and used a front hoof to kick him squarely in the head. It should have been a killing blow. Instead, Rikassa's hoof bounced off the giant, who shook off the attack like a dog shaking off water after a lovely lake swim.

That confirms it, thought Kara. There was definitely jötnar in Jarius' family tree. The giants were great when it came to brawn but not so valuable when it came to brains. And as Rikassa's kick made thoroughly obvious, it would also make him harder to strike down because jötnar had skin like stone. It would take a deft touch. There were only a few vulnerable places she could assail and do any damage.

Jarius beckoned in a "bring it" sort of way, and Kara obliged. She threw Rikassa into a steep descent, flicked her sword, and then bade Rikassa to fly up, up, and away. This left Jarius gaping at his right ear, which now sat on the ground like a leftover potato chip. He roared his anger to the sky.

12

The butler met Marc and Gaspard at the door, but before the butler could say a word, he was elbowed out of the way by a miniscule eighty-year old woman who had more than a little practice in getting her way.

"So?" Adelaide demanded, pulling her dressing gown tighter to fend off the slight chill of the evening. She craned her neck left and right. "Where's Kara?" she demanded.

Marc didn't answer. He simply turned and stared out into the night sky, perusing it for any sign of Rikassa and Kara. He didn't know for certain that Kara would have called for her horse, but it seemed likely.

"Guards!" Marc called, still exploring the sky for any sign.

Two guards double-timed it. "What is it? What happened?" said one. "You veered in here like the hounds of hell were at your heels."

"Not quite the hounds, but close," said Marc. "Are there sharp-shooters on the roof?"

"Yes, sir. Kara ordered it until the Northeast vamps bugger off."

"Tell them to expect a flying white horse."

The second guard's face wrinkled in confusion. "Sir, we are not familiar with that code phrase..."

Marc glared at both of them. "It isn't a code phrase. It means exactly what I said. Kara's horse is unusual."

"The horse *flies*?"

"Yes, and I don't want her or Kara shot. Understand?"

The guards nodded in unison. "Yes, sir." One craned his neck to speak into his radio. "Uh, Checkmate, Blue Eagle? This is Guard Post Three. You have orders to watch for a flying white horse. If you see one, do not, I repeat DO NOT shoot it. Copy?"

Silence.

"Checkmate? Blue Eagle? Copy?"

"Guard Post Three, this is Checkmate. I gave up drinking three years ago and LSD two years before that. I haven't seen a flying white horse in a long time."

"No, I mean it. Marc says that Rikassa can fly and Kara will be riding her."

"Oh. Why didn't you say so in the first place? Roger. Checkmate out."

The guards returned to their positions, one shaking his head. "First it was ghosts, then a freakin' large lizard, and now flying horses. God *damn* but this is more interesting than desk duty."

Back in the mansion, Gaspard used both hands to smooth down his already perfect hair, taking a moment to collect himself and then turned to Adelaide.

"You are up late, Miss Adelaide," he said, proffering his arm, which she took. "Let's gather in the sitting room, shall we? And Marc, are you back? Would you ring the kitchen? I believe we could all use a cup of tea."

Adelaide released Gaspard's arm. "I'm not drinking tea until you tell me what happened to Kara. Why isn't she with you?"

Marc returned and explained, "As we left, Jarius attacked. Kara stayed behind to fight him while I got Gaspard to safety."

"Jarius? That enormous man? He's a goliath! Even with her special skills, she can't beat him alone."

"You have so little faith in me," said Kara, walking in, back in her civilian clothes, both sleeves shredded, shoes dangling from one hand. She gave the high heels a disgusted look and dropped them on the floor.

Gaspard closed his eyes with relief and then turned to her, teeth clenched. "Ah, my darling. I wish we could have stayed and witnessed your triumph." He shot Marc a look. "Or, stayed and *helped* in some way."

"Marc did what he was supposed to do. He got you home while I fought off the attacker. Don't be mad at him for doing his duty."

"We shouldn't have run!"

Kara whirled on Gaspard and got right up in his face, so mad she was vibrating like a plucked guitar string. "Stop being such a baby! You are my responsibility and you don't have the right to throw a hissy fit when all we are doing is protecting you!"

Gaspard met her eye-to-eye, nose-to-nose. Ten seconds. Fifteen. Thirty.

He pulled back, straightening his tie. "What is that hum?"

"It's Kara. You got her so angry that she's literally oscillating at a B flat," remarked Adelaide, leaning over to take Kara's hand. Kara took a step back and allowed Adelaide to guide her to the couch. Adelaide motioned for Kara to lie back and began massaging Kara's right foot and calf. Kara groaned, closing her eyes in bliss.

"Thank you, Adelaide. That feels heavenly." Kara opened her eyes and pointed at Gaspard. "And I am never, ever, for any reason, wearing heels again. Got me, French boy?"

Gaspard didn't hear her, transfixed as he was by her sexy feet and the way she had groaned in pleasure at Adelaide's touch.

"Gaspard?"

"I hear you. You shall never wear heels again."

"Exactly."

"Exactly," he repeated, still staring at her calves.

Despite the serious events of the evening, Marc bit his lip to keep from laughing and nudged Gaspard back into the present as the tea arrived, accompanied by vanilla butter cookies. The cookies' aroma wafted through the sitting room, making Kara's mouth water. She grabbed three as soon as they were on the table.

Reclining with her tea and cookies, Kara forced herself to stay silent. She held her teacup in both hands and took tiny sips, waiting for Gaspard to begin.

"Somehow I, and all of us here, have become the center of an investigation, nay, a conspiracy, within the vampire community. I don't know who started it, why it started, or who is involved, but the Assembly sent Simon here to ascertain my strengths and weaknesses."

Adelaide crinkled her nose. "What is it they hope to find?"

"It seems some vampires have decided that because Kara is with us that I am building up muscle. They don't know what Kara is, exactly, but they recognize her as something special and believe her presence is a clue that I will be making a grab for power."

"Which is ridiculous!" Kara broke in. "I am here to protect Gaspard and his seethe, not set off a war."

"Vampires don't think that way, Kara," said Marc. "Everything is about gaining power."

"Yeah," snorted Kara. "So I've heard."

"But we learned a very important thing," said Gaspard. "Simon is weaker than he appears. None of his seethe interfered with our visit. In fact, they tacitly allowed it."

Adelaide asked, "How did the Assembly know about Kara? It isn't like you had a welcome party and sent out invitations."

"Someone has been keeping an eye on us, Adelaide, and reporting back."

Marc shot a look at Kara. She lifted an eyebrow in return and waited while it hit him.

He punched one fist into his other hand. "The new vampires! The Mistress of South Texas."

Kara touched her nose and pointed at him. Got it in one.

Gaspard said, "Yes, I believe so."

"But why?" asked Adelaide.

"We've had some interactions in the past. We didn't agree on a few things and parted company. It is safe to assume that she doesn't like me."

Marc narrowed his eyes. "Is this because of Paris?"

Gaspard nodded. "Naturally."

"Is someone going to tell me what in Odin's name happened in Paris?" Kara exclaimed.

No one replied because a scream erupted from outside, followed by a high keening and a rustle of trees and leaves being disturbed from their nightly slumber.

Kara jumped to her bare feet and was first out the sitting room door, gun drawn, followed by Marc and Gaspard, and despite Gaspard's warning glance, Adelaide came along as well.

"All of you, do not go out there!" yelled Kara at the staff who ran to see what was happening. "Let me see what is going on first."

She turned off the lights and waited for a second for her eyes to get used to the dark. Then she retrieved her flashlight from her thigh and dialed it to the lowest possible glow.

Still holding her gun in her right hand, Kara leaned her back against the wall and used her knee to push the glass door open. When nothing happened, she crouch-walked into the blackness.

Listening closely, she dropped to her stomach and belly-crawled forward, hearing nothing. Her sense of smell, however, told her something was out there. She rolled horizontally about two feet and hugged the side of a planter, peeking around it to see if she could determine the threat. The stench of the Grunch reached her nose, and she followed the smell until she found what she was looking for.

A pile of bones, mangled meat, and stripped skin lay in the middle of torn black tactical gear. The flattened grass showed where the Grunch had departed. Kara used the flashlight to study the mess, certain the Grunch was gone. A twisted name tag was still connected to what was left of the shirt.

Kara did a quick sweep of the area but, as expected, found nothing more. The Grunch had ambushed the guard, killed him, and left with military precision. It was murder. She murmured a prayer to her sisters to take the guard's valiant spirit to Valhalla and walked back to the house.

Other guards had run from the front of the house and waited for Kara to approach, the skinny guard from the prior day's training exercise looking particularly traumatized. Kara concentrated on him, a burning wrath emanating from her posture.

"Why was Sarge on patrol without his partner?"

The guard hung his head. "Is he dead?"

"Yes, he is. Murdered by the Grunch. I repeat my question. Why weren't you with him, or at least someone with him?"

The skinny guard's voice was tight. "My wife called about the baby. I asked Sarge to wait, but he insisted he go alone. He wouldn't delay. He said he'd be fine."

Kara's voice rose. "Let me be clear. None of you are fine on your own. You were distracted and he got cocky and now he's dead. Patrols will resume, this time in four man teams. If you didn't realize it before, the Grunch is out there, and he appears to be far more intelligent than we gave him credit for. Now, someone call the coroner and give me Sarge's address. We'll need to inform his family."

The skinny guard raised his hand, tears welling in his brown eyes. "I'll tell his wife. I've known her for years. She was friends with my mom, my aunt, and my cousin's entire family. In fact, we might be related several times removed on my father's side. She's known for her lemon cheesecake and can whistle the Star Spangled Banner." His face crumpled. "Ohmygod. Poor Marjorie, and it's all my fault."

Kara put her arm around him. "It was all our faults, especially mine." Her lips were pressed thin and her eyes grim. "I'll talk to Marjorie with you."

13

Things were quiet the next evening. Sarge's body was taken care of and his widow and children informed. Gaspard made a generous deposit into their banking account and set up college funds for each grandchild. Beyond that, there was nothing else to do.

Kara was puzzled. The Grunch had lived peacefully for all this time, either hibernating or simply living quietly. Why would this happen now? The Grunch had a mate and eggs. Maybe it was protecting them. But from what? No one had gone back there. No one had threatened them. She hadn't even known they existed. She hesitated to believe it was her one intrusion on its territory.

She could use her sisters' advice. Kara had been away from them for months now, and she missed them. *Surely*, she thought, *Odin wouldn't mind if I talked to them*? Maybe she could reach Hildr, who was wise and the most thoughtful of the Valkyries.

Reaching Hildr or any of the others was an exercise in patience and meditation. Kara sat in the setting sun, lotus position, and tried to clear her mind. It was more difficult than she had imagined. Stray, disruptive thoughts intruded, and her mind wouldn't quiet.

Why would the Grunch attack now? What was Simon's next move? I wonder if Gaspard sleeps in the nude...

Kara shook herself like a dog coming out of a pond. Where in the hell did that come from? *Deep breath*, she thought. *Get back to it.*

How much of Marc's blood does Emmie have to drink to stay young? Is there any pizza left in the fridge? When can I go back home? Do vampires really have souls?

That last question is what got her in trouble to begin with.

I wonder what my sisters are doing. Did Sarge make it to Valhalla? We should get some dogs for security. I need to remember to look into that. I would have asked Sarge to do it, but he's not here anymore, dammit, because he got cocky and the other guards didn't go with him, and I should have emphasized it more, so it's all my fault.

It wasn't working. She couldn't stop thinking, and the guilt over Sarge's death haunted her.

She called Rikassa, and the beautiful white mare appeared, ready for a ride. Kara and Rikassa rode like the wind; in fact, Rikassa let herself loose for a few minutes and flew, hooves not touching the ground, the air whipping past, moving so fast that they were a blur to human eyes. Kara held her head down over Rikassa's neck, hugged her mane, and focused on the wonderful feeling of flying.

Rikassa slowed and Kara looked around trying to figure out how many miles they had gone, but lurched forward when Rikassa stopped suddenly, putting on the brakes like a Bugs Bunny cartoon.

Hildr stood in front of Rikassa, smiling at Kara. "You finally got to me," she said.

Kara dismounted and hugged her sister, holding her tight. "I guess the ride is what cleared my mind."

Hildr nodded. "I could feel you knocking, but you never got close enough."

Jealous, Rikassa nudged Hildr's hand. "Ah, of course! As if I would come without a gift." Hildr opened her hand and a pink apple appeared, a special kind found on the Asgardian plane. Rikassa snorted appreciatively and took her prize.

"What is it you wanted to talk to me about?" Hildr asked. Then she held up a finger. "But I cannot answer when you come home. Odin has not told me that information."

Kara sighed. "I didn't expect anything else. No, I wanted to talk to you about a situation here." Kara retold the whole Grunch story from beginning to end, from her visit to the swamp to the Grunch's first attack to the albino and Sarge's murder.

"You are missing something, sister," said Hildr, the rising moonlight glinting off her armor.

"I know I am, but what?"

"There is another player in this game."

"How do you know this?"

"You said it yourself. Why would a formerly quiet creature suddenly attack? It had successfully warned off the populace years ago. As long as they stayed away, he lived in peace."

"We think it has a mate and eggs."

"Okay, so he is protecting them, but why Gaspard and why now? Why a vampire and those who serve him?"

"Something happened to rile it, to make it angry," Kara reasoned.

"Yes, that is obvious."

"Do you think that my visit did that?"

"No, I do not. I think something else happened. Again, ask the right questions. The Grunch kills if it needs to, but stays away if it can. So why now? Why the vampire?"

"Something happened that angered it deeply, and for some reason, it believes Gaspard is at fault, or at least involved."

"That is what I believe, too, little sister."

"But what?"

"That, Kara, is what you have to find out."

"How do I do that?"

"Parlay."

"Talk to it?"

"Violence isn't working. Try a different approach."

"And when it eats me?"

Hildr grinned. "Then we will Choose you, and you will come home, in a manner of speaking."

Kara considered Hildr's words. Then she had a thought. "Ah, speaking of Choosing Hildr, did…"

"Yes, Kara," Hildr said, reaching up to stroke Kara's hair. "We Chose Sarge. He is with us."

"I miss you," said Kara.

"We miss you, too."

"Even Sigrun?"

"Especially her."

14

Hildr left and Kara mourned her departure as much as she did the first time they separated, but she shook it off and got to work. She mounted Rikassa and rode her to the place where she'd met the albino. She dismounted and waited.

Maybe a half hour later, the albino appeared. She didn't hear him come and startled when he was suddenly behind her.

"What brings you here, warrior lady?"

Kara bent on her knee so she could be at his height, /and show respect since she was asking a boon.

"I would like to speak to the Grunch."

The albino blinked at her as if he were trying to process her words.

"He's pretty testy. I'm not sure he will meet with you, and I certainly cannot guarantee your safety."

"I understand. But you can get me to him?"

"I can try, but mind you, I won't push hard. We've lived in peace for years, but being honest, it's more like a mutual détente than friendship or allies."

"I don't want to place you in danger, but I think it is important to try to communicate."

The short man nodded. "Come back here, same time tomorrow."

"Thank you."

The man gave a gap-toothed grin. "We'll see if you thank me tomorrow."

The next evening, Kara met the small man at the same spot. She left Rikassa waiting and followed the man into the swamp. Her breath was steady, her heartbeat slightly elevated. She hadn't told Gaspard where she was going so he wouldn't follow.

The small man, who Kara had nicknamed Moses, scampered along the swamp's surface by skipping from rock to log, occasionally getting his feet wet. Kara tried to follow his path but kept falling in. She studied Moses' technique and realized the secret was moving swiftly and not spending too much time on any one surface. She had to be light on her feet and couldn't hesitate.

She was more successful after that, not thinking about where she was going but simply following, mind as empty as possible. The water snakes slithered out of her path, blue herons stood to the side, and snapping turtles dove for cover. Even the nutria, the giant rats that lived there, slunk away.

Eventually, they reached the shell road. Moses tiptoed forward and Kara followed, concentrating on her surroundings. She thought she could smell the Grunch as they got deeper in but had not heard a thunk or slither.

Moses came to a halt and pointed toward a copse of trees swathed in Spanish moss. He whispered, "He's in there. I will go no farther."

"This is the creepiest place I've ever seen," said Kara.

"It's not that bad."

Kara wrinkled her face at Moses. "Yes, it is."

"Well, you may not want to build a summer home here..."

Kara looked at him sideways through narrowed eyes.

"I'll stop talking now, warrior lady."

The moss hung thick and the canopy above blocked out any starlight. The fog was denser here than anywhere she had been before. She couldn't see more than two feet ahead of her.

"Can I turn on my flashlight?" she asked.

"I wouldn't."

"Okay, then." She inhaled, smelling the stench fully now, and felt her way forward. One step, two steps, three... A low-hanging branch forced her to crouch, and despite all attempts to be silent, her feet crunched on the shells below.

She emerged in a clearing where the leaf canopy was torn open and moonlight bathed the area, allowing her to see more clearly. She saw the Grunch sitting at the entrance to an enormous cave. Kara had never heard about swamp caves and wondered how far back this cave went and if it was stable.

An animal's scream rose from a distance causing Kara to jump and the Grunch to back away. She got herself under control, and despite the adrenaline, stood still, staring at the Grunch, waiting for him to make the first move.

The Grunch sat down on its belly like a basking alligator, and Kara realized that this was the Grunch's way of showing her he was relaxed and meant no harm. She knelt on the ground to signal the same. The Grunch's red eyes followed her every movement, so she made sure to move slowly, not wanting to scare him.

She spoke. "I believe we have misunderstood each other."

The Grunch tilted its head.

"I mean you no harm, and neither does the vampire."

The Grunch's tail slapped back and forth. It clearly didn't believe her.

"We want peace between us. Co-existence. You are a worthy opponent for any warrior, but there is no need to be enemies."

The Grunch snorted. The smell of rot almost overwhelmed her.

"Did something happen to anger you? Something specific I could help with?"

The Grunch's eyes bored at her, until suddenly he sprang to all four feet. Kara held herself in check but clenched her fist on her sword. Having made up its mind, the Grunch turned and walked to the cave. He stopped at the entrance and looked over his shoulder at Kara. He wanted her to follow.

Kara had no interest in going into the dark cave with him. She considered her options. She had come all this way, and the Grunch hadn't harmed her. But, there were no birds here. No insects. Nothing. Even the natural residents of the swamp avoided the Grunch. Going into its home where she could hardly see, with no knowledge of the layout, would be the stupidest move she could make. By Grabthar's hammer, what was she to do?

She followed.

The Grunch led the way through a series of tunnels, and Kara felt as if she were walking up and down as if the tunnels had hills and were changing elevation. She had lost her sense of direction two minutes in, and the farther they went, the more apprehensive she became. She held fast, feeling the wet walls of the cavern with her fingertips, breathing in concentrated breaths of the icy air, and in the end, following the Grunch by the orange-red glow of its eyes and the unique *thunk-slide* of its gait. The air was thick with an odor so fetid it made her eyes water. She blinked to clear them.

What felt like an hour later, but was probably a few minutes, the Grunch stopped at the entrance of another cave on their right. He inclined his head, daring her to enter. Kara knew this is what she had come for, but she didn't want to go into that cave.

She stepped past the Grunch, who moved aside so she could pass. He made a small keening noise that raised her anxiety to another level. The entrance to this part of the cave tunnels was a graceful arch, making Kara wonder if it was constructed like that or a natural phenomenon. She could feel heat emanating from the room, which caught her by surprise.

"I'm going to use my flashlight, okay?" she said the Grunch. "I can't see as well as you can." The Grunch made another keening noise, and this time the same type of noise was returned.

"Your mate is inside?"

The Grunch stood still but grumbled deep in his chest. The grumble was returned with a higher pitched sound that settled into a hum.

Kara pulled her flashlight out and used the lowest setting to create a soft light, enough so she could see, but not too much to blind whatever was in there. Biting her bottom lip, she stepped inside.

15

A Grunch larger than the first was curled up around an egg. She stared straight into Kara's eyes, then she collapsed down and curled tighter to the egg. The egg itself was the size of an ostrich egg, ovular shaped and white with striations of blue. It would be easy to mistake it for some rare type of rock. The cave was small with just enough room for the Grunch to change position. Her mate stayed outside, past the doorway, but the two kept humming to each other.

Kara swept the flashlight around the room and realized she was witness to a massacre. Shards of broken eggs lay everywhere, dead Grunch fetuses, looking a little like large tadpoles, lay within the shards. Easily a dozen eggs were destroyed. The female cuddled around the lone egg left.

"What happened?" she whispered. The female Grunch couldn't lift her head. She was sick, Kara realized, and without a second's thought, she crawled over to the mother, showing her hands open and empty so as not to scare her. The flashlight lay on the floor continuing to provide a glow so Kara could see.

"What happened?" Kara asked again, reaching slowly down to feel the Grunch's scales keeping the Grunch's head to the left of her. The scales were hot and Kara realized the Grunch herself was emanating the heat to incubate the egg. *Fascinating*, she thought as she felt for injury.

The Grunch made a hissing noise when Kara got to the back right flank. Kara grabbed the flashlight from the floor and leaned over the mother to see what was wrong. Two of the Grunch's scales were askew, almost falling off, and there was a deep gash on the skin beneath the scales.

"This is going to hurt," she said to the Grunch, and she moved the scales aside so she could get a better look at what lay beneath. Kara gritted her teeth as she realized she was looking at a bullet wound and the bullet was still inside.

Kara removed her sword from its belt. Instead of extending to its full length, the sword shaped itself into a dagger. The Grunch squirmed away, making an almost inaudible growl. Her mate filled the doorway.

"I'm going to help, I promise," Kara said. She moved back up to the mother's head and cradled the enormous snout in her arms, ignoring the smell, seeing the Grunch as a mother, a female, a warrior, a kindred spirit. She looked directly in the mother's eyes and repeated, "I'm here to help."

The female Grunch hummed another song, the male answered, and the female rocketed to her feet. Kara froze, hoping she hadn't made a terrible mistake. The female stuck her snout in Kara's face, huffing snorts of air, smelling her, sensing what she could. She opened her mouth, showing her fangs, flicked out her tongue, and licked Kara's face, causing a searing burn as the acidic saliva touched her skin. The Grunch's maw was inches from Kara's face, and the smell of the Grunch's breath reminded Kara of the odor of dead soldiers left to rot on the field of war. The Grunch seemed to make up her mind, but before she sat, she brought a clawed foot up to her mouth, like a cat, and slowly sharpened the razor talons to a honed edge, reminding Kara that her trust would only go so far.

"Got it," Kara muttered. The Grunch made another deep-throated growl and shuffled around, bringing the egg with her. Now the Grunch's injury was forefront and center. Kara swallowed the lump in her throat and brought the dagger to the opening. Saying a prayer to Eir, the goddess of healing, Kara dug in with the point trying to reach the bullet. The Grunch hissed in pain, and the male squeezed farther into the small room, crooning calming sounds to his mate. To Kara, he gave a warning glare.

Even with the flashlight, it was hard for Kara to see, and she was about to intensify the flashlight's glow when the dagger responded to her unspoken need and glowed brightly, illuminating the wound. "Thanks, Eir," Kara said out loud. "Sorry, this is not going to be fun," she said to her patient and burrowed farther down until she could get the dagger under the bullet and force it out. Kara knew the excavation was exquisitely painful, but the Grunch didn't move or make another sound.

Kara let the bullet drop the floor and let instinct do the rest. She held the glowing dagger to the wound and watched as it healed right in front of her eyes. After a few minutes, all that was left was a pink, puckered scar.

"It's all done," Kara said and patted the Grunch's side. The mother Grunch sighed and fell into a deep sleep, cuddling the egg closer to her belly.

Kara moved back, taking one last look at the detritus around her, tears gathering in her eyes at the butchery. It was easy to tell what happened. Someone had come in here to take the eggs, or destroy them. The mother didn't have much room to move and wouldn't abandon her eggs. She fought. Somehow, she got shot, breaking off her scales, and then shot again, this time the bullet doing serious damage. Kara examined the walls, feeling her way with her fingers and found a few bullets embedded in the rock. A forensic examiner could have figured out how the battle, or more appropriately, the slaughter, happened by looking at the angles of the bullets' travels, but Kara didn't care. All she knew is that someone, or someones, had found this nursery, shot the mother, and broken all the eggs save one. Kara couldn't tell if the perpetrators survived or not, given that it was entirely possible that the male Grunch had come along and killed them himself, shoving whatever remained into the swamp. But she remembered Adelaide's story and guessed that they had gotten away; otherwise there would be skeletons at top of Grunch Road again.

Kara's foot hit something, and she stumbled, dropping her flashlight. There was a clang of metal against metal. Kara reached out and felt around for the mystery object. She retrieved the flashlight and peered around the floor until she saw it.

It took a moment to realize what it was. She examined it, noting that it was very old and well used. The gold had been worn away where a thumb and index finger had spent ages opening and closing it.

Kara's mind flew back to Simon's right hand patting his robe, and the same patting motion at the party right before he said he'd misplaced... his pocket watch.

"That bastard."

16

"So, you believe that Simon attacked the Grunch's lair, destroyed the eggs, and wounded the female," said Gaspard, leaning back in his desk chair. "And he did this *himself*?"

Marc expressed similar doubt. "Simon is shaped like a weeble-wobble and has the coordination of a walrus trapped on land. I have trouble imagining him able to pull off something like this."

"I didn't say he did it alone," Kara retorted, pacing in front of the couch, a part of her brain trying to ascertain what a weeble-wobble was. Sparks flew from her boots as she walked back and forth. Gaspard gave Marc a small nod. When Kara's back was turned, Marc pulled the couch back a foot. There was nothing they could do for the area rug. She either ruined another one or she didn't.

Kara was furiously trying to piece the puzzle together in her mind. "I am certain this pocket watch is his. It's more a matter of *why* did he do it? What was his goal? How did he know about the Grunch in the first place?"

Adelaide leaned on the chaise like a true lady of leisure, eating lemon cookies. She washed the last one down with tea and said, "Maybe he attacked it to provoke you."

Gaspard walked around the desk and snagged one of the lemon

cookies. He didn't eat much regular food, but lemon cookies with icing were his weakness.

"I think what Adelaide is saying is that Simon somehow, we don't know how, but somehow heard of the Grunch and deliberately provoked it hoping it would attack so he could see you in action."

"He," corrected Kara.

"What?" said Gaspard.

"You called the Grunch an *it*. It is a *he*. A thinking, feeling intelligent animal with a mate who has lost his children. He's not particularly cuddly, I admit, but he is a powerful adversary, and he should be respected."

Gaspard gave her a little bow. "I stand corrected."

"But how did he know the Grunch would come here?" asked Marc. "Do you think Kara's visit gave it some direction?"

Gaspard considered another lemon cookie but, with regret, backed away and returned to his chair. He sat back and put his feet up on the desk. "I don't know. That feels awfully coincidental."

Kara regarded Gaspard's feet, raised her eyebrows, and waved his legs off the desk. "That's gross. No one needs to see the bottom of your shoes. It is an insult in some cultures, you know."

Marc did a little Beyoncé head bob. "Testy, aren't we?"

Gaspard waved Marc to silence and lowered his feet with a hand to his heart. "As you command."

Kara didn't respond. She'd turned her back and continue to pace. Adelaide gathered the hem of her dressing gown and tucked it up under her hip in case an ember flew close.

"Remind me, where did we leave things with Simon?" Kara asked, skidding to a halt, sending a cloud of hot cinders into the air.

"He said he would send us a note," said Marc, rubbing his hand over the stubbly crewcut he always wore while he backed away from the sparks, batting away a few that had settled on his jacket.

"And, lucky for us, he has sent over that very note," said Gaspard, brandishing a piece of fine parchment. He held it out in front of him like a court herald and cleared his throat in the most pompous manner.

"Gaspard, in recompense for the members of my seethe lost to violence on your property, when we were supposed to be under your protection, and your inexcusable behavior last night, I demand two months of Kara's service. This payment has been approved by the Alliance, as you will certainly be notified shortly. I will be visiting tomorrow evening sharply at eight p.m. to collect her. Please see that she is ready."

"Oh, and I should mention," continued Gaspard, "that we did indeed get notification from the Assembly that I am to comply at once."

Kara was stunned into silence. Marc's mouth was open, and Adelaide was trying to hide her look of shock behind her left hand. Finally, Kara said, "What a snake. Who does he think he is dealing with that he can order me to do anything?" Her stomach roiled at the thought of Simon's presumptiveness and paced to let out some of her anger, gesturing with angry hands, pointing in the air, and stabbing forward as if Simon were right in front of her.

She wasn't done. "That bastard wanted this the whole time. This was his endgame. I'm not sure how he managed to survive the Grunch pair or how he attracted the male Grunch to the party, but somehow, he did, and the entire thing was an act to see how I, and you, Gaspard, would react to the danger. And I fell for it. Like an idiot. I'm going to break him in two..."

Gaspard broke in. "Kara! My darling, you must stop flinging sparks around."

Kara looked down at her feet. "Did I burn another rug?"

"No, but you were slinging sparks from your fingers—nice effect by the way—and you singed Marc's suit jacket and almost burned down my bookcase."

"Sorry. Really. I didn't know I could spark with my hands, but it doesn't change the fact that Simon Whitleigh has been playing us like a fiddle this whole time."

"No, it doesn't. But now that we know the game, we can play *him*."

Marc asked, "What do you want me to do?"

"Talk to Sarah and another sanguineer. See if they are willing to help out with a special request," replied Gaspard.

Gaspard pointed to Kara. "Kara, you need to go talk to your new scaly friend."

"And me?" asked Adelaide.

"Get some rest. You will want to be here tomorrow night. Marc, Kara, let's discuss the details."

17

They were ready by seven o'clock, early for a vampire's circadian rhythm. Additional cameras were mounted in inconspicuous spaces to make sure any and all action was recorded. Chairs were positioned in the back veranda just so, and attending sanguineers took their medicine at exactly seven-forty-five. Marc had called the hotel and formally requested the number of visitors for that evening, explaining in a soft, humbled voice, that Gaspard wished to ensure he had appropriate nourishment and security this time. He was told there would be two attendees, Simon and his second-in-command, the hulking Jarius. Based the events of the past, Marc prepared for three.

Kara met the guests personally at the gate flanked by other guards, who had been kept in the dark about Simon's involvement with the Grunch. Kara was afraid if the guards knew that Simon had been the cause of the Grunch's rampage, and therefore, Sarge's death, they may not be able to perform their jobs with equanimity. She would explain later. They wouldn't like it, but they'd deal.

As suspected, Simon brought two companions, Jarius and a female vamp Kara didn't know, which made Kara wonder who this vamp was and why Simon brought her. The new vamp had bronze skin, dark eyes, full lips colored with a deep red lipstick, and an emaciated frame. If Kara didn't know she was a vampire, she would have been worried about her.

Jarius' hair was brushed over to cover his missing ear. He made a double-handed fist and cracked his knuckles when he saw Kara, making sure she saw him point to himself and then to her. Kara scrunched her face in mock confusion, pointed to her right ear, and mouthed, "I can't hear you." Jarius' face went white with rage.

Ignoring Jarius and the new vamp, Kara stood at attention, displaying respect, and bade Simon enter. When they approached the main door, she had the butler ask for their weapons in a polite and obsequious manner. She bit her tongue the whole time and smiled through gritted teeth, but Simon was so smug that he didn't notice. He relaxed into the position of generous Master with a practiced air.

"We have not come heavily armed, but in the spirit of our renewed relationship with Gaspard, we will relinquish our guns." He motioned to Jarius and the woman, who both handed over the guns in their shoulder holsters. Kara knew that they had other weapons and that the two guns were the tip of the iceberg, but she pretended to be grateful.

"Thank you, Simon," she said. "We appreciate the opportunity to make amends and start again."

Simon waved his arms in what he must have thought was a magnanimous gesture. "Of course, my dear, and I cannot wait to get to know you better when you spend time with us." He patted her shoulder, and she managed not to flinch.

"It sounds delightful. Thank you," Kara replied, swallowing the acid that burned her throat while consciously unclenching her hands. As she ushered them in, Kara took a moment to get closer to the woman. She smelled different than other vamps, as if another power lay underneath her vampirism, co-mingling the scents. It reminded her of something. She let it stew in the back of her mind.

"You can see that the fire damage is still being cleaned up, so we will meet on the back veranda. All has been set up, including sanguineers for your pleasure," she informed them, widening her smile. The woman studied her in a disturbing manner, but Kara continued the prattle.

"You must forgive me for blathering on like this," she said with a coy look directed at Simon.

"I love your blathering, my dear, and I expect to have many long *conversations* with you in the near future."

Ewwww, Kara thought. *Just ewwww.*

They proceeded to the back veranda where Gaspard, Marc, and the sanguineers waited. The sanguineers were relaxed and unafraid. Marc stood behind Gaspard in a tan linen suit, a white shirt, and a navy and white striped tie. His stubble had grown magically into a full beard, but his hair was still crewcut short. He looked sharp and capable, but could not outshine his Master.

Gaspard wore a fitted twill three-piece suit in a shade of steel gray, which Kara had been informed was called "metal." His shirt was white, his tie a subdued check of blues and silvers, and the pocket square a solid blue to match the tie. His bespoke shoes were polished to a shine.

It isn't the clothes that make the man in this case, thought Kara. She studied the way he held himself, both at ease and alert. With his left hand in his pocket, his body posture spoke of calm, but when Kara looked at his eyes, she felt like a tuna being circled by a shark.

"Gaspard. I will refrain from saying 'we meet again,' as it is too cliché, but I believe you have been informed by the Assembly that my requests are within reason and should be carried out immediately." Kara shuddered at Simon's pompous, self-satisfied tone. He thought he had won.

"I have, Simon, and of course, I am willing to comply, as is Kara. We do need to discuss some of the particulars though, I am sure you can agree."

"Of course, of course."

"Please partake of some refreshment. We chose two of our most beautiful sanguineers, and they are prepared for you to drink deep, as an offering of renewal, peace, and friendship."

"How thoughtful of you, Gaspard. Miranda, please take your choice. I will be most satisfied with either of these lovely volunteers."

Miranda went for the one male sanguineer whose well-muscled bare chest was on full display along with his low hanging worn blue jeans, revealing the most gorgeous abs and hip bones Kara had ever seen. He had a five o'clock shadow, deep brown eyes, and looked pliant, but also dangerous, an aphrodisiac for a vampire.

This left the big breasted redhead for Simon, with pale, creamy skin lightly covered in a dusting of freckles. She wore a dress cut down to her navel to best display her spilling cleavage but the *pièce de résistance* was the high middle slit, allowing Simon access to her thighs. She crooked her finger at Simon, and he knelt at her side, bending his head to draw a long lick up her legs until he arrived at her femoral artery. Jarius stood behind his master's back, looking outward, facing Kara with hate in his eyes.

Miranda chose to latch on to her sanguineer's nipple. Simon knelt between his sanguineer's legs. He had pushed back her panties to finger her while he sucked. Kara couldn't watch but noticed Marc and Gaspard had no such discomfort and instead gawked like teenagers. Simon was polite enough to ensure that the experience was pleasurable for his sanguineer, and Kara heard her orgasm. Miranda's gentleman seemed pleased and sedated, falling asleep in the chair, but not sexually satisfied, and Kara, Gaspard, and Marc all realized at the same time that Miranda had not done more than take a sip or two. Kara leaned in to warn Marc that something was odd about Miranda.

Simon rose from his knees, closed the woman's thighs and kissed her on the lips with his bloody mouth. She accepted his kiss and held his face with both of her hands, as if to keep him there as long as possible.

Kara thought she was going to throw up. Instead, she worried about Miranda.

"What is it that bothers you, Kara?" whispered Marc.

"She smells wrong."

"In what way, Kara?" Marc was on edge.

"There's something..."

Simon stood, sweeping his arms in a grand flourish, wiped his mouth with a handkerchief, and then dabbed at the already closing fang marks on his sanguineer's thigh. He held out one arm, helped the sanguineer to her feet, and caught her as she stumbled in his arms.

"What is wrong?" he asked, concerned. "I didn't take too much."

"I think she is overcome by your attentions," said Gaspard. "Marc, will you escort the lady back to the house?"

Marc nodded and retrieved the sanguineer from Simon's hands and walked her back to the house. It was clear the woman was not altogether right on her feet. Kara crossed her fingers.

Miranda peered at the sleeping man and then looked to Gaspard and Kara. The realization hit her in the very next second and she cried out, "Master, the sanguineers were drugged. This is a trap. They are bringing the Grunch to you! Run!"

Simon and Jarius were dumbstruck, Jarius' face ugly with anger.

Miranda vamped out completely, dropping her fangs and spilling saliva from her mouth. Kara did a head smack as she realized Miranda's scent was similar to a *völva*, the Icelandic name for a seer.

18

Jarius grabbed his master's arm to drag Simon back, but the sedative in the sanguineers' blood took effect, and Simon got disoriented and fell to the ground. Meanwhile, Marc ran back to the veranda from the house with a squad of guards bearing bo staffs and semi-automatics. The guards circled the jötnar and vampire and harried them with the staffs into the center like sheepdogs driving errant cattle.

This left Miranda for Kara, who she was hoping not to kill if she didn't have to. It was bad for business if visiting vampires died every time they came to Gaspard's compound, and she couldn't really blame the vamp for being suspicious. Miranda was a seer, or at least had similar talent, and had sensed that something was off. How she foresaw the Grunch's involvement, Kara did not know and didn't care. What mattered now was that an angry, fully-vamped out, emaciated woman with two-inch fangs was running toward her.

Before Kara could give them a command, the guards trained their guns on the active threat, targeting Miranda, the exact thing Kara didn't want them to do. This momentary diversion allowed Jarius to bulldoze two of the guards to the ground. He swiveled and grasped Simon's arm, dragging him along the lawn. He was slow, but he made progress. Simon gathered enough energy to crawl.

Kara screamed, "Hold them! I'll take care of her!"

Kara withdrew her gun and fired two quick shots at the vampire, which hit dead center, tearing a hole in Miranda's chest. The vamp didn't seem to notice and leapt on Kara, arms outstretched, scrambling for Kara's neck.

Kara twirled out of the way at the last moment, forcing Miranda to recover and make a quick turn. The bullet holes had closed already. *Crap, damn, shitfuckpisshell*, thought Kara, using all the new swear words she'd learned since coming into Gaspard's employ.

Kara unsheathed her sword and sliced Miranda's arm. The vampire responded by pulling a long knife with an angled blade from her skirt and charging again toward Kara. Kara heard Gaspard yell, "Kara, she has kukri!" She had a second to think, *no shit, Sherlock*, and then Miranda was on her. Kara parried as Miranda struck. Miranda blocked Kara as Kara sliced in quick diagonals, forcing Miranda to back up. Kara whirled in a circle to use her momentum to slice Miranda's neck, but the fast-moving vampire foresaw her move and ducked, swiping the kukri at Kara's feet, forcing Kara off-balance.

Back and forth the women went, until both were bleeding from multiple cuts. Gaspard raised his voice over the melee to reach Marc. "Can you get in there and help her?"

Marc danced out of the way of the battling women and yelled back, "Not if I don't want to be shish-kabobbed! Why don't you do it, boss?"

"I've got the same problem," Gaspard admitted, pirouetting in a graceful arc to avoid being slashed to ribbons.

Transfixed by the sword fight, Gaspard and Marc had turned their attention away from Jarius and Simon and didn't notice that the effects of the sedative were wearing off. Simon could stand on his own, which left Jarius free to attack. Gaspard and Marc were alerted by the sound of a shot and the scream of a guard as Jarius tackled the guard to the ground, cracking the guard's skull. Simon grabbed another guard, twisted his neck in one motion, and dropped the body on the ground in a heap. The remaining two guards shot multiple rounds at their attackers, hitting Jarius, but Simon simply dodged them, as he turned on maximum vampiric speed and sprinted past the guards, running toward Gaspard and Marc, Jarius lumbering behind, a bullet in his thigh.

Gaspard and Marc whirled to face their attackers, forced to trust that

Kara could handle Miranda. Jarius dove for Marc while Simon stalked Gaspard. Kara spared a single look in their direction and was shocked to see that Simon grew taller as a vampire, longer in the body and the legs, giving him leverage that even Gaspard, who was naturally tall, didn't have. His face lost the fishy lips and fleshy cheeks and became elongated and angular, the epitome of the old movie Nosferatu.

"What the HELL?" Marc exclaimed. "That's cheating!"

"Shut up, Marc, and pay attention. Look behind you!" Gaspard yelled back, dodging and weaving away from the new Simon.

Marc swiveled to see Jarius bearing down. Jarius remained a gargantuan and Marc, smaller than Jarius by well over one hundred pounds, relied on his speed and athleticism to escape Jarius' grasp. Even wounded, the giant was formidable. Kara wasn't sure Jarius was even aware of the bullet in his leg and fired a shot in the giant's direction, hitting him in the foot. Jarius howled in pain. There. Now he knew.

A heavy blow between her shoulder blades drew Kara's attention back to her more urgent situation, and she staggered as Miranda jumped on her and pinioned her to the ground, squeezing her neck. Kara didn't have the leverage to keep Miranda away. Miranda's saliva dripped onto Kara's face, and Miranda's blood seeped from her cuts into Kara's. Kara could feel the vampire's feel-good hormones sinking into her, and Kara became concerned, realizing this may be the last battle of her life. The very thought that she could be taken out by the wiry Twizzler of a vampire pissed Kara off, but for the moment, she couldn't think what to do.

The vampire's blood was sapping her resistance, and Kara could feel her arms giving out. Another drop of Miranda's saliva dripped onto her face, and Kara's sluggish brain started working at full-speed again, reminding her that there was another concerned party waiting for his cue. Gathering what was left of her strength, she screamed, "GRUNCH! It's your turn!"

The air filled with the tell-tale *thunk*, *slither* pattern followed by an enormous roar that could have come out of an African lion, if the lion were seven feet long with scales, red eyes, and talons. The roar ended in a hiss of rage as the Grunch came calling.

Miranda relaxed her grip on Kara's neck to look toward the sound, giving Kara a moment to grab a breath. Kara was irritated with herself for even being in a losing position, and as her aggravation grew, she had an idea. She focused on her hands, fueling them with her fury, pushing her ire into them until she could feel the full force of her power flowing through her fingertips. She felt a need for violence deep in her belly, and for the first time in her life, she purposefully urged her feet and hands to spark.

Kara didn't just spark. She flamed. She flamed like a dragon robbed of his gold, and her fire caught Miranda by surprise. Miranda toppled backward, screaming at the top of her lungs, rolling back and forth to extinguish the inferno, but Kara had caught Miranda's hair as well as her clothes. Kara noted absently that vampires really do go up like candles with short wicks.

Kara's neck was sore and her breathing ragged, but she turned toward the scene playing out in front of her, ready to fight if necessary.

Jarius and Marc were both bleeding from the head, and Marc was holding his left arm to his side. Jarius was tiring and moving slower than he had before, blood seeping from his leg and foot wounds. Gaspard and Simon were engaged in a hand-to-hand battle unlike any Kara had ever seen. Both master vampires, they moved like the wind, their forms blurring in front of even her enhanced eyes. Simon's visage was terrifying, his face stretched long, his mouth agape, and one of his hands had transformed into a something like a grappling hook, which he used to snag Gaspard's clothes.

Gaspard was almost as ghastly. His cheekbones stood out against his face. His lips were bloodless, his fangs extended, and for some reason that Kara couldn't fathom, he was barefoot, his shoes discarded to the side. Gaspard's arms were more muscled than Simon's, but Simon's ability to alter his shape gave him an unexpected advantage. Gaspard extended his right arm and slapped Simon's head to the right and then backhanded it to the left. Simon's wingspan was now double Gaspard's, but Gaspard used this to his advantage, stepping into Simon's center and hitting him with a flat palm mid-chest, knocking Simon on his back.

From the ground, Simon watched Jarius snap a kick at Marc's face and miss when Marc ducked out of the way. That was all the Grunch needed. Moving as fast as a snake, the Grunch snatched Jarius' bleeding leg and snapped it off at the knee. Jarius wailed in pain, but this lasted for the merest second as the Grunch chomped off his head. Marc collapsed to the ground, not moving.

Simon saw the Grunch coming, red eyes glinting with anger, fetid breath wafting across the lawn, and abandoned his battle with Gaspard to scramble away from the Grunch. Seeing Gaspard finally clear of Simon, the two remaining guards took aim, not sure if they should target the Grunch or Simon. Kara stopped them.

"Watch," she said.

The Grunch took his time. He stalked Simon, batting at him with his talons, playing with him like a big cat with a mouse. Simon screamed, "Gaspard, stop him! I'll give up Kara! I'll get the Assembly to back down. Anything you want! Don't let him do this!"

Gaspard peered down at the vampire, who was once more in his potato form. "I can't do anything about this, Simon. This is personal for Mr. Grunch. And good on you for recognizing that this Grunch is the male. I called him an *it* before and was corrected. I wonder how you knew his sex? Could it be that you have seen him before? Could it be that it was you who destroyed the Grunch eggs and shot his mate? I'm thinking it was."

"No, no, I don't know what you are talking about!" Simon tried to shove himself backward, but the Grunch and Gaspard kept coming.

"I think you do," said Gaspard. He pulled out the pocket watch. "In fact, I think you lost this in their den, where you attacked them. Tell me, how did you overcome them? I cannot believe you managed to get away."

Simon panted. "I had help. Three other vampires came with me."

"Were these some of my new vamps from South Texas, Simon?"

"Yes. We had tranquilizer darts loaded with high doses of zolazepam, an anesthetic used on reptiles. We doubled the normal amount used for crocodiles. Even that wasn't enough. They still fought back, and we shot the female twice. Even wounded and drugged, she managed to do damage. She got one of my group with her tail, knocking him unconscious. We had to drag him out of there. The male, uh, the guy Grunch, couldn't squeeze into the birthing room, which made it easy to shoot him in the face with another dose before we exited. He was completely paralyzed. We actually climbed over his body, and he couldn't do a thing." Simon cackled like a madman at this thought.

The Grunch shoved his snout into Simon's chest, knocking Simon over onto his back for a second time. The Grunch stood over Simon, lowering his head so that it was inches away from Simon's face. Simon screeched and shook from his head to his toes.

"Why did the Grunch attack the party?"

"He smelled me. That is what we were counting on."

"The better question is why?" asked Gaspard, knowing he couldn't keep Simon alive much longer. The Grunch was getting antsy.

"You are amassing power, and the Assembly is worried. I was assigned to create trouble for you and force you to recant your loyalty to the Assembly. Our spies heard the stories about the Grunch and Grunch Road and found a local who knew where they holed up. Then they explored a bit to isolate where the mated pair lived. You're adjacent to its home, so it was a natural connection. I'd draw the Grunch out, sic him on you, and maybe kill a couple of your people, sacrifice a few of mine, and that would be all it took. You'd either be excommunicated or you'd claim *loup seul* status, but either way, I'd be awarded Kara."

The Grunch had lost his patience. Gaspard backed away, bowed, and said, "He is yours."

Kara was surprised when the Grunch didn't kill Simon. Instead, the Grunch grasped him by the waist with his enormous jaws and headed back to the swamp. Kara watched them go and then laughed deep from her belly. Gaspard turned to her, confused.

"He's taking him back to his mate."

Gaspard's eyes opened wide. "That poor bastard."

Kara choked on her own laughter and sputtered, "I wonder if he will be food for the little one."

"It would be fitting," Gaspard agreed and turned to walk to the house.

"Gaspard, where are you going?"

Gaspard turned around, mouth set in fierce almost-smile, eyes hard. "Do you have one of those knives and lighters? I've got a couple of spies to kill."

19

Jarius' remains were boxed up, along with charred Miranda fragments, and sent to the hotel with a note explaining that Simon would not be returning. Gaspard instructed the North-eastern vampires to leave the city immediately, go back to their home, and determine their next leader.

Gaspard also sent a message to the Assembly along with digital, untouched recordings of the evening's events, demanding that the person or persons in the Assembly who had assigned Simon to his task come forward immediately. The Assembly's quick response washed its hands of the whole thing, saying that Simon had lied, was acting on his own, and none of the Assembly members held Gaspard ill will.

Upon reading their letter, Gaspard muttered, "But, of course," and passed the note to Kara. Kara frowned at the implication. It meant that Gaspard still had unknown enemies in the Assembly. She had no idea who they were or how many of them existed. This was not a happy thought.

Adelaide said what Kara was thinking. "Gaspard, this should be taken as a warning. The Assembly, for reasons unknown, is against you, or at least some of its members are. They are playing a shell game. This is a game of chess that we've been playing as a game of checkers. They are after you, my boy."

Adelaide, Marc, Emmie, Kara, and Gaspard were collected in the sitting room. Gaspard and Adelaide shared a plate of lemon cookies paired with Lady Grey tea. Emmie sat next to Marc, petting his arm. She hadn't reacted well to his limp form being carried into the living room after his battle with Jarius. Marc had fed from instinct only, unaware of his surroundings. Sanguineers lined up to provide blood until he was fully conscious. Gaspard wouldn't eat until he knew Marc was okay. Kara was exhausted and let Adelaide run the show. Hours later, everyone was in better shape and in bed.

Kara was so tired that that she almost couldn't shower, but she stunk so much from Miranda flambeau that she couldn't relax without getting clean. Her thoughts wandered as the water sluiced down her body, and she scrubbed herself clean with the vanilla-honey body wash some nice person had placed there. Her hands roamed her stomach scar, which angled down from her left mid-section to her right hip, a slash made by a right-handed warrior. After all that she had been through in the last several weeks with Gaspard, seeing how he reacted with strength and cunning, but also compassion as he had for the Grunch when the truth was known, she wondered if vampires might indeed have souls. If so, why couldn't she see them as she could with human souls?

She was too tired to give it any more thought and fell into bed, asleep almost instantly, but not in the deep sleep she craved. Instead she dream-walked, her mind leaving the room, walking down the hall and into the master suite. She could feel the lush carpeting under her feet, smell new paint in the hallway, and experienced no self-consciousness about entering the suite uninvited.

Kara had never been in Gaspard's room. There were no windows, just paintings, all of them with bright suns as if to replace his lost sunlight. Gaspard lay in bed, curled into a ball, his left hand pillowing his head, his right clenching and unclenching the sheets, his tension breaking through his sleep to the physical world.

Kara's dream body walked closer and sat on the edge of his bed. Gaspard whispered, "Kara?" in his sleep and then surrendered to the daylight, going completely still, sleeping the sleep of the dead.

But some part of Gaspard must have recognized her, for his dream-self rose to meet hers. In this dream, Kara was unsurprised. This felt completely natural.

Dream Gaspard sat up and reached for her. He caressed her cheek, dragging the back of his hand down to her neck so he could feel her pulse. Kara dropped her head back, reveling in the feelings aroused by that one touch. Gaspard's hand closed around her neck, keeping her next to him, making an unmistakable claim.

Kara's dream-self lifted her head and met his lips. At first the pressure was gentle, but they both increased the depth of the kiss, and she didn't even notice when she wound her arms around his neck, pulling him closer. He left her lips and nuzzled behind her ear, licking a path of hot flame down her neck, giving her a love bite right where her pulse now galloped. The love bite was a hint of what was to come, but even that much was enough to overwhelm her. She leaned back, and he licked his way down her cleavage, finally seizing a nipple, sucking hard.

Dream Kara gasped at the pleasure. She was certain she'd never felt this way before. Not with any of the men she'd bedded, not with any of the women she'd caressed in the dark. This was a new experience, and as Gaspard's dream-self moved to her other nipple, Kara's conscious mind panicked, pulling her backward from Gaspard's room back to hers, slipping back into her body, waking her with a jolt.

He has a soul. Gaspard was a vampire with a soul. She'd seen it.

Kara lay there panting, recalling the feelings of the dream, her desire and Gaspard's unmistakable soul. She still felt his touch and marveled at this revelation. *Oh, Odin*, she thought. *You were right.*

What was she thinking? She had a job to do and that was all. She swore no such dream would happen again and even the fact that Gaspard had a soul wouldn't affect her. But that didn't keep her from pleasuring herself to relieve the heavy ache between her thighs.

She was glad this was a fantasy and Gaspard wasn't aware of any of it.

Back in his bedroom, Gaspard did the impossible. He broke through the daytime death and opened his eyes, his body raging with desire, thoughts of kissing Kara strong and real in his mind. He could smell her scent and his fingers tingled with the memory of her skin. He could taste her on his tongue and hear her moans.

But before he could contemplate this fully, he was pulled back down to the land of the undead, slumbering without thought or memory.

The next evening, Gaspard was chipper, well-rested, with no recall of the dream of Kara in his bed. Kara, on the other hand, was grumpy, as no amount of tossing and turning had completely washed him from her mind.

"Kara, my love, what is wrong with you tonight?" Gaspard asked, leaning over to brush an errant cracker crumb from her shoulder. He stopped in surprise when Kara recoiled from his touch.

"I'm not your love," she snapped, standing up to create distance between them.

Gaspard teased, "Maybe not now, but a man can hope."

"Yes. A man could hope, but you're not a man, you're a vampire."

Gaspard grew silent. He gave his jacket a tug to smooth its already perfect lines.

"I'm sorry you feel that way, Kara. I thought we were further along than that. I obviously was wrong. Please excuse me, I have work to do." He gestured to the door and shuffled some papers.

Ashamed of her behavior but unable to explain why to Gaspard, Kara adopted a cool air of indifference and strode to the door. Before exiting, she turned slightly and said, "What do you want to do with the Assembly? Adelaide is correct. This is a game of strategy, and we don't even know who is sitting across the table."

Gaspard didn't look up from his paperwork. "That's what I have you for, Kara. Do your job and come up with a plan. Marc can brief you on what we know about the sitting members of the Assembly. All I want is to be left alone with my present territory. We need to convince them that I am not interested in expansion. Go figure it out."

Kara knew it was unreasonable for her to feel hurt by his curt tone. She deserved it. She regretted her outburst but thought it might be for the best to establish firm boundaries. She was on assignment, and her charge was in danger. She couldn't afford emotional entanglements if she was to do her job effectively, and what could it lead to anyway? A vampire and a Valkyrie? Unheard of.

"Yes, sir," she said, slipping through the door without a look back.

20

Gaspard dropped his pen and loosened his tie. What was going on with her? He'd thought they had developed a friendship, affection even. Her demeanor this evening was cold, heartless, and... disappointing. He rubbed his eyes in frustration. How had this happened? One moment he was drinking with a nice guy in a bar, the next minute he's got a mythological warrior princess in his service, and the minute after that he was imagining that same woman writhing beneath him in ecstasy. He was losing his damned mind. He needed to focus and remember who he was, a master vampire. He decided to call for Sarah, a sanguineer he enjoyed very much, and for the first time since he learned of the dangers of blood addiction, he was determined to seduce his blood meal.

While he waited for Sarah's arrival, Gaspard thought more about the situation with the Assembly. Someone there had it in for him and was spreading rumors about his desire for additional territory. He wanted none of it. Keep your domain small and tight, controllable and loyal. That's all he wanted.

Well, that wasn't *all* he wanted if he was honest with himself.

He got back to work, pleased when Sarah knocked on his door.

21

Kara sat in Marc's office staring at four pictures of vampires that were each hundreds of years old. In fact, one, the Greek, was rumored to be one thousand years old. She'd been looking at the same photos for three hours.

"How many sit on the Assembly?" she asked.

"Either seven or nine," Marc replied.

"So, we can only identify four of them? We don't have any information on the others?

Marc stretched, yawned, and said, "It is a secretive society, Kara."

"Do we know anything about the support staff? Their firsts? Assistants? Is there anyone we can connect to Gaspard?"

"I don't have that kind of intelligence, Kara," said Marc as he sat back in his chair in frustration. He kept rubbing his head, a sign that he was getting fatigued.

"Let's stop for this evening," Kara suggested. "We need to be clear-headed to figure this out."

She sat on the loveseat by the fireplace and flicked the gas on, kicking off her shoes and curling her legs under her. She preferred wood to gas, but had to admit that the convenience of flicking a switch was nice at times. Marc sat down next to her, his leg bumping her knee as he flopped down. He threw his arm over the back of loveseat, over her shoulders, and leaned his head back.

The door flung open with a thundering crack, jolting them both out of their seats. Gaspard stood in the doorway, studying the two of them, his face darkened with anger.

"Gaspard! What's wrong?" asked Marc.

Gaspard schooled his features, but his mood was communicated to the entire staff, and all the vampires shrunk down wherever they were, hoping they were not the focus of his ire.

Behind him, Sarah stood, face flushed, hair mussed, carrying her shoes. Kara was struck dumb.

"I heard you were up here together for several hours," said Gaspard. "I am surprised you have not come down to report."

"We needed a break, Gaspard. We also need to get more intelligence. We are missing the current names of at least three, possibly more, of the Assembly members and know nothing about the staff or hierarchies within the old ones' seethes. We were coming down to tell you in a moment..."

"Well, you didn't," Gaspard snapped. Sarah, her flush melting away, took a small step back until Gaspard caught her hand.

"My future, our future, the future of this seethe, and our security rests on untangling this conspiracy! If you need additional information, then determine a way to get it. Don't bother me with the details. Get. It. Done."

Sarah shrank away and pulled her hand out of his. Before he could stop her, she backed down the hall and fled upstairs to her room. He felt ashamed at having scared her. He sighed and reached up to rub the back of his neck.

Emmie and Adelaide walked around the corner to see what was going on. Emmie flew to Marc's side while Adelaide went to Kara's.

The look on Adelaide's face and the sight of Emmie clinging to Marc's arm was enough to knock Gaspard into his right senses.

"I am sorry. I guess this mess got to me more than I realized. If you will excuse me, I must go apologize to Sarah for frightening her."

Kara was numb. Here she was dreaming of sex with this man, worrying that she had rejected him and caused him pain. Obviously, she was mistaken. She was embarrassed at her weakness and drew herself to her full height, stalked out the door, brushing past Gaspard with an icy stare. Adelaide shook her head at Gaspard in disbelief.

"You've really messed it up now, my boy," she said as she exited. "She requires a soft hand and patience, but you had to go and push. Now look what you've done."

"What are you saying, Adelaide?"

"Gaspard, I am an old woman and have seen many love affairs stop and start. Your feelings for her are obvious and admirable. You have chosen well, but you need to woo her, take your time, show her your soul. She won't believe love with a vampire is possible until she sees that depth."

"She does not seem interested."

"Of course she is, but she's a warrior, used to being in control at all times. Love is the exact opposite of that. It is letting go, trusting another, sailing free with no rulebook. She's scared, Gaspard."

"Kara isn't scared of anything."

Adelaide snorted. "Not of any monster, no, but she's afraid of failure. She's afraid of getting emotionally entangled with you and forgetting her duty."

"*Merde. Demonschmidt.*"

"What does that mean?" asked Adelaide.

"Nothing. Just an old swear word I used to use when things really went to hell."

"Sounds like a story. I look forward to hearing it someday." Adelaide patted his cheek. "You'll figure this thing with Kara out, I have no doubt."

Gaspard looked at Marc. "Marc, I'm sorry…"

"Don't worry another moment, Gaspard." Marc headed for the door whistling a tune. It took Gaspard a moment to recognize it.

"What's love got to do with it? Marc, you bastard."

Marc's laughter rang down the hall.

The butler appeared, drawing all attention to him with a small "ahem."

By this time, Gaspard was smiling and ready to go find Sarah to beg her forgiveness. He had not seduced her as originally planned, only taken a drink. It had been a lovely, gentle encounter, not a rash physical coupling. At least he had been honorable in that.

"What is it?"

"There are vampires at the door, sir."

"Who are they?"

"They say they are from the Northeast."

"I told them to leave."

"At the risk of sounding obnoxious, sir, it is obvious that they didn't."

Gaspard strode down the hall into the entranceway. Marc and Kara were already there, staring at the contingent of vampires on the stoop and beyond. There was at least a dozen.

"What is it you want? I told you to leave my city," Gaspard said, looking worryingly at the lightening sky. "You should not be out. It is almost daybreak."

"We have no place to go," said a young vampire who was closest to the door. "We can return home to the rest of the seethe, but we have no master. You killed ours in lawful battle."

All the vampires knelt on one knee. "We acknowledge you as our new master, as required by vampire law. You are now the Master of New Orleans and the entire Northeast region," said the young vampire. The others murmured in agreement.

"Holy hand grenades," whispered Marc.

Kara pinched the bridge of her nose, took a deep inhale, and turned to Gaspard. "Now the Assembly will never believe you aren't interested in power and territory. Perhaps Simon achieved his goal after all."

"Master?" questioned the kneeling vampires as a ray of weak sun peeked out above the trees. The vampires scuttled closer to the door, squeezing into the shadows.

"Gaspard?" said Marc.

Gaspard looked at the sky and said, "Marc, show our new family inside and get them situated before full light."

Marc gestured the vampires inside and took them to the basement for the day. Gaspard headed upstairs toward his bedroom.

"Gaspard."

He looked down at Kara.

"What do you think happens next?"

"They're going to hunt us down, Kara. I was warned long ago that a war was coming. I'm afraid it has arrived. I'm glad you are here. We're going to need your sword."

"What kind of war?"

"Between vampires with souls, like me, and those without. We are on the brink of what Odin called the Soul Wars."

Kara let that soak in, her bet with Odin taking on new meaning. What did it mean that some vampires had souls and some didn't? How did that happen?

She studied Gaspard and recognized that now was not the time. The sun was rising and he was exhausted.

She put her hands on her hips. "Well, I only have one question."

Gaspard dragged his hands across his tired eyes. "What's that?"

"What are holy hand grenades? And can we get some?"

PART III

SOULS RISE

1

Gaspard's boots crunched on the icy snow as he walked through the 11th Arrondissment, the Jewish sector of Paris. The reek of fear was thick and the shadows so dense they were permanent fixtures, impervious even to the sun. The sidewalk's stains hit Gaspard's nose with the telltale stink of old blood, punctuated by motes of new blood, the only remains of residents picked off one-by-one. The sun sank behind the Paris buildings, and Gaspard pulled his hood up as he traversed Parmentier Street, mulling how the world had gotten so ugly.

Thud. Gaspard heard what had become an all too common sound. The sound of a boot hitting the abdomen of a man. Another thud. Laughter from onlookers.

"Please, stop! He's my husband! He's done nothing!" cried a woman. She carried bread and cheese and proffered the rarities on bended knee to the soldiers. A second soldier snagged the food, then put out his right hand and strong-armed the woman back.

"You will be beaten, too, if you interfere! Step back, old woman. Your husband is a traitor and a spy." Another woman, who had the sagging skin of someone who'd lost a lot of weight too quickly, hauled the crying woman into a shop doorway, saying, "Don't be stupid! Your children need you. They can't lose you both!"

One last kick to the head finished the fun for the German soldiers, who withdrew several yards to lean against their car, a German-registered Peugeot, and to share the bread and cheese. No one dared approach the bleeding man in the street who lay there, unmoving.

Gaspard could hear the man's heartbeat slowly fade. Compelled by the blood scent and his revulsion of the man's mistreatment, he strode into the street and cradled the man as one would a baby, carrying him off.

"Halt!" came the order from behind him. Gaspard walked toward a nearby alley.

Gaspard heard the clicks of rifles being readied. From the corner of his eye, he saw the remaining townspeople scurry into their homes and lock their doors. Gaspard, three soldiers, and a dying man were the only ones left in the mouth of the alley, hearts either pounding or failing.

Gaspard lowered the dying man onto the concrete, rose to his full height, and pushed back his hood.

"Who the hell are you?" demanded one of the soldiers looking at Gaspard's sharp features, pale skin, and reddened eyes.

Gaspard took a step closer. "I'm hungry." He lunged for the soldier, cracking his neck with one twist, sinking his incisors into the carotid artery to drink while the blood still pumped. He hadn't swallowed much when the next two soldiers were upon him.

Gaspard swung one arm and backhanded the shorter soldier smack in the face, dropping him unconscious on the ground. The third, backpeddling as fast as possible, raised his gun and took a wild shot, which went over Gaspard's head. Gaspard reached him in the blink of an eye, pressed him up against the alley wall, and pulled his head to the side, stretching the man's neck almost to the breaking point. Taking his time, Gaspard bared his fangs at the soldier, letting the man see what was to come. He was rewarded by the sound of urine hitting the street.

Gaspard broke the skin on the soldier's neck, sucking like a lover, making sure the man stayed conscious throughout. Gaspard took only enough to weaken the soldier but not enough to kill.

He straightened the soldier's neck and placed his mouth at the man's collarbone, drawing his tongue up to the ear in one long blood-scented lave, allowing his breath to wash over the man. When he was certain he had the soldier's undivided attention, he whispered, "Tell your superiors what happened because I'm declaring it open season on Nazis." He pushed the man out onto Parmentier Street and watched him stumble to the Peugeot.

Gaspard turned to the beaten man who lay on the ground. Gaspard held his head and drank deeply, not the cause of the man's death, but hastening its arrival. He briefly considered turning the man, but relinquished the thought as fast as it came. It would be cruel to doom a man to eternity in the hell that now lived on Earth. Better for him to take his chances with whatever lay beyond.

He left the unconscious soldier where he was and turned to leave, catching a swift movement in the corner of his eye. The movement came from above, and Gaspard looked up at the fire escape, wondering who had been there. He climbed the fire escape, scanning the rooftops. He saw no one, but he felt someone there.

"Come out!" Gaspard yelled. "What is it you want?" His voice echoed in the darkness.

Silence. The snow swirled from the parapets in clouds of pure cold. Even Paris's pigeons were hiding, although Gaspard couldn't imagine where the birds could roost in safety. Icicle teeth grew long and pointy from the gutters, threatening impalement to those below, and the moon was a wan, joyless scythe in the sky.

Gaspard didn't wait any longer. He leapt to the ground and returned to his apartment, where he sat in his chair and waited for the inevitable. The inevitable came a short ten minutes later. *Word traveled fast*, Gaspard thought.

The vampire thugs threw open the door, hauled Gaspard up by the shoulders, threw a hood over his head and marched him into a waiting car. Resigned to what he knew was coming, his stomach in knots, Gaspard bit his tongue and stayed silent, swallowing the snarky remarks that floated through his brain.

Numerous twisty turns later, the car stopped somewhere in what Gaspard guessed was the fifth arrondissement, the Latin Quarter. He could smell the Seine and hear the noisy clatter of bistros serving what limited food remained. Still blinded, he stumbled down dank stairs permeated by the odor of yesterday's garbage and was shoved into a cold room with a concrete floor.

He felt the Master's presence. How could he not? The Master's aura filled the room and pressed against Gaspard's resolve. Someone removed

Gaspard's hood, man-handled him into a chair placed above a drain in the center of the room, and tied his hands behind him.

"Arnaud. You could have asked me to come. Politely. I would have. There was no need for all of this subterfuge." Gaspard crossed one leg over the other to appear casual.

The Master of Paris held silent, but his long, lithe body was shaking with rage. He wore a fine suit, unusual in fabric-rationed France, with flat front trousers cuffed at the bottom. The material was a suitably somber gray with white chalk marks and a double-breasted blazer. He'd removed his Fedora and placed it safely out of the way on a hook installed on the back of the door. Gaspard glanced at Arnaud's feet, expecting to find two-toned spats, and was shocked to see that the vampire wore what looked like black leather German military boots.

Finally, Arnaud spoke, almost a whisper, as if he was hanging onto his temper by a thread.

"Did you or did you not send a message that it is, how did you say, 'open-season on Nazis'?"

"I did."

Gaspard didn't see the blow coming. One moment he was in the chair, the next on the floor, chair broken, blood streaming down his face from his forehead and nose. Since he had drunk his fill earlier, the blood was rich and red.

"They were beating a man, threatening his wife, and laughing openly about it. Germans. In *your* city. Why do you let them? What happened to you, Arnaud, that you would let them invade Paris unchallenged? Your forces are formidable. You could beat them!"

Arnaud's long fingers reached for Gaspard, pulling him to his feet only to launch a vicious attack of fists and feet until Gaspard was down and stayed down, the blood from his body flowing out as fast as he had gotten it, down the drain for the city's rats. Gaspard could hardly see by this time, his eyes were so swollen, and his ears rang from the repeated blows. But he heard Arnaud hissing at him in anger.

"You *ibécile*! We *could* beat them, *some* of them, but more will come. They are like cockroaches, scuttling in and out, hiding in the corners and cracks of the city. We cannot take on the entire German army, so I brokered an agreement. We don't bother them. They don't bother us. We co-exist, exactly as our former Prime Minister Reynaud intended, that chicken shit coward."

"It is our current Marshall Petain who is the coward," countered Gaspard, through swollen lips. "He's the one who invited the Germans in."

"Doesn't matter. French government is all the same, whether republic or monarchy. Weak. Shallow. Without pride or dignity. We would have fought beside French forces if they had stayed true. Now the Germans hang swastikas from our buildings and ransack our art."

Gaspard wiggled himself to a seated position on the floor and pushed back until he could lean on the wall, his hands still tied behind his back. "Then why are you working with the Nazis? Why not help the Resistance?" he said, eyes flaming despite the injuries.

"It is better to co-exist than start a vampire hunt in the city. We have lasted this long. This too shall pass."

"Are your people *helping* them?"

"No. We neither assist nor hinder."

"Semantics. If you aren't fighting them, you're enabling them. They have overpowered the great Arnaud? What has this world come to?"

"You have no right to judge."

"Are you having me followed?" asked Gaspard, changing the conversation's direction.

"No, but maybe I should."

"How did you get the news about my actions so fast?"

"A member of the seethe saw you and reported back."

"Incredible coincidence."

Arnaud leaned down into Gaspard's face. "Let me be clear. We are waiting this one out, and you don't get to change that by issuing threats! You do not speak for me. You do not speak for Paris, and so help me, if any of mine are killed because of your stupidity today, I will hunt you down and behead you myself. Am I clear?"

Gaspard nodded, struggled to a standing position, and wiped his bleeding nose on his right shoulder. "I'll remember, Arnaud, if you'll remember that I took this beating out of respect for your position as Master of Paris." Gaspard broke the ropes that tied his hands with one twist, stepped into what was left of Arnaud's space, held his hands up, and brushed both of Arnaud's shoulders, as if he was dusting off his best man's suit before the wedding.

Gaspard pivoted to leave, staring the guards down until they moved out of his way, got halfway up the stairs, and said, "I wouldn't be too sure some of your seethe aren't helping the Germans. That vampire who reported to you? If he wasn't there to spy on me, why was he there?"

Gaspard was indeed in the Latin Quarter, and he was beaten, swollen, and weakened with blood loss. Soldiers filled the coffee shops, drinking the only real coffee left in Paris, studying the French waitresses with half-lidded eyes. When he saw one of the soldiers slap a waitress on her derriere, he had his mark. The waitress grimaced at the slap but didn't protest. Gaspard swore he would do the protesting for them both.

His opportunity came when the soldier needed to relieve himself. The soldier sauntered to the back of the shop, unbuckling his belt and trousers before stepping into the loo. Gaspard had stolen into the alley behind the bistro and slipped in the back door. Once the soldier entered the lavatory, Gaspard followed, locking the door behind him.

"What the fuck!" was all the German got out. Gaspard pulled the man toward him and in one motion, sunk his fangs into the man's neck and lowered him to the seat of the toilet. He drained the soldier dry, taking pleasure in the thump of the heartbeat and how it dwindled to silence. Gaspard left the soldier on his throne, exiting as silently as he had come. Already healing and high on the caffeine-laced blood, Gaspard stole away into the night.

2

Thumbing his nose at Arnaud's command, Gaspard worked with the Resistance. Several months into his tenure, Gaspard was snatching French Jews off a train, pulling their thin frames toward him, then handing them to members of his team, working fast. Some of the Jews had already been in the car for several days and were dehydrated and starving. Gaspard could feel their bones beneath his hands and smell the desperation, along with the smell of human waste, in the air.

The Resistance had damaged the rails to ensure that the train would stop, but already German engineers were pounding out the bend in the tracks so the train could get back on course. The traitorous French government was deporting thousands of families, and they were on a strict schedule. Gaspard saved as many lives as he could, but he was limited by resources available. He could pull people off the train, but then where would they go? The Resistance had limited assets, and every member was in constant fear of being arrested. Members saved bullets for themselves, preferring a quick, self-induced death to months of torture and the possible shame of folding under pressure and releasing information about their colleagues and network.

Once again, Gaspard pleaded with Arnaud.

"Arnaud, I know you don't want to become personally involved, but could you provide a safe house, somewhere we could put people before getting them out of the country?"

"No. I will not become involved or involve my seethe. Since you do not recognize my authority as Master of Paris, I name you Outcast, a Loup Seul. You are on your own. I will do you one favor. I won't kill you." Arnaud held up one long finger. "Unless you kill some of mine, then I will do exactly as I promised."

Gaspard flashed back to this conversation again and again as he snuck people out of the Drancy internment camp or pulled them from a train.

Damaging the rail lines was a losing proposition as guards now stood all night watches to ensure the Resistance couldn't get near them. The Resistance leaders figured they had one last chance to use the tactic, damaging the rails farther down the tracks, past the guard watch, taking the risk that the train would careen off the rails altogether once it gained speed. Gaspard waited in the shadows until the train appeared. Gaspard heard it before he saw it, the tinny sound of metal on metal, followed by the rushing sound of wind being displaced by the moving train. He closed his eyes, trusting his ears more than his vision, and waited.

It was going fast by now, and a fetid odor accompanied it on its journey. Small hands reached out between the cracks in the wooden slats, and the sound of fingernails scratching on the doors was audible to his vampiric hearing. The train hit the bent rails and swung right to left in wild motions until the last car broke free and tumbled down the hillside. The train screeched to a halt, sending fiery embers into the air, and Nazi guards exited the dining car to examine the damage, some with napkins still tied around their necks.

Several of the Resistance dashed after the tumbling train car hoping to save those inside. Gaspard used shadows to conceal his presence and jumped to the nearest door, opening it in one fast motion. Bodies, alive and dead, tumbled from the open car as Resistance snipers shot the oncoming guards. A burly Resistance member stood behind Gaspard and another yet behind him, creating a chain to pass children and weak adults down the hillside.

There wasn't enough time. Suddenly, the train started moving, gaining speed at a fast pace, the engineer desperate to escape the attack and panicked about being late. A few guards and prisoners lost was one thing. Not being on time was unforgiveable.

Grabbing one last child by the waist, Gaspard swung the tiny girl to waiting arms. He turned to get her brother but wasn't quick enough.

Gaspard dropped all pretense of being human and used his speed to follow the train and grab the boy. He was forced to leave the parents behind but caught a glimpse of their grateful faces as their children escaped.

"Who are you?" asked the boy.

"No one," responded Gaspard, handing the boy to the burly man. The man, who up until five minutes ago considered Gaspard an ally, now looked at him with suspicion. Gaspard recognized that his time with the group was already over. He had to find another way. He refused to sit idly by. He needed information, and there was one place he could get it.

3

He headed back into Paris and disappeared in the shadows. Hunched against the cold, he walked and walked, thinking about how to push Arnaud into the fight. He arrived at his destination, a small bar down a side alley with the romantic name of Le Bar des Ecrivains, the Writers' Bar, and stepped in, hoping the usual vampire crowd and real whiskey would be there. As soon as he entered, he realized at least one of those two things was there in numbers.

"Gaspard, I would welcome you, but Arnaud says you are Loup Seul," sneered a small vampire with a thin, oiled mustache that made Gaspard's skin crawl. "It seems you want to waste your time getting us into this war. We will survive it as we always do and step out of the wreckage stronger. We have only to wait and harvest the leftovers."

"That makes you a scavenger. You're nothing more than a vulture feeding on carcasses on the side of the road," Gaspard said.

The oily mustache vamp hissed, sounding like a strange cat. "I would kill you, but Arnaud has said we are not allowed. You disgust me."

"The feeling is mutual," said Gaspard as he retreated to the back of the bar.

Gaspard couldn't help but admire the way Arnaud's reputation preceded him, so much so that this creep of a vampire wouldn't try to kill Gaspard because Arnaud wouldn't condone it. Word on the street was that those who tried to oppose Arnaud got one chance. Gaspard assumed he'd already had his one. After that single chance, Arnaud would hunt you down. One vampire took to preying on prostitutes, and the controlling Madame in Paris petitioned Arnaud to stop him. When a conversation didn't work, Arnaud took it as a personal offense. Pieces of the offending vampire turned up in trash cans throughout the city, surprising sanitation workers whose trash cans kept exploding clouds of ash when opened in daylight.

For the millionth time, Gaspard wondered how he could get Arnaud to put that strength behind the Resistance. Still having no answer, Gaspard found an out-of-the-way seat with his back positioned to the vampire clique and signaled for a whiskey, grateful when the bartender nodded it was available. Alcohol ran low Paris, but the barkeep kept them in drink in return for protection from the detested turncoat gendarmerie, the National French police.

The mustachioed vampire was holding court. Gaspard used the shadows to conceal himself further, hoping that the vampires would forget about him as soon as he was out of eyesight, and listened closely.

"I snuck a whole family out from underneath the gendarmerie's nose," the mustached vampire cackled. "Those caped stuck-up German wannabees didn't see me coming," he said, referring to the French police uniform with its decorative, and altogether useless, cape.

"Bet they didn't search too hard for them," said a red-haired, skinny vampire. "They wouldn't want to get their gloves dirty." The entire table snickered, ridiculing the long, white gloves the police wore to look distinguished to their German occupiers.

"So, you're stealing Jews from the Germans?" asked another vamp. "When are you doing it?"

"The best time is right before transfer from the Drancy internment camp to the trains. It's best to seize them in the crowds as they are herded into the cars. No one misses a few Jews here and there. We dress in, ah, procured uniforms, point the prisoners in a different direction, and that's it. *Voila*! The Jews are too scared to ask questions, and the real guards are bored. No one cares."

"Where are you hiding them?" asked the vamp.

"I keep them at an estate," the vampire replied. "It's not much, but the Nazis don't bother us, thanks to Arnaud, so we are safe." He opened his eyes wide and held his right hand to his heart. “There are many of us who are doing what we can.”

The red-haired vampire chuckled.

The questioner bit his lip as if considering the opportunity. “Who else is doing this?”

The vampire mentioned an entire enclave that resided south of Paris in Orléans. Ten vampires in all.

That was Gaspard’s destination.

4

Traveling to Orléans was not as easy as Gaspard had hoped. He needed to avoid both Nazis and his new vampire watcher, assumedly assigned by Arnaud. He had to be careful of using too much energy as he couldn't be sure when he would drink fully, having only sipped from locals before his departure. Nevertheless, he resorted to pulling shadows to him so he could slip onto the night train down to the original Orléans.

His thirst skyrocketed with the exertion. The bald head of the man in the seat in front of him wavered like jelly, the seat weaving back and forth in his vision. His throat burned like he'd swallowed sand, and he could smell the cut on the finger of his seatmate. The hour-long ride seemed endless.

He exited the train and retained his composure until he was out of sight of the watchful soldiers. The Nazis used the Orléans train station as a major logistical hub, so it was well policed and always busy.

He walked several blocks, slipped onto a side street, and waited for someone to come along so he could take a sip or two. He felt bad preying on the unsuspecting, but there was no way he could face the task ahead without sustenance.

I'll take a little bit and then find another, he promised himself.

He peeked around the corner and noticed a man moving toward him, a blob swaddled in a bundle of clothing. Gaspard scented the air. The man was bleeding, the smell enticing and pungent. He couldn't help himself.

"Sir." He stepped out of the shadows, hardly more than a shadow himself.

The man jumped back several feet.

"I'm not doing nothin'! I'm allowed to be out at night. Delivering something to Commandant Schmidt."

There was something forced about the peasant accent, and Gaspard realized the voice wasn't a man's but the husky voice of a woman. She held out her hand so Gaspard could see her identification card. He gestured for her to put it away.

"I only meant to assist you. You appear to be bleeding," said Gaspard.

"How did you know that?"

"Let me see."

The woman held out her other arm. Even in the dark, he could see the bruises and cuts. One cut was a deep, clean slice, and it was bleeding as if it had cut an artery. *A knife did this.* Blood pulsed from the cut and flowed in rivulets down her arm with an exquisite slowness, giving in to gravity at the elbow where it fell in long streams, slowed even more, and finally trickled to the ground, each drop an audible sound to Gaspard's ears.

She swayed on her feet. "Isn't nothin'. Just a scratch." She attempted to pull the arm back, but her strength was depleted.

Try as he might, the scent overwhelmed him. He could taste the molecules on the air, imagine the rush as her essence hit his mouth and the tang of fresh blood. Without another word and with the speed of a snake, he grabbed her, drew her arm to his mouth, and sucked.

The woman was too scared to scream and too weak to pull away. He swallowed a great gulp straight from the bleeding cut and then, thoughtless and driven by thirst, he clamped down on the wound and took his fill. It wasn't until the woman was on her knees, mewling, that he heard her cries to stop. He dropped her the rest of the way to the ground, aghast at what he had done, horrified at his actions, stomach cramping at the same time. Suddenly, the blood he'd swallowed wasn't so sweet.

"Oh, *ma chéri*, I am so sorry," Gaspard whispered, kneeling next to her. "I swear I never meant to hurt you. How can I make this right?" She didn't respond but pointed toward a building across the street.

"You want to go there?"

"*Oui.*" Her word no more than a breath.

Gaspard gathered her in his arms and crossed the empty street, guilt eating at him for what he had done. He entered the apartment building, bypassing the broken elevator as she gestured to the second floor. She indicated a door down the end of the hall, and he approached, unable to enter.

"I need an invitation, *ma chéri.* I promise to find a way to make this up to you."

"Knock." Her voice was small and faint.

He reached out an arm and rapped on the door. It opened slightly, an older woman peeking one eye through.

"Sophie! Oh, my God, what happened? Come in, come in."

Gaspard brought Sophie in and placed her on a threadbare couch. The only heat in the room came from a feeble fire in the fireplace burning what looked like trash and a chair leg. One look around confirmed Gaspard's suspicion. A chair lay upside down, a leg removed, off-kilter at the foot of the dining room table next to its murderer, the axe. In addition to the sofa, there was a worn rug and a queen-sized mattress on the floor, covered with what looked like hand-stitched quilts, and a Victorian armchair covered in an elegant chintz. Some books remained on the shelves. They felt misplaced with their bright red and green leather bindings.

"Sophie! What happened? Monsieur, did you find her like this?"

Gaspard's eyes drifted to the ground. "No."

The older woman looked at him with hard eyes, unafraid and defiant. "Did you cause this?"

Gaspard shuffled his feet and cleared his throat.

"Partly, Madame. She was already cut and bleeding..."

"He drank from me, Aunt Gigi," Sophie whispered.

Gigi whirled around, placing her body in front of Sophie. "You are one of those blood drinking monsters! Get out! Get out right now! I rescind your right to enter!"

Gaspard felt the pull backward and bowed his head further. "I obey, but I will be back with food and drink for you. I am sorry about what happened."

"She may die, and it will be all your fault, *vampire*," Gigi made the sign of the evil eye and placed one hand on Gaspard's chest and pushed. Gaspard fell backward out the door and landed on his back, feet splayed. The door slammed shut.

Gaspard picked himself up and smiled despite the dire circumstances. Gigi was a firecracker, no doubt. He couldn't remember the last time someone *shoved* him. He liked her.

Nevertheless, his heart hung heavy with his crime. He descended the stairs and went back out in the snow, which had now turned to a cold sleet. Commandant Schmidt, Sophie had said. He wondered who that was. He hugged the wall of the apartment building and pushed forward toward the only light visible, about a block away. The strains of a waltz and the sound of raucous voices told Gaspard he'd found the local German watering hole. This building had electricity, which meant it had been specially wired. The buildings surrounding the establishment were dark, probably because the Germans had rewired the power to service the train station.

Using the energy of Sophie's blood, Gaspard pulled shadows to him and slipped into the bar. Even with electricity, there were plenty of shadows to hide in, and Gaspard went unnoticed. He sat in a corner close to the entrance and watched the scene, evaluating the opportunity at hand.

The bar was packed from stem to stern with German soldiers drinking, eating, and, as he studied the winding staircase, otherwise entertaining themselves with the scantily-dressed French girls who wandered the room. A few of the soldiers were beyond their limit and passed out on the tables, and those who weren't were well on the way to achieving the same state. One soldier, who was still able to stand, pulled a raven-haired girl onto his lap, grabbed her face, and kissed her while fondling her right breast. The girl suffered through the assault, and when he pushed her up and pulled her toward the staircase, she walked with him. Only Gaspard noticed the pained resignation on her face.

Gaspard turned his attention the unconscious soldiers collapsed at the back of the room because there was a back door right nearby, and Gaspard wanted an easy exit. Casting a glamor that he hoped would trick the drunk eyes in the room, he traversed the saloon at a sedate pace until he sat at the table directly behind the inebriated men. The only person who seemed to see anything was the pot-bellied man serving drinks from behind the bar, assumedly the proprietor. Whatever the owner thought he saw, he seemed to dismiss it when a leggy blonde pushed past him with a tray of bottles and a patron toppled his draft beer on the bar.

Gaspard had used a lot of energy, and while Sophie's blood had satiated the gnawing hunger, he knew that using too much energy was unwise. He stayed still, continuing to observe. He became wary when the pot-bellied man strolled out from behind the bar, weaving his way in and out of the tables, looking for all the world like he was simply working the room, but Gaspard could tell he was coming his way. Gaspard tightened his thigh muscles and tensed his abdomen, preparing himself for battle. He put his weight on the balls of his feet, ready to spring.

The man gave him a long look. Gaspard met the man's eyes, letting a bit of the vampire bleed through. The man pulled up short, eyes wide with alarm. He held out his hands in a gesture of peace and sat across from Gaspard.

"What brings you here, Monsieur? I know most of the vampires around here, and you are a stranger," the proprietor said.

"I need food for a woman and her aunt. I have wronged the woman and need to do what I can to make things right."

"What woman?"

"A woman named Sophie and her aunt, Gigi."

"Sophie? She's my best cook. She'd better come back. I'll never find another cook as talented as she is. What did you do to her?"

"I hadn't eaten in a while, and she was bleeding. I was not in control."

"She isn't dead?"

"No, and she was badly cut before I found her. There was a knife wound on her wrist, quite deep."

"That bastard! Which arm?"

"Her left."

"Ah, good, she's right-handed. When can she come back to work?"

Gaspard curled his upper lip. "Not until I say so. Who's the bastard?"

"The Commandant. He's taken a liking to her and insists that she belongs to him. So far, she's the only one who has been able to put off the inevitable. The Commandant seems to like the chase. None of the other girls can refuse, and I can't either, except to make sure that they have clean rooms. It sickens me, but what can we do?" The man gave a shrug.

"Right now, I don't have time to debate your options, although I assure you they exist. I need to get back to Sophie. You believe this Commandant cut her?"

"That is the only thing that makes sense. We have no choice; he is the law here."

Gaspard tried to keep his patience. "I'm going to take one of these sleeping gentlemen out for a bite, and you are going to get me food to bring back to Sophie and Gigi. I am certain you have bandages. Provide those, too."

"But if the Nazis find out, they'll kill me."

"What's your name?"

"Vachel."

"Little cow? Appropriate."

Vachel pulled himself up to his full five feet six and threw Gaspard an indignant look. "No need to insult me, sir! I am trying to survive."

Gaspard patted the man's belly. "And doing very well, I see. Why don't you do something brave for a moment and help me out?"

Vachel pouted, turning his head away from Gaspard. "You are asking me to take chances with my life!"

"You mistake me. I'm not asking anything, little cow. I'm telling you, and if you don't help me, I'll kill you myself."

"You wouldn't dare! Arnaud knows me!"

Gaspard's face darkened as leaned in to Vachel. "Believe me, Arnaud knows me, too."

Vachel winced, and he gave a grudging nod.

"Meet me in ten minutes out back with the food and bandages, and don't fail me, Vachel. It will not work out well for you."

"I'm a dead man either way, but for Sophie, I'll do it." Vachel leaned in, and for a moment, the hardened shell of the man softened, and his eyes reflected his true concern. "Take care of her, vampire. I'm trusting you."

It was no more than a second, but Gaspard knew he'd seen inside Vachel, and that he'd seen someone much deeper and more thoughtful than the uncaring bar manager he pretended to be. Gaspard stored this information for later, curious about what Vachel was hiding.

Vachel reassumed his crusty armor and walked toward the kitchen. "A round on me!" he yelled, pulling everyone's attention to him. The soldiers lifted their beer mugs with a hearty huzzah and the alcohol flowed even more freely than before.

Gaspard grabbed the closest snoring lump of smelly Nazi and dragged him out the back door. He pulled the man toward him and lowered his fangs, puncturing the neck with a small sucking sound. He drank his first mouthful and jerked back in distaste as the man's alcohol-soaked blood bubbled up. Gaspard pursed his lips and then dug back in, making it a quick feeding. He dropped the man in the snow when the back door re-opened, whirling to face whomever came out. He relaxed when he saw it was Vachel, who handed him a bag.

"Here. This is what you requested. Tell Sophie she owes me, as do you. You know how much money I lost by providing a round to that crowd for free?"

"My heart bleeds for you."

Vachel crossed his arms.

Gaspard sighed. "Thank you, Vachel. I do, in fact, owe you one."

Gaspard hurried down the street and up the stairs to Sophie's apartment. He knocked, left the bag in front of the door, and hid around the corner. Gigi opened the door a slit, showing one eye and the barest sliver of her body.

"Where are you, vampire? I know this must be your doing. If you think you can make up for what you did to Sophie with this, you are mistaken."

Gaspard revealed himself but stayed several feet away. "I don't think I can undo what I did, but I can do what is necessary to make it right. There is food in the bag, and bandages."

"Where did you get them?"

"Vachel."

Gigi snorted in disbelief.

Gaspard bobbed his head in acknowledgment. "He's a little prickly."

"I'm shocked you got anything out of that man."

"You might be surprised. I think he has a soft spot for Sophie."

Gigi gave a wheezy snicker of disbelief. "Thanks for the supplies.

This will help." The door closed, and the old mortise lock clicked into place.

Knowing he had done what he could, Gaspard made his way to the basement, grateful to find it unoccupied. Nervous that the sun would show through the cracks in the walls, Gaspard felt along the floor, finally finding what he'd hoped for. He pulled the creaky trap door up, overwhelmed by the smell of earth and rotting potatoes that spewed forth. *Better than nothing*, he thought and lowered his body into the subbasement as the first rays of the sun splashed onto the streets.

5

Gigi opened the bag Gaspard gave her, stifling a yawn at the same time. She'd stayed up watching Sophie sleep and checking the girl's cuts regularly. Though she wouldn't admit this to Gaspard, his feeding from Sophie had probably saved Sophie's life. His saliva's clotting properties helped the deep wound heal a lot faster than it otherwise would have.

She grabbed a cloth and, blessing the gods that allowed them to still have running water, bathed Sophie's arm with soap and bandaged it with the clean cotton strips Vachel provided. Sophie slept through the entire thing, her chest rising and falling with deep, even breaths. A healing sleep, Gigi's mother would have called it.

Gigi ate some of the bread, cheese, and one of the four hard-boiled eggs from the food bag and was delighted to find a barley/chicory mix that could be used for coffee, with a small jar of real sugar. Rations were scarce, and the price for food on the black market was outrageous. A liter of milk cost almost thirty francs! Where was she or Sophie supposed to get that kind of money? All the men were either imprisoned or dead, and only the women and children were left. Scavenging for food had become the women's main pastime. One neighbor roasted pigeons she caught in the park. Others kept guinea pigs and used them for stew. It was a new normal in France and foreign to the gourmands of the French populace accustomed to the delights of their traditional cuisine.

Gigi scoffed at her own foolishness. There was a time when she too believed that she couldn't live without butter.

Thank goodness Sophie had the job with Vachel. As much as she disliked that little cow, working as a chef in the "German saloon" gave Sophie access to food that she could sneak home. They ate better than most people, relatively speaking.

She knew Sophie had been out again meeting with other women who fancied themselves Resistance fighters, passing along information she overhead in the bar. Gigi had no time for that nonsense. As she told Sophie, better to keep your head down and let things play out. They'd been through hard times before and survived. They would survive this, too. Gigi pressed her palms to her eyes, overcome with fatigue and worry.

She had lied to Gaspard when she called him a monster—well, it was more akin to stretching the truth. Several generations ago, her family had been employed by a vampire who they had considered a fair task master. That vampire was true-dead, and she herself had never provided blood to any vamp, but she knew they weren't all evil. Unfortunately, the actions of the current Orléans vampire residents left much to be desired. The last thought she had before falling into a fitful sleep was that Gaspard may be able to help those poor families.

Gigi tossed and turned on the mattress, tangled in the blankets, murmuring indistinguishable words.

When Sophie awoke, she caught the word "vampire" in Gigi's ramblings, and the night before came back to her, streaming into her memory in fine detail.

The vampire, Gaspard, was it? Right. The vampire drank from her, swallowing the blood already flowing from her arm from the knife wound Schmidt had given her.

Remembering the encounter with Schmidt was painful. Sophie held her bandaged arm and recalled his thin lips, a slash across his face, making his visage more stark and uninviting. His face was flushed from where she'd slapped him, and she knew she'd overstepped by looking at his eyes. They gleamed black and cruel, and it appeared as if someone else was looking through his eyes at her. His own eyes, a deep brown, remained, but underneath those irises were the black ones that peered out at her like a snake eyeing dinner. They seemed to hover there, layered beneath, or maybe on top of, Schmidt's human eyes. It was one of the spookiest things she had ever seen, and it made her shiver all over again.

She shook herself to dissolve the memory and opened the bag on the floor, realizing that it must have come from Vachel, although she couldn't fathom why he would provide such a kindness. She ate two of the hard-boiled eggs, saving the last one for Gigi, and swallowed the crusty bread with water.

Seeing the chicory mix, she pulled a pot from the kitchen, added water, and threw another chair leg on the fire. Leaning close to the dying embers from the night, she moved her hands in short jerky motions so as not to burn herself, and pooled them together to create a hot spot. She blew on the embers, wishing them to life, carefully adding tiny pieces of the brown bag that had held the bread, for kindling. She bit her lip in concentration, willing the flame to dance and not smoke. When the fire caught, she leaned back on her heels and exhaled in relief. Smiling for the first time in days, she stuck the pot in the fireplace to heat the water.

The coffee was horrid, even with the sugar, but it didn't matter. She thought about her next steps and sipped the hot drink, grateful for its warmth despite the bitterness. When it was done, she roused Gigi and let her know she was leaving.

"Are you going to meet those other women again?" Gigi asked.

"Yes, I think so."

"You're going to get yourself killed! You already risk yourself by giving them information. There is no need for you to pick up a gun."

"We women are the only ones left, Gigi! We must fight if we hope to see our men, boys, and families again."

"What are you going to do tonight?"

"That farmhouse two miles out of town, on the southern border?"

"The one where the vampires are keeping the Jewish families."

"Schmidt wanted me to go with him there last night. He wanted to show me something. I refused, not because I don't want to see the place and get the lay of the land, but because I know better than to go with him on my own."

"He didn't take that well?"

"He slashed at me and caught my wrist with his knife. He was so angry that I thought he was going to take me forcibly, but something made him stop. I'm not certain what it was. He's always been annoying, but last night he was dangerous."

Sophie continued, putting her hand to her chin. "Maybe he didn't want to lose control in front of his men. You know, the story would spread that the only way Commandant Schmidt can get a woman is by dragging her kicking and screaming."

"I don't know, Sophie, but this is worse than I thought. I can't lose you, too. Please, if you can't keep away from Schmidt, then let's go somewhere and hide. Please Sophie, I beg you."

"And how would we eat? My employment with Vachel keeps us fed, my dear aunt."

Sophie squatted in front of her aunt, who stayed on the mattress on the floor. She cupped Gigi's face in both hands and kissed the older woman's forehead. "I promise to be careful."

Gigi grabbed both of Sophie's wrists, taking care not to press on her wound. "I know what to do. The vampire, the one from last night?"

"Yes?"

"He owes you, and he brought us this food. We may be able to trust him. If he went with you, he could protect you."

"Aunt Gigi. The vampire bit me. Forgive me, but I'm finding it a little hard to trust him after that."

"He didn't bite you; he drank from an open wound. Big difference."

"Really? How so?" Sophie arched an eyebrow at her aunt.

"It's like eating beef. You eat it, but you didn't kill the cow. He took advantage of what was already there..." Gigi trailed off. She tilted her head in thought and began again, almost talking to herself her voice was so quiet. "He drank your blood, and his saliva entered your bloodstream. That's been known to have some side effects..."

Sophie tensed, her voice strained, "What kind of side effects?"

"It may have linked you, bonded you in some way. That could be useful."

"Bonded to a vampire? Like marriage bonded, slavery bonded? What the hell, Aunt Gigi?" Sophie didn't swear often, and she bit her lip to stop the torrent that threatened to pour out.

"Nothing so serious. More of a connection, an affinity for one another. I've known of trustworthy vampires before, and if I am right about the emotional connection, having him with you would keep you safe and..."

Sophie cocked her head. "And what?"

Gigi blew out a huge breath. "It would make me feel better."

"Really? You pulled that card?"

"I know it's the only one that will work," said Gigi with a sheepish grin. "I love you, girl."

Sophie hugged her aunt tight and whispered, "I love you, too. You're all I have left. How do I find the vampire? How do I use this so-called 'emotional connection'?"

Her aunt pulled back from the embrace and looked her in the eyes. "Wait until dark. He'll find you."

Gigi's hunch was rewarded by a knock at the door as the moon peeked over the horizon.

"Madame, Mademoiselle. May I speak to you for a moment?"

Sophie gave her aunt a salute, which her aunt accepted with a gracious nod of her head. Sophie called out, "Do you swear not to do harm to me or my aunt?"

"I swear."

Gigi whispered, "I don't think that works with vampires."

Sophie made a face and threw her hands up in a "do you have a better idea" gesture.

"It doesn't work on most vampires, but it does work with me." Sophie and Gigi could hear the amusement in Gaspard's voice.

Gigi muttered, "Damn vampires and their hearing."

"I heard that, too," said Gaspard through the door.

Sophie threw the door open. "Alright already, come in."

Gaspard entered, brushing dirt off his clothes. "Pardon me, I slept in the root cellar and do not have a change of clothes."

"We have some that may fit you. Go in the closet in the bedroom off to the right. Some of my husband's clothes are in there," said Gigi, as she stood up to look the vampire in the eye.

"*Mèrci*, Madame. I am even more in your debt, and Miss Sophie, I am truly sorry about last night."

As Gaspard disappeared into the bedroom, Gigi turned to Sophie and whispered, "See, he is our debt. That means he feels honor bound to help us."

"He's going to need to feed again, Gigi, and how is he going to do that? I'm not volunteering," replied Sophie in a normal voice, knowing Gaspard could hear her no matter what.

"Help you how, Madame Gigi?" Gaspard asked, exiting the bedroom in frayed, but clean clothes. "And Sophie, I will not drink from you again." He winked. "Unless you want me to."

Sophie rolled her eyes, but there was a little upturn at the corners of her mouth.

Gigi turned to face him, pulling herself up to stare at Gaspard eyes. "Gaspard, isn't it?" Gaspard nodded.

"Well, Monsieur Gaspard, my niece is a hot-headed bundle of stubbornness, and she is going to check out a farmhouse nearby, and I am asking you, as part of your debt repayment, to go with her and keep her safe."

"Why are you going to this farmhouse, Sophie?" Gaspard asked, taking a corner spot on the sofa, throwing a hand over the back.

Sophie made a face and said, "Commandant Schmidt wanted to take me there last night. I refused, which is what led to my knife wound. That's all healed up, by the way." She paused. "Why is it all healed up? Did you have something to do with that, vampire?"

Gigi answered. "Vampire saliva has clotting properties."

Sophie turned back to Gaspard. "Then it seems I owe you as well."

Gaspard changed the subject. "What do you think is at the farmhouse?"

"Captives. Jews. Schmidt and some of your friends are holding Jews there as blood slaves."

Gaspard jumped to his feet. "I assure you, they are not my friends. In fact, providence is with us, Mademoiselle Sophie. These vampires are exactly the ones I came to see."

"I'm confused," said Sophie.

"The Master of Paris is an honorable vampire, but some in the seethe aren't, and I believe that Arnaud—that is the Master's name—is letting some behavior slide so as not to aggravate the Nazi army. I find it reprehensible, but then again, I'm not managing a huge seethe during a war, so maybe I'm wrong. Maybe his approach is the best, but what I do know is that keeping blood-slaves, and that is exactly what I feared they were, is immoral. If Arnaud can't stop them, maybe I can."

"Did you tell this Arnaud that you were coming here to investigate this?" asked Gigi.

"Oh, my dear woman, no. He needs complete deniability, which he has because I left Paris without consulting him. Whatever happens here is on me."

Sophie wrapped herself in her old coat and shoved her feet into some too-big galoshes. "Well, vampire, let's see how to get you some food and go investigate."

6

Gaspard held the door for Sophie and escorted her outside. Snow had fallen during the day, and the dearth of townspeople was obvious from the lack of footprints. There should have been small prints from happy, playing children surrounded by larger prints of their parents, shivering but smiling at their kids, sipping coffee and chatting with one another. Instead, the ground was painted an uninterrupted white, a few candles flickered in windows, a couple of streetlamps emanated a gentle glow, and all was silent. Gaspard wished he could stay there in that moment and not do what he suspected he had to do.

The farmhouse lay two miles out of town, and with the snowfall, there was no way for them to walk that distance. Instead, they proceeded to the saloon where German guards were drinking once again and listened from outside a window to the surprisingly monotonous conversation.

"Ach. I hate this place. I want to get back to Germany and real food," said one.

"The French are famous for their cuisine, but I see nothing edible here. I need a good wurst and roasted potatoes, enough to fill my belly until I burst!" roared another.

A third groaned. "Stroganoff. My mother makes the best stroganoff."

"Yech. That's a *Russian* dish."

"You making fun of my mother's stroganoff? Shithead." The thud of a fist hitting a table followed.

"Don't call me a shithead!" The thud of a fist hitting a face followed that. Soon a full brawl broke out, and Sophie and Gaspard saw their chance. They snuck in through the back entrance and scoped out their prey.

"There!" said Gaspard. "That big one is about to push that scrappy guy right toward us. He's got some fancy stuff on his collar, which means he's an officer. He may have keys."

The big guy shoved the smaller guy, who fell on the ground only a few feet from Gaspard and Sophie. Sophie crawled forward and pulled the half-conscious man out into the snow. She ruffled through his pockets but came up empty.

"Nothing!" said Sophie, throwing up her hands. "I can do this a better way. Stay here."

Gaspard watched her back disappear through the door and took the opportunity to feed on the officer. He pulled the man toward him and sunk his fangs into the man's neck. The man moaned as Gaspard sucked, and through the blood connection, Gaspard could see into the man's most recent memories.

An emaciated man wearing striped pajamas with bare feet in the snow bowed in front of the officer. Gaspard felt the officer's exultation at finally being the one in power. All his life he'd been the small one, the helpless one, and now he had control. He reached down and pushed the prisoner's head forward and down, shoving it into the snow. The power tore through him, and he closed his eyes with the rush. This filthy Jew's life was literally in his hands, and he swallowed with the feel of it. The Jew was struggling to lift his head and take a breath, but he hadn't eaten in days and was too weak. The officer sat on the man's back, using both hands to press the man's face into the ground while he rubbed his groin back and forth on the man's buttocks and lower spine. As the Jew crumpled with his last breath, the officer reached his height and collapsed over the dead body.

Gaspard shuddered with revulsion as he lived through the experience, nauseous with horror at the man's pleasure in taking the life of an innocent, fragile man and his sexual excitement at doing so. Gaspard's loathing made him pull away, but when he looked at the officer's face, Gaspard made a choice. He sunk his teeth into the man's neck once again, drawing the man's blood into his mouth and not stopping until the Nazi's heart stopped beating.

Gaspard dragged the body into the pine trees behind him and buried it in the snow.

One down, he thought.

Sophie was waiting outside the back door, rubbing her hands to keep warm. "Where were you?" she hissed.

"I had to put that Nazi on ice," said Gaspard, waggling his eyebrows.

"Now? In this moment, you find humor?" asked Sophie.

"In every moment, *ma chérie*, or what is the point in living?"

Sophie shook her head, a small smile on her face. She held up her right hand, showing Gaspard the keys she'd swiped from one of the men inside.

"How did you get those?"

She gestured to her chest. "Décolletage. Boobs."

"Ah, but of course."

"The problem is figuring out which car the keys belong to," said Sophie.

"Not so hard, I should think. There are only seven cars and two are Volkswagen Kűbelwagons, monstrosities those are. Three of the cars are Peugeots. The other two are Mercedes. Let me see the key."

Sophie handed Gaspard the key, and he knew from the lion crest that it was a key from a Peugeot. Keeping low, he ran to the closest Peugeot, clambered in and turned the key. The little Peugeot 202 engine sputtered to life. Sophie raced to the passenger side, climbed in, and gave a whoop.

"First try and we got it!" she said.

"*You* got it, Sophie, my dear. Now, let's get out of here," said Gaspard, backing the car out of the spot with the agility of a motorcar rally champion. He veered off to the right and despite the danger of slipping on ice, raced to the farmhouse, cranking the heat as high as possible.

Gaspard snuck a glance at Sophie during that short ride. Her hood was back, and her hair tumbled around her shoulders. Her cheeks were flushed with excitement, and despite all the danger, all the death and suffering, she was smiling like a child on her first sled ride. Without thinking, he reached for her hand, and she squeezed his fingers in return. There was a tug in his chest, an ache of affection followed by a sharp stab as he was assailed by a sudden vision of Sophie shot and bleeding. He pushed the vision away but grasped the tenderness, holding it close. She turned to stare at him, eyes wide, holding a hand to her heart.

"My aunt warned me that we could have a connection because you drank from me."

"It's more than that. I drank from you, but I also healed you from a grievous wound, drew you back from death. It joined us. I've apologized for drinking from you, but now that I feel your heart, your emotions, forgive me, but I can't regret it." He looked away, uncertain of her response.

Sophie gazed out the passenger window. "I feel off-kilter and overwhelmed. But everything about this world is so irrational, so beyond belief damn awful, that feeling so close, well..."

She stopped speaking, and Gaspard stayed silent, waiting for what she would say next.

She blew out a breath. "I guess what I am saying is that I don't regret it either."

The car's strained engine whined as they slid on black ice, which destroyed the moment and pulled them both back to the present. Gaspard shifted the three-speed transmission to its lowest drive and inched along in the darkness.

The farmhouse rose in the distance, and Gaspard did a three-point turn to place the car in a get-a-way position, parked it on the side of the road, and killed the engine. They would walk from there.

Gaspard stepped into the snow and gave a quiet curse. "*Mérde*!"

"What's wrong?" Sophie swiveled her head back and forth, trying to spot the danger.

"Nothing. Nothing, *ma chérie*. I don't feel the cold the way you do, but my feet are wet and icy. I can't feel my toes."

Sophie put both hands on her hips and sent him a glare. "That's it? You're a vampire. Put your big boy pants on and deal with it."

"My big boy pants? How delightful! I shall remember that saying."

Sophie shook her head and gestured toward the farmhouse. "Let's go, vampire."

Gaspard peered ahead of them. "Behind the main house is a barn. I can see people going in and out of it. That is where we should start."

"How can you see that?"

"I fed from a farmer."

"What?"

"He ate a lot of carrots."

"Now you're kidding me."

"Of course, I am. Vampires have excellent night vision. It comes with the package."

"How can you joke at a time like this?" asked Sophie.

"I am usually quite a serious person, Sophie, but something about you brings out my lighter side."

"In another time and another place, I would joke with you. Now, I'm wondering what horrors lay in that barn."

Gaspard focused on the entryway to the barn, watching figures go in and out. The snow swirled in the air, forming small tornadoes, which marred his vision. Ice formed on his eyelashes, and he glanced at Sophie and noted she was shivering despite the galoshes and coat. Now that they were closer to the barn, they stopped talking and listened to the silence that hung heavy in the air, broken intermittently by the howling of the wind. The gray sky blurred with the white snow, erasing the horizon so the barn seemed to hang mid-air, as if physics didn't apply in this place.

They hunched down and moved forward one foot at a time in a silent, deliberate manner so as not to interrupt the quiet, keenly aware that any sound might give them away.

Five more yards. Two more yards.

Crack! A tree branch broke in the distance, and both vampire and human covered their mouths to stifle their cries of alarm. Gaspard's normally slow heartrate sped up to almost human levels, and he heard Sophie gasp as she ducked, hands covering her head. Gaspard grabbed Sophie by the shoulders and rotated her to look at him. Her eyes were wide, pupils dilated, and frost gathered on her nose and lips. Gaspard focused on her eyes and took a deep breath, then let it out, motioning for her to copy him. Ten inhalations later, her eyes were normal and her breathing even, but she was still shivering.

The trees lay heavy around the farm but disappeared near the barn itself, a perfect defensive strategy. It was impossible for anyone to sneak up without being noticed.

Well, he thought, *almost impossible*. Full from his night's feeding, Gaspard held Sophie's hand and pulled shadows around them. The pair shuffled as lightly as they could to the barn, praying that the poor visibility would keep any guards from noticing footprints. They reached the barn with only seconds to spare as a figure in black approached the barn entrance with a retinue of three following. Gaspard studied the figure and pulled up short, pressing his back to the barn.

The man had a shadow. At night. And it was huge, casting a shape on the ground and barn walls that dwarfed the actual size of the man himself.

Sophie leaned down in the snow and used her finger to write *Schmidt*, making sure Gaspard understood, and then erased it with a brush of her hand.

Gaspard pushed Sophie back against the wall as well, mind racing. He knew that he would be facing vampires, but he hadn't counted on facing a demon.

7

A demon riding a Nazi. A demon-Nazi. A Nazi-demon. Whatever. Gaspard knew they needed to get inside the barn, but he was afraid to enter with the demon and his host in there. He leaned down and wrote *demon* in the snow. Sophie scrunched her face in confusion. Gaspard wrote *demon inside Schmidt*. Sophie's mouth dropped open.

Gaspard could see that Sophie had a million questions, but there was no way to answer them now, especially as he watched Sophie shudder with the cold. His priority was getting inside the barn to both see what was going on and to get out of the weather, which was worsening with every minute.

Gaspard motioned for Sophie to follow him to the back of the barn, but she stumbled, so he picked her up and carried her. He was looking for another entrance and was rewarded by the appearance of a hayloft, although the high doors were shut. He propped Sophie against the wall, motioned for her to hold, jumped as high as he could, floated for a moment in front of the doors and pried one door open, hoping the sound would be drowned out by the wailing wind. He dropped to the ground where Sophie stood, ashen and unfocused.

Gaspard wrapped shadows around them, holding Sophie close to his chest. She was a block of ice, and he knew he didn't have a moment to waste. He leapt to the hayloft and slipped them both inside. They landed in a pile of cold hay, but they were out of the wind, and it was a few degrees warmer.

"You there! Go close that hayloft door. The wind must have blown it open," commanded a voice that Gaspard recognized. It was the mealy-mouthed mustachioed vampire of before, still looking like a bank robber in a silent movie.

A man, a guard of some sort, not a vampire, clambered up a ladder at one end of the barn and climbed into the hayloft. Gaspard held the shadows and slid farther from the door, burying them both in between hay bales. The guard scrambled on all fours to the doors, grabbed the swinging one, and latched it closed from the inside. He never looked toward the corner where Sophie and Gaspard hid.

Sophie stirred, and Gaspard placed a finger on her lips, holding her down so she wouldn't sit up or cry out. Sophie's eyes opened, glanced back and forth, and nodded her understanding. Gaspard released her, piling more straw around her body and scrambled to the edge to look over.

In the middle of the room was a pentacle with blue candles placed at each point and a bowl of water in the center. Demonschmidt—as Gaspard decided to call the unnerving joining—stood next to it, hands clasped behind him, head down as if in deep meditation. Gaspard counted ten vampires hovering around him and several flunkies hanging on the periphery.

As disturbing as that was, it was the stalls that shocked him. Every stall was crowded with people. Men, women, and children, emaciated, filthy and pale. Even from up high, Gaspard could make out multiple puncture marks on several, confirming the theory that these people were Jews being kept as blood-cattle, slaves with no control over their lives. They had gone from one certain death to another.

In case he needed confirmation, Gaspard watched one of the vampires stroll to a nearby stall, reach in and extract a boy, a teenager by the looks of it, and throw him to the ground. A woman and man in the same stall cried out in protest but were silenced with a single look from the vamp.

The boy slumped to the ground, his dirty hair covering his face, his ripped pants revealing multiple bite marks. The vampire crouched down, lifted the boy's arm, punctured the wrist and had a snack.

"Christophe, you're dribbling. Stop being such a slob," said another vampire, rolling his eyes at his friend.

Christophe talked around his teeth. "I can't help it; this boy is flavorful."

"By the looks of him, he's almost out of flavor. You're going to have to find another juicy peach soon."

Christophe pulled his mouth away, held the boy's wrist in his hand, and gave a so-what shrug. The boy's hand flopped with the motion.

"There will be another," he said, pulling once again on the boy's wrist, completing the feeding only when the boy was dead. He threw the dead body into the stall, and Gaspard heard the moans of grief from the couple inside.

"Silence!" shouted Christophe, but the woman wouldn't stop keening.

"I said, *silence*!" Christophe ordered again, glaring at the couple inside.

"Put them in the circle," said a deep voice.

Gaspard knew this was the voice of the demon, which was confirmed when Demonschmidt's mouth moved again, this time speaking in high-pitched German. The disparity caused such vertigo that Gaspard closed his eyes, overwhelmed by the sense of wrongness, of the iniquity of two beings sharing a body.

The German voice, Schmidt, Gaspard assumed, asked, "Vine, why are we doing this summoning? You have enough power on your own."

"Did you not ask for power? For the ability to smite your enemies and command fear and respect in men?"

Schmidt's voice was meek. "Yes, but I didn't realize..."

The demon's voice, Vine's voice, cut Schmidt off, dismissing his host's soul as one would a pair of holey socks. He spoke to the assembled vampires. "I want my sister by my side. She specializes in turning arguments into battles, keeping wounds from healing, and protecting the soldiers she rules. She will ensure our victory and bleed our enemies dry. See to it."

Mustache vampire bowed low and deep to Vine, sweeping his right arm in a flourish, and asked, "My Lord, what is the plan? Once we have her, how are we to serve?"

Gaspard winced as Vine twisted Schmidt's neck in an unnatural manner and released a loud pop from the body's neck. Schmidt's right arm flew up to touch his neck and then jerked down again. The left tried to touch the neck as well and, for a moment, oscillated in the air as the demon and man struggled for dominance. Gaspard watched as the demon regained control.

The demon's voice echoed across the barn. "You will know when I want you to know, vampire, and not a moment sooner." Demonschmidt stalked toward Mustache and stared him down, forcing the vampire to sink into a bow once again and then fall to a crouch, his head so low he slammed it on the floor.

Gaspard slid back to check on Sophie, who was recovering and had more color to her cheeks. He motioned for her to look over the side, warning her with his eyes to be prepared for the horror below.

When Gaspard and Sophie turned back to the scene, Demonschmidt was walking out instructing, "Call me when the preparations are set. I want my sister here by dawn."

Three vampires stayed in the barn; the rest filed out behind Demonschmidt. As soon as they were gone, the remaining vampires grabbed a captive and fed their fill, throwing the bodies back in the corrals with the living. Watching, Gaspard experienced a stabbing pain in the middle of his forehead followed by a gnawing ache in his gut, and his anger grew. He rubbed Sophie's shoulder as she covered her eyes and turned away, tears streaming down her face.

After feeding, the three vampires didn't do anything to prepare for whatever ceremony Vine demanded but sat there chatting and smoking, like teenage vamps trying to fit in with the cool kids.

Gaspard pulled Sophie back to the far corner and whispered to her, counting on the snowstorm and wind to keep the lesser vamps from overhearing. "Weak," said Gaspard. "None of these vampires are Masters or even close to becoming one. Vine has gathered the lowest of the pack, which means he is not as powerful as they think. That's why he needs to summon another demon."

"Vine's a real demon?" Sophie asked, creasing her forehead in disbelief and wiping away her tears. "I can't believe they exist."

"Yes, and he's sharing Schmidt's body, which means Schmidt *invited* him in, creating Demonschmidt."

"Demonschmidt? It sounds like a swear word."

"It is one. For example, when you hit your hand with a hammer, you can yell, Demonschmidt! Much better than *mérde*."

Despite the cold and the stress, Sophie managed a wan grin. Gaspard lifted a hand and caressed her cheek, then grabbed both of her hands and rubbed them back and forth to help the circulation. He hid his face and held tight to his emotions so she couldn't see his growing fear that he was going to lose her, or sense his deepening feelings. It seemed so quick to Gaspard that he could hardly believe it. What would Sophie think? How would she handle love at first suck?

"We have to stop them from bringing in another demon," Gaspard said. Sophie lifted a graceful eyebrow as if to say, "no kidding." He bobbed his head.

"Okay, so that was obvious, but I think the way to start is by taking out those miserable three down there. Stay here and let me take care of them."

Sophie grabbed his arm. "Let me help you. I can't stand by and do nothing."

Gaspard winked. "I can do this. You rest, pretty lady."

Silent as an owl taking wing, Gaspard traversed the hayloft until he perched above the smoking triad. Without a second's hesitation, he leapt, landing on one of three vampires, shoving the vampire to the ground. Gaspard leaned down and jerked the vamp's neck in one swift motion, breaking his neck. The other two vamps, slow on the uptake, stumbled to their feet, one even managing an affronted "hey" before Gaspard was on them, snapping the neck of the second vamp.

The third vamp's survival instinct kicked in, and he grasped a rake in front of him, clutching it in both hands, shoulders hunched like a bully hoping to avoid a fight but knowing he was committed. Gaspard let out a sigh, flicked his hand out, snatched the rake out of the vamp's clutches, flipped it, and plunged the wooden handle through the vamp's heart.

The staked vampire turned to ash, but the other two remained alive, albeit unable to move since their nervous systems were disconnected from their bodies. They lay there, eyes googling, trying to form words with their useless mouths. Gaspard finished them with the rake as well and brushed the remaining ash away with a nearby broom. He wiped his hands and gave a thumbs up to Sophie, who was staring openmouthed from the loft. She gave him a silent salute.

The captives in the stalls reached out their hands to Gaspard and begged for their release, trying to kiss his hands with their gratitude, believing a savior had arrived in their midst. Gaspard held a finger to his lips and turned in a circle.

"Hush, my friends. We need to stop the ceremony first. Right now, I need a place to hide."

The man and woman in the stall with the murdered boy motioned him to their corral. "Come, Monsieur, you are much taller than we are, but we can hide you with the straw, and..." the mother faltered, "with our son's body."

"Thank you, Madame," said Gaspard, and he leaned down and gave the woman a kiss on the forehead. He entered the pen and noticed, to his complete surprise, that a tiny, scrawny girl clung to the woman's legs. Gaspard glanced at the mother in alarm.

"Is she bitten?" he asked.

"No," said the mother, her face cragged with grief and deprivation. "So far, they have left her alone, concentrating on my son. I fear they will fall on her next."

The father grasped Gaspard's shoulder. "If you can save her, Monsieur, just her, we would be happy. Don't worry about us."

"What's her name?" Gaspard asked.

"Isobel," said the father. Gaspard leaned down to Isobel who pulled back at the sight of Gaspard's fangs.

"Isobel, I know I don't look like it, but I'm going to try to help. Can you be quiet for us and not let the bad guys know I am here?" The girl nodded, pulled in closer to her mother's bony leg, and pointed to her brother's corpse.

"Yes, Isobel. We will kill the vampire who killed your brother."

8

Gaspard got situated in the corral, hiding his body with straw and the boy's remains. The smell of death was strong in his nose, and he had to stop breathing in order not to gag. As soon as he was well-hidden, he heard a shuffling noise from the barn ladder, and when he peeked through the slats in the wood, he saw that Sophie had scrambled down and was slipping into a stall across the barn.

What is she doing? Gaspard fumed. Now he had to take out one demon, seven vampires, and protect countless innocents including the one woman with whom he shared a strong emotional connection and had begun to treasure. He wished Arnaud was here. He knew the Master of Paris would be as shocked as he was. Say what you will, but Arnaud was honorable. Gaspard disagreed with the vampire's approach to keeping his seethe safe, but there was no way Arnaud would countenance this.

Gaspard shifted, ready to step out and run to Sophie, but stopped when he heard voices. Six of the vampires had returned.

One of the vampires let out a vulgar epithet. "Where are those three? They haven't done anything!"

"Bet they're in the stalls blood-drunk," said another, "probably passed out cold."

"Find them," the first vamp ordered.

The six fanned out, two staying in the barn to check the stalls, one climbing the hayloft, and the other three going outside. Three stalls down from Gaspard, a vampire with big ears stuck his head over the first pen's door, sending its occupants fleeing to the back, pressing their bodies against the wood wall. The wall creaked in protest, and Gaspard heard a crack as a floor beam came close to letting go.

Big-ears laughed, and Gaspard's body reverberated with the sound like a plucked guitar string strained to almost breaking. Despite his revulsion, Gaspard forced himself to hunker down under the boy's body, covering every inch of himself so he couldn't see what was happening but could only hear.

Gaspard heard a creak of rusted hinges and surmised that Big-ears had entered the first stall. Gaspard realized that Big-ears was a young vamp because he hadn't slowed or stopped his breathing and, in fact, was huffing and puffing as if he needed air. Gaspard recalled that time of his own afterlife. Breathing out of sheer habit, salivating at the smell of beef stew, glancing up for the sun. Behaviors left over from life, reluctantly abandoned.

A whine of fear split the air as Big-ears stepped closer to the women in the corral, followed by a slap as one brave captive stood her ground. She paid the price for that moment of courage when Big-ears roared like a lion with a thorn in its paw, whipped out a fist, and crunched the woman's nose. Gaspard heard it all, and though he couldn't see it, he could imagine it all too clearly.

Gaspard restrained his disgust and stayed still and silent. He twitched when a hand touched his, but it was only the little girl leaning against her dead brother's back, using her tiny body to further hide Gaspard from view.

The silence in the barn was broken by the slurping sound three stalls down as Big-ears lapped the blood pouring from the unconscious woman.

Gaspard's mind raced. *Where is Sophie? Is she well-hidden?* He sent up a prayer to God to keep her safe, not sure if God listened to the prayers of vampires, but hoping for divine providence if not for him, for her.

Big-ears stopped slurping and emitted a wholly unnecessary belch making Gaspard purse his lips in disgust even within the confines of his gruesome hiding place. The hinges creaked again, a few hulking steps, then a scrape as Big-ears considered the next stall. The next sound was a scratching noise, and Gaspard presumed that Big-ears had dragged the rake across the floor of the stall, searching for the missing vamps.

Gaspard's fangs descended to their full length as the stench of blood tickled his nose. He tried to hide this from the little girl, but she saw anyway and didn't flinch; just looked at him with old eyes and a mouth that had forgotten how to smile. Gaspard's belly clenched again, and a burning sensation rose through his chest and up his throat as his fury flared for the girl, her parents, and all the victims in the barn.

He decided to wait no longer. He tensed his muscles, ready to pounce.

"Hey! Who's this?" a voice across the room bellowed. "A lovely lady hidden in this refuse, looking like a meal on two pretty feet to me. How'd you get here, pigeon? You look like a vampire virgin, no bite marks on you anywhere... Ah!"

Gaspard leaped to his feet and pushed through the door in a millisecond, in time to see Sophie drag her hand across the vampire's face, something in her hand creating an enormous gash from his eye to his chin. The vampire tried to get the blood out of his eye but wasn't fast enough for Sophie, who had extracted a piece of rotting floorboard, held it aloft like a dagger, and slammed it into the vampire's chest, releasing a cloud of ash.

Gaspard's mouth hung open in amazement and delight, but this distraction was enough to let Big-ears capture Gaspard in a bear hug from behind. Gaspard pushed backward, destroying the door of the pen, and slammed the big vampire into the back wall, leaving a Big-ears-sized crack in it. The prisoners scurried out of their way, running into the middle of the barn, letting out a battle cry of the weary and worn, the hungry and hunted, the wail of people who had nothing to lose. One grabbed the rake, another the broom, and the others sought weapons where they could find them. Someone managed to create a flame out of old wood, and they lit the candles and created burning torches out of wood and straw. Sophie showed them the nail she'd torn from the floor and had effectively used to scratch the vampire's face. The children crawled on the floor finding more nails, sharp shards of wood, and stood by their parents.

Meanwhile, Gaspard battled Big-ears, stamping on the vampire's feet and head butting his nose. Big-ears released his grip, and Gaspard whirled around, caught a stake Sophie tossed in his direction, and ended it.

They had no more than that second as the four remaining vamps, including the reviled Christophe, charged in to see what was happening. The prisoners used their newfound weapons and their fury to attack the vamps as they entered.

A decrepit old man used whatever strength he had left to step forward holding a makeshift torch lit with the flame of righteous rage and shoved it directly into a vampire's chest. This vampire ran in a circle flapping his arms like a chicken with its head cut off before he collapsed on the ground and burned to dust. The old man dropped to the ground as well, dead with that one final act of defiance.

Gaspard sighted Christophe and shouted, "That one's mine!" Christophe turned to look at who was speaking and stopped dead in his tracks when he saw the unknown vampire. Gaspard's world tunneled down until all he could see was Christophe, who was still wearing the shirt with the boy's blood on it.

Gaspard charged forward, grabbed Christophe by the collar, and dragged the shocked vampire across the room until he lay, scratched and bleeding from the rough floor, in front of the boy's family and directly in front of the sister. Gaspard kicked Christophe in the belly and then on the side of the head.

"Take your revenge," he said to the family.

The mother looked at her husband and folded into his arms sobbing with pain and grief.

"Even now, we cannot," said the father.

"Why not?" asked Gaspard in disbelief.

"It is against Jewish law to take a human life."

"He's not a human! He's a vampire, and he tortured and killed your son!"

The man hung his head. "I do not want to become what they are."

A crack clipped the air, and Gaspard looked down in astonishment to see that the little girl had jumped with all her might onto Christophe's chest. She bounced again and again, using Christophe like a trampoline until the vamp's chest shattered and the vamp was true dead.

The little girl gazed at Gaspard, slowly grinned, and walked away on bloody feet.

9

"Gaspard! Watch out!"

Sophie's warning almost came too late. Gaspard had forgotten about the vampire in the hayloft and crashed to his knees when the vampire fell on his back.

No one turns my tactics against me, thought Gaspard. He motioned to the man holding the rake, who rushed forward and handed it to him. Gaspard took the handle, threw it over his shoulder, and used the rusted metal ends to scrape up the vamp's back. The vamp screamed and released Gaspard.

"That's it?" said Gaspard. "One scratch and you're screaming like a g..." Gaspard caught Sophie's eye, swallowed, and amended his sentence, finishing with "...like a *baby*."

"That hurt!" said the vamp.

"How long have you been a vampire?" Gaspard asked, hand on his hip, foot out in a relaxed "lord of the manor" fashion.

"Two days," the vamp.

Gaspard cursed. "Two days? Two days! What's your name?"

The vampire gulped. "Charles."

"How did you get involved in all of this?"

"They said I'd be strong," said the young vampire.

"Why did you want to be strong?"

"To protect my family."

Gaspard contemplated the vamp in front of him and decided. "I'm surprised you have this much control with only two days. It impresses me. It makes me think you have a chance at redeeming yourself. I'm going to make you a deal. Go to Paris and seek the Master of the City, Arnaud Bachelet, and tell him what has been going on here. Tell him Gaspard asked him to come with food and medicine."

"And if I don't?"

"I'll hunt you down to the ends of the Earth, yoke you by the neck to a horse, tie your feet to a tree trunk, and slap the horse on his butt. We'll call it treecapitation."

"Yes, I shall do as you ask. I swear." The vamp rose, unsteady on his feet with blood loss. He peeked out from behind his lashes, looked around at the captive families, and asked, "Can I have something to..."

"Eat? Surely you jest. Absolutely not. Go without or find an animal. It will do you good," replied Gaspard.

The vamp bowed his head and slipped into the night.

Without any guards, the prisoners gathered their dead, covering them with straw as best as possible. Many sank to their knees next to the corpses and rocked back and forth, praying. Some stared into space, listless and traumatized.

A giant shadow cast its darkness from the entrance, halting the gentle hum of parents consoling children and the rhythmic chanting of prayer. The shadow's voice boomed, "What. Is. This?" The sound echoed throughout the barn.

It was what Gaspard had expected. He turned to face the demon.

Schmidt's neck hung at an odd angle, his skin was gray, and at least two fingers appeared broken. The shadow behind him on the wall was shaped like a winged monkey with a tail twice as long as its body. The tail curled in and picked at the shadow's fangs, flicking whatever it removed to the side.

"Lord Vine, I presume."

"Yes, the original owner of the vessel is diminished. He will be gone soon." The demon wearing the Schmidt suit tried to straighten the head, but it flopped back down. "I will need a new body." Schmidt's eyes looked Gaspard up and down.

"Yours will do nicely," Vine said. "Why don't you invite me in to stay?"

"I don't like to share space," replied Gaspard.

"So don't," said Vine. "You can go, and I'll stay." The demon took two steps forward.

"You can't do that, demon," said Gaspard, taking small steps back. "You need a live host, and technically, I'm dead." Gaspard continued to back up, his brain forming and dismissing plans in seconds as he sought any way to defeat Vine. He heard scuffling behind him as the prisoners scooted back. Grasping for more time, he asked, "Why did Schmidt summon you?"

The demon stalked Gaspard, enjoying the hunt, and waved Schmidt's hand as if this detail was a trifle. "The Nazis sense the tide is turning. Hitler himself chose certain soldiers to be the recipients of a demon's grace."

The demon lunged and grabbed Gaspard by the left shoulder, pulling him straight up so that Gaspard was forced to stand on his tiptoes. "They were quite generous."

Choking, Gaspard gasped, "What sacrifice did you require?"

"The heart of an eight-year old boy." The demon ran a finger down Gaspard's right cheek.

Gaspard shuddered at the touch and struggled in the demon's grasp, pain lacing his upper back, shoulders, and calves.

"Why an eight-year-old?"

Schmidt's distorted mouth split into a revolting parody of a smile. "Because Schmidt had an eight-year-old son." Still holding Gaspard, the demon used Schmidt's left hand to cup the body's cockeyed, listing chin.

"You know, once my sister comes, I won't need a host at all."

"Why her?" Gaspard asked, sensing a presence behind him.

"She is equal to me in power. We are yin and yang, male and female. With both of us here, we will be able to hold our own bodies. Then we shall call our children."

"Your children? I thought you said you were brother and sister?" said Gaspard, feeling behind him for a weapon. He would take whatever he could find. A small hand slipped him a splinter of sharp wood.

"Does that really matter, little vampire? When a boy demon and a girl demon want to make a baby, they have a special hug..."

"Ewww. Just stop."

"I'm coming out now, little vampire. It's time to play." The demon opened Schmidt's mouth.

A black and red miasma spewed from the now lifeless void of Schmidt's maw and floated toward the center of the room. Gaspard took this moment to attack, flinging himself at the cloud and slashing his tiny stake at every mote. The motes landed on his hands and arms, stinging him like tiny wasps until they coalesced in a dense cloud and went for Gaspard's head.

"I need fire!" yelled Gaspard. Isobel snatched a burning torch out from a panicked adult's hand and darted to Gaspard, who grabbed the torch and yelled, "Run, Isobel! Run!" Gaspard waved the torch at and through the black and red murk, but to no avail. The cloud struck, pulsing like a beating heart, burning Gaspard's hair, fiery embers drifting to the floor. The pain rocketed through Gaspard as his entire face and skull were enveloped in the living evil of a demon's shade. Gaspard endured the stings, covered his face with his left hand, and closed his eyes, bringing the torch up so that it almost scorched his nose. The fire caught a few of the motes, and Gaspard felt the demon dust shudder in pain.

Gaspard squeezed his eyes shut as the motes attacked again. He knew better than to scream because he had to keep his mouth shut and nose blocked or the motes would have open access. He fell to the ground in a fetal position, hands over his face.

He'd forgotten his ears. Vine swam through Gaspard's ear canal into his nasal cavity, down his throat, and entered his bloodstream. Though Gaspard's blood did not pump as a human's, Vine could use the super-highway of arteries and veins to travel through Gaspard's body, burning him from the inside out, making him feel the literal fires of Hell on Earth.

It was as if someone had lit a firecracker inside Gaspard's body. He writhed in agony, screaming without being aware he was doing so until he could scream no more. Pain laced through his head as Vine slipped into Gaspard's brain and dove through every nook and thought, ravaging Gaspard's mind while killing brain cells, propelling Gaspard into a massive stroke.

Gaspard was paralyzed and helpless as Vine rummaged through his memories, flinging one aside and then another until he found what he wanted—the locked box.

Gaspard's mind recoiled at this invasion and fought to keep Vine from opening the box and releasing the memories. All souls keep an accounting of each pain and injury, every rent and tear, every grief and agony experienced during a mortal lifetime. Those experiences go into the box where mortals learn to live with them, but never forget.

In the boundary between life and death, each vampire is given a choice. Those who want to keep their souls must keep the box. They must live with the pain of those regrets and injuries for as many years as they live, adding to them as they continue to make mistakes. The resentments and hurts stay present and bleed for *eternity*. That is the cost of keeping one's soul.

Those who relinquish the pain, who choose to extinguish the agonies of mortal life, lose their souls in forfeit.

Vine extracted each painful memory, held it by the corners, and shook it out like laundry hung on a line. He examined each in detail, reminding Gaspard of all of it, all at once. Nothing was spared. Little hurts like burns and knife nicks. Big ones like his wife's and son's deaths. The loss of Henri. The scars on his neck and hands from being shackled to an ox in childhood when he was forced to lead the ox in proper rows while the ox tilled the soil. Gaspard now crumbled under the boy's fear of being trampled by the giant animal.

Everything from the time his sister stepped on his foot to the times when he turned his back on friends in need. The shame of words said in anger and the prayers said in grief. The memories of sickness and plague, of loss and loneliness, of inequality and prejudice, all were removed and revealed, and there was nothing Gaspard could do to stop it. Vine fingered each memory, fondling them as one would a beloved pet, holding every hurt up for minute examination, the only purpose to torment Gaspard's soul.

Though the men and women around him didn't know what was happening, they could sense the anguish, and they hid in terror. Sophie did try to come to Gaspard's aid, but the demon's miasma burned her if she got too close.

Inside his own consciousness, Gaspard battled for his sanity. Vine pushed Gaspard's nervous system to its limit and beyond, breaking it, inadvertently creating an opening for Gaspard to think again as the physical pain shut down. While Vine continued to play with Gaspard's errors and mistakes, juggling them like bowling pins, Gaspard ignored him. *There is nothing new to me there,* he thought. *I already know each and every one of those memories. They are mine, a part of me. I'm not proud of them, but I do own them.*

Gaspard pulled away from Vine's fun and turned his thoughts to the families on the trains, to the Nazis in the streets, to Arnaud's lecture, to Sophie and Gigi, and only one thing remained: a burning desire to see this demon destroyed for its role in creating the hate-filled world in which Gaspard now lived.

Gaspard settled on what Vine hated most. Gaspard thought of love, his long-lost sister's smile, his parents who struggled to keep them alive and gave hugs that melted discomfort, the rolling hills and vineyards of Burgundy lit by the moon, the warmth of the sun, and the feel of a friend's hand on his shoulder from his mortal years. He thought of Sophie and her courage and spirit. He thought of Gigi's love for Sophie, a puppy's nose against his hand, the taste of finely spun sugar, and the richness of chocolate melting on his tongue. He thought of how even now in the pit of darkness, parents put their children's lives before theirs. He thought of sacrifice and honor and how it all meant something, even as he lay there being ravaged by a duke of Hell, certain he was headed for a true death.

Vine hated those emotions and broke through to show Gaspard war, disease, hunger, and agony. He gave him visions of the racks in Hell, the burning lava pits, the pitiless cold, and the absolute silence, all created to punish the wicked. He laughed when Gaspard winced and whispered in Gaspard's mind, "This is what awaits you, vampire."

Gaspard's thoughts raced as he struggled to find the good, to find the way to weaken his enemy. His soul shrunk in on itself, deflating like a balloon at the after party, shrinking under the pressure. He prayed once more for help.

The answer came in a flash of white Light, a living, breathing Light that streamed through the open doorway, its brilliance flooding the barn and soaking into the caverns of Gaspard's soul where Vine sought to defeat him.

Vine cowered at the Light's touch, and the humans covered their eyes in awe.

Gaspard was exultant. *That's right, Vine. If there is a Hell, there is a Heaven, and now I know that despite being a vampire, Heaven is open to me.* "Thank you, Vine," he whispered. "You have given me the answer I most wanted."

Vine spit acid flame in Gaspard's mind and withdrew. Gaspard regained control of his body as the Light flew through his bloodstream healing what was destroyed. Gaspard opened his eyes with a small smile.

Sophie grabbed him in both arms. "Gaspard! Gaspard, are you still alive? I thought we had lost you."

Gaspard gazed at her. "*We* had lost me, or, *you* had lost me?"

Sophie blushed. "Both."

Gaspard's smile widened and then disappeared as he saw the demon miasma, the demon dust that was the essence of Vine, dive for Sophie's head like a swarm of bees.

Isobel's father shot out of his hiding spot and threw his body to intercept. Vine crashed into him, infecting Isobel's father instead of Sophie. Vine struggled with the man's enduring spirit, a spirit newly strengthened by his certainty of what was to come, having seen the proof with his own eyes. The man gasped one last sentence, "Burn me!" and returned to the battle within, holding Vine tight.

"NO!" screamed his wife, running forward, but Isobel held her back, watching with steady eyes, and nodded to Gaspard.

Gaspard made one of the hardest decisions of his life. He motioned for Sophie to get a torch, and while she was doing so, he reached down and twisted the man's neck in one motion, killing him instantly to prevent the good man from feeling more pain. He seized the torch Sophie provided with a snap of his hand. He set the man's body on fire, starting with the head, before Vine could escape.

The head charred fast, leaving Vine no exit. The demon's dust filtered through the floor and disappeared while the man's soul lifted to the Light.

10

Gaspard and Sophie collapsed to the ground as did the other men and women around them, some hugging their emaciated children, others holding bodies of those who hadn't made it, either through the battle or before, dying of mistreatment, malnutrition, and despair. Some were silent, wrapping their minds around the glimpse of the Divine. One man bent his head and prayed, his mouth moving in silent words of thanks.

Isobel held her mother's hand while her mother sobbed. Isobel herself was stoic and dry-eyed. The little girl was little in age only. Her eyes were ancient, and Gaspard knew there had been irrevocable damage. He tried to hug her, but she pushed him off, refusing the embrace.

"Isobel."

Isobel turned her wide eyes to him. He tried to read them, to get a glimpse of what she was thinking, but her eyes were emotionless, blank.

"Some people are bad, and some are good, right?" Gaspard said. Isobel nodded.

"Your parents and brother were some of the good guys. Your dad was a hero."

Isobel's only sign that she heard was a blink of those empty, old eyes.

"Some vampires are good and some are bad, too. It isn't about whether we have fangs or not, or are Jewish or not; it is what we do with our lives that matters. Does that make sense?"

Isobel spoke, sounding decades older than she was, and what she said made his stomach curdle. "It makes sense, vampire, but you are wrong. How people perceive you, the stories they tell about you, what they tell their children, what they tell each other—that's what matters. That's what becomes reality."

"What stories are they going to tell about you, Isobel?"

"That I killed them all."

Isobel led her mother by the hand to an empty spot in the barn, sat her down, and petted her mother's hair. Gaspard wasn't sure if her mother noticed. He bit his lip to contain his sorrow for the life that Isobel could have had and what kind of monster she might become.

With a heavy heart, he allowed himself to be distracted by Sophie, who, ever practical, was organizing the former blood-slaves and planning immediate next steps. "Gaspard, we need to get these people to the main house. It is probably heated and may have food and blankets. They're cold and starving; some are so ill I don't if they can survive another night."

Gaspard said, "You're right, but let me go check it out first. I'll wave to you if it is all clear."

"And if it isn't all clear?" Sophie asked.

"If I don't come back in fifteen minutes, assume there is a serious problem and hunker down in the barn."

"You'd better come back. Be careful."

Gaspard stepped out into the snow, noticing that the flurries had died down, and sprinted to the house despite his fatigue.

The house was well lit, and a strong fire burned in the two fireplaces —one in the main room and the other in the connected dining room. Gaspard fed the fires more wood and stoked their flames before walking into the kitchen. The kitchen was large and well-stocked with pots and pans, but the only food Gaspard found was stale bread, until he opened a small pantry. The pantry was stocked with tinned goods, including fruit, vegetables, and condensed milk. A quick examination of the rest of the house revealed pillows, sheets, and blankets as well as some first aid supplies. The house had a trickle of running water, but Gaspard knew it wouldn't be enough and was glad when he located some wooden buckets so they could melt snow.

He went back outside and beckoned to Sophie, whose face lost its tension as soon as he appeared. She led the long line of prisoners inside. Once inside, Gaspard didn't do a thing and felt rather useless. Sophie and the remaining families divvied up chores, taking care of the children first, feeding them what they could, some of them so weak they almost couldn't chew and swallow.

They pulled in fresh snow for washing and drinking, and finally, every person fell into a deep sleep somewhere in the house. Sophie tended to the more severely wounded, but no matter her ministrations, three more people died within a few hours.

"Gaspard."

Sophie beckoned him from across the room.

"If you give some of these injured people a sip or two of your blood, would it save them?"

"I don't know, but right now I don't have any to spare." He grasped the back of a chair to keep from falling. The world was spinning, and day was coming.

"Sophie, my love. Day approaches, and I haven't had anything to eat for a while."

Sophie peered out the window and saw the light rising over the horizon. "Drink from me, Gaspard," she urged.

"No! I've done that once already, and I almost killed you. I can't do that again."

"We'll give you a little," came a voice.

A woman spoke from behind Gaspard, holding out her wrist. Three other women stood behind her as well.

"We are some of the newer ones here and haven't been as drained as the others. Take a little from each of us..."

"And me!" said Sophie.

The woman gave a wan smile. "And your lady. Will that get you through the day?"

Gaspard had no choice. His vision tunneled down to a single black spot, and he wobbled on his feet. He nodded a short assent.

Sophie was first. Gaspard sank his teeth into her wrist and sucked in a few sips, but her taste was so exquisite he had to fight hard to hold back.

"Take what you need," said Sophie, caressing the back of his head, but remembering his prior mistake, Gaspard lifted his mouth from her wrist and gave her a short bow, stopping way short of what he would have wanted. The other three women presented themselves one at a time, and he took care with all of them. He was about to hit the floor unconscious when the women caught him and dragged him into an inside closet that they buffeted with blankets stuffed into the cracks of the doors, ensuring that he wouldn't be touched by the dawn.

11

Flickers of starlight floated above the horizon, pushing the sun down until its next turn, the moon shining a light into the darkness, reminding the hodge-podge of refugees, vampire, and cook that there was more to Heaven and Earth than they could see.

Gaspard woke and poked his head out of the closet, noting that several more bodies were wrapped in sheets. These were the poor human beings who were so destroyed they couldn't make it one more day, their bodies sputtering their last breaths even as food and water arrived.

Too much damage, too much time. Gaspard bent to lay his hands on a small sheet-wrapped bundle that lay on its side.

He pointed to a man who seemed to be the one organizing the dead. "Sir, we need to take all of the bodies out to the barn. They can't stay here."

The man nodded. "Yes, we agree, but there are so few of us that have the strength."

"I'll help," Gaspard offered, grabbing hold of one body, lifting it over his shoulder. The perfume of death filled his nostrils, reminding him of mass cattle deaths from disease or the time when a sleeping sickness came through his village. The smell stuck to his clothes, already dirty from the battle the night before, and Gaspard wished for new ones.

Gaspard trudged to the barn—one step, two steps, three—and didn't stop until he reached the entrance where he placed the first body. Flies buzzed around the faces of the dead despite the freezing temperatures, and a putrid smell of rot permeated the broken-down barn.

One-by-one, Gaspard brought the dead to the barn, stacking them like hardwood. He emptied his mind of all thoughts, thinking only of Sophie and the other pleasures of life. Every time his brain tried to focus on what he was doing, he turned his mind away. Eventually, all the dead were in the barn, and the Jewish prisoners held a meeting. Jewish traditions demanded that the dead be buried, sent back to the earth, but the ground was frozen, and allowing human remains to rot was dangerous. To protect the lives of those still living, they had to let go of the dead.

The Jews, no matter how weakened or cold, stood in front of the barn and said a traditional prayer for the deceased while Gaspard set the building on fire. All the former prisoners stood with freezing feet, tears streaming down their cadaverous faces as they watched their friends and loved ones turn to cinders. Gaspard bowed his head, held tight to Sophie's hand, and sent a prayer to whatever being had helped him drive out the demon. *Please*, he thought, *please*. He didn't even know what that meant, but it was the best his brain could come up with. He figured a deity could understand.

Gaspard supported a woman back into the house while the others made their way at their own speed. It was then that he heard the sound he'd been waiting for.

Military-grade trucks barreled down the snow toward them. The former prisoners scrambled for cover, crawling if necessary to get in the house. Gaspard held his ground.

The first truck came to a snow-spraying stop in front of him, and knowing who it was, Gaspard tensed, crouching slightly, putting energy into his leg muscles, back tight, ready to vault into action if needed. Even when Arnaud exited the truck and walked toward him, Gaspard didn't relax.

"You summoned me, Gaspard?" said Arnaud, his voice like sandpaper.

Gaspard considered the Master's tone of voice.

"Not summoned, Arnaud. Respectfully requested your help."

Arnaud swept his arm out to the right. "And we have come. Allow us safe passage and we will distribute blankets, food, and water. We have medicines as well."

"No offense, Arnaud, but ten of your own vampires were involved in this horrid little show, so I'd like to examine the trucks myself."

Arnaud's white skin stretched until it was bordering on translucent, but, like the Master he was, he controlled his anger and replied, "By all means. But, Gaspard, I give you my word."

Gaspard gave a curt nod of acknowledgement but walked to the trucks and peeked inside for himself. He didn't smell anything unusual and didn't want to hold up the aid.

"Arnaud, we promise you and your team safe passage and bid you welcome." Gaspard walked several steps closer, his frustration with the Paris Master mounting even though Arnaud had showed up with assistance. "But if any of your vampires try to take a bite of one of these people, I will end it, and I do mean end it."

Arnaud placed his hands on his hips and glared at Gaspard. "End it? Is that what you did to the nine other new vampires? I understand from the fledgling you sent to me that none of the other fledglings are left!"

"No, none of them are left, Arnaud! Thanks to your insistence on not pushing the Nazis out of Paris, they got a foothold here, as I warned you. Ten of your vampires, vampires that should have been under your control, not only kept Jews as blood slaves, but they also got themselves enslaved to a demon!"

Arnaud stepped back a little. "What do you mean?"

"The oh-so-lovely Commandant Schmidt gave his body over to a demon named Vine. This demon slowly took over Schmidt's body and mind, bringing his special kind of punishment and chaos to our world. If you had been paying attention, you would have known that."

Arnaud leaned in to Gaspard's space so their faces were only inches apart. "Don't you lecture me, Gaspard! I have held Paris for over one hundred years, surviving plague and war and betrayal from my own kind. I have survived and maintained balance through monarchy and despotism. You have no idea what it takes to rule a city."

Gaspard's throat was so tight he spat in Arnaud's face. "I know that in this case, you let your city down."

"I did not."

"You did. You had a demon in your midst, Arnaud. A demon. Don't tell me that doesn't embarrass you just a little bit. It has to rankle."

Arnaud turned abruptly to the right, exposing his profile, revealing a thin scar Gaspard had not detected before. It ran from Arnaud's ear down his jawline ending with a little divot at the chin. Gaspard could only speculate as to what, or who, had managed to injure Arnaud badly enough to leave such a mark. He hoped he never met him.

Gaspard noticed Arnaud's long white fingers has sprouted talons, a sign that his temper was on the rise. Gaspard took a step back and then a second, wondering if he had taken things too far. Arnaud was a good guy who had made a bad judgment call. *He is right*, thought Gaspard. *I don't know what it is like to hold a city for over a century, and not just any city. Paris. Arnaud has held Paris.*

Arnaud straightened his shoulders and inclined his head a minute amount. "In point of fact, the presence of a demon in my domain does cause me much discomfiture. But it doesn't change the fact that you went behind my back and killed nine fledglings. I admit that you appear to have removed a demon, and for that service, I will not kill you now. One step in the wrong direction, however, and I promise I will destroy you and fling your ashes into the ocean without a moment's angst."

Gaspard was silent for a moment.

"Fair," he replied. "Let's get these supplies inside."

12

Gaspard helped the last prisoner onto a truck and held Sophie's hand as they watched Arnaud and his men move the former blood-slaves to a sanctuary farther south. The wagon train moved under the cover of darkness to minimize the chance of being caught by Germans, but with Arnaud there, Gaspard knew the people were safe. Several individuals on the edge of death had survived another day, which Gaspard took as a positive sign.

"Do you know where they are going?" asked Sophie.

"No, I don't, and it is safer that way," Gaspard replied.

"Do you think they will ever get their lives back again? Will this madness end now that the demon is gone?"

"According to Vine, there are other demons out there." Gaspard sighed. "I don't know. He was only one form of evil. The Nazis are evil unto themselves. The demons walked into a welcome and ready embrace. It makes me wonder if there are other forces at work here."

"More than demons?" Sophie asked.

"Possibly. Probably. I don't know. I do know that good and evil sparred in that barn and good came out on top. I have to cling to that."

"They used your body as their boxing ring," Sophie said. "I didn't think you would survive."

"I didn't either."

"We must get back and check on Gigi," Sophie said, turning her face up to his. "I'm sure she is worried out of her mind."

"I asked Arnaud to get a message to her."

"You did?" Sophie's face lit up. "That was so thoughtful."

"Yes, but I was being selfish. I wanted to keep you here one more night," Gaspard said, "For this..."

Gaspard bent his head down and placed his lips on Sophie's. He'd meant it to be a soft kiss, but the one touch flared his desire to life. He pulled her close, pressing his body against hers, relishing how her body responded to his touch.

They parted for enough time to get back inside the farmhouse. They tore each other's clothes off and lay on the rug in front of the fireplace, hands roving, mouths exploring. He yearned to know her body and soul. To learn what she liked and what she hated. Did she like to dance? What flowers would make her smile? What could he do to stay close to her and make her laugh every day?

He loved.

The fact that he loved astounded him. He'd been alive more than two hundred years and had never experienced this depth of emotion before. He thought he'd loved, but he now realized he'd experienced the most abstract notion of love. What he felt for Sophie dwarfed those intimacies by magnitudes. The blood sharing started this flame, but something else fanned it, and at that moment, he didn't care how or why it happened. He was simply grateful that it had.

He caressed her, starting with the soft skin on the side of her breast, easing down to the curve of her waist, ending with feather strokes on her hip. He slipped his hand around her, pulling her up by her waist to meet him even higher, even closer. It didn't seem close enough. He placed her down on the rug and followed the same path with his other hand, watching her face as he did so.

Her eyes were closed, one arm out to the side, the other gripping his shoulder. Her lips parted slightly, her breaths coming faster. He leaned in and kissed her again, releasing the kiss to place his thumb to his fang, breaking the skin. He pressed the thumb to her lips, thrilled when she sucked the drop of blood, almost sending him over the edge right then. She licked the wound as he would lick a bite.

He slid down to her breasts, wondering if he could ever get enough of them. They were beautiful and fit in his mouth and hands as if made for him and him alone. He sucked on her nipples and could feel the tightening in her thighs with each twirl of his tongue.

"Will you drink, Gaspard?" she asked, opening her eyes to stare into his.

"If you will allow me, my love, yes, that would be my greatest honor."

She lifted both hands to his face. "Drink, my dearest. Drink. Make me feel your joy both ways."

Gaspard sucked in a breath at hearing those words, and thoughts fled as his body took over and the physical want became too great. He slipped inside in one thrust, then pulled back and took it slower, going inch by inch. He leaned his body in to make sure he hit that sweet spot, and knew he'd been successful by her groan of pleasure. He tried to keep it slow, but it was impossible. She bent her legs around his thighs, pressing him closer, urging him deeper, and he obliged, moving with abandon, and at the exact point of release, he bit, joining himself to her at the neck and groin, the release racing like electricity to and from both ends of his body, giving him the longest orgasm he'd ever experienced. Sophie's equaled his as she came not once, but twice, as he pulsed inside her.

Spent, laying on the rug side-by-side, Sophie turned her head to grin at him. "I'm going to get cleaned up and then eat. Or maybe eat and clean up. I'm starving."

"And then?" Gaspard asked.

She crept her fingers up his thigh. "We do that again."

"I love this plan."

"There is something I'd like to try. Something I wondered..." she murmured. She blushed and averted her eyes. Gaspard turned her face back to his.

"Never hide your face from me, Sophie. What is it you desire?"

She leaned close to his ear and, on a whisper of breath, said, "I want you to bite me—down there. Have you ever done that before?"

His eyes were wide, and he developed an erection at the sheer thought. "No, my love. I have not, but I exist to serve, Mademoiselle. Your wishes are my command."

She giggled and ran naked into the kitchen to get enough nourishment to last the entire night.

13

When the first streaks of dawn appeared in the sky, Sophie woke to find Gaspard easing himself into the closet. She rose to give him a kiss and cover the cracks with blankets.

"I will not be able to protect you, *ma chérie*. If anyone comes during the day, you must run. Leave me here."

"Shhh... no one is going to come. You worry too much. I'll get things ready for our return home, and we'll leave together tonight."

"Don't work too hard. Save your strength. Take a nap," Gaspard said, fiddling with her hair until she noticed a faint whiff of smoke.

"Gaspard! You're burning! Get inside." Sophie jostled him into the closet and draped the blankets.

Sophie turned from the closet to survey the scene around her. The fire had died, and the room smelled stale and dank, an odor leftover from the crush of bodies before. Detritus lay everywhere, some from the medical supplies and food provided to the former blood-slaves, some from the demon and its followers. The main room had tall walls and an arched ceiling with rich merlot-colored drapes, dotted with an insignia in gold. The couch and loveseat, now pushed to the side, matched the drapes and blended well with the elegant fleur-de-lis wallpaper. *Someone*, Sophie thought, *once loved this house.*

A cabinet stood on one wall, its top shelf now crooked. She examined the wood and noticed rings stained into the shelf and guessed they were from crockery that once decorated it. A piano perched in the corner. Sophie pressed a key and winced at the sour note.

The brick fireplace was built into the wall, guarded by a wrought-iron screen to keep the embers contained. The luxurious bear rug, on which she'd slept, lay on the ground in front. She could imagine the lord and lady of the house making love there, just as she and Gaspard had done, whispering to each other after the children had gone to bed.

She turned to the hallway and climbed the long staircase to survey the bedrooms upstairs. One bedroom must have been home to two children, girls she guessed by the pale peach walls. The beds were twin size, and she could imagine the handmade quilts and soft linens once tucked into their corners. A ragged stuffed bear still sat on a tiny rocking chair near the closet. The closet was empty, as were the dresser drawers. A deep brown water circle on the top of the dresser still held a soft scent and hinted at a long-lost perfume bottle. She stepped on a small throw rug, and a few blue beads rolled off onto the wooden floor. Nothing of value was left.

Sophie circled the upstairs, entering each room, studying the master bedroom as if she could see the images of the man and woman who used to live there. Theirs was a private room, a haven at one time. Husband and wife each had separate closets, and the man had a tall bureau, while the woman had a short horizontal dresser with a mirror. The master bathroom had a large tub and, if she closed her eyes, she could imagine warm water and soft bubbles and how lovely it would be to have that luxury. The sink was cracked and in pieces, but the toilet flushed, as did the one next to the laundry downstairs, something that they had discovered yesterday to everyone's great relief.

The snow insulated the house, muffling outside noises, allowing her to hear the voice of the building that was once a family's home. The voice spoke of faint chamber music, squealing children sliding down the staircase on silver serving platters, honks from geese flying south, and a bustling kitchen. If she stood still, she could hear it, but that joyous voice was fading, overwhelmed by the stomp of boots and the horns of war.

She rested her back to the wall of the hallway, closed her eyes, and listened to the house's story.

Creak.

Sophie snapped awake. *Maybe I imagined it?*

Squeeeeak. The eerie sound of old hinges opening.

Where is it coming from?

Scratching, followed by the echo of breathing as someone entered the house.

Downstairs! Gaspard!

Sophie grabbed a broken lamp that lay on its side on the dresser and held it at the ready, prepared to swing at the first head she saw. She balanced on the balls of her feet and descended one step at a time, her heart beating like a hummingbird's, sweat gathering at her brow.

She reached the bottom of the stairs, crossed the hall, and pressed her back flat against the wall.

A tinny sound followed by streaming water. *Someone was putting on a kettle?*

Sophie ducked and flipped around the corner, holding the lamp high and saw…no one. She deposited the lamp on the floor, plucked up the fireplace poker, and crawled on hands and knees to the kitchen door. She pulled herself up, back again to the door, and let out a blood curdling cry as she rushed into the kitchen.

"Ahhhhhhhhhh!" screamed the little man, holding his hands up to protect his face. "Sophie! It's me!"

Sophie rubbed her eyes. "Vachel?"

"*Oui. Oui!* Your aunt told me where you were. Some vampire stopped by and told her everything. I came to help you get back. Look," he said, thrusting a brown bag into her hands, "I brought cookies. I made them with real butter. Can you believe it? Those Germans got their hands on real butter."

Sophie cocked her head to the side and examined Vachel from the corner of her eye. "What's the trick, Vachel?"

The portly pub owner clasped his hands to his chest. "You wound me! I am here to help. I brought a car. Why do you doubt me? Did I not provide food and bandages the night you were injured?"

"You did."

Vachel placed both fists on his hips and turned to face her, his belly thrusting forward. "I want my cook back. My business has gone to shit since you left."

"It's only been a couple of days."

Vachel shook his finger at her. "And they have noticed! No one makes cassoulet like you do."

"I'm having trouble believing this, Vachel."

Vachel deflated, his shoulders down, and he looked at the floor. He shuffled along the few feet that lay between them, and when he looked up, she was shocked to find that his eyes were bright with tears. He took her hands in his. "Sophie, they *notice* that you are gone. They *noticed.* They also noticed that their Commandant is *missing*. They are putting two and two together, Sophie, and it isn't looking good for you. I came to warn you. I can get you out of here. You aren't safe."

Sophie couldn't have been more dumbfounded than if Vachel had sprouted wings. Her go-along, get-along, what-can-you-do boss was *worried* about her.

"Did you get hit on the head?" she teased.

"Sophie. This isn't funny." Vachel snapped his words, angry for the first time since she'd known him. He marched to the boiling kettle and made a mug of tea, something else he'd brought with him, and attacked a cookie. Then another.

Sophie's stomach sank as she realized he was serious. She covered her face with her hands, embarrassed that she'd underestimated him.

"I'm sorry," she said, sliding onto a stool near him. She placed her right hand on his forearm. He didn't look at her. She used her left hand to choose a cookie and took a bite. The light butter cookie melted in her mouth bringing back memories from before the war. She closed her eyes in bliss.

"Oh, Vachel. These are delicious!"

The little man smiled. "I made five dozen. These are all that are left."

"Can I have another?" Sophie asked, fingers tip-toeing toward the bag.

"You can have all of them, but you must eat them in the car."

"I can't leave Gaspard," Sophie said.

"That maniac vampire is here?"

"Where else would he be?"

"I thought he'd have left with other vampires," said Vachel.

"And left me by myself? Don't be silly."

"And left you by yourself?" Vachel eyes bore into hers, then raked her body, noticing her healthy glow and then the bite mark on her neck. He blanched at the sight, clapping his temples. "Oh, Sophie. Tell me it isn't so."

Sophie rubbed her temples. "He's a great guy..."

"Who *eats* people!"

"He doesn't eat people. He drinks their blood. There's a big difference."

Vachel tore at his hair and paced the kitchen. "Sophie. Be reasonable. You can't be in love with a blood-sucking vampire!"

Sophie popped off the stool and got in his face. "And why not? Why can't I take happiness where I find it?"

"*Mon Dieu*! Sophie, he's going to want to make you like he is. He's going to turn you into a vampire, and then I'm going to lose you forever!"

Sophie closed her eyes, took a breath, and opened them again, bringing both hands up to cup Vachel's face. "I'm not turning into a vampire, Vachel, and you aren't losing me." She leaned in and kissed the tip of his nose, making him blush to his ears.

Sophie noticed the fading light in the kitchen and ran to the closet in the main room. She opened the door and Gaspard fell out, dead weight, like a corpse in a morgue.

14

"I think I brought him out too soon," Sophie said, covering Gaspard with one of the blankets to make sure he didn't burn in any remaining light.

Vachel tapped his foot. "Yeah, he isn't done yet, like a pie in the oven. Leave him here, and let's get moving."

"I can't, Vachel," she said, holding Gaspard's head in her lap.

"Yes, Sophie, you can. He's tough. He'll survive, but you are only human."

Sophie repositioned Gaspard's head on the ground and stood to face Vachel.

"And where am I supposed to go? You said they noticed that the Commandant is gone. Do you think they are going to leave me alone, ignore what happened?"

"When your aunt told me about the demon, something that other vampire explained to her, his degradation in his behavior finally made sense, but the soldiers have no knowledge about the demon. They can't prove anything, Sophie. Come back and let things return to normal."

"When has proof ever made a difference to a Nazi? And you know as well as I do, Vachel, there is no normal left in the world."

Vachel rubbed his cheeks with his hands and took a deep breath.

"Sophie, your aunt agrees. You are to come with me this minute. We have no time to argue."

"Stop ordering me around, Vachel. You don't own me."

"I'm your employer, I might remind you, and in these times, it is hard to find a good job. You may want to remember that."

"He's right."

Sophie and Vachel turned to look at Gaspard as he came to life, stood, and dusted off his clothes.

"Were there any pants or shirts left upstairs, Sophie?" he asked.

"Unfortunately, no. How are you feeling?"

"Confused. Why is Vachel here?"

"Your vampire friend told my aunt everything that happened. Vachel came to bring me home."

Gaspard rolled his neck, wincing at the pop. He considered Vachel.

"I'm impressed. Didn't think you'd have the... what's the slang? Didn't think you'd have the stones to do it."

"I need my cook back, and I'm not a complete asshole."

"No. No, you are not." Gaspard stepped toward Vachel and offered his hand. "Coming here was very brave, and I thank you."

Vachel took the hand, shook, and wiped his hand on his pants. "Yeah, well, it's Sophie."

Gaspard nodded. "Exactly. It's our Sophie."

Lightening flashed in Vachel's eyes. "No, vampire. She's *my* Sophie. She can never be yours."

Sophie pushed between them. "First, as I have already said, I don't *belong* to anyone. Second, I decide who I'm with, and I'm with Gaspard."

Vachel proffered both his arms, straining to reach Sophie with his words, pleading for her to understand. "That can't be," he whispered. "With him, you have no life. This war will end, and what will you have to show for it? A life lived at night, no children, no friends." He turned to Gaspard.

"Gaspard, you said you owed me a favor. This is what I ask, that you release her from this fairytale she's concocted in her head. Convince her that she'll be better off with me."

"He's telling the truth, Sophie," said Gaspard. "It is a lonely life. Maybe I'm being selfish, wanting to keep you by my side."

Sophie shook her head. "I can't change my heart."

Vachel stepped two steps closer to her and with a tenderness no one would have guessed he had, held her hands and looked in her eyes.

"Sophie, I *love* you."

Sophie didn't know what to say, so she said nothing. She pressed her lips together, staring at the ground, both stunned by Vachel's pronouncement and dismayed that she had to hurt him.

"And I will always hold you in my heart, Vachel."

"But you do not love me." Vachel's words were tinged by bitterness, and he dropped her hands.

Sophie touched his shoulder, wanting to make it better, hating that she'd injured him so deeply. "I am so sorry, Vachel. You are a good man, braver than I knew. I see you in a whole new light now, and I would like us to stay friends."

Vachel rocked back, struck by her words. "Stay friends, Sophie? Stay friends? When you choose Gaspard and a life of darkness over me, when I have taken care of you as best I could, and offer you protection and pledge my undying love?" He snorted. "Undying was a poor choice of words."

"I do choose Gaspard," Sophie said, as quietly as she could, holding her hands out in supplication, hoping he would forgive her.

Vachel held his stomach like he'd been punched in the gut, breath labored. He turned his back to Gaspard and Sophie and walked to the kitchen, coming out mere moments later holding his coat.

His face was stone, all the softness gone. Whatever love he'd once held, it was extinguished. The sight broke Gaspard's heart, and he closed his eyes against the pain. Sophie stepped toward Vachel, arms out, pleading. "Vachel, don't be like this, please. It hurts me to see you this way, so hard and unforgiving. Where's the Vachel who came through that door with cookies and tea?"

"He's gone, Sophie. You killed him." Vachel turned and walked out the door, closing it behind him with a soft click. Gaspard and Sophie heard the car start and listened as it drove away, neither saying a word.

When they couldn't hear the car any longer, Gaspard enveloped Sophie in his arms and held her as she cried.

15

They were still holding each other tight when they heard the plane.

"That's a bomber!" Sophie said, eyes wide in alarm.

"Stay here!" Gaspard ordered, and he ran outside. It was full night, but Gaspard's vampire sight made it possible for him to see the planes, a full squadron he guessed. He rushed back in.

"It's the Allies. They're doing bombing runs. We must get to safety. I'm sure this farmhouse has a cellar. We need to find it."

Gaspard pulled Sophie's arms and together they ran around the house searching for the entrance to the cellar they assumed was there. They finally found it under the stairs, a small door, but big enough for them to crawl through. Freezing air blew up toward them when they opened the door. It was a root cellar, which meant it was nothing more than a large hole in the ground.

"Gaspard, it's very cold," Sophie said, looking up at the ceiling like she could see the planes herself.

"Wait a moment," Gaspard said, and sprinted to the main room where he grabbed blankets and the bear rug. "Get down there, Sophie. I'll push these down after you."

Another plane swooped over them, engines growling. That was all the encouragement Sophie needed. She crouched and peered into the cold, dark space. "Good news. There's a ladder."

She turned onto her stomach and squirmed down until her feet hit the first step. She descended one step at a time, but Gaspard wasn't fooled into thinking she was calm. He heard her breath coming out in ragged waves and could hear the pitter patter of her heartbeat.

Sophie got to the bottom and yelled up, "Throw down the blankets!" Gaspard shoved one in and then another, the bear rug going last. Then he copied Sophie's technique and climbed down the ladder himself, pulling the door closed after him.

He'd been so worried about the cold that he'd forgotten about the darkness. It was pitch black, and though Gaspard could see fine, Sophie was blind. Her breath ceased being ragged and advanced straight to panic, claustrophobia setting in.

"Gaspard?"

"Shhhh. I'm here, my love. Hold onto me." Gaspard wrapped a blanket around her, placed the bear rug on the ground, and threw the second blanket around them both.

They waited. And waited.

"Perhaps it is safe?" Sophie asked. "There haven't been any bombs. Maybe we were wrong?"

Her question hovered in the darkness for a millisecond, and then giant pops resounded through the night. The pops got louder as the planes bombed nearer their position until they were full-on booms.

A boom resonated above their heads.

Another.

The ground quaked, and dirt shook free of the walls.

Another boom, louder than the previous ones. The sound reverberated in their ears and Gaspard knew the next one would be...

BAM!

The cellar vibrated with the energy flowing through the ground. Rocks fell on their heads and loosened dirt fell in chunks around them, hitting the floor and spraying up a fine dust. Sophie screamed, and when she breathed back in, she coughed hard as the soil entered her nose and mouth.

She didn't have time to recover. The next bomb landed directly on the farmhouse property, close to where the barn's ruins lay. The farmhouse rattled on its foundation, and they could hear the slide and crash of furniture upstairs. The cellar collapsed on one side, forcing Gaspard and Sophie to scramble away. As the last shockwave rolled over them, a huge cracking noise rebounded through the air as two big tree branches fell on the house, one thrusting straight through to the cellar.

The whining of the plane grew fainter and then silent as the plane flew into the distance, back to wherever it had come from. Gaspard released Sophie from his embrace, and they both sat back with their backs to the remaining dirt wall.

"Do you think it is over?" Sophie asked, working hard to control her trembling.

"I don't know. Let's stay here another minute."

Another plane zipped over their heads, and they braced for the explosion, but nothing happened.

"Surveillance plane maybe," Gaspard said. "Doesn't sound like a bomber now that I listen to it."

"I'm going up," Sophie announced. "I can't stay down here anymore."

"Sophie, no. The surveillance plane could have dropped paratroopers. We need to wait a little longer to be sure."

Sophie crawled on her hands and knees until she found the ladder, which, mercifully, was still intact. "I can't, Gaspard. It's a tomb down here. I've got to get out."

"Okay, Sophie, but let me go first… Sophie!"

Sophie rushed up the ladder leaving Gaspard scrambling to follow. He grabbed the blankets and rug and shoved those through the opening one by one and then, finally, squeezed his body through the door, which was smaller and compressed from the weight of the tree. It took him several minutes to struggle through.

He stared dumbfounded at the remains of the house. The stairs were partially collapsed, and now Gaspard could see the rest of the giant oak that had fallen and come so close to killing them. Soot and grime covered what remained of the center wall, and when he managed to clamber over the chunks of plaster and look toward the main room, he saw the sky. The roof and walls were decimated. Trees from the surrounding forest were either gone or on fire.

"Sophie! Where are you?" he shouted into the night. It was almost dawn, and though he could feel the sun, it was so cold there was no way

Sophie would be able to survive in these temperatures without warm clothing. He darted this way and that, his heart in his throat, his brain screaming that danger was here.

He found her only a few yards from the house.

She was standing still in front of a soldier, an Allied paratrooper by the looks of him, her hands up. The soldier was speaking English with a smattering of French. He looked like he was eighteen and as frightened as she was. Sophie was shaking hard, both from fear and cold but bravely stood tall telling the soldier that she was no danger to him. Gaspard heard her voice on the wind and watched as she moved her arms in a gesture of peace. She took one step...

Gaspard's world slowed, and no matter how he tried, he couldn't move fast enough. The frightened soldier shot her in the stomach. Sophie collapsed to the ground, her blood staining the snow in a wide pool of dark red.

"Noooooooooo!" Gaspard ran to Sophie's body, throwing himself toward her still form, hoping against hope that this nightmare wasn't real.

A bullet ripped through his body, knocking him to the ground, and a second hit his calf. He tried to crawl to her, but the sun peeked over the horizon, blistering his skin, setting his clothes ablaze. Gaspard gritted his teeth against the pain, but when the cascading blood flowing from his wounds boiled, burbling up to release steam in the air, it was too much. He could smell his seared skin and realized he'd be ash if he kept going. Practically unconscious from the pain, Gaspard rolled his charred body to the left until he hit the burnt beams of the barn. He crawled in amongst the destruction, burrowed down amongst the ruins, and cried pink tears for his love.

16

Gaspard rubbed his eyes as he crawled his way out of the wreckage to stand in the night, bare-footed, filthy, and grieving. He stayed on his knees and crawled to where he'd been shot, clutching his left side where the bullet was still embedded in his body. When he couldn't crawl, he slithered, searching for Sophie's body.

He couldn't find it, and he realized he'd never find her given the foot of fresh snow that had fallen during the day. Gaspard collapsed into a small ball, holding his side and staying still with his eyes squeezed tight as if he could will this reality away. He stayed there for quite a while, his mind roiling, but he moved when the bullet in his body wiggled closer to his back. The bullet squirmed, creeping closer toward his skin. Every millimeter was agony, and Gaspard shrieked when his body ejected the bullet, shoving it through his skin, creating another open, throbbing wound. The cold snow numbed the pain somewhat, but Gaspard knew he needed blood to heal.

Gaspard staggered to his feet and lurched forward, wobbling with pain and blood loss. He teetered one step and then another, concentrating on putting one foot in front of the other, not thinking of anything beyond the next step and Sophie.

He tumbled to the ground when he heard voices. The voices spoke English, and he assumed he'd come upon Allied soldiers; maybe one of them was the one who shot Sophie. With as much silence as he could muster, he crept toward the camp, hope alive that he would find Sophie, that maybe she wasn't dead but was laying in the American's camp injured.

The soldiers wore white and gray winter gear, and several huddled over a fire warming their hands. Gaspard counted three tents, one bigger than the others. He scooted around the camp, ignoring his wounds, until he was behind the large tent. Using energy he didn't have, he pulled shadows around him and groped his way to the tent flap where he peered in, praying that Sophie was alive.

There was no sign of Sophie, but Vachel sat in a chair, tied to the main tent pole.

"Vachel!" Gaspard hissed.

The man looked up, revealing his bruises and the dried blood that ran from a cut on his temple. "Gaspard?" he asked, disbelief on his face. "Get me out of here!"

"Hold on. I am injured also."

Gaspard gave up any pretense of silence. He pushed his way through the tent flap, worked his way behind Vachel, and untied the knots, releasing the pressure on Vachel's shoulders.

"They beat you?" Gaspard asked.

"No. My car flipped over on an icy spot. That's how they caught me." Vachel turned to look at Gaspard.

"What the hell happened to you?" Vachel asked, looking at Gaspard's devastated body. "And where's Sophie? Is she alright?"

Gaspard didn't have to answer because a soldier was outside the tent and leaning down to enter. Gaspard scuttled to the side to the immediate left of the opening, and when the soldier came through, Gaspard grabbed him, sunk his teeth into his neck, and drank. It took all of three seconds. Vachel stared, dumfounded.

Gaspard didn't kill the man, though he wanted to because he blamed the Americans for Sophie's death, but he held himself back and only took enough to help the healing process. Satiated for the time being, he lay the soldier on the floor of the tent and covered him with a sleeping bag. He seized Vachel's hand, and the two ran out of tent.

"Hey!" yelled a soldier, noticing the ruckus behind him.

"The prisoner is getting away! I think there is someone else with him," yelled another.

Gaspard ducked as a bullet flew overhead. He pressed Vachel's head down, hissing, "Duck!"

"Don't shoot! In this darkness, you're likely to hit one of us!" said the first soldier.

"Get a move-on. Stop talkin' and start doin'."

Gaspard recognized the drawl of the American Southwest.

Vachel was out of breath, huffing and puffing with the exertion, but Gaspard's strength had returned, and he yanked Vachel along with him.

"We can't stop, Vachel. We must keep going!"

"Where's Sophie?"

"Run!"

The soldiers crashed behind them using a flashlight to throw light into the darkness, following the footsteps the two Frenchmen, vampire and human, left behind.

"That way! Get 'em!"

Gaspard knew they were done for if they didn't reach the road. He bent down, scooped Vachel into a fireman's carry, and flowed through the woods at vampire speed, gliding through the trees, taking in a moment of joy as he ran flat out. He got to the road, pleased that the Peugeot was where he'd parked it. He threw Vachel into the back, dropped into the driver's seat, snatched the keys from the hiding place where he'd put them before, and roared off, leaving two baffled American soldiers behind.

They careened down the road, and Vachel gave a whoop of triumph. "Where's Sophie?" he asked again. "Is she safe?"

Gaspard didn't answer, focusing on driving. Vachel grabbed the steering wheel, yanking so hard they almost veered off the road.

"Where's Sophie?" Vachel demanded.

Gaspard stopped the car. "She's dead."

Vachel once again turned to stone.

"I'm so, so sorry. Bombs rained down on us, and she wouldn't wait. She couldn't take being down there any longer. She ran out, and an American soldier saw her. She tried to tell him she wasn't a threat, but when she took a step toward him, he shot her. Then he shot me, twice." Gaspard's voice broke at the retelling.

Vachel slammed his fist into Gaspard's ear and followed with an uppercut to Gaspard's chin. Vachel scrambled over the middle and lay into Gaspard with everything he had. Gaspard didn't defend himself. Taking the beating was a relief, a way to show penance for Sophie's death. *I deserve this*, he thought. *Hit me as much as you want. I let her get killed. I wasn't good enough.*

Vachel landed another punch to Gaspard's gut, slamming Gaspard back against the door. The latch let go, the door opened, and the two men tumbled to the ground, Gaspard on his back, Vachel still flailing away with a strength fueled by grief and anger.

"She rejected me for you, so you were to keep her safe! You bastard! You blood-sucking villain! I hate you! I hate you!"

Gaspard huffed as another violent punch landed in his gut. "I hate myself, Vachel. I loved her, too!"

"You barely knew her!" Vachel grappled Gaspard into a head hold and pulled back on Gaspard's neck, using his body weight to pull tight. Gaspard thought his head was going to pop off as his neck snapped and popped with the pressure, but he bore it, taking the pain. In the end, Vachel knew his efforts were futile. Gaspard didn't have to breathe, so cutting off his windpipe was pointless. He released Gaspard's neck, battled his own weariness to get to his feet, and gave Gaspard a last kick to ribs.

"How could you have let this happen? How? I'm glad you will live a long time, vampire. You have forever to remember the gift you had, and lost."

While Gaspard lay on the ground, once again bleeding and aching, Vachel got in the car and drove away. Gaspard dragged himself to his knees, stood, swaying on his feet, and began the long walk back to town.

17

Le Bar des Ecrivains was Parisian in all ways, including its claim that Alexandre Dumas once wrote at its corner table. Gaspard observed the patrons with their yellow-stained fingers, coarse laughs, and most significantly, the prize-winning wine and cognac they drank like water, finally flowing again now that the Second World War was over. The last time he'd visited the bar, it had been filled to the brim with vampires, one loudmouth in particular bragging about his ability to slip Jewish families out from under the German guards, which the vampires then used as blood slaves.

That hadn't lasted.

Gaspard felt at home here, sitting in the back, smoking a Quai D'Orsay cigar, drinking whiskey straight. He longed for Sophie and worried about Vachel. The last time Gaspard had seen him, he was rebuilding his bar. A bomb had smashed the pub to smithereens, and Vachel was back to ordering people around, although his eyes were tired and his spirit dimmed. Gaspard laid a headstone to Sophie in Burgundy on his old estate and found living quarters for the heartbroken Gigi, paying for a caretaker to ensure her sustenance and safety.

His grief forced him to think about his future, and after the initial pain-stoked paralysis lessened, he'd taken a new step to the New World, as he still thought of it. He now owned an estate in New Orleans, an irony he recognized. The most powerful vampire that lived there—correction, *used* to live there—was turned to ash by an unfortunate banana foster flambé incident.

Gaspard had jumped on the real estate left behind and informed the American and European Assemblies that he would be taking residence there. Once a hub of vampire politics, New Orleans had faded in importance, left to the misguided fantasies of Anne Rice readers. The power was in Washington, D.C., where the American Assembly gathered. All those lovely Senators and Representatives to control, not to mention visiting celebrities and unsuspecting tourists. D.C. was a veritable all-you-can eat buffet for vampires.

He had returned to France to arrange for the transfer of his possessions to Louisiana. It was time to say goodbye to France, and sitting in the alley bar seemed like the most appropriate way to do it.

One man, looking about fifty, had stationed himself toward the front of the bar. He wore rugged motorcycle pants and a leather jacket over a classic white T-shirt. He looked like James Dean, if James Dean had been allowed to age and had an eyepatch and a beard. Runes covered the man's jacket, and embroidered crows decorated each of his shoulders.

The man sensed Gaspard's gaze and looked up to meet Gaspard's eyes. Gaspard lifted his glass in salute, and the man smiled, picked up his cognac, and walked to the back of the bar.

"May I join you, friend?" the man asked in perfect French. His voice was gravelly and low like he'd been drinking scotch for hours and had just now shifted to cognac to finish his evening.

Gaspard nodded, gesturing to a chair. The man sat, leaned back so only two chair legs connected with the floor, and studied Gaspard through half-shut eyes.

"You have the look of a man saying good-bye," he said.

"Very astute," Gaspard replied. "You have the look of a man who wanders where he will."

The man laughed, a good belly laugh that caught the attention of the other patrons, who glanced over to see what was so funny.

"That I am! Harder to find other wandering spirits these days, but I've found a motorcycle lets me get around, and bikers are an interesting lot."

"What's your name?"

"Ah. My name. Isn't that a thing? Names matter, do they not?"

"It's just something to call you," replied Gaspard, gesturing to the bartender for a refill.

The man seemed to make up his mind. "You can call me Wulf," he said, pronouncing the Germanic way, with a "V" sound at the beginning.

"And you can call me Gaspard."

"Gaspard? Interesting name. It means treasure keeper. I wonder what treasure you keep? Maybe the treasure is a secret and you are a secret keeper, eh, vampiirrre?" he said, stretching the last word like a piece of delightful taffy.

"Ah, you see through my one secret. I have no other secrets."

The man gave another one of his hearty laughs. "Of course you do! Everyone does. That in and of itself is a secret worth knowing, eh?" The man tapped his nose and then pointed at Gaspard.

"I thought this war may have taken the heart out of Paris." Wulf continued looking around the room at the revelers. "It's a pleasure to find the heartbeat returning. Where did you hide during the war, vampire?"

"I didn't hide," Gaspard replied. "I was here, doing what I could."

"And only you could do it. Isn't that right?"

"What do you mean? You don't know me or my past. Let's turn the tables. Where were you, Wulf? Hiding? Fighting?"

Wulf's mouth twisted. "Collecting. Preserving. Learning. Planning for what is to come."

"What the hell do you mean by that?"

Before Wulf could answer, the door opened, and three men and one woman entered. The men were a little too sharply dressed for le Bar, but the woman...the woman was something to behold. Long dark tresses trailed down her back, green eyes snapped like emeralds, and it didn't matter what she wore because her presence was enough to attract attention. Her swaying walk dragged every male eye in her direction, and the poor men had as much hope to resist her as they had to resist gravity.

She was dressed up, too, wearing a red cocktail dress with black lace hose and sky high black heels. No jewelry though, Gaspard noticed, which was odd because not only were they overdressed, they were vampires, and vampires loved sparkle.

Wulf gave a low whistle, which she undoubtedly heard given her heightened senses. This was confirmed a second later when she looked over at their table and gave a minute smile of acknowledgment. She stared at Gaspard for a moment longer, and he placed both hands on the table, palms up, a gesture of peace. She nodded and took a table in the opposite corner.

"Who is *that*?" Wulf whispered, leaning forward, eye twinkling, eager for information about the mysterious woman in red and her three escorts. "Do I dare approach such a *femme fatale*?"

"I would advise against it," replied Gaspard, keeping his voice low. "She's a visiting vampire from the United States, and the men are paid muscle."

"She is your associate?"

"No. I've never met her in person, but rumor says she has gifts that other vampires don't, such as a knack for enthralling humans with a single look and an ability to cause hallucinations. I don't know how much of that is true or just good public relations."

"Can you do something special?"

"Why do you ask? And why do you think I'd tell you, a stranger?" demanded Gaspard.

"I was thinking it would be unfair if she can do these things and you can't."

"I can float if I jump high and can pause time when I do so, which can be handy. Why am I telling you this?"

"I have a trustworthy face," said Wulf.

Gaspard continued talking. It was as if he couldn't stop. "I only learned of her appearance in Paris yesterday evening. I can't imagine why she's here."

The answer revealed itself a moment later when a tall, graceful man entered. He had long white fingers like a piano player who had never seen the sun. His suit was tailored to fit his lengthy frame, and the crisp white shirt revealed pale flesh at his neck and chest. He walked like a man used to being in charge.

"Holy Moses, is that who I think it is?" asked Wulf.

"Yes. Arnaud Bachelet, Master of Paris. I think it is a bad idea for me to be here."

"Why, what could they want with you?"

"Nothing, and I'd like to leave it that way."

Wulf leaned back in his chair again. "Are you afraid, vampire?"

"Cautious."

Wulf glanced at the vampire party and nodded. "Sensible."

"This is my last night in France, at least for a while. Why on Earth did these particular vampires show up now?"

"Of all the bars in all the world, they had to walk into mine?" said Wulf, doing his best Bogie.

"Exactly."

When the woman in red turned her attention to Arnaud, it was as if a heavy weight lifted, and the slightly dazed men who had been staring at her turned back to their wine. Even Gaspard and Wulf, on the periphery of the power, felt the release.

"What's her name?" Wulf asked, forefinger on his lips as if in deep thought.

"Valeria Snow."

"Not originally American then?"

"Mexican, I think."

"Does she know you?"

"She may know my name because she has a seethe in Texas, close to where I am setting up residence. But Arnaud and I have history. He's one of the reasons I'm moving to America."

"Ah, a new beginning! How grand! Where are you moving?"

"New Orleans."

"Historical. Hot. Good food. Alligators."

"That about sums it up." Gaspard smiled at Wulf, feeling better now that Valeria Snow's attention was focused on Arnaud.

That lasted for all of a minute as Gaspard felt the weight of both Valeria's and Arnaud's gaze settle on his shoulders. Combined they were formidable, and Gaspard bowed his head under the pressure for a moment, then managed to bring his head up to stare at the power couple in front of him. He had changed over the last few months. He was wiser, more thoughtful, and aware of his growing strength, and by his will alone, he was able to counteract the gaze of both vampires. He was pleased by his increased power but also not stupid. He gave himself a mental shake and a reminder to be respectful.

Valeria and Arnaud walked to his table, flashing in and out the way vampires could do, making it look to the humans that they magically transported themselves from one part of the bar to the other, which, as Gaspard thought about it, was accurate.

Gaspard stood, and at six feet tall, he almost met Arnaud's height. Gaspard inclined his head, keeping his face neutral, adopting a look of complete indifference. Valeria was petite and maybe five foot three.

"Arnaud."

"Gaspard."

"What brings you to this particular bar this night?" Gaspard asked.

"Perhaps I wanted to say *au revoir* and *bon chance*," Arnaud replied.

Gaspard lifted an eyebrow. "You came to wish me goodbye and good luck? I highly doubt that."

"Or perhaps I thought you might like to meet our visiting American since you will be moving to the United States yourself. May I please present Madame Valeria Snow?"

"It is a pleasure, Madame," said Gaspard, once again inclining his head, lifting her right hand to his lips. She smelled like strawberries, bruised and over ripe, combined with a touch of dead things, like rotting leaves or a flowerbed gone to seed. It was as if everything about her was a tiny bit past its prime, a step too far gone.

Valeria simpered, batting her eyelashes like a Southern belle born and raised and attending her first debutante ball. A Southern belle with fangs. Now that she was up close, he could see that her complexion was a lovely caramel, dark for a vampire.

"I hear you will be taking over the seethe in New Orleans," she purred, placing her hand on her hip to highlight her curves. Gaspard couldn't help but notice that the curves were indeed luscious.

He dragged his eyes away. "I do not plan on taking over as much as relocating. Those who want to join me may, and those who do not can petition another seethe."

"Ah, a gentleman. I've never understood that sentiment. I would take the city for my own, by force if necessary, and every vampire in it. But, I've always been told I'm a bit... aggressive." She licked her lips.

"I like aggressive," whispered Arnaud in her ear, but loud enough for Gaspard to hear. Gaspard couldn't help but roll his eyes. Arnaud ignored him and turned his attention to Wulf.

"Who is your friend, Gaspard? He isn't a vampire, but I don't think he's human either. Who are you, mystery man?"

Wulf stood, studying Arnaud with his one eye, not offering a hand, not speaking, certainly not announcing his heritage or pedigree. The moment dragged on until Gaspard broke it by saying, "We've just met. Wulf, may I introduce you to Arnaud Bachelet, Master of Paris, and Valeria Snow, Mistress of Southern Texas."

"It will soon be all of Texas, but yes, that is accurate... as of now," Valeria said with a flip of her hair.

Wulf switched his gaze to Valeria and took a step back, as if he had been pushed. He recovered his balance and rubbed one of the runes on his jacket. Wulf's face was a mask as he looked at first one, then the other, vampire. At last, he opened his mouth.

"I see you."

Valeria laughed, waving her hand. "You are very strange, sir. Of course you can see me. I'm right here. Gaspard, your friend is quite odd. Tell me, sir, how did you lose your eye?"

"Mistress Valeria, I'm sure he lost it in the war; so many have lost an appendage. The bombs were quite clever at tearing people limb-from-limb, piercing eyes, lancing ears, expediting pain and madness."

"Why doesn't he answer?" she asked.

"I'm afraid his French isn't very good. Please excuse him," Gaspard said, reaching for anything to explain Wulf's behavior. Wulf returned to his seat and said nothing further.

"You didn't answer my question, Arnaud. Why are you here this evening?"

"As I said, it is to introduce you to Valeria," Arnaud snapped. "She's interested in establishing an alliance with you prior to your arrival in America."

"Why?"

Valeria spoke up. "There are a number of factions within the South that need..." She tilted her head as she searched for the correct word. "Monitoring. Guidance. Parenting. Their current leaders are sloppy and allow behavior that I would not nor, do I believe, would you. Arnaud tells me you are a clever man."

"Arnaud paid me a compliment?"

"I said you were clever; that is true enough. Perhaps I should have used the word devious or backstabbing," Arnaud replied, crossing his arms as he leaned back in his chair.

"I never backstabbed. I didn't agree with your position, and I was vocal about it. You knew exactly where I stood."

"You killed nine of my vampires in one night."

Gaspard leaned across the table. "They were pretending to offer Jewish families refuge and then penning them in a barn to use as a food supply. It was no better than the camps."

"They were the walking dead regardless."

"You let them fall into the hands of a demon!"

"Which is the only reason you're alive, Gaspard, as even I find that particular detail distasteful. Did I not come to your aid?"

"You did." Gaspard leaned back and crossed his arms over his chest.

Arnaud sighed. "I am far older than you, Gaspard. Perhaps my view on the sanctity of human life has changed over the years. I've seen many generations come and go."

"You let Nazis take over your city."

"Yes. And no. Really, Gaspard. Don't assume you know everything. Maybe one day you will make similar choices to mine when you oversee a major city and all its inhabitants. If you ever get that far."

"Boys, boys, this is in the past. Gaspard, let's talk about the future," Valeria purred, sidling over to Gaspard, stroking his arm. "Let's all sit. We have so much to discuss."

Gaspard held out a chair for the lady and gestured for Arnaud to take a seat. The silent Wulf looked on.

"What did you mean by bad behaviors?" Gaspard asked Valeria, keeping an eye on Arnaud.

She leaned in, as if sharing a secret. "The vampires in our neighboring states are weak. They cannot control their seethes. I've heard stories of rampant blood-taking going unchecked, and in Mississippi, the vampires are in a war with the werewolves. Mundane citizens are getting caught in the crosshairs. By working together, we can bring peace and order."

"Why doesn't the American Assembly do something about it? I'm sure they have interfered in such problems before."

"They don't care about anything outside of Washington."

"I've done a lot of research and haven't heard anything about this. I've spoken to a few of my soon-to-be neighbors, and no one reported anything of the like."

Valeria pursed her lips in irritation. "Are you accusing me of lying?"

"No, of course not, but perhaps we can get together when I'm settled and can see for myself what is happening. I don't want to make any rash decisions."

"I'm offering you an opportunity, Gaspard. The southern United States is ours for the taking. I'm approaching you out of respect. Your activities of late have reached American shores. There are some who would rather a vampire of your potential not come to the USA."

"My potential?" Gaspard asked.

"You are a Master, that much is clear, but killing nine vampires and repelling a demon in one evening? That's impressive. Don't underestimate yourself."

Wulf stared at Gaspard in shock, giving a low whistle. "You exorcised a demon?"

Gaspard shuffled his feet under the table. "I had help."

"Exactly," said Valeria. "The humans loved you. You inspired them, made them want to serve you, and engendered *loyalty*."

"I think you are misunderstanding the situation..."

"*I* think this discussion requires something special," Wulf interjected, suddenly speaking French like a native, which drew looks of ire from both Valeria and Arnaud.

"Please, allow me to provide a round." Wulf rose and headed to the bar where he asked for four empty beer mugs. When he turned to return to the table, the mugs were full with an amber liquid.

"The barkeep has a special vintage that I really enjoy. It is a honey-wine, a special mead, that I can't always find," he said as he passed the mugs around the table.

"This is delicious," said Valeria, after taking a sip. "It tastes, well, don't be offended my suddenly chatty Wulf, but it tastes like blood to me."

"Really?" said Arnaud. "I think it has the bouquet of a merlot, or maybe a fruitier wine from Alsace. There's something about it I can't place. I must ask the barkeep where he got it. Gaspard, what does it taste like to you?"

"Honey-wine? It tastes exactly like I expected it to. It's sweet and heavy on my tongue. I couldn't drink a lot of it. No offence, Wulf," Gaspard remarked, looking at Wulf for an explanation.

"None taken! It does taste different to different people," Wulf said. "I find that it often tastes like what each of us likes best. You are right not to drink much of it, Gaspard. It is quite a dangerous thing, this mead. It makes you more of who you are."

"What do you mean by that?" Arnaud asked, sniffing the mead once again then rolling it up to the light. Gaspard recalled that Arnaud was a wine snob and appreciated that the vampire hadn't lost this human fascination.

"I don't mean much of anything. I'm glad you like it. Let's make a toast. To allies!"

"To allies," the other three responded, but Gaspard eyed Wulf, wondering what he was up to and why all the vampire and demon chatter didn't seem to faze him. Who was this guy?

18

Gaspard cursed himself for sitting with his back to the wall. Normally a preferred observation post, the position was currently detrimental. He was cornered with Wulf on his right, Arnaud and Valeria across the table, and no way to escape. All he wanted to do was leave. He decided facing Valeria head on, unflinching but respectful, would be his best approach.

"I am no threat to other vampires, Valeria."

"A vampire with your strength is always a threat."

"This makes no sense. I'm not even there yet."

"That is the way of things," Valeria snapped. "Don't be naïve."

Their conversation was interrupted when a man slammed back first onto their table, a barrel-chested man landing on top of him, throwing wild punches.

"Don't talk about my mother, you jackass!" screamed the burly guy as he slapped the other man across the mouth. Two teeth went flying.

"That's.... gurgle gurgle mummmpf..."

"What? I can't hear you, you foul-mouthed cocksucker!"

"He said, 'That's not what she said last night,'" said Wulf. Gaspard threw him a baleful look.

"You aren't being helpful, Wulf," Gaspard muttered.

Wulf had big innocent eyes. "I was simply making sure that they have adequate communication."

Another splatter of blood squirted up in the air, and Gaspard knew at that moment that it was all going to go to hell. Valeria's fangs dropped as she opened her mouth and caught blood droplets on her tongue like a child in her first sun shower. Blood splattered on her face as well, and she wiped it from her eyes with her hands, licking her palms and smacking her lips at the taste.

"Cognac," she commented. "A good chaser to that honey-mead."

Multiple things happened simultaneously. Arnaud attempted to grab Valeria's arm and pull her out of the bar. Her bodyguards grabbed Arnaud, and Valeria ignored it all while lunging for the bleeding man on the table. Wulf nudged Gaspard, pointing at Valeria. "I think that mead went to her head."

"It is unusual for a Master or a Mistress to act like that, without self-control. What was that stuff?" Gaspard asked, elbowing a drunk patron out of the way, then dodging the man who followed.

Wulf never answered because he and Gaspard had to avoid glass as beer mugs went airborne. Even the small pretzel bowls were tossed high and became tiny aerial missiles that collided with brawling bodies. Gaspard heard the crash of wine bottles and barstools overturning as every patron joined the fight. One hard-core patron, wearing a white T-shirt stained with sweat, pummeled his way through the crowd while protecting his hard-earned cigarette.

Gaspard and Wulf leapt to relative safety on top of the bar and observed from above. The humans punched each other hard enough to leave bruises and break bones, but all came to a stand-still when they saw Valeria. The once hypnotizing vampire fed on their friend, rubbing her face in the blood like a cat. That was enough to drive them toward the exit *en masse*, creating a traffic jam at the door as they rammed forward, shoving and pushing each other in a scramble to get out first.

Gaspard observed it all, but he was most enthralled by Arnaud. The man's long pale fingers became talons, a trick Gaspard had seen before. Arnaud moved with grace and speed, ripping three of the hulking, but human, bodyguards to shreds. The men went down and stayed down. A fourth fled. Arnaud still wore his suit and white shirt and didn't get a speck on him.

Bastard.

His admiration of Arnaud's fighting skills and nefarious ability to stay clean came to an end when a fifth bodyguard unzipped his skin, let it fall to the ground, stepped out, and grew several feet.

"What is *that*?" said Gaspard, looking at the bumps and pockmarks on the creature's skin. The giant was a mess of a whole lot of ugly, and he was too big to be human. Gaspard had never seen anything like it, and he wasn't afraid to admit the thing intimidated him.

Wulf narrowed his eyes and didn't reply but raised his hand and spoke, "Thurs of Jötenheimr, by what right and by what magic do you appear thus?"

Thurs turned to Wulf, eyes widened in shock, and fell to one knee, head bowed.

19

Gaspard's heartbeat dropped from its normal twenty beats per minute to fewer than ten in one second, decreasing what blood pressure he had, making him a touch dizzy. He knelt on the top of the bar and moved with great care as he slid off and behind the counter. He held onto the bar counter to keep himself steady.

"I ask again," Wulf thundered, his voice rumbling around the room. The only other beings left in the place were Arnaud, Valeria, and Gaspard. Valeria was blood drunk, walking in lazy circles as she rode her mead-cognac-blood high. "What are you doing here?"

Gaspard spared a glance for Arnaud, who looked as surprised and wary as Gaspard.

"What is a jötnar, a giant from the Norse realms, doing here on Midgard working for a vampire?"

The giant bowed his head even lower. "I was assigned to serve as a guard to Valeria Snow, my lord," replied the giant.

"By whom?"

"The Vanir, my lord Odin."

Gaspard and Arnaud exchanged glances. Arnaud mouthed, "Odin?" Gaspard lifted his shoulders and held his hands palm out. He mouthed back, "I didn't know."

Wulf, or Odin, stepped into the air and floated down to the floor. He approached Thurs and gestured for the giant to stand up.

"Let's all take a seat," Odin said. "Except her." He pointed toward Valeria, who was still walking in circles.

Arnaud took Valeria's arm and guided her outside. He came back in a moment later saying, "My driver will take her back to my home. She will be safe. I'm surprised to see her this incapacitated."

Odin made a wry face as Arnaud took his chair. "She has a hard time keeping her passions under control, and while you have kept *her* safe, I see glimpses of her future, and it is quite *unsafe*, at least for you, Gaspard."

"My head is spinning. Are you really Odin? *The* Odin?"

Thurs slammed his massive fist on the table with such force he broke his chair and plopped to the floor. Even sitting on the floor, his head reached taller than Gaspard's.

"You doubt the All-Father?" Thurs stood to his full height and loomed over Gaspard, a massive fist at the ready.

"Easy big guy," said Gaspard. "I'm just taking a moment here."

"It's okay, Thurs," said Odin. "It's understandable."

The giant collected two chairs, one for each cheek, and kept his eye on Gaspard. Gaspard didn't like the look and slid his chair closer to Arnaud.

Odin bobbed his head. "Yes, I am Odin, la de da, the All-Seeing, Father of Thor, etcetera, etcetera, but I still like being called Wulf. It's my traveling name."

"Forget it," said Arnaud. "If you are truly Odin, then we shall call you by that name, if only to remind us of your power. Wulf is a motorcycle drifter. Odin is the King of the Norse pantheon. I'm still a skeptic, though." Thurs cast him a look. Arnaud looked back. "I can't help it, I'm French."

Odin stared at Arnaud for a moment. He seemed to make up his mind about something and said, "I will do what I can. You must believe."

He stood, and the motorcycle jacket melted away, as did his riding pants. He appeared in a nimbus of light in full body armor with a horned helmet and a spear. The ravens from his jacket morphed into real birds, one perched on each shoulder.

Gaspard looked at the creature in front of him and no longer doubted. The man previously known as Wulf had grown so his head reached the ceiling, and his arm muscles bulged in a way that made it clear the spear was not for decoration. Deep white scars crawled out from under the eyepatch, and his beard and hair grew longer and fuller. Gold bands wrapped around the ends of his braided mustache. But it was his presence that sealed the deal for Gaspard. He sensed the power of the god pressing in on him from all sides, and from the looks of it, Arnaud felt the same. The power felt like he imagined it must feel like at the bottom of the deepest oceans, or on top of the world among the stars. It was cavernous, dizzying, and yet, Gaspard knew that if he could stay there for a while, just a moment, he'd learn secrets, ancient secrets. He tried to stare down into the blackness, but the vision winked out.

He almost cried out with the loss.

Thurs was once again on the ground, trembling.

Odin was in Wulf form.

Arnaud had recovered and was placid as ever, his long fingers stroking his chin.

Gaspard studied Odin, examining the ravens stitched into the shoulders of the jacket. *Hugin and Munin*, he thought. *They're real.* He also noticed a new detail. Odin's belt buckle was a startlingly realistic looking wolf. *Fenrir*, he realized. He decided to ask the only question that made sense.

"Why is the Ruler of the Norse pantheon in a hole-in-the-wall bar in Paris?"

"Ah! Now we get to the heart of it. Get up, Thurs. It's alright," said Odin, patting the giant on the shoulder.

"Before I answer that, I need to understand one thing. Thurs," Odin said, turning to the big guy shaking like a leaf in a strong wind, "tell me why the Vanir sent you."

"Who are the Vanir?" Gaspard asked.

"The Vanir are one family of gods and goddesses in the Norse pantheon. The other are the Aesir, which is the group I am in. Freya, my wife, belongs to both. Make sense?"

Gaspard and Arnaud both nodded, but the look Arnaud sent Gaspard said, *No, I don't know. This is way out of my league*. Gaspard agreed.

Gaspard asked, "And what is Midgard?"

"Earth, your world. That is what we call it."

"Interesting," Gaspard and Arnaud said at the same time, pretending they understood, nodding sagely.

"Freya herself asked me to cross the plain into Midgard," said Thurs, directing his attention to Odin. He acted as if the other two weren't there.

"I assumed as much, but why?" asked Odin.

"She said that trouble was coming, trouble that could shake the Tree. She enlisted my clan to assist her. We are to watch and report back to her what we learn about the vampire race here on Earth."

"She sees more than I give her credit for," mused Odin. "She foresees the trouble, too."

"Didn't you say that Freya is your wife?" asked Gaspard.

"Yes," Odin replied.

"Don't the two of you *talk*?"

"We try to have a date night every decade or so," Odin said. "See a movie. Take in a play."

Arnaud nodded, as if this made sense to the old vampire, and asked, "What Tree?"

"Yggdrasil, the Tree that holds the Nine Worlds, including this one. I have seen the same signs as my clever wife. The vampires of this world are now of two clans, those with souls and those without. The system hangs in the balance, and you, my young friend," Odin said, pointing at Gaspard, "are at the center of the war to come."

"Why me?" asked Gaspard.

"Why him?" asked Arnaud.

"That I do not know. Perhaps because you are moving from Old World to New. Perhaps because you were touched by the divine. Yes, Gaspard, I know about that."

Arnaud turned to gape at Gaspard. "The divine?"

Gaspard blushed, hating that he still did that on occasion. "It was, you know, sort of a long day. Things happened. We destroyed a demon. The Light rushed through me, healing me of my wounds. Blah, blah, blah..." He waved his arms to indicate there was no real story to tell.

Arnaud continued to gape, finally managing, "And you didn't *tell* me this?"

Gaspard hunched down in his chair. "It was personal."

"Did the Light... did the Light... can we...?" Arnaud stuttered with the gravity of the question.

"Yes, Arnaud. Heaven is still available to us."

Arnaud made the sign of the cross, sat back, and stared out the window into the night. Anyone who knew him would notice that a tension they didn't know he carried, that he didn't know he carried, was gone, and his sharp eyes had softened. He placed his palms together in prayer and mouthed a few words.

"So, what we do matters?" he asked.

"What we do matters," said Gaspard.

"What you do matters very much," said Odin, "and that is what we need to discuss."

"Tell us more," said Gaspard.

"There are fewer vampires with souls than those without. Vampirism seems to attract humans in exquisite pain, pain they'd like to forget. Giving away their soul is an easy solution."

"If they don't have souls...?" asked Gaspard.

"Heaven is not available," said Odin.

"Where do they go?"

"They don't go anywhere."

"What do you mean?"

Odin leaned forward. "I mean that they cease to exist. They don't move on. They don't go forward. They never find out what happens next. They end."

Arnaud broke in. "That doesn't sound like much of a punishment."

Odin smiled. "That's because you don't know what could happen next."

It was Arnaud's turn to lean forward. "And you do? Tell us."

Odin chuckled. "No can do."

"Oh, come on!" said Gaspard.

Odin's face turned serious. "Boys, everyone has a different path. It is not for me to decide what happens next. I can only tell you there are possibilities, an indefinable number of possibilities, and your actions make your path."

"Free will?" Arnaud scoffed.

"Something like that, yes."

"So why are you here?" asked Gaspard.

Odin grinned. “Because when the time is right, I’m going to send someone to help you, Gaspard.”

“Who?”

“I have someone in mind. I think you’ll like her. Her name is Kara.”

PART IV

SOULS UNITE

1

Kara removed a gun from the dead soldier's hand and called to the woman's soul. "Come to me," she whispered, concentrating on the heart chakra where the soul resided. The woman's soul was confused and clung to its body, but with patience, Kara retrieved the soul and sent it to Valhalla. The woman deserved the honor for her courage. In this life, she was an Afghani and a resident of Kandahar. She'd provided translation services to the United Nation coalition forces and had been targeted by her own family for aiding the enemy.

Bodies and pieces of bodies lay strewn across the countryside, some so covered with dust that it was impossible to tell if they were male or female. Discarded weapons lay beside these silent figures, some emptied and useless, others waiting to be picked up again. The landscape spoke of war unending, differences never settled, and hate for no reason other than a different name, a different tribe, a different accent to the same language.

"Sisters, to me!" cried Sigrun, the eldest of the Valkyries. Dozens of armored warriors wielding golden swords and riding breathtaking horses flew across the night toward the border of Pakistan. The Valkyries knew this area well, having visited for centuries, collecting souls from the area's legendary conflicts and conquests.

The fighters scrambled over rock and briar, crossing into Pakistan. The dead rotted where they lay, and the Valkyries concentrated on searching for worthy souls.

A smoky black body lay on the ground, covered in dirt and soot, burned past recognition. Next to it lay another male figure, but this one was missing its head. Hildr and Kara discovered the head several feet away, cleanly severed, and bent to examine it. It was Kara who noticed the fangs.

"Uh!" she grunted, jumping back in one leap, scowling at the sight. "I hate vampires."

"I know," said Hildr, walking back to the vampire's body.

"Can you blame me?"

"No. You witnessed the worst vampire Gorge since the Middle Ages."

"Dirty, soulless, disgusting things," said Kara. Then, "Hildr, what are you doing?"

"I'm looking for his soul."

"He's a vampire. He doesn't have a soul."

"Sigrun says otherwise," replied Hildr, still studying the body.

"I love my older sister, but on this, she is wrong."

Hildr cast Kara a look. "Don't let her hear you say that."

"She's out of touch. She's leading now, not collecting. When was the last time she ran into a vampire?"

"I have no idea." Hildr stood up and wiped her hands on her thighs. "Nothing there. I wonder where it went."

"They don't have souls. There was nothing to find."

"And I told you, Sigrun says there are. Let's get back to the group."

Kara mounted Rikassa, a white mare with a flowing mane and luxurious tail, a Wild One, horses that only served Valkyries. Kara followed Hildr back home, thoughts of Baidoa, a Southwestern town in Somalia, raging through her mind. She could smell the smoke still.

The camp had been dark, everyone asleep. The women and children slept outside on the dusty ground, or if they could find a space, under one of the white tents provided by the refugee aid organization. Children groaned in pain, and mothers wept watching their children suffer. Several hundred had died in the last week from malaria. More died from malnutrition or dehydration, but they had no other place to go. The other camps were full to overflowing, and conditions there were just as bad.

Kara prowled the perimeter, offering what protection she was allowed. As a Valkyrie, her role was limited, but she could drive off evil to save the innocent in some cases. There were rules, laws, provisos and such, but she did what she could. Children were always considered innocent. Odin himself assigned her this region to patrol.

There. A scrape. The tinny sound of metal on metal, the rasp of bone on bone. Kara stalked in noiseless steps, sword drawn, looking for the source. She closed her eyes to better focus on what her ears told her since the darkness created shadows that could trick even an experienced warrior.

A clack. A rattle. Wind brushing by her cheek. And a pungent, vile scent. She hunkered down behind a rock. *What was that smell?*

More clacking sounds and the stench became stronger, a musty smell that reminded Kara of walking into an attic after many years, but this was accompanied by a side serving of decay. An eerie wind disturbed the ground at her feet, creating dust swirls that rose into the air and plugged her nose. The children's moans escalated into full-throated cries. The mothers rocked the children while the hairs on the back of their own necks stood up and a primal instinct told them to flee. But, flee where? There was nowhere to go.

Wild dogs howled at the moon, and entire flocks of birds rose from the Qudhac trees, wheeling away into the night sky. A small rodent ran across Kara's foot to dive into a burrow, and yet, there was nothing specific to sense. Nothing human, nothing animal. In fact, it felt like a black hole had descended from space and settled on the ground, sucking all life and energy in, creating a void.

Kara tracked the emptiness closest to her, lifted her blade, and leapt toward it, slashing her sword from upper right to down left, knowing she had made a good cut. The wounded void creature roared, shifted in her direction, and Kara's eyes finally fixated on her attacker, a gaunt mask of bone, fangs, and bloodshot eyes that undulated toward her, emaciated hands outstretched.

Kara cut left to right in a straight horizontal line, severing the vampire's hands at the wrists. She thrust her sword forward, pierced the vampire's side, and lunged to the right using both hands, cleaving it in two. Both halves crumpled to the ground, the vampire not dead but no longer a threat.

She stayed low and used her hearing and sense of smell to locate the other vampires. She assumed there were more; they liked to travel in packs. Now that she knew what to look for, it was easy to find them, and once she did, she ducked to the ground in dismay. There weren't three of them, or four, as she had assumed. There were *hundreds*, and their combined lack of life force had coalesced into the void she'd sensed.

Battery-operated security lights flashed as the vamps' movement tricked them to life. The refugees didn't even have time to scream. The vampires attacked *en masse*, seizing bodies big and small. The blood ran in rivers, and all Kara could see was a writhing horde of vampires feeding as a single body. Piranhas couldn't strip prey with any more efficiency.

Even Kara, trained, strong, and used to the unexpected, had never seen anything like this. The word for it came to her mind.

Gorge.

This was a Gorge.

The last known Gorge had been in 1348, during the Black Death. Vampires congested the filthy European streets and indulged as packs under cover of the bubonic plague. This led to a concentrated vampire scourge by what remained of the populace, culminating with Van Helsing in the late nineteenth century.

After that, the Assemblies bulked up in power and influence and policed their own.

Kara issued a cry that echoed to her sisters in Valhalla and jumped into the fray, hacking her way through vampires, leaving as many of them true-dead as she could, incapacitating the rest. Valkyries arrived to help her, and they tore the Gorge to pieces.

It was still too late. More than half of the refugees were dead, and the rest were dying. Kara looked around and saw a leg—just a leg with a tiny foot and five little toes attached. A woman's head lay at her feet, hewn from her body by teeth and claws. A mangled infant pierced by multiple sets of fangs hung from a tree branch, and an aid worker was collapsed at the bottom of the tree, dying while trying to save the child. Kara collected the aid worker's soul. The child's needed no collecting; it traveled on with ease.

A cry led them to a lone living boy sitting at his mother's feet, trying to wake her up, but the gaping wound in her chest said that she never would. Kara bent down and saw that her heart was gone, carved from her chest in a mess of ragged skin and bone.

Kara cradled the toddler, rocking him to and fro. Something pinged in her head, a memory, telling her that this skeletal boy was four, though he was no bigger than an average two-year-old. Tragedy upon tragedy. She held back tears by concentrating on her anger.

The Valkyries set the parcel on fire, scouring the corruption from the land. When all was cinders and smoke, they left with the one survivor, giving the child to a family in a bucolic area of Ghana who had always wanted a son.

Kara's thoughts returned to the present when Rikassa dove into the Asgardian plane, angling at warp speed, sheering past Heimdall, the guardian of the Rainbow Bridge, who spilled his dark roast with the force of the fly-by. The big man shook his fist at Kara.

Kara yelled, "Sorry, Heimdall!"

The guardian grunted. "No, you're not."

Kara dismounted and brushed Rikassa, who stretched her neck out to make sure Kara got every angle.

"You are a vain horse, Rikassa."

The horse threw her a look.

"It's okay. You should be vain. You're beautiful." Kara hummed a calming tune and patted Rikassa's rump.

"Let me get your tail."

Rikassa turned so Kara could brush the luxurious white tail, releasing a small rumble from her chest to express her content.

"In another life, I think you were a cat."

Rikassa tossed her head.

"Oh no! Not a house cat, nothing so mundane. A lion, perhaps. Or a cheetah."

Rikassa snorted.

"They are powerful animals. You shouldn't look down on them."

Rikassa's nose twitched.

"Okay, good. You think about it."

Rikassa gave Kara a head bump and ran off to pasture.

At dinner that evening, the sisters recounted the day, and Hildr mentioned the beheaded vampire.

Sigrun asked, "Was there a soul left?"

Hildr poured herself another glass of mead. "No. I looked for it, but there was nothing there." She gestured for Kara to pass the bread basket.

Kara handed her the basket, as well as butter and honey to spread on the thick slices. "I don't understand this insistence that vampires have souls. They don't. They are all soulless, nasty creatures."

Sigrun said, "Why do you think they are soulless?"

"They're out of the natural order of things. Dead but not. They exist in between."

"They started as people, Kara," Sigrun said. "What happened to the souls they had when they turned?"

Kara pressed her hands on the table in irritation. "I don't know, Sigrun, but I do know that no one with a soul could have possibly participated in a Gorge."

Sigrun's voice was mild. "People with souls commit evil all the time."

Kara snapped back, "Not like that."

"Exactly like that."

Kara stood with such violence that her chair screeched on the floor. "If you can find a vampire with a soul, I'll eat my hat."

Sigrun smiled. "Little sister, you don't have a hat."

The smile made Kara more aggravated. "I'll do dog duty for a month." Dog duty was shorthand for taking care of Odin's pet wolves. It was the most unpleasant job the Valkyries had to do.

"Dog duty. Hmmmm, maybe that. But I get to pick the task. It may be dog duty. It may be something else," said Sigrun.

A voice rang through the hall. "No. I get to choose."

The sisters stood and bowed their heads to Odin, who had entered the hall while they were arguing. He approached Kara, and despite her height, she had to look up at him. Odin in his true form had muscles upon muscles and towered over everyone else. His one eye studied her.

"So, taking care of the wolves is called dog duty?" he inquired, looking around the room. Kara and the rest of her sisters squirmed.

"It's...it's...a joke?" Kara stammered.

"Interesting. I shall have to consider that. But I don't want to get away from the topic at hand. If Sigrun can find a vampire with a soul, I get to pick a task for you."

Kara might have been looking up, but she was still defiant. "Yes, All-Father, because I know there is no such thing."

"It's a bet?" said Odin arching one eyebrow.

A part of Kara's brain was screaming at her to stop right there, shut up, stop talking. This is Odin; you don't make bets with a god who sacrificed an eye for wisdom. That cautious part was overwhelmed by the young rebellious part that led her to say, "It's on."

Kara thought she was safe after ten years. She knew she was safe after twenty. She had forgotten it by the time she arrived in Paris.

They were scouring an urban battlefield this time, another terrorist bombing in another major city. This time Paris, late in the evening. Hundreds injured and the number of dead had not yet been counted. They walked among the populace unnoticed, searching for worthy souls. Hildr found a security guard who had died with shrapnel in his back, covering a young woman with his own body. Kara called the soul of a chef of a nearby café who had ensured every patron got out before the bombs went off, going down with the restaurant, his life's work.

All that was left were scars. Buildings left their imprint but stood no more. Bodies lay abandoned as loved ones searched for them, crying for help, praying their family members or friends were alive. The Valkyries attended many such scenes, but it never ceased to hurt. Their job was to find the good within the evil. The souls that loved, lost, protected, and sacrificed, no matter the cost. The ones that placed others above themselves.

Sigrun stood in the middle of the Paris rubble, eyes scanning over the combat zone with experienced precision. The epicenter was a dance club, and the front of the club was torn to pieces, but the back wall remained. Sigrun motioned to Kara to follow, and they proceeded to the rear. The wall leaned at an acute angle but was still upright.

The back door, torn off its hinges, lay at an odd angle several feet away. There were sooty, bloody footsteps leading from the empty door frame to the street. Dozens of them. This is how the only survivors escaped. Sigrun walked toward the door where an old woman knelt, weeping silent tears.

There was one body crushed beneath the door, hands still grasping the sides. The Valkyries watched as the ancient woman touched her hand to her lips and then to the dead man's forehead peeking out above the door's upper edge. Crying and bent, the woman's face reflected years of pain but also goodness and hope. There was something about her that caught their imagination, but before they could speak on this, the woman said, "Goodbye, my friend," and rose to her feet with the help of her walker. A young man came to her side, and she made her way down the alley and back to the street.

"It's as if he ripped the door from its hinges and then died," Kara said, getting closer to look at the body. The tall man wore a finely made suit, had pale skin, and long artist's fingers.

"That's exactly what he did," Sigrun replied. "It took an enormous amount of strength."

"Was he killed by the blast?"

"No, by this." Sigrun rolled the man over onto his side. A scrap piece of lumber pierced his back on the left side going through his heart but stopping short of bursting through his chest.

Sigrun called to the man's soul, beckoning it, crooning to it. Kara bent down to assist but then sprung back in repulsion.

"That's a vampire!"

"Yes," said Sigrun. "He died saving others."

"Impossible. Vampires don't have souls. They cannot be collected to serve."

"They do and they can, and this comes directly..."

"No! It's a perversion!" Kara pulled her sword ready to slit the body in two and then fourths, and then into as many pieces as she could. Her hate for vampires surged in her belly, her revulsion flowing out in waves from her heart center. Her sisters came running, feeling her distress.

"No!" ordered Sigrun.

"Kara! Stop!" Sigrun ordered again.

Then, as Kara swung down, Sigrun made a choice. She swept her sword right to left, slicing Kara's body not enough to kill, but enough to hurt and leave a scar. As Kara fell to the ground, eyes wide in shock, Sigrun pulled Arnaud's soul out of his chest and sent it to Valhalla.

2

Gaspard dragged himself into his own home at sunset, tired after visiting the Northeast vampires, who he now ruled. Marc trailed after him, weary as well. Their visit was productive but required more attention to detail than either would have thought. Simon kept his seethe in the dark about many things, and no one knew passwords to computers or log in credentials for financial spreadsheets. The mundane world once again lorded its ugly head over the supernatural. One evening, a Northeast vampire spent six hours on hold with tech support to reset the security questions on an account. They were glad the company had offices in India so they could call them at night. And the banks! The banks required proof of death, but how was that possible when the original owner was eaten by an oversized lizard's one remaining baby? There was simply no way to explain that. They resorted to forging a death certificate.

"Gaspard! You're back. We are so glad," said an older woman wearing a long navy blue skirt, sensible shoes, a pale peach blouse with a bow, and an armful of gold bangle bracelets, which jingled when she walked.

"Adelaide. We are so very glad to be home. You look lovely as ever," said Gaspard, leaning down to grasp the woman's hand and bring it to his lips. He had missed her.

"Always the charmer! I'm glad to see Boston didn't take it out of you." She turned her attention to Marc, holding her arms out for a hug.

"And you? How are you doing? Your aunt will be happy to see you."

Marc gave Adelaide a bear hug and a kiss on the cheek. "It is good to see you, Adelaide, and in fact, I'm going to see Aunt Emmy right now."

Gaspard continued to his office, eyes roving, hoping to see the one person he'd really missed. He'd left for Boston without getting a chance to talk to her, and he wanted an opportunity to clear the air. He waited for her to appear, but she was a no-show. He put paperwork away, removed his suit jacket, loosened his tie, and called for a sanguineer, one of his volunteer blood-donors.

Still no Kara.

Marc ambled in, rolling up a cuff on his shirt. He'd changed, visited Aunt Emmy, and gotten a meal. Now, he was ready to get down to work.

"Where's Kara?" Gaspard grumbled.

Marc lifted one eyebrow.

"I don't know, Gaspard. I just got home, too, remember?"

Gaspard held up his hand in a gesture of apology. "I know, Marc. Sorry."

Marc said, with a hint of a smile on lips, "Why don't you send someone to fetch her?"

"Fetch her! Are you mad, Marc? One does not *fetch* a Valkyrie unless one wants to get one's head cut off in a quite literal way."

Marc shrugged, enjoying teasing his boss about his crush on Kara. "I am certain she will appear when she's ready."

Gaspard scowled. He hated that he was this needy, this vulnerable. He stood up, knocking over his chair, and stalked from the room, grumpy as a cat in a rainstorm. If she wasn't on the main floor, then she might be in her favorite place in the mansion—the training facilities.

That was exactly where he found her, working up a sweat while fighting hand-to-hand with four of the security staff. It didn't surprise him that the four mortal men were on the losing side of things. Watching them spar made Gaspard understand two things. One, Kara's speed was too fast for the mortals to follow, and two, once she got inside, you were done for. She pulled her punches, of course, but the men got smacked around a bit. She snapped her right wrist forward at one man's jaw and followed up with what would have been a fight-ending jab to the throat.

The man held up his hands in defeat and tapped out, motioning for an ice pack.

The other three joined together to take her on all at once, but the technique was a failure from the get-go. Instead of encircling her, which might have stood a chance, they came at her from the same direction, lock step, like the British army in the Revolutionary War. It didn't work then, and it didn't work now. Kara took a single step forward to meet them and hit them open palm—one, two, and the three men flew back like cartoon villains. If it wasn't for their protective vests, the strikes, even at a fraction of her strength, could have killed them. Kara believed in training by fire and that pain was a dependable teacher.

Gaspard watched her at work, his heart beating a little faster, which, he admitted, still wasn't all that fast, but it was yet another annoying indication of his admiration for this woman who'd fallen into his life. He schooled his features and let out a low whistle, attracting the attention of both Valkyrie and vanquished.

Gaspard's heart leapt when Kara smiled at him, walking over with her arms out for an... embrace? Startled, Gaspard held out his arms, then Kara seemed to reconsider the hug and changed to a handshake. Gaspard winced as they came together in something that wasn't a hug or a handshake, more like a one-armed football tackle.

I'm French, dammit, thought Gaspard. *This won't do. Time to put on my big-boy pants.*

Reclaiming his well-deserved reputation for charm, Gaspard lay both hands on Kara's shoulders and gave her a kiss on each cheek, left then right. *There*, he thought, *that is proper*.

"It's good to see you, Gaspard." Kara grabbed a towel to wipe perspiration from her brow. Gaspard noticed the guards in the background studying them, and noticed that they wheeled around when he caught their eye, consumed by an urgent need to talk about the New Orleans Saints.

"Are you finished here?" Gaspard asked. "May I accompany you to my study where I can tell you about my visit to the Northeast? Simon Whitleigh left quite a mess."

"That doesn't surprise me, but was it successful?" Kara wiped her neck with the towel. Gaspard almost didn't answer as he watched the pulse in her neck.

"Gaspard?"

"Ah, yes, it was, but we were at the mercy of a nerdy computer geek, a human, who helped us crack into Simon's network. The man was a secrecy nut and completely unconcerned with his possible true-death. No one there is prepared to lead."

"What are you going to do?" Kara asked, rubbing her legs. Gaspard forced himself to look away.

"I may send Marc there. He's ready."

"Interesting thought. I look forward to hearing more. I'll meet you in your study, Gaspard. Let me get cleaned up," Kara replied.

"I shall await your presence."

Ha, thought Gaspard. *I can contain myself.*

"After we talk about your visit, I will leave for Washington, DC," said Kara, "so it is good you are back."

"Washington!" Gaspard said to her retreating back. "Why?"

"I'll tell you in twenty minutes!" she yelled over her shoulder.

Gaspard grimaced at his own powerlessness in her presence, but that didn't stop him from watching her derriere as she departed.

3

Kara felt much better after her shower and a change of clothes. Seeing Gaspard again was both a pleasure and a problem. She wasn't sure how she should act around him and hoped he didn't suspect her feelings went beyond respect. She couldn't love a vampire, even one with a soul.

She recalled her dream from the week before. In it, she had dream-walked to Gaspard's room, where his dream-self caressed and kissed her. She closed her eyes in memory, feeling the softness of that touch all over again and her astonishment that he had a soul. She'd become too afraid in her dream to take the lovemaking very far and had snapped awake, but it had felt real. Her face reddened with embarrassment. *He mustn't know*, she thought.

She gave herself a sharp rebuke, adopted a pleasant but blank face, and knocked on the study door. It swung open at her first touch.

She entered to see the object of her fantasy lounging in his desk chair, tie loosened and at ease. His dark hair was loose, and the one silver streak that ran from temple to tip was less obvious than when he wore it back in a tight queue. He looked to Kara like he didn't have a care in the world.

Gaspard gestured for her to sit. She chose to stand, which caused a spark of annoyance in his face before he let it pass.

"The Northeast contingent is used to a heavy-handed type of leadership," Gaspard started, leaning forward to place his arms on his desk to look at Kara directly.

"I'm sure they are," Kara responded. "Simon was a heavy-handed kind of guy, and his part-jötnar bodyguard was a bull-headed moose. Neither known for their subtlety."

"Did you say part jötnar?" Gaspard asked, eyes quizzical.

"Yes, I figured that out when I fought him in the hotel parking lot. His skin was very hard, and his mulish behavior was typical. He looked human, but I'm pretty sure he had some giant, jötnar, in him. It's a mystery why a member of the Jötenheimr would be serving a vampire. It is something I plan to ask my sisters..."

"The Vanir asked them to keep an eye on the vampires," Gaspard said. "I bet Jarius was an unintended consequence."

Kara's jaw dropped to the floor. "The *Vanir* asked the Jötenheimr to keep an eye on vampires? Are you kidding me?"

"No, not kidding, *ma chérie*. When I met your boss, we also found out that Freya had foreseen battles ahead between vampires with souls and those without. She'd asked the giants to act as bodyguards to the soulless ones and report back. They were her spies."

Now Kara sat down. "Freya. The Jötenheimr. Odin. Me. I've been so focused on myself I never thought of the bigger picture."

Gaspard wrinkled his brow, which made him look like a confused puppy, Kara thought, especially adorable. She shook herself again.

"Didn't Odin explain all of this to you? He sought me out in Paris, saying that he'd seen signs of a war between vampires with souls and those without. Freya had as well. Freya dispatched the giants. Odin sent you to me."

"Paris. Odin sought you out in *Paris*. Of course, he did," said Kara, rising to pace, although now she knew enough to watch out for sparks flying from her heels. She'd burned a lot of rugs that way and recently had used the sparking power to kill a vampire. She didn't dare let it get out of control.

"Tell me," Kara said. "Why do some vampires have souls and others do not?"

"As we turn, it is a choice we are given. Keep our souls and keep our pain, or abandon our souls and lose the pain, and the guilt, sadness and shame that come with it."

"Everyone has pain."

Gaspard shrugged. "But some pain is harder than others, and we have long lifespans. Our pain can last for centuries, sometimes gathering dust and losing its impact over time, other times gaining in intensity until it consumes us. When we turn, we take that risk. Or, we choose not to take the risk and live soulless."

"This was a game. A game played over decades, maybe hundreds of years. What else happened in Paris? You've mentioned it a few times. I have a right to know." Kara rubbed her hands over her eyes in resignation, realizing that Odin had played her. *I'd been so young*, she thought. *So hot-headed and sure of myself. And so wrong.*

"I don't know if the word 'game' is correct, Kara. Odin believed a war was on the horizon. I'd recently lost Sophie, a girl I loved desperately, and had a long-standing disagreement with the Master of Paris, Arnaud. It was a delicate time. Odin met me in a bar the night I was to leave for New Orleans."

Kara stuffed her jealousy at the mention of Sophie down where Gaspard couldn't see it. She smiled a full-on smile as she pictured Odin and Gaspard in a bar. "A vampire and a god walk into a bar... That sort of thing? That must have been a surprise."

Gaspard grinned right back at her. "It was one of the most extraordinary meetings of my life. He served us honey mead."

"Ah, his favorite brew. The dwarves perfected the fermenting process. It loosens lips and convinces the drinker that he, or she, can trust Odin."

"Well, it worked with me. I spilled my whole life, but he seemed to know a lot about me anyway."

"He did. He's Odin," Kara replied.

"There's one other thing, Kara. He said this war could shake the Tree."

A stab of alarm raced across Kara's stomach, directly in line with the scar she'd gained by her stubborn disrespect of her Valkyrie sister, Sigrun. It was that quarrel that landed her here, on Midgard, Earth, serving a vampire.

"The Tree? Yggdrasil? The Tree that connects the nine worlds? That Tree?"

Gaspard nodded. "The very one."

"Oh, Odin. Why didn't you tell me?" Kara looked at the ceiling but spoke to the sky. A shadow formed in the air, gaining shape and substance as it floated down on a non-existent breeze. As Kara reached out to capture it, she realized it was a leaf. Leaves were falling indoors in Gaspard's office. It wasn't even the strangest thing that had happened in the last two weeks.

Gaspard dashed around his desk to examine the leaf with her. It held one sentence on its broad face. "You wouldn't have believed me," Gaspard read aloud.

Kara hung her head, considering her Odin's words and her behavior. She wouldn't have believed him. She never thought anything could shake the Tree. Now she understood that a vampire war was coming, and Odin had placed her directly in the middle of it, depending on her to make a difference. Her shame grew to pride and determination.

"I have to go to Washington," she said, hurrying to the door.

"Why?" said a bewildered Gaspard to her exiting back.

She peeked her head back in. "We got an email from someone who says they can give us information about what is going on, but the writer said that only a face-to-face meeting will do."

Gaspard followed her out into the hall and grabbed her elbow.

She looked at his hand.

He removed it.

"Kara, this could be a trap."

"Certainly, but we won't know until I get there."

"I'm coming with you," Gaspard announced.

"No, you aren't," said Kara, whirling around to face him, hands clasped in irritation, as if she were trying to keep from striking him. "I can't protect you while searching for this mysterious informant, and I need to travel during the day."

"I don't want you going alone." Gaspard said this in a quiet voice, and despite her concerns, it touched her heart.

"Let's agree to this. I'll go, and when I have an idea what's going on, if I need you, I will call. In the meantime..."

"...let her do her job," finished Marc, as he strolled back down the hall. "I've said it to you before, Gaspard. You must let Kara do her job. She's terribly good at it."

Gaspard glared at Marc for his interference. Marc whistled while he waited for Gaspard to come to his senses.

"Fine," Gaspard snapped. "Go alone. But I want daily reports."

Kara smiled and shot him a salute. "Aye, aye, captain."

Gaspard gave her a regal nod and turned to Marc. "Marc, we need to review our finances. Let's go over the books and check on the investments."

Kara was surprised to see Marc frown. "I think that's a good idea. We may want to sell..."

"Absolutely not."

Kara asked, "Sell what?"

"Some land in France," Gaspard replied. "Leave it alone, Kara. Go, as you say, and do your job."

Kara made a small bow and backed away, heading upstairs to pack.

4

Kara arrived in D.C. early the next morning. She'd taken her own form of air travel, a ride on her horse, Rikassa, whose sole purpose was to serve her Lady. Horse and rider were bound so closely that when Kara was sent to Midgard to protect Gaspard, she'd been allowed to take Rikassa with her. It would have been unthinkable to do anything else.

"Hello, and welcome to the Holiday Inn at the Washington Capitol," said a chipper voice from the vicinity of the front desk. Kara scanned the counter and registration area until she spied a tiny young woman, maybe four foot, nine inches, smiling up at her from the other side of the desk.

"Hello. I have a reservation for tonight and would like to check in," said Kara proud of herself for remembering the phrases Marc had taught her. She'd never stayed in a hotel before.

"It's too early to check into your room, but we can store your luggage and park your car for you," said the young woman.

Kara hesitated. "Uh, I don't have a car."

"No problem. I thought you might have a car since I didn't see a taxi pull up to the front. Guess I must have missed it. How'd you get here?"

Everything Marc told her flitted through Kara's brain. She found nothing to help answer that question.

"Hello? You okay?" The tiny woman tapped Kara's elbow. Kara

stopped herself from stepping into a fighting stance at the last minute, foot back and forth, fists up and down, swiveling back and forth at the waist.

"Hey, you having a seizure or something?"

"No. No. I'm fine." Kara considered calling Rikassa to rescue her from this situation. Rikassa snorted in Kara's mind. "Shut up," Kara muttered.

"Excuse me?" stammered the front desk clerk.

"Not you! I'm sorry." Kara reached for any excuse. "I'm just...tired."

The woman relaxed. "Of course, you've arrived quite early. Tell you what?" The woman leaned in and whispered, "I'll let you check in promptly at noon, before our other guests. You come back then, and I'll get you into your room." She gave Kara a wink.

"That's nice of you." Kara swallowed hard and kept her composure.

"If you have your luggage, I'll be happy to store it." The tiny woman walked around the desk, head sweeping back and forth looking for Kara's suitcase.

Kara pointed to the small drawstring gym bag she'd slung over her shoulder.

"Oh, right. You are only staying overnight. Would you like me to hold it for you anyway?"

Kara searched her memory for what Marc told her to do in this situation.

"Yes, that would be nice, thank you."

The tiny woman held out her hand, and it took Kara a beat to realize she was asking for the backpack. Fumbling and thinking that this whole thing was awkward, unnecessary, and altogether too hard, she shoved the backpack toward the woman with such force that the small woman stumbled backward.

"Wow!" said the woman, recovering her balance. "You must work out."

"Yes, I do," said Kara. "Sorry. Gotta go." Kara fled, propelling her way through the rotating doors and out into the fresh air.

"Wait! You forgot your claim tag!"

Kara heard this last statement from outside the door and waved. "I trust you," she yelled and then ran off toward the stone buildings and green grass of the National Mall.

The informant asked to meet at the Jefferson Memorial, located at the southern tip of the Tidal Basin between the Lincoln Memorial and the Washington Memorial. The closest metro stop was the Smithsonian exit, but even that stop was distant, meaning Kara had to walk or take a bus to visit the memorial of the third president of the United States.

It was past cherry blossom season, but Kara could imagine all the trees dressed in pink and white, sprinkling petals over visitors, creating a carpet at night when no one was there to see. She wondered what Jefferson would have thought about the war to come. He had been a spiritual man, she decided, and he would fight to protect the innocent who would get caught in the crosshairs.

She entered the memorial, gazed at the nineteen-foot bronze statue of the man, and stopped to read the inscriptions on the walls. She examined the quote on the Southeast Portico.

"I am not an advocate for frequent changes in laws and constitutions, but laws and institutions must go hand in hand with the progress of the human mind. As that becomes more developed, more enlightened, as new discoveries are made, new truths discovered and manners and opinions change, with the change of circumstances, institutions must advance also to keep pace with the times. We might as well require a man to wear still the coat which fitted him when a boy as a civilized society to remain ever under the regimen of their barbarous ancestors."

"I wonder if the world is ready to understand the nature of vampires, truly understand them?" she said out loud in the empty dome. "How will humans react? What laws would they change? What amendments would they add?"

"They most likely wouldn't get the chance to do any of those things," said a man, from behind her.

Kara recognized the voice and turned to face its owner, lowering her head in acknowledgment of his preeminence.

"Odin. My lord."

"My lovely Kara," said the one-eyed man, dressed in a moderately well-fitting blue suit with a red tie, as any good Washington regular would. He could have been anybody. A congressman, a lawyer, an investment banker. He melded in with the commuters streaming from the metro stops, stomping up the sidewalks to their various offices, each one staring at the ground or talking into a cell phone. He stepped forward and lifted her chin so that they looked in each other's eyes.

"I was…" Kara searched for the word.

"Young, my dear. Young. That is all, but I would ask you to remember what I sacrificed this eye for the next time you want to make a bet with me," Odin said, tilting his head and tapping his nose with his index finger, a small smile on his lips.

"It wasn't that long ago that we made that bet. How come I feel so much older now?"

Odin took Kara's arm. "Walk with me."

They walked arm-in-arm as if he were an older gentleman approaching retirement, secure in his federal pension, and she was his niece, visiting from Montana.

"Sometimes growing older isn't about years," Odin said. "It is about knowledge. It can come quickly, as it has for you. It usually arrives with a deeper understanding that not only were you wrong about one thing, but you are most likely wrong about others, and your mind expands. That is growth, true growth, and I'm proud of how you've handled yourself during your time on Midgard."

He continued. "Gaspard had a similar experience. Despite being a well of power and clearly a Master, he'd lived his two hundred or so years in Burgundy, ruling a small village that became a small town. His problems were the equivalent size. Then, he arrived in Paris, and in a series of months, he encountered hunger, a global war, sheer hate, genocide, fell in love with a girl, lost her, and learned that he was going to be at the forefront of the Soul Wars. He is a much older man now than when I found him in an out-of-the-way bar."

"The Soul Wars. Very romantic," remarked Kara. "And what is this about falling in love? Was this about a woman named Sophie?" She uttered the last in an embarrassingly sharp tone, and she was horrified by her lack of composure.

Odin smiled. "Do I detect a note of jealousy? Love is a good thing, Kara. In fact, it is the *only* thing. You would do well to remember that."

Before she could respond, he placed a finger on her lips. "Hold onto that thought. We'll talk about that later. But to get back to your first point, yes, the Soul Wars, for that is what it is. We are battling for the soul of Midgard now. If the soulless gain too much power, and there are a lot of them, then they will have no checks, no balances. They will run amok, and our human friends will never have the chance to make laws, change laws, or enforce new policies, as President Jefferson advocated, because they will have been subjugated while they weren't looking."

"An entire world of slaves?"

"Basically, yes, and that would indeed shake the foundations of the Tree. It is ironic that your contact chose the Jefferson Memorial for your rendezvous, isn't it? The memorial of the man who wrote 'all men are created equal.' He believed those truths to be self-evident, but if the soulless are in charge, mankind will be stripped of everything and nothing will be self-evident because truths will hide behind shadows."

"How is Gaspard involved?" Kara asked.

"He's the tipping point. If he falls, then others will as well."

They walked on in silence, Kara deliberating all that Odin had said. She turned to ask another question, but Odin interrupted her.

"Oh look, an intact cherry blossom," he said, pointing to the ground.

Kara bent to retrieve the flower, wondering how it could be there. When she stood up, Odin was gone.

5

Kara spent the rest of the day wandering the National Mall, enjoying the sights and sounds, examining memorials, watching for tails, marking out escape routes, keeping anyone suspicious in her line of sight. She found the last to be difficult. It was Washington, D.C., after all. Everyone looked suspicious.

At ten p.m., she situated herself in the dark rotunda of the Memorial, wishing the damn thing wasn't so *round*. She preferred corners where she could have walls to two sides of her body. The set meeting time—eleven p.m.—came and went, and at eleven-thirty, Kara decided this had been a waste of time and readied to leave.

"You are loyal to him," came a voice, deep and throaty in the silence. Kara slid several feet to the right, ducking low, moving position, her hand on her sword hilt. She padded along the wall of the dome, her training telling her to keep moving, keep moving.

"Who are you?" Kara asked, looking for the speaker. All she saw was shadow and an occasional flicker of movement. It was as if the natural dark had turned true black, a complete absence of light that weighed like a stone in Kara's mind. The gloom was a physical blanket that draped the dome, playing on the natural instincts of living beings everywhere to seek illumination, scratching at that primordial knowledge that the dark was the Devil's playground.

The voice was right in front of her, following Kara's every movement, lower, higher, right or left. Kara gave in and stood still, realizing that this creature could see her as if it were full daylight. Kara closed her eyes, controlled her breathing, and *listened.*

The heartbeat was slow, far slower than a human's, and if she concentrated, she could smell blood on the creature's lips. Vampire. Kara mentally triangulated the location of the vampire's blood-soaked mouth and created a mental picture of the vampire's height, and thus, its head. If things went sour, that was her target.

"Why did you ask me here?" Kara asked, hand still on her sword.

"Tell Gaspard it is Vachel."

"Who is Vachel?" Kara demanded.

"He'll know."

"Why did you ask me here? Who are you? Why help Gaspard?" Kara's voice grew in strength and pitch as her temper rose. The voice pulled back. Kara estimated the voice was on the other side of the rotunda. Thanks to the parabolic harmonics, Kara could still hear the voice clearly; in fact, it sounded as if it were right next to her ear, but Kara could tell by the lack of smell that it wasn't.

"I'm a friend, and I wanted to see the woman who protects him."

"Why?" asked Kara.

"I'm curious."

"Tell me about this Vachel."

"Vachel was a pub owner in Paris during World War II. Gaspard knew him. What Gaspard does not know is that immediately after he and Vachel parted company, Vachel met up with a vampire, a vampire you know as the Greek."

"The Greek! He's ancient."

"Yes, and wily. He would have sucked Vachel dry, but Vachel did the unexpected," said the voice.

"What did he do?"

"He promised to serve the Greek for two hundred years if the vampire would turn him." The voice sounded wistful.

"Vachel wanted to be a vampire?"

"Yes. To avenge the death of a woman they both loved. He held, and still holds, Gaspard responsible for her death."

"Why?" asked Kara.

"That doesn't matter. What does matter is that Vachel has been waiting a long time to get his revenge. He's planned and plotted. He's gathered allies."

"Who?" Kara demanded.

"A female vampire from Texas, Valeria Snow." The voice shifted again, moving toward the entrance, getting ready to leave.

"Wait! Who else? You said allies, plural." Kara released her sword and stepped toward the voice, still not knowing if it was male or female.

"Tell Gaspard Luc failed. Henri is back."

The voice left in a swish of wind. Kara stood, stupefied, followed by fury at herself for not having foreseen Henri's return. She should have guessed. Henri was Gaspard's brother, turned into a vampire without Gaspard's knowledge, thought long dead. He had proved his death to be nothing more than a rumor by showing up at Luc's mansion, determined to murder his brother in retribution for ancient misfortunes he attributed—falsely—to Gaspard. Luc was their father, and he was supposed to have brought Henri to justice for breaking vampire laws, specifically for drinking from children.

Now, this Vachel was back from the dead as well. *What was it with this vampire*, thought Kara, *that so many of his so-called friends come back from the dead wanting to kill him*?

Kara felt the ominous wet blanket of darkness lift and starlight beamed once again into the rotunda. Kara returned to her hotel, finally checking in and gaining access to her room. The tiny woman from before was long-gone. Kara considered what she had been told and knew she needed to talk to Gaspard, but she wasn't sure this was something she could say over the phone or in an email. She showered, ate something from the nearby candy machine, and decided to leave that night, surprising the night clerk who had only given her the room key an hour before.

6

Rikassa winged back to New Orleans at her normal hurricane speed, dropping Kara off at the front door, nearly giving the guards heart attacks as the white horse descended from the sky. The roof snipers had been warned long ago not to shoot any flying horses, an order they took seriously, but they hadn't been ordered to warn the ground crew when one approached, and they got a perverse joy out of watching the ground guards almost wet their pants.

Kara gave Rikassa a loving pat and slid her an apple she drew out of nowhere. Rikassa nuzzled her Lady and went on her way. Kara wished she could have taken her four-footed friend into the house with her. She could use some backup.

Delaying the inevitable, Kara dashed to her room to change clothes, buying time to consider how to break the news about Henri's return and the appearance of somebody else from his past, and how they were colluding against Gaspard. Not to mention the Greek's involvement, which meant the tacit approval of the Assembly. She wondered if any members of the Assembly had souls. That would be an angle of investigation for another time. The implications of a completely soulless Assembly made Kara shiver.

She couldn't help but wonder if Odin knew any of this already or if she needed to report to him in some manner. She decided it was likely he either knew before or knew now by following her conversation with whatever means he had. She tried to remember if Hugin or Munin, Odin's ravens, had been hanging around the memorial. She didn't recall seeing them, but spotting black birds in a black rotunda was a mighty hard trick, even for her.

Gaspard wasn't going to take Henri's return well, and Adelaide would be absolutely beside herself. Kara made a note to have someone drop by Lisette's house to give her a warning. Lisette was a former sanguineer Henri brutalized the last time he was in town, using her to gain access to Gaspard. Perhaps Lisette needed to go on a vacation.

Taking her time, Kara examined the bottles of what she called "smelly stuff" on the counter. She'd never used any of it and had no idea if it would smell good or not, but a little moisturizing seemed to be in order, and it was an especially good way to delay going downstairs.

The first bottle smelled like rose petals, and Kara put that one back. The second smelled of vanilla, with a hint of ginger—an earthy scent she enjoyed. She slathered the lotion all over her and then sprayed the body mist on to boot. When she stopped sneezing, she worried she'd put too much on and used a towel to wipe as much off as she could.

It was all a little much, she thought, as she sat naked on the edge of her bed. Every minute since she'd arrived at Gaspard's mansion was frantic. They were either being attacked or planning a defense for when they were next attacked. Her feelings for Gaspard slipped in somewhere amongst the crazy nights, and occasional days, and her mind whirled with anxious energy. Her weaknesses were evident, cracked open for all to see after being under constant pressure, and she worried she wasn't good enough. What would happen if she failed? If Gaspard died? It was too much to consider, and Kara shook the thoughts away.

She dressed in her customary black racer back t-shirt and jeans; donned her sword, shield, and gun; and made her way downstairs, taking deep cleansing breaths. She plastered a smile on her face and entered the study.

She could tell by the slight flush to his cheeks that Gaspard had just fed. As she walked in, he sniffed, then looked up in surprise, staring at her with a slight smile. He took a deep breath, holding it for a moment, then exhaled with an audible growl. Marc followed his lead and took a sniff, eyeing Kara with alarm.

He and Marc were conducting business with someone on a speaker phone, but Gaspard disconnected the call without apology.

"I asked for a nightly report, but that didn't mean you had to rush home personally. What brings you here so quickly, and why do you smell like snickerdoodles?" He walked toward her, inhaling like a blue tick coonhound getting a scent. With every step, his body became more languid, his eyes more seductive, and when he licked his lips, it was more than she could take, and she bolted to the side.

"You enjoy port, don't you Gaspard? Perhaps a drink would be a nice way to start the debrief?" Kara uncorked a few decanters and bent down to absorb their rich aromas, which had the other advantage of hiding her eyes from the predator to her front.

Gaspard's eyes lost their gleam, and he pulled away, giving her space, for which she was intensely grateful. He was dressed for business this night, wearing a navy suit, silver tie, and a white shirt. The silver tie complemented the silver streak in his hair. It was one of Kara's favorite looks.

"Kara. What. Is. It?"

Kara turned to face Gaspard and decided brazen and brash was her best option, also usually her only option, but she was glad to realize that she knew there was a choice. *See*, she thought, *personal growth*.

"I met a vampire. I don't know if the vampire was male or female. It, for lack of a better pronoun, said that it was a friend of yours."

"You didn't get any more information than that?"

Kara held up a finger. "Wait. Be patient. The voice also said one person was behind Simon's attack, the Texas spies, and the tacit approval from the Assembly. In fact, it seems the Greek is his key to the Assembly."

"Did this mysterious voice say who this person was?" Gaspard asked, left hand on his hip, right hand clasping papers in a model of the modern businessman.

"Someone named Vachel."

Gaspard sank into the chaise lounge and let the documents fall to the floor. Marc scrambled to pick them up.

"How could it be?" Gaspard whispered.

"That's not all." Kara knelt to look Gaspard eye-to-eye. She knew this part would kill him. "The voice also said Henri is back. Luc failed to destroy him."

A voice shrieked from the hall, "I knew it! I knew that bastard would resurface! I'm going to tear him apart with my own hands!"

Adelaide stormed into the room, right hand in a fist, left on a cane. "I knew Luc couldn't kill his own son." She was so distraught that her face was red and her already unsteady legs quivered.

Marc hurried to Adelaide's side and helped her to a seat on the couch. "It seems you were right, Madame. I had my doubts as well, but calm yourself. Here, have a drink." He walked to the decanters and poured a sherry, which he handed to Adelaide. She took one sip and placed it on the side table.

"Who is Vachel?" Kara asked. "I know Henri's past and his game, but I don't know anything about Vachel and why he would hate you so much. You seem to have a knack for stirring enmity in past acquaintances."

Gaspard poured himself a small bit of port, held quiet for several moments, studying his shoes. When he spoke, his voice was soft.

"Vachel and I once loved the same woman, a French girl named Sophie. She was brave and beautiful, and she was killed by an American soldier during World War II. Prior to her death, she, Vachel, and I had a confrontation. She chose me over Vachel, and he felt it was my responsibility to watch over her, to protect her. I agree with him on this point and regret to this day that I failed. He never forgave me. I never forgave myself. I lost track of him after the war. I didn't know he had turned vampire." Gaspard's face was stony, but Kara noticed a very small tic at his temple.

"The voice also said that a vampire from Texas, Valeria Snow, was involved. I'm assuming she is the source of the spies?"

"Yes, that I figured out already. Odin warned me about her long ago, when we met in that bar, and her spies admitted to their true purpose when I, ahem, confronted them." Gaspard's eyes glittered a bit at the memory. Marc coughed to hide his laugh.

"I wasn't there. What did they say?" asked Kara.

Marc interjected. "Our Master..."

"Your Master," Kara retorted.

Marc rolled his eyes. "Fine, Gaspard, my Master, confronted them in the billiards room downstairs after the Grunch debacle. You were working with the guards to clean up the outside and remove the remains of Jarius and that seer witch."

Marc shifted a little in his stance, making the most of his time in the spotlight. "There was a crowd of bystanders, other vampires mostly. Gaspard played those young guns like a fiddle. They weren't ready for his strength of will, and when he confronted them, they fell on their knees begging for their lives in seconds. Gaspard drew one of your knives across each of their throats, not enough to kill, but enough for them to get the idea. Despite their injured vocal cords, they managed to name Valeria Snow, Mistress of Southwest Texas."

"It would have been nice if you told me!" Kara crossed her arms over her chest.

"Yes, we should have," said Gaspard. "That was my error. I apologize."

"We should have sent spies in return."

"She would have killed them. We did send her people back, hermetically sealed in pieces in an overnight delivery box. I got the idea from an old French vampire I knew. I think I mentioned him to you, Arnaud, Master of Paris."

"I appreciate his style," Kara said, rubbing her temples. "Again, why wasn't I told this?"

"Marc and I went to work with the Northeast vampires, and it slipped my mind," said Gaspard, returning to a standing position with a small flourish, fixing his cuff links. "Then you left for Washington, D.C., to meet with your mysterious informant. Besides, this way we have confirmed this tidbit of information from two sources. It makes me think your informant, whoever it is, is telling the truth."

"So, let's review what we know," said Kara, returning to the safe ground of strategy before she strangled Gaspard and Marc with her bare hands. "This Vachel guy is out to get you. He's been plotting his revenge for years, nay, decades, and recruited your lunatic brother to join him. He works for the Greek, so he has access to the Assembly and has some influence with them as well. In the meantime, Valeria Snow wants your territory, is in league with the bad guys, and presumably has information about us, me, and our security protocols. Not to mention that you have an entire new vampire seethe to rule."

"That seems about right," said Gaspard, who had moved to stare out the window into the night, hands clasped behind his back.

Kara paced the room. "And if we don't shut this down quickly, it could lead to an even bigger war that could shake the very foundation of the Tree."

"The Tree? Odin's Tree? Yggdrasil?" asked Adelaide.

"Exactly that tree. How did you know?" asked Kara, curious that her friend recognized the reference.

"I read," snapped the older woman, still brooding over the news of Henri's return. She fluttered her hand in apology to Kara for her tone. "And when you told me you were a Valkyrie, I made sure to refresh my memory of Norse mythology."

"Well, short version, some vampires have souls, like Gaspard. Others relinquish their souls when they turn. This situation we now find ourselves in is the first battle of the Soul Wars, as Odin calls them. If we don't stop this now, it is entirely possible that the soulless vampires will gain in power and enslave the world."

"Oh, is that all?" Adelaide downed the rest of her sherry.

7

"So, what's the first thing we do?" asked Marc, holding pen and paper, ready to make a list. Kara shook her head. *Virgos, they always organize, even when dead.*

Kara stopped pacing long enough to check the floor. No sparks. That was a good thing; she was gaining some control. She snapped her fingers.

"First, we change security protocols around here given that Valeria probably knows a lot about us. Second, we get your vampire seethe in shape and on guard. They're going to need to fight. Third, you bring some of the best, most experienced warriors from the Northeast seethe down here to help us."

Marc scribbled, nodding at her instructions.

"The fourth is up to Gaspard."

Gaspard turned around. "What is that?"

"You have to find Luc. He is undoubtedly around somewhere. Tell that father of yours to get his butt in gear and help fix what he broke."

"I shall endeavor to locate him," Gaspard replied, face grave. "But I will refrain from saying he has to get his butt in gear."

"Whatever." Kara waved his words away. "He owes us."

Adelaide held up a finger. "Wait. Do you think we can trust this informant?"

Kara put her hand on Adelaide's shoulder. "As Gaspard said, the information about Valeria Snow's involvement was correct. Besides, I don't think we have any other choice."

Marc turned to face Gaspard, whispering in his ear so the ladies couldn't hear.

"We'll figure it out, Marc," said Gaspard.

"What is it?" Kara demanded. "Don't leave out one more piece of information."

Marc replied. "The recent expenditures are straining Gaspard's finances. He needs to liquidate some assets, especially if we are going to expand our home base here. We'll need more weapons, certainly, but we'll also need more sanguineers, which means food and other necessities for humans, which we will then have to protect."

Gaspard's face pinched with fury. "That is private business, Marc!"

"They have to know!"

"It is my responsibility! I will take care of it!" Gaspard stepped into Marc's space, but the lieutenant stood his ground. Barely.

"Gaspard! This is my job. Let me do it."

Gaspard took a step back, but his face remained closed, and the tips of his fangs peeked out from his lips. "That seems to be a refrain around here." He stared at Adelaide and Kara. "This goes no further, understand?"

Adelaide cleared her throat. "I may be able to help with that."

"How?" Marc asked. "You don't have any money left."

Adelaide squirmed in her seat. "Actually, I do. When I was searching for money to restore my property, you know, before the whole ghost thing made it almost impossible, I asked a friend for help. He placed several pieces of my jewelry, including a rather impressive sapphire, up for auction. I just learned that it sold."

Gaspard raised his hands to object. Adelaide held up her hand to stop him. "I now have shy of three million dollars. Let me help."

"No." Gaspard's voice was rock hard.

"Gaspard, please, I ask again, let me help. When we get through this, I have an idea about what to do with our properties that we will both like, but we need to survive first."

Gaspard snapped. "I will think about it." Kara could tell that was all

Gaspard was willing to bend, but she had faith in Adelaide. That woman never lost a fight.

Marc nodded to Adelaide. "It is a generous offer, Madame. We will discuss it later."

"Ahem."

Kara, Adelaide, Gaspard, and Marc turned their attention to the entranceway.

"There is a vampire at the front gate asking to see you, sir," the butler said to Gaspard. "Security has asked for Kara."

"Did he say who he was?" Kara asked.

The butler nodded. "Security reports that his name is Luc."

Gaspard held his arms wide and faced Kara. "Found him."

"Oh, for Odin's sake..." Kara marched through the front door. There was hell to pay for Luc's failure to kill Henri, and she was going to pay it. Her muscles were loose and ready, her sword was on her left hip, and her shield camouflaged on her back as a small disc attached to her belt. She reached the gate, focused and hungry to hurt the man whose actions hurt Gaspard.

When she got there, she stopped in shock.

The guards at the front gate held a limp form dressed in black, lank hair hanging forward over the man's face. He wore one black boot, unlaced. His other foot was bare, its white skin noticeable even in the flood lights. She motioned for one of the guards to pull back Luc's head and stopped short at what she saw. His face was a mass of bruises, and his right ear hung by a strip of skin. Most shocking was his mouth. His incisors were gone, pulled out by the root. The once powerful vampire was defanged.

Kara barked orders. "Bring him up to the house. Carry him, please. He's seriously injured. And call ahead to tell them we will need three pints of bagged blood. I'm not sure even that amount of blood can fix all of this damage."

Gaspard waited at the open door, worry on his face, as the guards carried Luc's body into the house and lay him on the couch in the office.

"He said who he was?" Kara asked the guards.

One of the guards answered. "Yes'm, barely, and we radioed up. Then he fainted straight away. We didn't know if he was friend or foe."

"He's both, but he's toothless now," she said.

"Literally," agreed the other guard. "Who could do this to a vampire?"

Kara's face was grim. "Any sadist with pliers and time. The bigger questions are why and how did they capture him? Luc could teleport, or something close to it, when we last saw him. I would've thought he could get away from anyone."

Marc scowled. "This stinks of the Assembly to me. Kara, you said the Greek was involved? I'm betting he was a part of this. Who else could be strong enough to subdue an old vampire like Luc?"

"Only Luc can tell us," Kara replied.

8

Gaspard couldn't believe that a vampire of Luc's age and power could be in such a state. He'd have taken Las Vegas odds that this couldn't happen.

He shook himself back to reality when Kara yelled, "Where's that bagged blood?" Marc's aunt, Emmy, hurried in with three bags, heated to mimic body temperature. "How are we going to get this down his throat? He's not conscious enough to swallow." She directed this last question at Gaspard.

"I'm going to start him off," answered Gaspard, grabbing the letter opener on his desk. He'd used this same letter opener once before to do almost the same thing. He sliced his wrist with the letter opener and placed it at Luc's mouth, dribbling in his blood to rouse his father. Luc was still.

Gaspard knew he didn't have long, so he said, "If this offends your sensibilities, then turn away now." He sliced his tongue using the same letter opener and lay his mouth directly over Luc's, shoving blood down Luc's gullet like he was feeding a baby bird. Gaspard's lifeblood, blood of Luc's blood, dripped down Luc's throat and, at last, Luc sucked, capturing Gaspard's tongue with his.

Gaspard disentangled himself and held out his hand for a pint of the warmed blood. He punctured it with the letter opener, motioned for

Kara to lift Luc's head, and streamed the blood into Luc's mouth, letting it trickle so the weakened vampire had time to swallow. Luc took all three pints before he opened his eyes.

"Luc, what happened?" Gaspard asked, still holding the remains of the last bag. "Who did this to you?"

Luc stared into Gaspard's eyes. "My son, I failed," he whispered. "I couldn't kill Henri. I tried, but..."

"I know. That's for later. How did you come by this state?"

"The Greek. He chained me while Vachel and Henri had their way. He's too powerful, far older than I. There was no way to fight back, even when they took my fangs." If he could, he would have cried like a baby, Gaspard realized. It was a stunning realization, confronting your own father's mortality.

Kara stepped in with a question of her own. "Why would the Greek have it in for you?"

"For no reason in particular. He's bored and crazy. He's been alive for over a thousand years. He's toying with us, and with Vachel and Henri, too, although they don't know it. It's all a game to him." Luc's head fell back, his strength depleted, but some of the bruises were fading, and his ear was stitching itself back together, which was a good sign.

Gaspard issued an order to Marc. "See that Luc is placed somewhere quiet, lay fresh clothes out for him, and we'll let him rest until sundown tomorrow. He'll need more bagged blood then, if he is to survive."

Marc kneeled at Luc's side, mouth open, eyes blinking fast as he stared at the holes in Luc's mouth. "Will his fangs grow back?"

"I don't know. This is uncharted territory. For now, let's do what we can."

"I have a question," said Kara.

"What?" Marc, Adelaide, and Gaspard said at the same time.

"If the Greek is so powerful, how did Luc get away? Did he truly escape? Or was he released?"

Gaspard cast his eyes to the floor, thinking this through. "In other words, can we trust him?"

"You can't. You already know that." Adelaide's eyes were flinty. "He let Henri live. That's reason enough not to trust him."

Gaspard's thoughts tumbled through his head. His instinct was to trust Luc, but at this point, he would be stupid to give in to blind emotion.

"It's a fair point. Kara, can you place two guards at his room's entrance? He's so weakened that I cannot imagine him rising until tomorrow full dark, but..."

Kara clenched her teeth. "Better safe than sorry. I'll make sure they search him, too. Check for wires or any kind of transmitter. Until we hear his story in full, Luc Rochon is the enemy."

Marc made sure Luc was safely tucked away, and Kara assigned a guard rotation to watch his door for the next twenty-four hours. Guns holstered, bo sticks at the ready, the guards were under orders to kill on sight if Luc rose earlier than planned.

The house retired for the day, but Kara stayed awake in her room, considering this new development. She thought of the one person she knew who might have answers. It was late for vampires, the sun almost up, but she took a chance and logged on to her computer, clicking on her email.

Luc Rochon showed up today at Gaspard's mansion, severely injured. What do you know about this?

A message came right back from the informant.

I am glad he got to you. I wasn't sure if he would.

How did he escape? Kara typed.

A human servant loosened his chains and donated blood, just enough to get him on his feet, then snuck him out to the street, and the rest was up to him.

How do I know you aren't lying?

No response. Kara clicked refresh. Then again. A third time. She paced behind the chair. Four steps toward the closet. Four steps back. Nothing. Five steps toward the closet. Five steps back. Still nothing.

Scuff, scuff across the carpet. Six steps this time. Kara stomped out a spark before it could catch. She didn't look at the monitor, pulling in air through her nose and letting it out through her mouth for another twelve steps. Finally...

I can attest to his injuries. He was neutered as a vampire. They pulled out his incisors.

How do I know you didn't do it? Kara struck the keys with such force that she broke the H key.

You don't.

ow do I know I can trust you? The H was gone, but the informant seemed to understand.

You don't.

Crap, thought Kara. She couldn't really argue the informant's point. Unless he or she was willing to come forward and reveal who they were, and it didn't seem that was the case, she'd have to decide what to believe and what not to believe. The informant's story could be verified by Luc's recollection...unless they were in on this together. Kara's mind lurched from possible deceit to lie to untruth to half-truth. Sleep, she decided, was the best approach.

She closed her eyes and drifted, an image of Gaspard floating behind her eyelids. He was in a house of some kind. It seemed old. There was a fire crackling in a fireplace and a brown rug. Gaspard was naked, his body entwined with a woman's. He ran his hand down the woman's side, and Kara watched as the woman shivered with his touch. Kara's stomach clenched in response. She tried to leave, not wanting to see this intimacy, but her vision held her fast.

Gaspard pulled the woman to him, kissing her deeply, then moving his thumb to the woman's mouth. Kara heard the woman say, "Will you drink, Gaspard?"

Kara's breath came faster, both with jealousy and arousal. She watched as Gaspard bit the woman's neck and entered her at the same time, and Kara wished she was the one in Gaspard's arms.

The woman's gray eyes opened wide with her release, and Kara heard Gaspard breathe her name, "Sophie."

9

Was her vision real? Sophie died during the war, which meant her vision, if it were true, was from Paris during World War II.

The rest of the day passed in a broken and fitful sleep, so when Kara woke at sundown, she was worn out. She decided to go for a ride to clear her head. She dressed, weaponed up, and called for her horse.

Rikassa was happy to see her and rubbed her head and neck against Kara like she was a cat marking her territory. They rode at the back of the property, far from the main house, and Kara mentally saluted the Grunch family who lived deep in the swamp. She wasn't going back in there to see how they were doing. She assumed the Grunch would find her if he or his family needed help. She and the giant reptile monster had a live and let live agreement.

Rikassa let go as they reached the farthest part of the property and lifted off into the air. Kara threw her head back, closed her eyes, and wished her sisters were there to share in the cool evening air. She could use their advice.

"We are here," said Hildr.

Kara snapped her eyes open and hooted in joy when she saw that Hildr, Sigrun, and a Valkyrie she didn't know were flying beside her. Rikassa whinnied her greeting, too, and the race was on.

The four flew so high and so fast that they risked losing access to oxygen. Kara glanced at Sigrun and noticed her horse's hind quarters were only a streak of light as they flew around the world and back again. Kara hadn't flown like this since she'd left Valhalla, and doing so with her sisters alongside her filled an empty spot in her heart.

They landed on Gaspard's property and dismounted so the horses could play with one another. The Valkyries sat together in a circle.

"It is so lovely to see you. I see we have another sister," said Kara.

Hildr motioned toward the new Valkyrie. "She joined us after living a long life on Earth. She has taken the name Astrid."

"Astrid?" said Kara. "A beautiful name. Tell me about yourself, Astrid."

The Valkyrie smiled. "There's not much to tell."

Sigrun held up her hand. "False modesty. You led an interesting life."

Astrid acknowledged Sigrun's censure with a bob of her head. "I was a police officer in France. Not one of the regular police. I worked for a special branch that investigated the paranormal, the odd and the interesting. I had a good run. Saw a lot of ugliness, but good as well."

"What made you go into that line of work? I didn't know there were paranormal teams."

Astrid replied, "I saw some things in my childhood that I couldn't get past, emotionally, I mean. So, I decided to deal with it by getting involved. Finding the monsters. Eradicating them from the face of the Earth. Killing them all, if I had to."

Kara rocked back at the vehemence in Astrid's words.

Sigrun interrupted the exchange. "Now, Kara, let's get to the business at hand. What is it you need to know?"

"Will you join me in the fight if it comes to it?" Kara asked, starting with her most important question first. "Will Odin allow you to help?"

In response, Sigrun rose to her feet and drew her sword.

"What? What are you doing, Sigrun?" Kara asked, voice loud with alarm.

"Let's spar, sister."

Kara jumped up, eager to play with her sister again. Hildr and Astrid sat on the ground arms wrapped around their legs, ready to enjoy the show.

Kara attacked, drawing her sword lower left to upper right, using her speed, trying to get inside Sigrun's space. Sigrun parried and took a step back. Kara attacked again, upper right to lower left. Again, Sigrun parried and took another step back.

"What's wrong, Sigrun?" Kara asked. "Why do you not fight?"

"I'm letting you get warmed up, Kara," teased Sigrun, who then launched an attack that forced Kara to peddle backward like a poodle on stilts.

Down stroke, upstroke, thrust. Repeat. Kara couldn't stop Sigrun's rhythm and paid the price by slipping on the ground and falling backward. Hildr and Astrid cheered them both on and yelled for Kara to get up. Sigrun gave Kara a little bow and moved back so Kara could get to her feet. Sigrun also shrunk her sword to the size of a matchstick and whistled while she used it to pick her teeth.

Kara bit her lip in irritation and whipped out her shield to harry Sigrun with short strokes, pushing Sigrun in a circle that she couldn't get out of. Rikassa neighed and raised her hooves in the air for her Lady. Sigrun's horse grunted and shoved her shoulder into Rikassa's side.

Sigrun ducked under Kara's sword and scrambled behind, attacking Kara from the back. Kara struggled against the stronger woman's power and technique. "Come on, Kara," Sigrun hissed. "Win."

Kara knew she couldn't win. She'd battled Sigrun in training hundreds, if not thousands, of times. Her older sister was their leader for a reason. Kara panted with the effort of staying upright as Sigrun held the flat side of her sword to Kara's throat, using it to choke her younger sister.

"Haven't you been training, Kara? How do you train your guards? If the soulless are coming to play, how are we to *win*? You've been asked to lead a battle that can shake the Tree. Giving up is not an option!" Sigrun whispered all of this in Kara's ear.

Kara's thoughts slowed down. She knew how she'd trained her guards, but it never occurred to her to fight her sister that way.

"Okay, Sigrun," Kara said. "If that's what you want."

Kara slithered out of Sigrun's grasp, executed a tight twirl, and in one smooth motion, withdrew her Glock and shot her mentor in the chest. She then followed up with a sword thrust that would have pierced Sigrun's neck.

"Shoot and stab," Kara said, as Sigrun lay on the ground, stunned and gaping like a fish. "If you were a vampire, I'd have set you on fire, too."

Sigrun jumped to her feet, not wounded in the least, and pounded her sister on the back. "That's what I was looking for! New thinking and a passion to win. Yes, Kara. If it comes to a fight, we will fight with you."

10

Luc woke with a start, turning his body to and fro, trying to figure out where he was. His instinct was to huddle down in a small ball, a far cry from his once proud demeanor. Panic flashed through his body, and he ran his tongue over his incisors or, more appropriately, where his incisors used to be. It all came back to him.

He must be in Gaspard's house. He'd found the house almost by instinct, like a homing pigeon seeking its nest, the one safe place it knew. He couldn't bite, so getting food was difficult, and he resorted to cutting animals with a knife and sucking the blood as best he could.

The Greek. The Greek had the power of a thousand years and the mindset that went with it. The Greek had gone insane—wildly, terribly, classically mad. The years had piled up, and for the Greek, the years wore heavy, each new language a new burden, each new government, border, army, or state was change over change over change. Given his speech, his mind must have shorted out sometime in the 1600s when he came to the New World.

"Luc, Luc, lucky Luc, dancing Luc," the Greek has sung while skipping in circles around the dark room where Luc was prisoner.

"Ye don't want to tell me?" the Greek asked.

"Tell you what?" Luc had managed, with a rasp. He honestly didn't know. It took Luc several days of this torture to realize the Greek wanted nothing.

"Hold, sir! If you shall not renounce the devil, then let us put your feet to the fire!" the Greek had exclaimed.

Luc discovered the Greek meant that in a literal sense. The Greek placed the torch to Luc's feet and watched him burn, then fed him blood to restore him whole. Luc felt sympathy for Prometheus, wondering if the Greek vampire had gotten this idea from the hero's tragic story.

"Ah, sir," the Greek would say as he entered the room the next evening. "How do you do? I am at your service. May I introduce my friend and confidante, Vachel."

That was the first-time Luc saw Vachel, but he had learned Vachel's history during those tortuous days. Something about a woman. A woman named Sophie, a lover, a beauty, but to Vachel, a queen.

A soft knock on the door brought his mind back to the present. The door opened without his bidding it to do so, and he faced three armed guards.

"We've been instructed to bring you to Gaspard. If you so much as twitch, we will kill you."

"I am not Gaspard's enemy," Luc said, holding his hands out in front of him, entreating them to believe him.

"Not my call, vampire. Let's go."

"Allow me to change, please. I see fresh garments have been provided."

The guards waited in the room, forcing Luc to undress and dress in front of them. Another humiliation Luc had to absorb.

When done, Luc stepped into the hall in his bare feet, for no shoes had been provided, and did as they bade. He walked in the middle of a three-point team, covered in the front and back, and he could tell by their discipline that these guards were well trained. *It's the Valkyrie*, he thought. *Good for Gaspard.*

Luc's primary feeling was humiliation when the guards shoved him into Gaspard's office. And regret. He admitted to both. It was an unusual feeling for him, and he squirmed as he stood in the center of the room and took in the scene.

Gaspard sat at his desk, a massive wooden thing that fit his powerful personality. The Valkyrie stood to Gaspard's right, right hand resting on her belt. She reminded Luc of a white tiger with her blond hair, but it was her gaze that signaled the predator. She stood loose and ready, seeming relaxed, but her gaze gave her away. She would strike if he messed with a hair on Gaspard's head. He saw more than a bodyguard's duty in her eyes. She had the ferocity of a woman in love.

A man stood to Gaspard's left. Vampire, Luc concluded, and was proved correct when the man bared his incisors.

Luc straightened himself and adopted a relaxed posture, belying what he felt in his belly and the shame that stabbed at his brain.

"May I sit?" he asked.

"Yes," said Gaspard. "No," snapped Kara.

Luc elected to stand.

"How did you feed me?" Luc asked, so uncomfortable that he was, for him, babbling. Another wave of self-disgust hit him.

"I fed you myself, blood of your blood," answered Gaspard, tilting back in his chair, holding a pen to his lips, considering his father. Luc noticed the gray pinstriped suit and red tie and how they molded to Gaspard's body. *No off the rack for him*, Luc thought.

Luc sighed, shoulders rising and falling, and watched the Valkyrie shift her weight to the balls of her feet. "Madame Valkyrie," Luc said, "I swear that I am not here as an enemy, but as a friend."

She didn't move a muscle. Not a smile, not an upward curve of the lip, not a blink.

Gaspard rose and placed a hand on the Valkyrie's shoulder. "Kara, stand down. He's defanged and beaten. He's not a threat."

Kara, now Luc knew her name, flicked an eyebrow at Gaspard but acquiesced. Gaspard said, "Luc, sit on the couch. Marc, please call for two pints of bagged blood." Marc, the well-muscled man who stood to Gaspard's left, didn't reply but did walk to the door and whisper instructions to whomever was there.

Gaspard unbuttoned his jacket, brushed non-existent lint off his trousers, and with a graceful, fluid movement, lowered himself to the chaise. Luc waited.

"Start at the beginning, Luc."

11

"I brought Henri to the Assembly, as promised," said Luc, studying his toes, as he was unable to look Gaspard in the eyes. "What I didn't know is that Henri's game was larger than I realized, and he had allies I couldn't have dreamed of. They captured and imprisoned me."

"The Greek?" said Gaspard.

"Yes, and an old enemy of yours, Vachel."

"How did Vachel become a vampire?"

"He left you after the battle in Orléans, furious to his core. Mere minutes after he'd left you, he came upon a stranger holding a woman in his arms. It was Sophie."

Gaspard's face stilled. He motioned for Luc to continue.

"It was the Greek. The Greek was monitoring southern France for the American Assembly and had traveled closer to Paris to see firsthand what was going on. He was old even then and had the speed and stamina that came with it. He'd seen Sophie in the snow and collected her. He likes to *collect* things." Luc shuddered.

Luc's feet bounced a nervous rhythm as he continued. He saw out of the corner of his eye that Kara had moved behind him, into what could only be called a good beheading position.

"For whatever reason, the Greek decided to turn Sophie, and when he saw Vachel, he thought he had the perfect first meal, but Vachel surprised him. He entreated the Greek to turn him, too, and promised indentured servitude for two hundred years if the Greek would help take you down. He fixated on revenge for Sophie's death and then Sophie's turning, which he despised, saying it was wrong to deprive Sophie of the sun. The one redeeming feature of this situation was that he'd be with her in death, as he couldn't be in life, and you would never know. He gloried in depriving you of her presence."

Marc retrieved two packs of blood from a person at the door and handed them to Luc. Luc stared at the bags, wanting to drink but unable to puncture them. Marc leaned in, plucked a hole in the bags with a sharp pocketknife and handed Luc a straw. Luc felt the heat rise in his face, but he didn't refuse the nourishment. He sucked them down like a two-year-old slurping a juice box. When he was done, he resumed his story.

"He's been plotting ever since. Somehow Vachel learned of Henri, and the two teamed up."

Kara broke in. "Where was Sophie in all of this?"

"Nowhere, as far as I know. She seemed a bit actor in this play, never coming to terms with being a vampire."

"That doesn't surprise me," mused Gaspard. "Did you see her when you were captive?"

"No. Never saw her, never smelled her. When I had the temerity to ask about her, the Greek said he'd 'lost' her sometime in the past, stating, almost offhandedly, that she had walked into the sun. He talked about her as one would a doll or a prized painting, something he'd acquired and then misplaced."

Luc cleared his throat. "Vachel was obsessed with her though, always talking about how she would be back. He...he," Luc coughed, "he extracted my incisors when I told him that the Greek said she was dead. Do you know that I was so starved by then that I barely bled? He ripped my fangs out with a pair of pliers, and Henri looked on, a ravage joy on his face!" His voice dropped to a whisper. "It was...painful."

Gaspard's face was pulled tight, his white skin stretching over his cheekbones. He was a second away from vamping out. He walked to the window, standing there for a whole minute without speaking. When he turned back around, his face was back to normal.

"Sophie was turned and never tried to find me." Gaspard stated this fact without emotion.

"I can't pretend to know what happened during those years, my son, but a vampire who walks into the sun must feel she has few, if any, options."

"How did you escape?" asked Gaspard.

"A human man loosened my chains and fed me, making me promise that I would pay him a large sum of money, which I didn't have, but he thought I could get."

"And did you?" asked Gaspard.

"I robbed two convenience stores. I'm not proud of it, but I was indebted. Then, I made my way here to warn you."

"Too easy," spat Marc.

"Maybe so, but it's what happened all the same."

Kara spoke up. "Where does Valeria Snow come in?"

Luc grimaced. "She is to provide soldiers for Vachel and Henri's army in exchange for Gaspard's territory. She was pleased when he beat Simon and inherited the Northeast. More for her. That woman is insatiable."

"I remember her well," said Gaspard, earning a look from Kara. "No, nothing like that Kara, darling, but she was alluring and knew how to use her assets. Quite powerful in her own right."

Luc noticed the epithet and squashed a smile. His Gaspard was in love.

Kara interrupted Luc's thoughts by getting to the point. "What is this army, and when it is coming?"

Luc turned in slow motion, not wanting to trigger Kara's sword arm and gazed at her. "I don't know when. Henri wanted to kill Gaspard. He failed. Vachel is interested in humiliation and then death. Valeria wants power."

"What does the Greek want?" Kara asked.

"To see how the game plays out."

"You rotten, lying, scoundrel! You cur!" The door flew open, smashing into the wall with the force of the entry, leaving a deep divot where the door handle hit the wall. A fuming Adelaide, brandishing her cane, rampaged at a whopping two steps an hour toward Luc. "I knew you couldn't kill your son."

Luc stared at the tiny, elderly woman as his brain made sense of what was happening. "My dear, I am sorry..."

"You, sir, have no honor. You are foresworn. I am ashamed to be your descendent."

Nothing that had happened in the last several months hit Luc as hard as those words. He doubled over as if hit in the gut, and he closed his eyes to avoid Adelaide's. Adelaide was his direct descendent on her mother's side, a Rochon through and through. Thinking of it that way, her fury amused him, pleased him even. This feisty woman was the last of his line, but what a way to end.

He stood, uncomfortable in his bare feet, uncomfortable at facing his descendent, and tugged at the hem of his shirt. "Madame, I am indeed foresworn. I promised to kill Henri but could not. I was unaware of his allies, a stupid misstep I have paid for."

"Paid for how?" Adelaide demanded.

Luc looked at Kara for permission, which was given with a curt nod. He approached Adelaide and opened his mouth. The old woman gasped and held a hand to her lips.

"Who would dare do this to you?" she asked. She held her hand up to his face, her anger cooling somewhat at the sight of the two holes where his fangs had been.

"Vachel and Henri. They were...unhappy...with me."

"You are much stronger than either of them," Adelaide protested.

"But not the Greek. He's a thousand years old, and with his muscle behind them, I was caught like rabbit in a snare." He shook his head, sickened at his own stupidity.

"So, what are you going to do?" asked Adelaide, glaring at him, thin, wiry arms crossed across her drooping bosom. "Lay down and die? Be unmanned? Or fight back?"

"That depends on what Gaspard wants," Luc said, turning to his son. "And Kara."

Gaspard approached Luc in steady steps, eyes locked on Luc's until Luc had to struggle to hold his head up. Gaspard reached his father and placed a hand on his shoulder. "Gear up for battle, *mon pére*. If it is a fight they want, then we will give it to them. But we do not fight fair. I know Vachel. He'll be stuck in the past. We will use Kara's techniques, a combination of old and new, and take them by surprise."

Kara's eyes glittered. "Shoot, stab, and flame?"

"As you wish," said Gaspard, with a toothy smile that made Luc shiver.

12

It started with a soft click of a door opening, a back door, very early in the morning when day staff were getting up and night staff headed to bed. Kara strained to hear more, but that one sound was enough to have her jumping out of bed, where she'd settled a few moments before, and make her way down the stairs on silent feet.

The lack of sound was so ominous that Kara drew her sword, holding it high above her left shoulder. As she turned the last corner into the kitchen, she saw a man standing inside, back pressed to the door.

He could be staff, she thought, but there was something tickling her senses that told her he wasn't. The man was dressed in a black t-shirt, pressed blue jeans, and slip-on black shoes. He had a mustache and short dark hair, broad shoulders, and piercing eyes that studied the inside of the house. He whispered something, and Kara realized he had an earpiece in his right ear.

Kara leapt from her hiding place and held her sword to his throat. The man's face was frozen in shock as he tried to stammer out a sentence.

"How did you get past security?" Kara demanded.

"I don't know what you're talking about. I work here. I'm a gardener!"

"A gardener with pressed jeans? Need the pleat to help you to prune the roses? And what is this?" Kara pressed the sword tighter against the man's neck and reached for his earpiece, holding it up in front of his face.

Daytime kitchen staff streamed in, stopping dead when they saw Kara in full armor and sword to a man's neck.

Kara put the man's earpiece in her ear and heard a voice saying, "We've been compromised. Repeat, we've been compromised."

"Damn straight you've been compromised," Kara hissed. "You are on the wrong side of things, boys and girls. That I promise." Then she dropped the earpiece and squashed it with her right foot.

"Look lady, I don't know what's going on," said the man. "I'm a hired hand. Asked to break into the house during the day and identify how many people—humans, that is—are in the mansion. My job was to blend in and count. That's it."

"How did you get past security?"

"With the lawn staff at your back guard shift change."

Kara growled and reminded herself to button that up. "How many more of you are there?"

"None, now. The attack is supposed to come at sundown. Listen, I'm not a part of that. They needed a human to do a human census, that's all."

"Why?"

The man squirmed, eyes shifting left to right. All he saw were human onlookers, now aware of what was happening and readying to take him themselves, if needed. One, a chef, held a long butcher's knife and looked like he knew how to use it.

"To capture as many humans as possible to hold as collateral. Needed to know what the kitty is."

Kara rolled her eyes. "These guys are so stupid," she muttered.

"Lady, they may be stupid, but there are a lot of them," said the intruder.

"Yeah, I know. But now you work for me, got it?"

The man tilted his head to the side, as much as he could with the sword to his throat, and asked, "How much?"

"How much do you like your head?" Kara asked.

"A lot."

"Good, get into this cupboard," said Kara as she dragged him to a mid-sized pantry and threw him in, locking it from the outside.

"But Kara, I need things that are in that pantry," started one of the cooks, who stopped, mouth open when she realized that everyone was looking at her. "Uh. Never mind. More important things. Gotcha."

"Everyone, we've discussed what to do in this type of emergency. Go do it. I think we have some time before the wheels come off..." The knife-wielding chef gave her a thumbs up for using the idiom correctly. Kara winked. "But by noon, I want everyone gone, using escorted vehicles only."

Operation Paris was in motion.

Kara jogged to the back gate, where two men guarded the entrance.

"Anything strange going on?" she asked, making them jump at her unexpected visit.

"No, ma'am, everything normal," said one of the guards.

Kara stepped forward and grabbed the man's left ear. "Everything is not normal. A spy entered the mansion after coming through the back gate. He came in at the shift change with the lawn service, which means you failed."

The two guards scrambled to say something, anything. Their mouths flapped open and closed, and their faces turned red.

"I'm sending an extra set of guards to help you since the two of you aren't enough. And, by the way, we're in Operation Paris, so put your big-boy pants on," Kara said, enjoying the use of that phrase. "We've got incoming."

Operation Paris called for escorted removal of all human staff to safe houses miles from the mansion. By noon, all humans had evacuated, and Kara and the security team were left, surrounded by sleep-dead vampires. Kara patrolled the house one more time, rattling doorknobs, making sure the entrances to the vampires' rooms were locked from the inside and bolted. She triple-checked Gaspard's room and ran smack into Emmy and Adelaide as she turned to return to the main floor.

"What are you two doing here?" Kara exclaimed, hands out wide like wings, as she stared at both ladies in exasperation.

"We're not leaving," Adelaide said, and Emmy nodded.

"Do you realize what is coming at us this evening? Vampires, lots of them, possibly giants, and potentially other creepy-crawly monsters of the night. Ladies, you need to be safe."

"We are safest here with you," said Emmy. "And with my nephew.

Besides, the attack is supposed to come at sundown, and you need some sleep. We can keep watch while you rest."

Kara did need rest, but she was so keyed up she didn't believe she would sleep, but Adelaide and Emmy were right. She'd be no good to anyone if she headed into the belly of the battle exhausted.

"Okay," Kara relented. "But keep watch from the upper windows, and I'll alert the guards. They are working in rotations now anyway so they don't tire either. Dogs are walking the perimeter, so don't go outside, and for Odin's sake, stay away from the flamethrowers. There are two in the kitchen and two in the dining room."

"Flamethrowers? Kara, are you serious?" asked Adelaide.

"Very."

"Can't I pick one up? I want to see if I'm strong enough to hold one," Adelaide said, eyes wide with excitement. Emmy bounced on her toes next to her.

"No!"

"You never let us have any fun," Adelaide pouted, arms crossed over her bony chest.

Kara ignored them and entered her room with a small sigh. It was coming, and for that, she was grateful. She didn't realize how tiring it was to prepare for an emergency in a continuous manner, waiting for it to arrive. It was better to face it, and in a few hours, she would.

She lay down on the bed thinking that she might rest but that she wouldn't sleep, but the Sandman had other ideas and took her under right away. Her dream-self did something it had done once before, sliding out through her bedroom door and in to Gaspard's where he lay, unmoving, unaware. But if his body was unresponsive, his dream-self wasn't, rising to meet her in a warm embrace.

What is it, Kara? What brings you to me in the middle of my torpor?

Operation Paris is underway. The battle is about to begin.

Now?

Tonight. We intercepted a spy infiltrating the house. They wanted to count the humans and, I am sure, get a better sense of the floorplan and where your room is. Most vampires sleep in the basement. I think they would be surprised to find you sleep on the top floor.

Where is this spy now?

Locked in a cupboard.

Ha! Our enemies failed and now we have warning. Are all humans evacuated?

Yes, but Emmy and Adelaide are staying.

Dream-Gaspard smacked his nonexistent forehead with his nonexistent hand. *Of course, they are.*

Gaspard's dream-self faded and drew back toward the bed like a puppet on strings. *I must return, Kara. I'm...*

He was gone. Kara, too, felt the pull of her body and slid back into her physical self while she slept on.

She woke two hours later, refreshed but wary. Had she actually spoken to Gaspard? Would he know about Operation Paris when he woke? Was the dream real? She reminded herself to deal with what was, not what might be. If he knew, he knew. If not, she would tell him when he woke. It was early for him yet, not quite four p.m., too early for him to rise.

"Kara." A knock at the door.

"Gaspard?" Kara opened the door, her eyebrows knitted in confusion.

Gaspard was unusually dressed in sweatpants and a t-shirt. His arms were pale and lean, muscled in all the right ways. She dragged her eyes back to his face, which was drawn. He pushed past her into her room.

"Operation Paris is underway?"

Kara nodded. "I guess my dream was real."

"I dreamt that you came to me and that the battle had begun. I dreamt that my people were dying, and I didn't wake up. I couldn't do anything, sleeping on and on while all around me innocent people died." He ran his hands through his loose hair, pacing across her floor, nervous energy from his nightmare needing release.

Kara stopped him mid-step with a hand to his chest. "The battle has begun, but not in the way you think, and no one has died. I expect the fun stuff to happen after sundown. You haven't let anyone down. All is prepared."

"The humans?"

"Evacuated."

"Except Adelaide and Emmy," Gaspard said with a rueful smile.

"Exactly. Peace, Gaspard. Relax."

Gaspard swallowed and rolled his shoulders. "I'll get dressed."

"I'll meet you in your office. The rest of the troops won't be awake yet. We can strategize."

13

Kara had donned her armor to impress upon her troops that the battle was nigh. Her armor gleamed in the fading sunlight, her hair was a nimbus of white gold and her manner, posture and movement conveyed authority. Each of her steps bred certainty and pride to her squad. She would lead, and they would follow.

Gaspard watched her rally her team with a sense of satisfaction. If it was to come to this, at least he had Kara by his side. She may not know how he felt about her, but she was still in his corner, ready, willing, and able to lead a battle that they may not win. Seeing her speak to each man and woman with a hand on a shoulder and a nod of confidence was like watching an eagle soar. She was in her element, and as far as he was concerned, he'd never seen anything more stunning than her in action.

He had donned black clothes and carried no weapons except for his fangs, speed, and strength. The guards were surprised to see him up with the sun still shining, but most seemed inspired by it. They knew the power it took for a vampire to wake before sundown.

He perceived the exact moment the mood changed. He held himself still and closed his eyes, sensing the air. He caught a perfume he'd only smelled once before, a scent of strawberries too long in the sun, and knew who came to his door. He made sure his face was blank when Kara walked in.

"You won't believe who is here waving a white flag," she said.

"Valeria Snow."

Kara startled. "How did you know?"

"I can smell her stench."

"She does have an unusual smell. Like jam, but jam I would never want to eat," Kara agreed. "Like wet leaves, maybe."

"What did you mean that she is waving a white flag?"

"She wants to parlay. She seeks your audience," Kara said, crossing her arms. "By the way, Marc is up."

"Good about Marc," Gaspard said. "You don't think I should speak with Valeria?"

"No, I think you should speak with her, but only if Marc and I are here. I don't trust her. This could be an assassination attempt."

"Not her style. She's underhanded and sneaky, not direct. Show her in. We might as well hear what she has to say."

Kara grunted her assent, readying herself for what might come.

Gaspard waited for several minutes before Marc walked in, hands out in a what-can-you-do gesture. "Mistress Snow insists on seeing you alone. Kara refuses. Valeria tried to...I don't know...seduce Kara?"

"I take that it failed."

"Valeria tried to put the whammy on her, and Kara..." Marc trailed off with a suppressed smile on his face, looking down at his shoes.

"Kara what?" Gaspard prodded, grasping both arms of his chair to keep from wringing Marc's neck. "What did she do, Marc?"

"She laughed."

Gaspard sat up straight. "She laughed in Valeria's face?"

"She laughed. She guffawed. She doubled over in tears." Marc said in a dry voice. "I fear Mistress Valeria is quite put out."

Gaspard pinched his nose. "Oh dear, that won't help things."

"Kara's not known for her subtlety, or political skills, Gaspard," Marc said, as he made himself at home on the couch. The wrinkles at the outer corner of Marc's eyes told Gaspard that Marc was feigning complacency. His assistant was coiled and ready for action.

Gaspard shooed him off the furniture and instructed, "Go down there and rescue this situation before it goes completely wrong. I will see

Valeria with Kara and you present, and she may bring two of her seethe as well."

Marc hauled himself off the couch with an "aye-aye captain" and headed back outside.

Gaspard watched Marc double-time to the front gate through his window and shifted his gaze to the ceiling. "You better know what you are doing, old man. You're taking quite a risk here, betting that we can win. What if I fail? Is there a Plan B?"

A speck drifted from the ceiling, sailing by Gaspard's nose, and floated down toward the floor. Gaspard caught it in his hand where it turned into a leaf. Gaspard read the note out loud. "You are Plan B."

Gaspard crumpled the leaf in his hand and released it to the floor. "You mean there was a Plan A and it failed?"

He looked out the window and saw Kara and Marc, along with two other guards who were armed to the hilt, walking up the drive. Valeria was in the center with two of her associates, taking mincing steps in what Gaspard knew was a purposeful attempt to annoy Kara. By the look of Kara's face, she was succeeding.

Gaspard sat in his chair again and smoothed his hair, assuming the air of a Master who was unconcerned about the battle to come. He forced his hands to still and schooled his features into a mask.

Marc entered first and shifted to execute a perfect bow toward the woman in white behind him, announcing at the same time, "Mistress of Southwest Texas, Valeria Snow, to parley for peace."

Gaspard rose to meet the lady, strolling around his desk and taking two steps toward her, which forced her to take five steps toward him. The only sign that she noticed this small slight was a twitch of her nose, but Gaspard knew he'd won the first point.

Kara took her place at his right hand; Marc positioned himself at the left. Valeria's guards mimicked them, playing the role of Kara and Marc's opposites.

Gaspard held out his arms and leaned in to kiss Valeria's cheeks, left then right.

"Valeria, my dear! How long has it been?"

"It is lovely to see you, Gaspard. I'm sorry that it has to be under such circumstances," said Valeria, shaking her head at the shame of it all.

Gaspard frowned and gestured for her to sit. "Under what circumstances, Valeria?"

"Oh, come now, Gaspard. Let's not play games." Valeria pouted like a debutante wearing lipstick to her first ball. "You know what I mean."

"I really don't." Gaspard sat on the couch with Valeria, angling his body so he faced her. Kara moved behind the couch, still to Gaspard's right, but took her hand off her sword hilt and placed it on the butt of her gun. Valeria's guard mimicked her again, keeping his eyes on Kara's right hand. Gaspard watched Kara mock the guard by wiggling her fingers, daring the guard to act first. The guard, a vampire, took the bait and jumped forward like an offensive lineman going off-sides. Kara's mouth twitched in a grin as the guard checked himself and retained his position, although his fangs dropped a little as he did so.

Good for you, Kara. Keep them off balance.

Gaspard returned his attention to Valeria, who had lost her pout and found her glare. "Gaspard. This won't do. I have come, wearing white, as a symbol of my good faith and a desire to avoid bloodshed through negotiation."

"You are wearing a sleeveless white mini-dress with a plunging neckline and boots I last saw on working girls downtown. I didn't know they made white platform vinyl kinky boots. Wherever did you find those things? This looks like a dress to seduce, not converse," said Gaspard, keeping his face calm.

Valeria flipped her long dark hair over one shoulder. "Why cannot it not do both? And I will ignore your working girl comments as, in fact, I did take them from a working girl, after I drained her dry. Those girls really should take more care in who they associate with."

"How old was she?" Gaspard asked, forcing his voice to remain calm.

"She was young, maybe seventeen. Oh, forgive me. Seventeen is 'underage' these days. So, we'll say she was eighteen." Valeria licked her lips and batted her eyelashes. Gaspard heard Kara make a low snarl.

Valeria flicked her eyes toward Kara. "Keep your guard on a leash, Gaspard. Thanks to my spies, I know what she is and what she can do, but I also know that she wouldn't want any harm to come to you, and my guards have orders to kill you first, no matter what."

"I'm bored, Valeria."

"Fine," Valeria said with a roll of her eyes. "I want your territory. All of it. I'm expanding my horizons. By this time tomorrow, I shall be the Mistress of Texas, all of it, and with the addition of your territory, I'll be in perfect position to take the rest of Louisiana and then the entire southern border of the U.S. Who knows? Maybe I'll work my way up the east coast as well."

"My territory recently expanded, in case you didn't know."

"Whatever do you mean?"

"The Assembly's attempt to intimidate me didn't work. I killed Simon Whitleigh, and his seethe pledged loyalty to me," said Gaspard.

Valeria's eyes grew big. "I had not heard that," she said in a slow, low voice. "Vachel and Henri failed to inform me. I was told you scared him off, not that you killed him and claimed the Northeast."

"Vachel and Henri aren't known for their caring, sharing personalities, Valeria. Surely you must know they can't be trusted. And thank you for admitting your involvement with the little cow and my long-lost brother."

Valeria waved Gaspard's words away. "You knew I was. I didn't tell you anything you didn't know."

"I held out hope that it wasn't true," Gaspard replied, standing. He turned his back on his guest and took a seat at his desk. Kara didn't move, but Marc shifted to stand next to Gaspard.

"Those conniving bastards. They will pay for this betrayal," Valeria muttered to herself. She rocketed to her feet, her sudden movement almost leading to her death as Kara withdrew her gun and placed it to Valeria's head. Valeria's guard simultaneously shoved his gun against Kara's temple, and Marc pushed Gaspard back and placed his body in front of his Master, blocking Valeria's second guard's aim, who had sighted Gaspard.

"Stop!" ordered Gaspard. "Enough. Kara, stand down."

Kara withdrew her gun but shot Gaspard a displeased look. Valeria nodded to her guards, who also holstered their weapons.

"*Détente*," Gaspard said. "Valeria came to offer a deal. What is it, Valeria?" Gaspard worked his way around Marc's body, earning a glower from his second, and placed himself directly in front of Valeria. "Out with it. What did you come to discuss?"

Valeria huffed once and said, "Yes. To business. I came to offer you a chance to leave with your people, avoiding any bloodshed, and in exchange, I will acquire your territory in a bloodless coup."

Gaspard did a long slow blink. "You must be joking. That's your offer?"

Valeria placed a hand on her hip and cast Gaspard a disgusted glance. "It's a good offer. Henri and Vachel will be here shortly. My proposal is a peaceful transition of power. I'll hold Vachel and Henri off, and you and yours can leave before anyone is hurt."

"So, I can run from them forever?"

"You can hide, retreat, retire. Choose a word, but it will result in the same outcome. I own what is yours, and you live to see another day."

Gaspard laughed a bitter laugh. "You *know* me. You know what happened in Paris and Orléans. What about that history makes you think I would take your offer?"

"Your desire to protect the innocent, of course."

"I've done so already. Anyone here is a professional and understands the risks," said Gaspard.

"Except I know where your safe houses are and have teams positioned to take them and kill everyone inside if they don't get a call from me in an hour."

Gaspard's stomach clenched, and his vision grew dark as his anger boiled over. "Let me be clear, Valeria. If you touch so much as one hair on anyone under my protection, I will not only kill you, I will kill you one square inch at a time so you can feel the extent of my fury."

Kara backed away from Valeria, and Gaspard watched her out of the corner of her eye. She needed time to send security to the safe houses to check on what Valeria said, so Gaspard decided to make a diversion.

Moving with all his speed, Gaspard grabbed Valeria by the upper arm, pulling her in front of his own body. Marc followed suit, grabbing the closest guard, and striking him with a stinging blow to his right wrist. The guard's numb fingers couldn't hold the gun, and Marc stole it from him in one smooth move. When Valeria stumbled into Gaspard's arms, the guard who was supposed to be watching Kara turned his head away from his subject to train his gun on Gaspard.

The entire attack took less than thirty seconds but was enough for Kara to use her earpiece to issue quick orders to the security teams outside without Valeria or her guards noticing.

Valeria's face was red and her voice a vicious bark. "Really, Gaspard, if you wanted rough foreplay, you could have asked."

Gaspard held her firm and dragged her back so they were behind his desk, creating yet another barrier between him and her guards. Marc shoved his disabled foe onto the floor and tied his hands with an electric cord from a nearby lamp. With the second guard's focus on Gaspard and his mistress, Kara had the opening she needed, but unlike Marc, she didn't pull punches. She simply stepped behind the second guard, withdrew her sword, and sliced his head off in one glorious, exquisite movement.

Valeria hissed at Kara, leaning forward trying to escape Gaspard's grasp, but he was stronger and held her fast. Kara fixed her eyes on Valeria and strode forward, sword outstretched, and with extreme gentleness, placed the very tip of the sword on Valeria's neck.

"You were saying?" Kara asked.

"I was saying," said Valeria, straightening as much as possible in Gaspard's hold, "that I was going to offer you a bloodless exchange of power, but now I see that is impossible, as you have shed first blood." She flicked to the head and body on the floor, leaking fluids all over the rug. Gaspard sighed. Yet another rug to be replaced.

"Yeah, it's a shame," said Kara. "But we thought about your offer for the exact amount of time that it deserved and rejected it." She cocked her head and listened for a moment to a conversation no one else could hear.

"Ah, and your threats are meaningless now. My teams disabled yours, and our safe houses are secure. It doesn't seem that you have a lot of people in your employ, Valeria. Having trouble finding followers? Only two vampires per safe house?" Kara made a *tsk tsk* noise. "That was terrible planning."

"I have many more, and you'll see them soon, you bitch."

"Hush. No name calling." Kara sheathed her sword and took control of Valeria from Gaspard. "See, Gaspard, now would be a good time to have Wonder Woman's magic lasso. Maybe I should have been an Amazon."

Gaspard's laughter was as much a chuckle of relief as it was sick humor, for he heard something that neither Kara or Marc heard yet.

Valeria heard it, too, and grinned. “Now, we’ll see what you think about my resources.”

From outside, Rikassa blared a warning. The battle was about to begin in earnest.

14

Valeria took advantage of the momentary distraction to break free of Kara's hold. She whirled to face Kara and drew her long nails down Kara's right cheek, missing Kara's eye by a millimeter. Kara snapped her head back, reached for her sword, swung the blade in a swift left to right cut, and was rewarded by a peal of pain as Valeria lost both hands at the wrists. Blood streamed from the stumps, forming pools of the red thick liquid on the floor.

Kara readied to strike again but didn't have to. Gaspard pulled Valeria back into his arms and sunk his fangs into her neck. He drank her energy and power in, making it his own while her one remaining guard watched on in horror from the floor.

Valeria's body shrunk in on itself as Gaspard drank. Her face withered, resembling a rotten apple left in the sun. Her arms, torso, and legs shriveled into desiccated sticks until all that was left was a scarecrow—limp, dry and paper thin—hanging from Gaspard's mouth. As Gaspard finished the last drop, the guard on the floor gave a gasp, and Gaspard's head snapped back. Kara and Marc watched as Gaspard's blue eyes went black, all black, no irises at all, and the guard on the floor mewled as if in pain.

Gaspard turned his coal eyes to the guard, who was crumpled up in a fetal position, and said, "Did you feel that?"

The guard gave a jerky nod.

"I now own you and all of Valeria's seethe, land, and power. Who is your Master?"

The guard whispered, "You are. We all felt it."

Kara listened to her earpiece again. "Gaspard, the vampires we subdued at the safe houses are bending on one knee, swearing their loyalty to you. They are doing their best to explain what has happened. Our teams want instructions."

"Tell them to return here and bring Valeria's vamps with her. They are no threat to us now. In fact, I think we will use them to fight on our side. We could use some cannon fodder."

A whistle of wind streamed by the windows followed by the crack of two bullets shot from the roof. Then two more. An eerie wail grew in volume until it ended with a tumultuous smack as whatever it was the snipers shot hit the ground. Kara ran, headset on. "Blue Eagle, Checkmate? What did you just shoot?"

"Big, black, and ugly, ma'am. Oh, here's another one." Kara made it outside to see the second figure plummet to the ground with a resounding *thunk*.

"It's a sylph!" she said. "Sylphs are peaceful, and I've never seen one this color or with talons. What in Odin's name is going on?"

She didn't have time to figure it out as gunshots rang out around the entire compound. Kara saw two bright flares of lights as the guards at front entrance enacted Protocol 911 and burnt a pack of vampires to crisps. More disfigured sylphs flew through the air, picked off one by one by Blue Eagle and Checkpoint.

Calling Rikassa, Kara flew to the back of the mansion and saw the flood of vampires swarming the compound. Intermixed were humans with machine guns moving in careful, practiced motions. *Mercenaries*, thought Kara. *Well-trained ones.* "Team, there are humans involved. They aren't friendly, but try not to kill many of them, please."

"Do our best, ma'am, but they are hunkering down with MP5s," came the response.

"Let me see what I can do," Kara responded, sending up a silent call.

A whoosh of wings a moment later told her that help had arrived.

"Sigrun, can you, Hildr, and Astrid deal with the humans? They're mercenaries and are working on three-round bursts from MP5s. I don't want to kill them, but we can't have them shooting at our people."

Sigrun nodded once, and the three Valkyries rose in the air, winking out of sight as they sought to disable the mercenaries. It didn't take but a moment for Kara to notice the bark of the machine guns lessening.

"This is Checkpoint. There are invisible flying things out there, but they seem to be snatching guns out of the enemy's hands. Assuming those are friendlies?"

"They're my sisters, Checkpoint. Don't shoot them. It will merely piss them off."

"Don't shoot the Valkyries. Got it. Checkpoint out."

While the Valkyries dealt with the human threat, Kara turned her attention to the inhuman threat on the ground. Her troops were holding, but she saw bodies lying on the grass from both sides. She dove for a dense area of fighting, leaping off Rikassa as soon as she was close to the ground.

Gaspard and Marc were in the fray, ripping, tearing, and clawing their way through lesser vampires, and as Kara watched, a host of vampires turned on their own, fighting to protect Gaspard. *Valeria's seethe*, Kara realized. *Gaspard turned them all with a thought.*

A heavy hit to her lower back sent her sailing several yards, tumbling over and over until she rooted her hands in the ground, stopping the downslide and righting herself. A gargantuan grinning *naked* jötnar loomed in front of her carrying a club almost the size of her body.

"Oh, yuck! I can't un-see that. Haven't you heard of pants? And truly, how big are your women?"

The jötnar slammed his foot heel first, sending ripples of earth throughout the grounds, toppling friend and foe alike. Kara ran between the giant's legs, striking at the Achilles tendon of his right foot, only to make a useless shallow scratch. Jötenheimr skin was notoriously hard with only a few vulnerable spots, mostly around the face, which she couldn't reach without Rikassa. She sensed that Rikassa was helping the snipers by kicking the attacking sylphs in the air. It was like skeet shooting. Rikassa punted them up in an arc, and Blue Eagle and Checkpoint used them for target practice.

Kara didn't have time to wonder why there were so many disfigured sylphs raining down on the battlefield. She had to immobilize this giant on her own. The giant turned to catch her, but Kara used her speed to zoom out of his way and climb the tallest tree she could. Climbing the tree required concentration, and Kara had a hard time scaling the stately oak when the giant's paw kept fishing for her body within the branches. An index finger poked down, almost knocking her off her branch, followed by a thumb as the giant attempted to pluck her from the tree. Kara needed him right above the tree for her plan to work, so she slithered and squirmed horizontally as she worked her way vertically.

When she reached the apex of the tree, she knew she had to act fast. Balancing on the top, she whistled to the giant and waved her arms like a ground controller bringing in an airliner. As soon as the giant was in shooting distance, Kara gathered her energy. She pulled the life energy from the tree to further magnify her power, apologizing to the dryad who lived there, and pushed the energy outward.

The resulting fire caught the giant right in the gonads, and since Jötenheimr, she now unfortunately knew, were hairy, the giant's private parts lit like dry leaves on a hot day. The giant fell to his knees with a resounding crash beating at his doo-dads with frantic swipes of his hands.

"That's it, Tiny," Kara yelled from her perch, punching her fist in the air. "I don't care how big you are. When someone lights your nuts on fire, you're going down!"

Kara's victory cry stopped short when she looked to the sky and saw more sylphs approaching. From her vantage point high in the tree, she could see that three of them carried passengers. The riders bent down over the sylphs' backs so low they would be invisible from the ground, but Kara could see them from top of the tree. She bellowed a warning, but no one could hear her in the fray and din of battle. She called to Rikassa, who abandoned her game and flew to her Lady. Kara leapt onto Rikassa's back, humming "Back in the Saddle Again" as she flew to meet the riders in the sky.

15

Kara flew directly toward the shadowed figures, hazarding a guess as to who they were. She didn't know how they had corrupted the sylphs and gotten them to do their bidding. It had to have been black magic, which disgusted her, but it was a clever trick nevertheless. The sylphs kept her snipers busy fighting the air battle, and they provided coverage and air travel for the three individuals behind this whole mess.

Her stomach tensed as she drew closer, peering into the night to verify her hypothesis. She mentally called to her sisters and felt them break away to join her. They were at her side a moment later.

"Who are those three?" demanded Hildr.

"The real enemy," Kara replied. "I think that..."

Kara didn't finish her sentence because one of the magicked sylphs dodged in and swiped its talons over Rikassa's hindquarters. Rikassa reared at the pain and lashed out with her hooves at the offending creature. She made contact with a crack of her foreleg, and the sylph plummeted. Other sylphs attacked the Valkyries *en masse*, a gusting, beating cacophony of wings, talons, and wind as they batted, scratched, and scored the horses.

"We have to go down!" yelled Sigrun, as her horse suffered another laceration, this time across the stomach. "We can't risk the Wild Ones!"

Kara's sword snapped back and forth, but there were simply too many sylphs. Gripping her sword tight, she gave her sister a curt nod, and the four Valkyries descended to the earth, each of their horses bleeding from multiple wounds. Kara dismounted to examine Rikassa's injuries, frantic to stop the bleeding. She recalled how she had healed the female Grunch with her sword and prayed she could recreate that feat. She motioned for her sisters to watch and pulled the sword, forming it into a dagger. She whispered a prayer to Eir, the goddess of health and healing, and was grateful when the dagger began to glow. She placed the dagger on Rikassa's hind leg and watched as the wound closed. Kara let out a sigh of relief, closed her eyes, sent a message of thanks to Eir, and healed Rikassa's other injuries. Able to breathe again, Kara turned to see how her sisters were faring and stopped short at what she saw, all the air she'd taken in let out again.

Sigrun's horse lay on her side, her belly wound deep enough that Kara could see organs among the glistening blood on the grass around her. Sigrun was on one knee next to her mount, weeping, talking to the horse in a soft voice, caressing her mane. The horse panted in pain but managed to lift her head to nuzzle her rider one more time. The bonds between horse and rider broke, tearing apart like a seam giving way, but with a physical flare of light that hit the Valkyries like an electric shock. Kara, Hildr, and Astrid wept with Sigrun as the four women watched their brave comrade pass on. The beautiful beast's body faded away until it was there no more.

Kara's throat closed as guilt flooded over her. It was all her fault. She shouldn't have asked her sisters to help. The thought of losing Rikassa made her physically sick and tore at her heart. She couldn't imagine how Sigrun felt, but she wished more than anything that she could go back in time and undo the damage done.

Sigrun turned her tear-stained face to her sisters and said, "Let's go make them pay." Kara could only nod in response.

Leaving the other horses to recuperate, the four sisters raised their swords to the sky and charged into the thick of the battle, slashing this way and that, taking down enemies with full swings and the briefest movements, their dance a ballet to anyone who watched.

Kara heard a voice howl. "Henrrrrrriiiii!"

Luc, still weak, pointed a gun at his own son. A small man stood beside Henri, but behind them was a middle-sized, average-looking man. He was dressed in a jarring mixture of colors and clothes. He wore a toga with pantaloons and hunting boots and covered the whole ensemble with a suit jacket, complete with pocket square and matching tie. On his head, he wore a Baltimore Orioles baseball cap. Kara knew she was looking at the three passengers, Henri, Vachel, and the Greek.

Henri smirked and said, "Father! How did you get away? We were having such a fun time together, father and son bonding and whatnot. Glad you got here in time for the end game."

Luc didn't answer. He fired.

His aim was true. The bullet hit Henri in the stomach, toppling him over onto the grass. "I promised I would kill you, and I will," said Luc, stalking toward his writhing son.

"Oh, no. You won't," said Vachel, in a calm, measured tone, as if he were reciting a grocery list. He pushed his way between the fallen Henri and Luc. "See, Henri and I have an agreement. He gets to kill you. I get to kill Gaspard. I would hate to renege on my promise."

"Oh! There you are, Gaspard," Vachel said, clapping his hands together in delight at the sight of his enemy. "Haven't seen you since you failed Sophie, after she rejected me for you. Ironic, isn't it?"

"I didn't know she was turned, Vachel. Why didn't she get in touch with me? Why didn't you both get in touch with me?"

"Because you let her die and then deprived her of the light! You are responsible for her first death and responsible for her true death. She missed the sun so much that she walked right into it. I lost her twice because of you."

"But, I didn't know..." Gaspard voice was gentle, but his gaze was hard as he took another step toward Vachel.

"She blamed you, nevertheless, as did I, and why on earth would I want to share her with you? She'd already chosen you once. It was much more fun to deprive you of her presence. She never got used to being a vampire. She was always too good for us."

"That is true," said Gaspard, nodding in agreement, moving yet another step closer to Vachel. "She was better than both of us."

"Gaspard! Watch out!" shouted Luc. At the same time, Kara threw her body in front of Gaspard, sword drawn.

Henri had tugged Vachel out of the way and taken the front position, smiling an evil grin at them both. He seemed unsurprised that Kara protected Gaspard's body with her own.

"Thanks to the Greek here," Henri drawled, gesturing to the man twirling in circles behind him. "I heal well. A little of his blood is powerful enough to heal even the most grievous wounds. Think on that, Father!" Henri lifted his voice to carry to Luc.

That was the last of the talk.

Henri bore a sword he'd gotten from the Greek, and the battle began anew. Henri slashed and stabbed at Kara, but she held him off, jabbing at him while she juked left, slicing at him while she juked right. He couldn't get a clean blow and neither could she.

"You won't kill Gaspard on my watch," said Kara, holding Henri back with a strong parry.

"You are probably right, my dear Valkyrie. Yes, I know what you are. Valeria told me. Quite a coup for Gaspard to have a Valkyrie in his service. I am quite curious as to how that happened." Henri danced back as he taunted Kara.

"Well, you may have noticed that Valeria isn't here, Henri," said Kara, swinging the sword downward toward Henri's head. Henri met her sword and slipped out from under using his sheer strength. Kara retreated several steps to take a breath. Henri's eyebrows knitted together.

"Did you kill her?" he asked.

"No, Gaspard did. Didn't you notice that her vampires are fighting for our side now?"

Henri glanced around him, taking his eyes off Kara for a moment, but a moment was all she needed. She rushed toward Henri, getting inside his reach and stabbed toward his body—only to miss as he sashayed to the side at the last moment. Vachel and the Greek crowed from the sidelines.

Around them, the battle waged on. Sigrun carried a battle axe she'd gotten from somewhere and was hacking vampires with every swing. Hildr had both sword and shield out and fought three enemies at the same time. Even Luc grappled with a human mercenary who'd gotten to the front lines. Gaspard's fangs were down, and his face stretched to a bloodless mask of alabaster skin as he beheaded a vampire with his bare hands, ripping the skin and bone apart with a squelching rupture of sound that made Kara's hair stand on end.

But nothing compared to the colossal boom that exploded above them, and the spit and tongue of flame that lashed out, setting trees and bushes on fire, turning a few vampires to briquettes in the blink of an eye. Kara's eyes roved to the source and saw Emmy and Adelaide working together to balance a flame thrower on a patio table. They covered their mouths with their hands when they realized that they could have barbequed their allies and scuttled back into the house, leaving the jumbo-sized weapon where it was. Kara inwardly berated herself for even mentioning the flamethrowers to the two women. She was relieved when a brigade of Southwest Texas vamps unrolled hoses as others brought fire extinguishers to contain the damage. It took brave vampires to run toward fire, making Kara wonder if the Texas vamps weren't too upset about the change in leadership.

Kara considered using her own flame, but there were so many friends and associates around her, she couldn't take the risk. *Sparking is good when facing a giant's genitals*, she realized, *but it isn't so good for up-close work.*

A human man ran in between Kara and Henri, and the two combatants got separated by a stream of knives and bo sticks, followed by the inevitable fall of wounded bodies. Time slowed down, and Kara took stock of the carnage. A head rolled by her left foot. An arm flew in a graceful arc in the air. Luc's mercenary issued a howl of pain as Luc smashed his kneecap. A guard at her side stabbed a vampire in the neck while his partner sawed off the vamp's head and flicked a lighter to the body, searing it to well-done in less than a moment. She wanted to cheer but couldn't as another vampire attacked the two-man team from behind, ending them both.

I must finish this, Kara thought. There are too many casualties.

She had an idea. She knew it wasn't a great idea, but it was an idea nevertheless. She asked Njord, the Norse god of the wind, to help her, and then whistled a piercing sound that ground everything to a halt.

16

The battle raged like a hurricane—loud, unpredictable and a swirling monsoon of motion and noise—until Kara's whistle. As the sound pierced the air, all the players on the field froze as if someone had paused a video game.

Kara sought Henri, their eyes met, and they held still in the silence. *Not quite silence,* Kara corrected herself. Kara could hear hearts beating. Breath sucked in and out. Someone heaved, vomiting their last meal at the feet of their enemy.

Kara stared at Henri, who stared back, his sword at the ready.

Kara bent at the knee, sword across her legs on its broadside. She looked up at Henri and said, "I call for an official challenge."

Henri's eyes grew wide. "A duel?" Henri asked, his voice giddy with the idea. The Greek did a jitterbug behind him.

"Yes, we fight each other as the gods intended, strength against strength." Kara cocked her head, trying to get a read on the vampire. Would he accept? If he did accept, would he follow the rules? He had no honor and his word was meaningless, but if their one battle could stop the chaos around them, it was worth the risk.

"Sword against sword," replied Henri.

"Done. Midnight tonight."

"Kara!" said Marc, standing with one foot on a broken vampire in front of him. "We can't trust him! This is craziness! Gaspard, tell her!"

"We will trust in Old World rules here," Kara replied, her voice ringing out over the battlefield, carrying easily as Njord gave her another assist. Kara felt Njord's touch on her shoulder as he blew by, and it strengthened her resolve.

The Greek, a human guard at his feet and another one dead in his arms, hopped up and down in pleasure. He nodded his assent and then said, "Old World rules, if Gaspard agrees. I'll bring the marshmallows."

Gaspard released the neck of the vampire he'd been holding, who dropped to the ground, dead weight with several broken cervical vertebrae. The overpowered vampire's tongue protruded in and out, and her eyes rolled around in her head, frantic as she realized her brain couldn't send commands to her body. Gaspard jerked his chin to the bisected vamp and raised his eyebrows at the Greek. The Greek gave a toothy smile, clapping his hands in joy at the execution to come. Gaspard made a gallant bow to Sigrun, who didn't even look down as she held her battle axe one-handed and used it to cleave the vampire's neck, ensuring the vampire was true dead. The Greek giggled a manic sound of happiness.

Gaspard swung his gaze to Kara, asking her with his eyes to reconsider. She shook her head no. He looked around the grounds at the bodies strewn across the grass, closed his eyes, and nodded his assent.

"I agree. Old World Rules. Winner takes all. I have full faith in Kara when it comes to sword-fighting." Kara knew Gaspard well enough to know that his calm exterior covered an internal firestorm of anxiety, but he would not show doubt in front of the enemy.

"So be it," cackled the Greek. "Posthaste. Expeditiously. At once. Double-quick. Straightway."

"Two hours," said Gaspard.

The Greek pouted. "Yea, merrily sir, two hours. Damn the torpedoes! Light the fuse! Throw the grenade! At last, my darling, at last." He bowed like an actor center stage to an applauding audience, unaware or uncaring that friends and enemies alike had no idea what he meant.

The insane vampire whirled around, grabbed Henri and Vachel's hands, clicked his heels three times, cried, "There's no place like home," and disappeared in a puff of fuchsia smoke. The deformed sylphs crept away, and the guards and vampires made their way back to wherever they came from. Kara could hear her guards whispering to themselves about their dead comrades, wrapping their arms around each other as they moved the human bodies to a makeshift holding area so they could pay their respects.

The Valkyries collected several souls, sending them on to join other heroes in the great halls of Valhalla. Gaspard's staff hauled the dead or dying vampires to an open yard for sunlight to take care of in the morning. Others helped the injured, providing first aid or rushing individuals to the hospital, depending on the extent of their injuries.

Kara, Gaspard, and Marc walked back in the house where Adelaide met them.

Kara glanced at Adelaide and reached out a hand to the woman's face, the face old for the first time since Kara had met her.

"Kara," Adelaide said in a small, tiny voice, so unlike her usual tone. "Child. No."

"It is the best way, Adelaide," Kara replied, stopping to wrap the woman in a hug, forgetting the blood and brains splattered all over her armor. "Oops, sorry, Adelaide."

"You think a little blood and guts bothers me, young lady?" Adelaide's voice increasing in pitch. "You go off and promise a duel to the death without thinking about anyone else? You do not need to bear this burden alone. Gaspard, tell her you will not allow this!"

Gaspard flicked a shard of bone off his arm and stepped out of his shoes, motioning for the others to do so, too. "Don't get blood on the carpets. Emmy will kill us."

Kara shot him a look, and Gaspard winced. "Ugh. Poor choice of words. Sorry."

"Gaspard!" Adelaide rapped him on the hand like a nun in Sunday school.

"Adelaide, Kara decided to do this, and I respect that. Of course, I'm worried, but we will back her all the way."

"Thank you for your trust, Gaspard," said Kara.

"I trust you to do your job, Kara," Gaspard said, getting a wan smile out of Marc.

"Finally, he learns," Marc commented, leaning against the wall, picking flesh from his incisors. Emmy frowned, raised a warning finger in the air, and made him wait to dispose of the bloody pulp until she handed him a trash can.

"What I'd like to discuss," said Kara, drawing to her full height as she turned to the two elderly troublemakers, "is why you two decided to lift a flamethrower, carry it out to the back porch where you could have been shot, and then thought it was a wise idea to release its power *over our heads*?"

"We wanted to help!" Adelaide said, backed up by her co-conspirator, Emmy, who nodded like a baseball player bobble head toy.

"Didn't I tell you to stay away from those things? As it is, you set a tree or two on fire. Luckily, we had extinguishers to put them out."

"We got a few vamps, too!" Emmy protested. "We weren't completely useless."

"Yes, you did get a few vamps, and thank you, but next time maybe we can settle on something less likely to mutilate our friends."

Adelaide *humphed*.

Their banter was interrupted by a pounding on the inside of the pantry door. Kara rubbed her eyes. She'd forgotten about the spy. He'd been locked in for hours now.

"Can I please come out?" the man wheedled. "I need to pee."

"Let the man out," Kara instructed Emmy, "and then send him out with the others to assist in the clean-up. Let him see what his side wrought tonight. Maybe he'll think better the next time someone suggests he become involved in a vampire war."

Emmy opened the door, and the man flew out gesturing right and left asking wordlessly where the closest restroom was. Emmy pointed, and he sprinted in that direction. Empty peanut butter and jelly jars lay overturned on the floor of the pantry. Kara winced. Chef was going to make her pay for that. The burned trees, grass, bushes, and flowers were of no account to the master of the kitchen, but a mess on the floor? Unforgiveable.

"I need to prepare," said Kara, walking toward the stairs.

Gaspard caught up with her. "Kara."

"Yes?"

"Let me help you."

"Let you help me what?"

"Prepare."

"You understand what's involved?"

"I do."

She studied him for a moment, and it hit her this might be the last time she saw him. If she was killed, she wouldn't die the way a human would. She'd follow her sisters to Valhalla, but that would be her last foray to Midgard. Her last foray to Earth.

Gaspard waited in front of her, making this his offer, her choice. His eyes held no guile. No teasing. Just honesty.

She took his hand.

When they entered her room, Kara didn't turn on the lights but began the process of reversing her armor and stripping off the clothes beneath. She had bruises everywhere, and as she sat to remove her body gear, she realized she ached everywhere as well.

Gaspard didn't look at her, allowing her privacy, but went into the bathroom and drew a bath in the sauna tub. Kara could hear the water flowing and the rustle of bath salt parchment paper being opened. She removed all her clothing, wrapped a silk robe around her, and waited.

She heard the bathroom door open and raised her head.

Gaspard had removed his clothes and was wearing a fluffy white robe.

"Where did you get the robe?" she teased.

Kara realized Gaspard didn't hear her. He was staring at her, staring like she was his whole world. It made her uncomfortable.

"You are beautiful. Stand, my love. Let me worship you."

"Worship not necessary," she said, suddenly very self-conscious. "I repeat, where did you get the robe?"

Gaspard's eyes snapped back to her, and his mouth turned into self-satisfied grin. "I had it placed there in the hopes that one day I would need it."

"Sure of yourself, aren't you?"

"Ever hopeful, that's all. Come." He held out his right hand. Gulping, Kara took it, and they entered the bathroom together. Candles glowed from the rim of the tub, the sink, and the shelves. *Where did those come from*? Kara wondered, and then decided not to bother asking. The room was steamy and hot, and one look at the tub made Kara groan.

"May I?" Gaspard asked.

He was behind her, arms wrapped around her waist, hands on the tie keeping the tiny piece of silk closed. She hesitated.

"What are you afraid of, my love?"

"I'm not afraid of anything," Kara said, whipping her body around to look at him.

"Then, let me."

"Fine," she grumbled.

"Always so gracious," Gaspard teased.

Gaspard gave the cinch at her waist a gentle tug, and it loosened. With a light touch of his hands on her shoulders, he pushed the robe off, and it cascaded to the ground in a whisper of silk.

Instead of feeling of self-conscious as she thought she would, Kara felt like a goddess. Gaspard consumed her with his eyes, hungry for her, and she could see that his hands were trembling with emotion. She hadn't believed she could make anyone feel like that, especially Gaspard.

She noticed his erection. *Anyone would*, she thought, and asked, "Are you sure this is going to be okay for you?"

"Shush, my love. This night is for you and you alone." He gestured to the tub.

The water was hot, not scalding, but hot enough to seep into her tired muscles. As one particular cut on her arm hit the water, she hissed in pain.

"Let me see to that, *ma chérie*," Gaspard said. Kara held out her arm. Her body was already feeling better from the effects of the hot water, so when he touched her with his hands, rubbing soap into her open wound, she was amazed that so simple a touch could erase more discomforts. Gaspard brushed his hands up her arms and pressed his thumbs into her neck and shoulder muscles bringing such relief that she closed her eyes with the joy of it.

He removed his hands from her shoulders, and Kara almost cried out from their absence. She was rewarded for her patience by the exquisite feeling of Gaspard's hands in her hair. He massaged her scalp with all ten fingers, the experience something so indulgent, so sensual, she wasn't ready for it. His thumbs and forefingers seemed to reach into her and pull doubt and anxiety out and away. When he put pressure on the joints at the bottom of her scalp where her head met her neck, she did cry out.

"Easy, my love," Gaspard whispered next to her ear. "Let go. I've got you."

That was all it took. Kara did let go, let go of her fears, the crushing responsibility that this duel had brought, and her inhibitions. Gaspard was the magic she'd been missing, and she hadn't even known it.

With this newfound freedom, Kara turned her head and caught Gaspard's head in her hands, leaning in before he could say or do anything, to place her lips on his. He responded like a man on fire, pressing his lips into her like he couldn't get enough. Kara couldn't get enough either and slipped to her knees so she could get more leverage and explore his mouth with her tongue.

Gaspard pulled away, panting. "Kara, I can't keep control if we do this."

Kara held his cheeks in both hands and placed her forehead on his lips. "So, don't. Let's forget control for this night."

Gaspard shoved his robe off and slipped into the tub with her. Before she could think, he'd lifted her onto his lap, positioning her right where she wanted to be. He looked her in the eyes. "Are you sure?"

Kara responded by shifting her weight forward and sliding down his erection, the bath salts enhancing the lubrication so that her descent was complete and easy, enveloping him in a second. They stayed like that, not moving, until gradually Kara began the chase, moving up and down in slow, long motions.

Gaspard held her head to his mouth, kissing her without restraint, not letting her pull away even for a moment, such was his need for her. Kara felt the heat building and couldn't stay in control any longer. Gaspard responded to her excitement by lifting her up so she could plunge down, rubbing her pelvis against his as he held her hips fast.

The orgasm was unlike any Kara had experienced before. Instead of a pleasurable release, this sensation was an explosion from her body's core outward. For a split second, she thought she saw her own face, head thrown back, mouth open, and heard Gaspard's voice in her head saying, "Kara, Kara..."

She collapsed on Gaspard's chest as he slipped out of her. He rubbed the small of her back with one hand and caressed her cheek with the other. He used his toe to flick on the hot water so they could stay wrapped in each other's arms for a few more moments.

"Kara?"

"Ummmhumm?"

"Are you okay? Are we okay?"

Kara pulled back so she could look him in the eye. "Yes, we're good. Thank you, Gaspard, for showing me something so beautiful."

Pink tears gathered in Gaspard's eyes. He blinked them away. "Thank you, Kara, for trusting me."

Kara wiped away his tears with her thumbs and kissed Gaspard on each cheek. "I didn't know I could," she admitted. "You have loved before. I have not. This all feels impossible, like we've moved into an alternate reality, and when we walk out of that door, it all ends."

"It won't, Kara. You'll do what you must do, and we'll have eternity to figure the rest out. Henri is nothing but a... What's the phrase? A fly in the liniment."

"You mean a fly in the ointment. Marc used that phrase once and explained it to me."

"Whatever. It is a trifle. He's a temporary problem that you shall eliminate."

"I hope you're right, Gaspard."

"I am always right, Kara."

17

After the bath, Gaspard left so Kara could meditate. She dressed in tight black fighting pants and a tight black shirt, knowing that she'd pull her armor to her as soon as necessary. She sat on her knees, with her legs in a V-shape in front of her and her feet meeting in the back. She touched her middle fingers to her thumbs and began her meditative breath.

She floated right away, sinking deep within herself, centering, seeking calm. Her breath was deep and even, each inhale bringing in clarity, each exhale removing worry and self-doubt. Without the weight of anxiety, the answer she sought revealed itself. She must be simple but tricky. Stay true to her own beliefs. A battle ended quickly is a battle well won. She wouldn't dance with Henri tonight; she would strike. He would be the peacock; she would be the cobra.

She considered what she'd learned about herself in the last several weeks and months, about her capacity for change, her ability to share joy with others, her potential to love. She realized that she was only at the beginning of her journey and whatever lay ahead was an adventure she was ready to accept. But first, she had to face Henri.

She visualized his strokes and style. He was more of a fencer than she was, but he used a broad sword instead of a rapier. His footwork was fast but predictable, and his ego his weakness. He wanted a brutal and drawn out climax, a display to right the wrongs and perceived disgraces of the past. He had no intention of stopping with Kara. He'd move on to Gaspard, Marc, and anyone and everyone loyal to Gaspard.

Centered and ready, Kara left her bedroom without looking back. Whatever belongings she'd collected were unimportant. She needed to live to explore this new beginning with Gaspard, to reach deeper into herself and see what she could truly be. For this to happen, she had to win. For Gaspard's sake, her sisters', Adelaide's, and the humans around them, she had to win.

For the preservation of the Tree, she would win.

A crowd of Gaspard's followers gathered on the back lawn, some crying, others dry-eyed, all with their hearts in their throats. Kara bowed to them, a real bow, from the waist, and held it to show them that she respected their fears and the responsibility she carried. Her guards, faces serious, saluted.

Kara sat on the ground, as she was before, on her knees, in a meditative position. As she descended, she summoned her armor, and it appeared in a flash of light. The onlookers held their hands to their eyes to block the white and gold blaze.

She waited. The world around her was silent. Not a rustle of a leaf, not the buzz of a mosquito, nothing. All the witnesses and all of nature waited with her.

Kara's nose alerted her to a smell, one she'd scented before. Kara raised her head, and in the distance, she saw the Grunch and his family. The little Grunch wasn't so little, being about the size of a regular alligator. The female was huge, broader than her mate. The male stretched his front arms out and pressed his chest to the ground, like a cat, and Kara nodded her thanks. It was good to have allies.

A rumble reverberated through the air, like the sound of an oncoming Harley biker crew. Shadows approached from the east as Henri, Vachel, the Greek, and their mercenaries poured onto the grounds. Henri shadowed himself until he was positioned seven paces from Kara, then he dropped the shadows like a Vegas showman, held his arms wide, and took a bow. His retinue hooted in approval.

Gaspard advanced toward his once friend and brother, now his mortal enemy, his face stern and unmoving. "Flashy, Henri. You look like a cheap hack magician begging for applause at a local motel."

Henri growled, the sound coming from deep in his chest, like a wolf. Gaspard yawned in response.

Henri said, "You have agreed to this duel in the manner of the Old World, Gaspard, which means that you cannot interfere."

"I understand Old World honor better than you do, Henri."

Gaspard looked to Vachel and the Greek, who stood silent. The Greek had an amused smile on his face, but his eyes were wild, distant, staring at something that wasn't there. Vachel crossed his arms in front of his paunchy body and scowled at Gaspard.

Gaspard wore a suit as befitted the occasion. He reached for his pocket square, removed it, and held it in the air.

"So let it be." The pocket square drifted to the ground.

Henri studied Kara, who remained still.

"Aren't you going to get up and fight, Kara?" taunted Henri. "What are you doing sitting on the ground? You are asking to be beheaded."

Kara closed her eyes, breathing, and focused her attention to her hearing. She could hear his footsteps as he paced in a circle, could sense his befuddlement at her behavior. She could taste his blood-laced spit on the air.

For Kara, time slowed. Her heartbeat decreased, and she could feel the sharp sting of the grass where she knelt, hear the insects as they fed on the blood-saturated ground, and smell the sweat emanating from the humans in the crowd. She didn't see, but perceived, the appearance of two ravens with far-reaching eyes.

When Henri attacked, she was ready, alerted by the sound of his feet, the rustle of his clothing, and the sudden increase in his heartbeat.

He came at her with a wild, banshee yell, sword high in the air, closing the gap between them in an eye blink. He brought the sword down in a vicious arc, slicing the air with a whoosh of sound. He was within a foot of her body, the sword inches from her neck. It was a killing blow.

He staggered back, and then he toppled forward, jerked by the velocity of his own swing as his sword swiped empty space. He flailed trying to catch his balance, eyes wide with shock.

Kara had ducked at the last second, the sword missing her scalp by a millimeter, displaying such exquisite timing that even Gaspard had not seen her move. She brought her right foot up, using it to propel herself upward and to the left. In one beautiful arc, she severed Henri's right hamstring. She sliced his left hamstring with another strike and with two flicks, severed both of his Achilles tendons. Henri went down, flat on his face, howling in pain. He slithered forward a few inches, blood trailing after him as he tried to escape. Kara took one step forward, plunged her sword into and through his neck, reached down, and with a caress of her hands, set him on fire, blue and gold sparks flying into the air.

It was over in ten seconds.

The Greek clapped his hands together. "Brava! Brava! Well done." He hopped up and down on one foot, switching to the other in an insane dance, twirling around like ballerina doing a perverted version of *Swan Lake.*

Kara didn't watch. She looked at Gaspard, who was grinning from ear-to-ear. Kara shuddered at the sight and indicated he should stop smiling. With his fangs out, the grin was a horror show. Gaspard grinned wider and let saliva slip from his lips like a rabid animal. She brought her hand to her face in a face-palm of disbelief.

A questioning grumble drifted on the air. Kara looked at her friend and swept her eyes to Vachel, who was standing still, stupefied at what had happened to Henri and horrified at his mentor's deranged behavior. The Grunch ambled over toward the little cow vampire, taking his time, eyes focused on his prey. The baby Grunch followed his father like an excited puppy. Vachel sniffed the air and turned toward the stench.

One look at the scaly monster slinking toward him was enough to make Vachel forget about Gaspard and back-peddle as fast as his legs would carry him. The daddy Grunch nudged his son toward Vachel, and the little guy sprinted forward, fast as snake, and chomped down on Vachel's shin. The vampire gave out a shriek and hopped up and down trying to shake the baby Grunch off, but the tenacious Grunch progeny held on, sinking its sharp teeth deep into Vachel's leg. He mauled the vampire until the vampire was on the ground, missing a great deal of his lower limb, bleeding out and yelping in a high-pitched voice that turned into a keening as Vachel saw his future draw short.

The baby relented, letting go when he got bored of torturing and taunting his prey, and turned toward his father for instruction. The father rubbed his face against his son's in a gesture of approval, and with a grumble, warned his son back. The daddy Grunch winked at his offspring, took an enormous inhale, rose on his back legs, and blew.

He exhaled fire. Billowed flame. Hot as the sun and fast as the wind, the fire consumed Vachel in a stunning tableau of elemental destruction.

Dragon, thought Kara. *The Grunch is a type of dragon?*

Vachel's embers scattered to the ground as the proud father and son turned to leave. The baby scampered to his mother, talking to his mom in a high-pitched chitter. His mom nuzzled him and hummed her approval. The male Grunch turned his red eyes to Kara, opened his mouth wide, and let out a *huff, huff, huff* sound.

"You enjoyed that, didn't you?" she called to the Grunch. The Grunch let out another laughing *huff*. "I'm glad we could provide your young one with a hunting lesson," Kara finished, hands at her hips. The Grunch continued making his *huff-huff* laugh as the family sauntered away, the little one prattling on in his high-pitched voice the whole time.

By the time Kara returned her attention to the stunned crowds around her, the Greek had hopped on his magic mystery train and disappeared. Kara scanned the remaining onlookers with a stern eye. Several of those on Vachel and Henri's side averted their faces.

Gaspard stepped forward. "The Old World rules apply. Kara won the duel. Our discord is at an end. Return to your homes and do not come back. Those who oppose us will suffer the consequences."

A well-muscled vampire, looking like he'd been a pro wrestler before he died, bucked forward and went down on one knee.

"Gaspard, Master of New Orleans, Southwest Texas, and the entire Northeast, you are now our Master, too."

"What?" said Gaspard.

"The Greek ceded a small but important part of the mid-Atlantic to Vachel. Now that Vachel is gone, you are now also Master of that territory."

"And what is that territory?"

"The entire state of Maryland."

Gaspard exhaled a giant whoosh of breath and muttered, "You've got to be kidding me."

Kara couldn't help herself. The laughter bubbled out until she couldn't stand, and when she couldn't stand, she sat until she couldn't sit, and finally, she lay down on the ground rolling back and forth at the total absurdity of it all.

18

Gaspard sat in his desk chair mulling over the events of the last several weeks. His emotions ran from overwhelming pride in Kara, to shock that he had more territory to rule, to incredulity that only a few hours earlier he and Kara had made love.

"Gaspard?"

Kara stood at the office doorway, her sisters behind her. Gaspard blinked at the endless trail of blinding bronze and gold.

"Kara, *ma chérie*." Gaspard shook himself out of his reverie, straightened, and pulled at his cuffs. "My heroine," he said as he walked to the door. His emotions threatened to boil over, but he managed restraint and poise with iron will and iron will alone.

"I'd like to introduce you to my sisters." Kara gestured behind her.

"And I would like to meet them. What an honor, please come in."

A glorious goddess stepped forth, her brown hair short like Kara's blond. She had piercing blue eyes and cheekbones as sharp as glass. Her armor was all gold, though it was splattered with blood and muck.

"You already met Sigrun. My eldest sister and our leader. She lost her Wild One today in the battle."

"I am so sorry to hear that," said Gaspard, eyes soft. "That such a worthy companion died in this battle is a pain to my heart." Sigrun acknowledged this with a jerk of her head.

Gaspard continued. "Pardon me. My French manners would have me kiss the hand of such a beautiful woman, but I know from Kara that one doesn't take the sword arm of a Valkyrie without permission."

Sigrun held out her arm and clasped Gaspard's elbow-to-elbow, wrist-to-wrist. "It is an honor to have fought beside you, Gaspard. Odin tells me you your role in this play is not done."

"Oh, for goodness's sake, don't say that. I've had nothing but trouble since that man entered my life," said Gaspard.

"*Au contraire*, Odin doesn't make trouble. He follows it. The Norns determined your fate before you were born."

"Can you ask them if I can have a break?"

Sigrun threw her head back in a tired laugh. "I'll pass on the request."

A second goddess, slighter than Sigrun but no less luminous, elbowed Sigrun out of the way and advanced on Gaspard. Her face was serious, and she looked him up and down, like she was choosing a breeding stallion at auction.

"Mademoiselle?" Gaspard lifted an elegant brow at the Valkyrie.

Kara introduced her sister. "Gaspard, this is Hildr, my closest and dearest friend."

Hildr circled Gaspard while he stood there like a dog at Westminster. When she completed her examination, she leaned in close and studied Gaspard's eyes. She stood back, one hand on her hip, the other on her chin. Finally, she said, "You'll do."

Gaspard executed a short bow. "I am much relieved to hear so."

"Don't hurt her, or you'll have to deal with me."

Gaspard genuflected at the knees to communicate his respect. "I have been warned."

Kara hid her grin and gestured for the third Valkyrie to step forward. "This is Astrid, newly joined to us..."

She stopped as Gaspard gasped and held his right hand to his chest.

"Hello, Gaspard," said Astrid.

"Isobel?" Gaspard tried to keep his voice steady, but it broke at the end of her name.

"I'm surprised you recognize me."

"I could never forget your eyes," said Gaspard, reaching out his hands for hers. She placed them in his palms, and he pulled her toward him enveloping her in a tight embrace, his mind flashing back to the day in a barn in mid-winter in Orléans where he'd first met Isobel as a little girl. He'd fought a demon that night, and the experience gave Isobel demons to battle for the rest of her life.

"You wanted to kill them all," he whispered into her ear.

"And I did, the monsters anyway."

"I was afraid for your soul."

Isobel pulled back to look Gaspard in the eyes. "Reasonably so, but I found a path in the end. There is something I must tell you. Arnaud is dead."

Gaspard released her but held onto one hand. "I am...aggrieved to hear that. I never saw him again, after Paris."

"He was one of my best informants," she said.

"You were police?"

Isobel toggled her hand. "A special agent of a kind. He died saving people from a terrorist bombing in Paris. He died a hero."

Gaspard didn't notice that Hildr and Kara rocketed to attention at Isobel's statement. They shared a look of realization as they thought back to that infamous day when Sigrun cut Kara down. Sigrun caught their eye and dipped her chin in acknowledgment.

Isobel continued. "He speaks of you fondly."

Gaspard snorted. "I bet he does." Then, he reconsidered her words. "What do you mean, speaks, present tense? I thought he was dead."

Isobel smiled. "He is, but his soul is in Valhalla."

Gaspard took a moment to absorb her words and then the facts fell into place. "He had a soul," he murmured to himself. "And he died a hero saving others."

Isobel rewarded him with a gentle smile.

Gaspard raised her hands to his lips. "I am so happy to see you. You should never have seen all that you saw."

"But you forget I saw the good with the evil. You showed me," said Isobel, kissing his hands in return.

Kara broke in, pulling their hands apart. "This is a story I would like to hear some day, *Astrid*."

Isobel stood back and said, "A story I would be happy to share. Your Gaspard saved my life and the life of my parents."

"Not your brother." Gaspard sighed as he remembered the boy, beaten, suffering multiple puncture marks, the life literally sucked out of him.

"No. That is true, but you did what you could," said Isobel, a tightness at her eyes the only sign of her grief.

Sigrun broke up the reunion. "We must return, sisters. Kara. Gaspard. It was an honor."

Gaspard clasped his fist to his chest. "The honor was—and is—mine. I will not forget the sacrifice you made in this battle."

The Valkyries retreated, and Gaspard heard the pound of hoof beats followed by the rush of wings, the sound less intense than it should have been because of the lack of Sigrun's partner and friend.

Which left Gaspard alone with Kara. He hadn't been this nervous since, well, he couldn't remember. Maybe when he was seventeen, his first time with a girl. Maybe with Sophie. But this was different. Here stood a warrior. An equal—no—a better. The most beautiful woman he'd ever known, and she was his.

Her armor was gone, and she was dressed in black from head to toe, her white-blond hair a halo of light. Her back was covered in mud from rolling around during her laughing fit, a thought that made Gaspard smile. He held out his arms, and she stepped into them. He breathed her in, grateful she was alive, incredulous that she was there.

"Day is almost here, my love," he said. "And there is so much to do, so much to discuss..."

"Shush. I know. We will take the day to rest and regroup at sunset."

Gaspard wrinkled his nose. "That sounds like a superb idea. You reek, my dear. You need a shower."

Kara's eyes shot up. "But I had a bath only a few hours ago."

"We have time. I'll wash your back," said Gaspard, tugging arm to her room.

19

The next evening's sky was clear and bright with stars. Gaspard and Kara each sat on a chaise lounge on the back patio, admiring the clean-up job the daytime staff had done on the grounds. Kara sipped a glass of wine with her left hand, her right dangling over the armrest to touch fingers with Gaspard, who had settled into his chair to her right.

It was a rare moment of peace, and Kara relaxed into the light breeze, the chirping crickets and the flit of fireflies darting through the night air. Two ravens floated to perch in front of them on the back of a third, unoccupied chair. Hugin and Munin, Odin's eyes and ears.

Kara titled her head as she listened to a question that Gaspard could not hear.

"He's given me a choice?" Kara said to the ravens. They bobbed their heads up and down.

"I'd like to stay," Kara said, admitting something that she'd been afraid to say out loud. Gaspard brushed her fingers with his.

Kara jolted up, body taut with alarm. Gaspard catapulted from relaxed to alert at her movement.

"What?" he demanded. "What's happening? What's wrong?"

"What do you mean the immediate danger continues?" Kara said to the ravens. "We won. I know Sigrun said there was more to do, but does that have to mean battle? Didn't we shut the Soul Wars down?"

"There is still a risk?" she continued. "Why? How? Who takes up the mantle? Gaspard hasn't insulted anyone else that I know of." She turned to Gaspard with an accusing look. "Have you?"

Gaspard held his arms out wide. "How would I know? I didn't know about Henri and Vachel."

The ravens squawked, pirouetted into the air, and flew off.

The crackle of a walkie-talkie disturbed their privacy. Kara hadn't wanted to wear her earpiece but had agreed to carry the radio. She answered with a quick, "Report."

"Back gate watch. There's a woman here who says she's a friend and would like to see you."

Kara whispered to Gaspard. "Back gate? Maybe Lisette? We sent her away when we learned that Henri was still alive. She's most likely returned."

"Seems probable. She always entered through the back," Gaspard replied.

Kara hauled herself off the chair and clicked the radio on. "Detain her, but be polite. I'll be there in a second."

"Yes, ma'am."

She jogged down the grounds to the back gate and flicked on the walkie-talkie while she did. "Is she human?"

"We couldn't tell at first, so we asked her to remove her hood. She's a vampire, ma'am. We have three guards on her."

"Did she give a name?"

"No, ma'am. Says she prefers not to."

"I'm on my way. Be careful."

"Roger that."

Kara picked up speed and ran the rest of the way, coming to a stop a few feet before the gate. The vampire was wearing a gray cloak with a hood that had been pushed back so her face was visible. She was pretty with curling long brown hair, and something about her pinged at Kara's memory.

"Who are you and why do you come as friend? I don't believe I've ever seen you before," Kara said to the vampire.

"But we've spoken many times, Kara."

Kara recognized the voice. "You are our informant? The one I met in Washington?"

"The very one," said the woman with a soft smile. Her fangs were retracted, her hands held out to show they held no weapons.

Kara considered the situation, pausing long enough that the guards moved closer to the vampire, ready to jump if asked. One readied his bo stick in a rest position, poised to strike with extreme prejudice if Kara so much as twitched a finger as a signal.

"You can let her in," Kara said, after the long pause. The guards unlocked the back gate and ushered the vampire through. "Would you like one of us to escort you, ma'am?" asked the younger guard before the older one could give him an elbow in the stomach.

Kara gave the young gun a look that froze him in his tracks. "I've got this," said Kara.

As she walked away, she heard the older, more experienced guard say to the younger one, "She's a Valkyrie for goodness's sake. She no more needs our help than you need a hammer to eat soup."

"I was trying to be professional!" the younger one said.

"Next time, don't!" said his older partner.

"Don't be professional?"

"No. That's not what I meant. Oh, forget it."

Kara and the vampire smiled at this as they proceeded up the hill to the back patio where Gaspard waited.

"You've never told me your name," Kara said.

"Let me see Gaspard, and then it will all be clear," the vampire said, her gray eyes gazing toward the patio at the aristocratic figure waiting for them.

Gaspard walked to meet them and stopped dead ten paces away.

"Hello, lover," said the vampire.

Gaspard face drained of any color it had, his blue eyes widened in shock.

"Sophie?"

Sophie stepped forward, arms extended, and Gaspard folded her into his arms, his face a picture of confusion.

Sophie? The Sophie? Kara thought.

Gaspard stepped back to look at Sophie's face and held his hand to her cheek, rubbing his thumb over her skin. "How is this possible?"

Exactly right, Kara thought. *How is this possible?*

But Odin taught his Valkyries to deal with what was, not how or why it happened. When in the middle of battle, dealing with what was in front of you, no matter how implausible, was imperative. Keeping to that code, Kara stepped to Gaspard's right, assuming her position as his body-guard, his First. Arms loose at her side, weapons ready, face still as stone.

ACKNOWLEDGMENTS

Acknowledging people is a challenging process because there are so many individuals, in both small and large ways, who helped make The Soul Wars happen. I'd like to acknowledge the folks at Falstaff Books, John, Jay, Melissa and Jaym, for believing in this book, as well as my DragonCon family, who encouraged me to start writing again, and made me practice saying, "I am a writer," until I could say it without feeling foolish.

Last, I'd like to acknowledge Natania Barron for creating ridiculously awesome covers.

ABOUT THE AUTHOR

J.D. Blackrose is the fantasy pen name of Joelle Reizes. She loves all things storytelling and celebrates great writing by posting about it on her website, www.slipperywords.com.

When not writing, Blackrose lives with three children, an enormous orange cat, her husband and a full-time job in Corporate Communications. She's fearful that so-called normal people will discover exactly how often she thinks about wicked fairies, nasty wizards, homicidal elevators, and the odd murder. As a survival tactic, she has mastered the art of looking interested.

ALSO BY J.D. BLACKROSE

Tweety & The Monkey Man

Souls Collide

Souls Fall

Souls Rise

Cover Design by Natania Barron

ISBN Hardcover: 978-1-946926-35-7

ISBN Paperback:978-1-946926-36-4

This book is a work of fiction. Any resemblance to any person, living or dead, is coincidental. Except that bit about that guy. That's totally a thing.

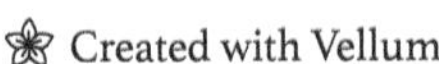

www.ingramcontent.com/pod-product-compliance
Lightning Source LLC
Chambersburg PA
CBHW030550310726
48979CB00011B/2094/J

* 9 7 8 1 9 4 6 9 2 6 3 5 7 *